CAMPBELL

NEW YORRS: PERILOUS SHIELD

"[An] imaginative
science fiction
novel."
—*Night Owl
Reviews*

FIRST TIME IN PAPERBACK

THE LOST STARS
TARNISHED KNIGHT

C

$7.99 U.S.
$8.99 CAN

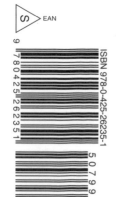

EAN

ISBN 978-0-425-26235-1

"Campbell maintains the military, political, and even sexual tension with sure-handed proficiency . . . [He] focuses on the human element: two strong, well-developed characters locked in mutual dependence, fumbling their way toward a different and hopefully brighter future. What emerges is a fascinating and vividly rendered character study, fully and expertly contextualized."

—*Kirkus Reviews* (starred review)

"Brilliant . . . Jack Campbell runs a strong saga shown from the viewpoints of the Syndicate at a time when the vicious totalitarian military regime teeters on the brink of total collapse."

—*Genre Go Round Reviews*

"Usually it takes me a few dozen pages to get into a new book and feel comfortable in the world. *Tarnished Knight* had me joining the wild ride right out of the gate . . . A true page-turner as Jack Campbell takes you from one cliff-hanger to the next before you've had time to readjust to the newest twist." —*My Bookish Ways*

"If there is at this present time a better writer of pure popcorn explosive-BOOM military space opera working in the field, I haven't found them." —Tor.com

"*Tarnished Knight* is a winner, with the right mixture of action-based military science fiction and political space opera."

—*The Guilded Earlobe*

PRAISE FOR THE LOST FLEET

THE LOST FLEET: BEYOND THE FRONTIER: INVINCIBLE

"An entertaining thriller with great space battles between the First Fleet and the aliens." —*Alternative Worlds*

"A very gripping read . . . It should satisfy longtime readers of Campbell's series and might even work as an entry point for new readers . . . If you have been reading the series to this point, there's absolutely no reason to stop now . . . *Very* pleased with the turn of events in *Invincible*." —SFFWorld.com

continued . . .

THE LOST FLEET:
BEYOND THE FRONTIER: DREADNAUGHT

"Campbell combines the best parts of military SF and grand space opera to launch a new adventure series."   —*Publishers Weekly*

"One of the best military science fiction series on the market."
                                             —*Monsters and Critics*

THE LOST FLEET: VICTORIOUS

"This is a series of fast-paced adventure. Battles take into account the vastness of space and the time involved in an engagement. Fans of Ian Douglas, David Weber, and David Drake will enjoy this similar quality series."   —*SFRevu*

"There are great battles and well-told military-life scenes, but the character tensions and the drama kick this from war story to high drama . . . Fans of military SF will love this series."
                                  —*Stranger than Truth: Science Fiction Society of Northern New Jersey*

THE LOST FLEET: RELENTLESS

"This exhilarating, action-packed outer-space military thriller will remind the audience of the battles in *Star Wars*."
                                             —*Midwest Book Review*

THE LOST FLEET: VALIANT

"Fast-paced and enjoyable . . . Readers who enjoyed David Weber's Honor Harrington books, Ian Douglas's Space Marines [novels], or Walter Hunt's Dark Wing series should also enjoy this series."
                                             —*SFRevu*

"The series is military SF, rigorously extrapolated in the classic tradition of hard SF. The laws of physics and the effects of relativity govern the battles and shape the action, while military virtues and ideals like honor and courage shape the conduct and personalities of the more admirable characters."   —*Sci Fi Weekly*

THE LOST FLEET: COURAGEOUS

"It's almost nonstop action and conflict . . . Jack Campbell does an excellent job with the space battles." —*SF Site*

THE LOST FLEET: FEARLESS

"Straightforward, solidly written military space opera . . . It's all good fun, and Campbell has actually given some thought to the problems of combat in space." —*Critical Mass*

"Another satisfying [Campbell] cocktail to slake the thirst of fans who like their space operas with a refreshing moral and intellectual chaser . . . The Lost Fleet deserves a berth on your bookshelf." —SF Reviews.net

THE LOST FLEET: DAUNTLESS

"A rousing adventure with a page-turning plot, lots of space action, and the kind of hero Hornblower fans will love." —William C. Dietz, author of *Andromeda's Fall*

"Jack Campbell's dazzling new series is military science fiction at its best. Not only does he tell a yarn of great adventure and action, but he also develops the characters with satisfying depth. I thoroughly enjoyed this rip-roaring read, and I can hardly wait for the next book." —Catherine Asaro, Nebula Award–winning author of *Carnelians*

"Black Jack Geary is very real, very human, and so compelling he'll leave you wanting more. Jack Campbell knows fleet actions, and it shows . . . [*The Lost Fleet: Dauntless* is] the best novel of its type that I've read." —David Sherman, coauthor of the Starfist series

"A slam-bang good read that kept me up at night . . . A solid, thoughtful, and exciting novel loaded with edge-of-your-seat combat." —Elizabeth Moon, *New York Times* bestselling author of *Limits of Power*

THE LOST STARS

TARNISHED KNIGHT

JACK CAMPBELL

ACE BOOKS, NEW YORK

THE BERKLEY PUBLISHING GROUP
Published by the Penguin Group
Penguin Group (USA) LLC
375 Hudson Street, New York, New York 10014, USA

USA | Canada | UK | Ireland | Australia | New Zealand | India | South Africa | China

Penguin Books Ltd., Registered Offices: 80 Strand, London WC2R 0RL, England
For more information about the Penguin Group, visit penguin.com.

THE LOST STARS: TARNISHED KNIGHT

An Ace Book / published by arrangement with the author

Ace Books are published by The Berkley Publishing Group.
ACE and the "A" design are trademarks of Penguin Group (USA) LLC.

For information, address: The Berkley Publishing Group,
a division of Penguin Group (USA) LLC,
375 Hudson Street, New York, New York 10014.

ISBN: 978-0-425-26235-1

PUBLISHING HISTORY
Ace hardcover edition / October 2012
Ace mass-market edition / October 2013

PRINTED IN THE UNITED STATES OF AMERICA

10 9 8 7 6 5 4 3 2 1

Cover illustration by Craig White.
Cover photographs: limestone © Martin Fowler / Shutterstock;
nebula © Kevin Carden / Shutterstock; metal plate © Eky Studio / Shutterstock.
Cover design by Judith Lagerman.
Interior text design by Laura K. Corless.

ACKNOWLEDGMENTS

I remain indebted to my agent, Joshua Bilmes, for his ever-inspired suggestions and assistance, and to my editor, Anne Sowards, for her support and editing. Thanks also to Catherine Asaro, Robert Chase, J. G. (Huck) Huckenpohler, Simcha Kuritzky, Michael LaViolette, Aly Parsons, Bud Sparhawk, and Constance A. Warner for their suggestions, comments, and recommendations. Thanks also to Charles Petit for his suggestions about space engagements.

CHAPTER ONE

TREASON could be as simple as walking through a doorway.

At least that was true anywhere ruled by the Syndicate Worlds, and when the doorway in question had stenciled on it in large, red letters the words *Unauthorized Access Forbidden OBSTLT.* CEO Artur Drakon, commander of Syndicate Worlds ground forces in the Midway Star System, had spent his life following rules like that and only partly because everyone knew that *OBSTLT* stood for *Or Be Subject to Life Termination.* "Death" was the sort of blunt term that the Syndicate Worlds' bureaucracy liked to avoid no matter how freely it meted out that punishment.

No, he had obeyed because there hadn't been much choice while the endless war with the Alliance continued, when disobedience could leave a path open for the enemy to destroy homes and cities and sometimes entire worlds. And if the enemy didn't destroy your home as a result of your rebellious behavior, and if you somehow escaped the long and powerful reach of Internal Security, then the mobile forces of the Syndicate Worlds themselves would rain down death on your world from orbit in the name of law, discipline, and stability.

But now the war had ended in exhaustion and defeat. No one trusted the Alliance, but they had stopped attacking. And the mobile forces of the Syndicate Worlds, the once-unassailable fist of the central government, had been almost wiped out in a flurry of destruction wrought by an Alliance leader who should have been dead a century ago.

That left the ISS, the Internal Security Service, to worry about. The "snakes" of the ISS were a very big worry indeed, but nothing that he couldn't handle now.

Drakon walked through the doorway. He could do that because multiple locks and codes had already been overridden, multiple alarm systems had been disabled or bypassed, a few deadly automated traps disarmed, and four human sentries in critical positions had been turned and now answered to him rather than to CEO Hardrad, head of Internal Security. All of this had been done on Drakon's orders. But until Drakon entered the room beyond he could claim to have been testing internal defenses. Now he had unquestionably committed treason against the Syndicate Worlds.

Drakon had expected to feel increased tension as he entered that room; instead, a sense of calm filled him. Retreat and alternate paths were no longer possible; there was no more room for uncertainty or questioning his decision. Within the next several hours, he would either win or die.

Inside, his two most trusted assistants were already busy at separate consoles. Bran Malin's fingers were flying as he rerouted and diverted surveillance data from all over the planet which should be streaming into the Internal Security Service headquarters complex. On the other side of the room, Roh Morgan used one hand to flick a strand of hair from her eyes as she rapidly entered false surveillance feed loops designed to fool the automated systems at ISS into thinking that everything still worked properly. Drakon was dressed in the dark blue executive ensemble every CEO was expected to wear, an outfit he personally detested, but both Malin and Morgan were clad in the tight, dull black skin suits designed to be worn under mechanized combat armor. The skin suits also served well on their own for breaking and entering, though.

Malin sat back, rubbing his neck with his right hand, then smiled at Drakon. "ISS is blind, sir, and they don't even know it."

Drakon nodded as he studied the display. "Malin, you're a wizard."

Morgan stretched like a cat, lithe and deadly, then stood up, leaning against the nearest wall with her arms crossed. "I'm the one who got us in here and entered the deception loops. What does that make me?"

"A witch?" Malin asked, his expression and voice dead-pan.

For a moment, Morgan tensed, then one corner of her mouth curled upward as she gazed at Malin. "Did I tell you that I'd calculated the lowest possible cost to fire a single shot from a hand weapon, Malin?"

"No. Why should I care?"

"Because it came out to thirteen centas. That's why you're still alive. I realized killing you wasn't worth the expense."

Malin bared his teeth at her as he drew his combat knife and balanced it on one palm. "This wouldn't cost a centa to use. Go ahead and give it a try."

"Nah." Morgan stood away from the wall, flexing her hands. "I'd still have to put some effort into it, and like I said, you're not worth whatever energy it would take to kill you. CEO Drakon, we should eliminate those four sentries. They could still betray us."

Drakon shook his head. "They were promised that if they played along, they and their families wouldn't be killed."

"So? If they were stupid enough to believe the promise of a CEO—"

"It was *my* promise," Drakon interrupted. "I made a commitment. If I violate that, I won't be able to count on anyone else's believing I'll do what I say."

Morgan shook her head with a long-suffering look. "That's the attitude that got you stuck out here in the back end of nowhere. As long as they're afraid of you, it doesn't matter whether or not they believe you."

Malin pretended to applaud, his palms clapping together silently. "You know the first workplace rule for Syndicate Worlds' CEOs. Very good. Now think about the fact that we *lost the war*."

"I operate the way that works for me," Drakon told Morgan, who was pretending not to have heard Malin.

She shrugged. "It's your rebellion. I'll check on the assault preparations and get the troops moving as planned."

"Let me know if any problems develop," Drakon replied. "I appreciate your support in this."

"That was always a given." Morgan started to leave, now ignoring Malin's presence completely.

"And, Morgan . . ."

She paused in the doorway.

"The sentries will *not* be killed." He said it flatly and with force.

"I heard you the first time," Morgan replied, then continued on out.

After the door closed, Malin looked at Drakon. "Sir, if she notifies the snakes of what we're planning, she'll end up in command and you'll be dead."

Drakon shook his head. "Morgan won't do that."

"You can't trust her. You must know that."

"I know that she is loyal to me," Drakon said, keeping his voice even.

"Morgan doesn't understand loyalty. She's using you for her own purposes, which remain hidden. The moment you're no longer useful, she might put a shot in your back. Or a knife," Malin finished, raising his own knife meaningfully before resheathing it with a single thrust.

Morgan has told me the same thing about you, Drakon thought as he considered a reply to Malin. "Morgan realizes that she couldn't count on the snakes rewarding her for turning us in. They'd be just as likely to shoot her, too, no matter what agreement they had reached with her. Morgan knows that just as well as I do. But I am keeping an eye on her. I keep an eye on everyone."

"That's why you're still alive." Malin shook his head. "I'm not suggesting that you get rid of her. As long as she's alive, you need to have her where you can watch her."

Drakon paused, eyeing Malin. "Are you advising that I take care of the 'as long as she's alive' part?"

"No, sir," Malin answered.

"Then you'd better not be planning to take care of that yourself. I know it's common practice with some CEOs' subordinates, but I don't tolerate those kinds of games on my staff. It's bad for discipline, and it plays hell with the working environment."

Malin grinned. "I will not kill Morgan." His smile faded, and Malin gave a worried glance upward. "We can take down the Internal Security Service on the surface, we *will* take them down, but if the mobile forces in this star system aren't also neutralized we'll be sitting ducks. From what I know of the mobile forces commander, CEO Kolani, she will support the Syndicate government and the snakes."

"As long as we eliminate the ISS snakes on the surface, CEO Iceni will handle CEO Kolani and the mobile forces." *I hope.*

"Sir," Malin said with exaggerated care, "if I may, I understand that you and CEO Iceni have agreed to run things here jointly. You are justified in believing that it is in her self-interest to stick to that agreement. But how will you run things, sir? I know how unhappy you are with the Syndicate government—"

"Sick to death of the Syndicate government," Drakon interrupted. "Sick of watching my every step and every word." It felt strange to be able to say that, now that the snake surveillance gear was neutralized. "Sick of bureaucrats a hundred light-years away making life-and-death decisions about me."

Malin nodded in agreement. "There are many who feel the same way even though few have dared to say it, even in private. But I am unclear as to what system will replace that of the Syndicate."

"Are you?" Drakon smiled wryly. "Me, too. Iceni and I couldn't talk about it before this, before we had these surveillance systems short-circuited. Too great a chance of being caught by the ISS. We both agree that we want to get out from under the merciless thumb of the Syndicate. We both agree that the Syndicate government proved its incompetence, and that we can't depend on that government to defend this star system or to keep us safe. That's always been the argument, that we have to accept tight controls on everything we do in exchange for security. You and I and everyone else knows how false that proved to be. And now we know that the Syndicate government is moving to try to maintain control by replacing CEOs wholesale and executing anyone whose loyalty is doubted in any way. It's revolt or die. Beyond that . . . Iceni and I will talk when the snakes are dead."

"The Syndicate system failed, sir," Malin agreed. "The control has always been there, but it didn't provide the promised security. I strongly advise that you consider another way of governing."

Drakon eyed Malin, knowing why he hadn't brought that up in front of Morgan, who would surely have reacted with derision at the idea of anything less than an ironfisted dictatorship. "Your advice is noted. Our priority for the moment is survival. If we achieve that, we'll think about how to run things without repeating the mistakes of the Syndicate. I don't want anyone like the snakes working for me to keep the citizens in line, but I also know we need order and that means some control. Now I need to talk to Iceni so she knows this surveillance node is blinded, and so we both know the other is getting ready to move."

"Do it in person, sir. Even though we should've blinded ISS, they might have some security taps we're not aware of yet."

"Let's hope not." Drakon nodded farewell to Malin, then made his way out through the multiple layers of security that had protected the main surveillance node. The sensors watched him but saw nothing, feeding routine images of empty hallways and sealed doors to their masters at ISS, the men and women responsible for the very broad range of actions categorized as Internal Security on Syndicate Worlds' planets. He passed by the armored room where two of the turned sentries were pretending to see nothing. Then a little farther along before he reached the new, concealed access that had been painstakingly dug into this building from a neighboring structure, a task that itself had been a very delicate operation, requiring diverting and spoofing various alarms and sensors as well as the cooperation of those co-opted sentries. Walking down a roughly hewn passage, Drakon entered the basement area of a shopping center, ignoring surveillance cameras there which had also been blinded, then went up a set of stairs and through an EMPLOYEES ONLY door whose lock combination had long since been compromised.

The ISS snakes are going to be in for a real shock in a few hours, Drakon thought. *For over two hundred years, the snakes have been staging surprise arrests and security sweeps. Now we'll see how* they *like surprises.*

It would have been nice to be able just to hit the snakes right now, but Drakon knew the process was like a long line of dominoes that had to fall in turn, each knocking down the next as the plan progressed, as sensors and spies and surveillance gear all over the planet were spoofed or silenced, as military forces loyal to Drakon began to move under cover of those actions, as rebellion gathered without the knowledge of those who could still inflict terrible damage to this world if not taken by surprise. So he kept to the plan, which had been unfolding slowly for months now and would soon begin moving very quickly indeed.

That was why Drakon wore his executive suit despite his dislike for the garment mandated for all CEOs. No average citizen seeing him could tell by his outfit whether he was assigned to overseeing manufacturing or sales or administration or any other aspect of the integrated economic, military, and political system of the Syndicate Worlds. Having spent almost his entire adult life in the ground forces, risking death and leading troops, Drakon didn't care for the thought of being outwardly indistinguishable from someone who had spent the same amount of time in advertising. He had once even suffered the indignity of being mistaken for a lawyer.

But he knew that he had to appear to conform to routine right now in order to avoid tipping off the ISS. Drakon walked briskly but without any sign of concern by storefronts and out of the mall, then turned to walk past the outside of the nondescript building that secretly housed the ISS surveillance relay facility. It took practice to look truly casual when you were guilty and strolling past those charged with enforcing laws, but no one reached the rank of CEO without plenty of experience at doing so.

The citizens he encountered on the streets automatically moved aside when they saw the CEO-level executive suit, some eagerly seeking eye contact on the chance that a CEO might take notice of them, but just as many striving to avoid attracting his attention. Citizens of the Syndicate Worlds learned their own lessons, and one of those was that the attention of a CEO was a double-edged sword which might bring benefits or calamity.

Watching the citizens react with mingled fear and fawning submission, the first real and the second probably faked, Drakon thought about Malin's recent words. What would come next? He had been consumed with figuring out how to kill the snakes without having half of this planet blown apart, and what he had said about not being able to discuss the matter with Iceni was true. They had barely been able to risk the few, occasional, and brief meetings in which coded phrases and words sketched out the agreement to cooperate in taking down the snakes, saving their own hides, and perhaps giving this star system a chance to survive the ongoing collapse of the Syndicate empire. Midway would either get caught in the death throes of the Syndicate Worlds or get free of that tyranny and look out for itself.

But after that? All he knew was the Syndicate way and, as Malin said, that had failed. How else did you keep things running without everything's falling apart? The Alliance way? He had learned little about that, and what little he had heard Drakon mistrusted.

Drakon shook his head with a frown, causing nearby citizens to freeze like rabbits that had seen a wolf and now hoped to avoid notice. He couldn't afford to think about them at the moment, or about the details of what would replace Syndicate rule here. He had to keep his mind centered on getting through the rest of this day alive.

More than a few of the citizens warily watching him walk onward probably wondered why a CEO was in public without bodyguards fencing him off, but it wasn't unheard of for some CEOs to travel occasionally without guards. Drakon had made a habit of that over the last few months, casually mentioning in ways that were certain to get back to Internal Security that he could take care of himself. The snakes wouldn't question a CEO's being arrogant and self-assured, though in Drakon's case his ground forces training and the equipment hidden in his executive suit gave him strong grounds for feeling able to handle most threats as long as he kept varying his routine to make assassination plots difficult.

It took fifteen minutes to reach the office of CEO Gwen Iceni, the senior Syndicate Worlds' official in the Midway Star System. But Malin had been right. Any message could be intercepted, and any code could be compromised or broken. If ISS learned of their plans at this point, with Drakon too far committed to pull back, it would trigger a disaster.

Human bodyguards and automated security systems providing layers of protection for Iceni all passed Drakon without hindrance despite the hidden weapons on him. If Iceni was planning to betray him, it would probably be after his forces had dealt with the snakes that both he and Iceni needed to have cleaned out. And she had surely reached the same conclusion about him, that he would not strike her yet because he needed her to handle those mobile forces still in this star system.

But all of the screening still took time that he didn't have to spare, so that Drakon had trouble not showing any irritation or anger as he walked into Iceni's office.

That office had the grandeur expected of a star system CEO's workplace but on a level consistent with Midway's modest wealth. There was an art to such things in the Syndicate Worlds' hierarchy. Too much ostentation would have attracted too much attention from her superiors, wondering how much extra Iceni might be skimming off tax revenue and what her ambitions might be, while too little pretension in the size and furnishings would have signaled weakness to both superiors and subordinates. Now Iceni, appearing calm, waved Drakon to a seat, then checked her desk display. "Security in here is tight," she said. "We can talk freely. You didn't bring any bodyguards. You trust me that much?"

"Not really." Drakon gestured in the general direction of the ISS headquarters complex. "There's a small but real chance that one of my bodyguards might be partly turned and providing information to the snakes on my movements. Right now, those bodyguards are watching the entrance to my command center, thinking that I'm inside it. Do you trust your bodyguards completely?"

"I don't have to," Iceni replied, not really answering his question. "By the time I do something that might alarm the snakes, you'll be doing your part. Are your people ready?"

"We'll hit the four primary ISS sites on this planet at fifteen hundred, just as planned. I'm personally leading the assault on the main ISS complex in this city, and three trusted subordinate commanders of mine are leading attacks on the secondary complexes in other cities. ISS substations everywhere will be hit by squad-level forces at the same time."

Iceni nodded, then glanced upward. "What about the orbiting stations and other facilities off-planet?"

"I've got people ready everywhere the snakes are, except on the mobile forces units, of course."

"Those are my problem. You have a lot of soldiers moving around. You're sure the snakes won't be alarmed?"

He hadn't sat down despite Iceni's offer, being too keyed up to carry that off well. But he couldn't show any weakness in front of another CEO, any nerves, or Iceni would surely focus on it like a wolf seeing a stag stumble. Instead, Drakon shrugged in a show of indifference. "I can't be certain. It's a very big operation, so it's possible the snakes will see something. But it shouldn't be enough to alarm them. We had to rush things over the last few days because of the order from Prime, but everything had already been planned out."

Iceni twisted her mouth slightly. "Fortunately for us. I had been warned that the central government was sending out orders to have star system CEOs hauled in by the ISS for loyalty checks, and that quite a few of those CEOs were not being seen again after disappearing into ISS custody; but I didn't expect the government to send that order here as quickly as it did. Even before you and I launched this plot we wouldn't have survived such an interrogation session."

"You think I have the wrong kinds of skeletons in my closet?" Drakon asked.

"I know that you do. I did my homework before I made any offers to you, just as I'm sure you did your homework on me before you responded. But we didn't start planning rebellion any too soon. That order to the ISS is still held up in the comm systems, but it could pop free at any time; and then we can both expect invitations we can't ignore from CEO Hardrad."

"And he'll also have questions about how that order got held up in the message system," Drakon noted dryly. "But you did keep it from being delivered for a few days, giving us time to act on our plans. As long as Hardrad doesn't see that order for a few more hours we'll be all right. The ISS surveillance systems are disabled while still appearing to be functioning, so we can finally talk freely. The snakes should assume everything is quiet until we launch the attacks. Are you still guaranteeing to handle the mobile forces in this star system?"

"I'll take care of the warships."

"Warships? We're going to start using Alliance terminology now?"

"They did win the war," Iceni replied, her voice tinged with sarcasm. "But it's not just an Alliance term. We used to call them warships, too, before the bureaucracy 'redefined' and 'relabeled' them. We're going back to our own older terminology. Changing what we call things will be a clear signal to the citizens and our forces that we are no longer subject to the Syndicate Worlds."

"After we win, you mean."

"Naturally. I've got a shuttle lifting me to C-448 in ten minutes. I'll use that heavy cruiser to rally the other warships here to us."

"What's CEO Kolani's status?" Drakon asked. "Any change?"

"Not yet. She's still in command of the flotilla and still committed to the government on Prime."

Drakon frowned upward, as if he could see through the building and up through intervening space to where the small flotilla orbited. "You'll take her out?"

"That option fell through," Iceni replied in as casual a tone as if she were referring to a minor business deal. "Both agents of mine who were within reach of her have already been neutralized by Kolani's security, so assassination isn't one of our choices."

He felt a chill run down his back at the thought of what that flotilla could do to this planet. "You promised me that you'd handle the mobile forces." Morgan's words came back to mock him. *If they were stupid enough to believe the promise of a CEO . . .*

"I will handle them," Iceni said, her voice hardening. "We can't wait for better options. Even if that order from Prime hadn't forced our hands, another high-priority message came in this morning when that courier ship popped in from the hypernet gate, then popped out again after sending its messages to us. CEO Kolani has been ordered to take almost all of the mobile forces here back to Prime immediately. We *need* those forces to defend this star system once we achieve control. I've kept that order stuck within the comm system, too, but a high-priority message can't be held up forever."

"How certain are you of success with taking over the flotilla?" Drakon asked.

"Certain enough. Some of the ships are already mine, including C-448. I have enough individual unit commanders committed to me to be able to beat Kolani. If Kolani refuses to go along with us, then she goes down, along with any warships that stay loyal to her. It's not ideal. We could have used every one of those warships, and now some are likely to be destroyed. You just hold up your end and wipe out the snakes, then keep a lid on the security situation down here while I'm busy up there. We have to maintain order. The mob may take the destruction of the snakes as a license for anarchy. Once we've declared independence, you and I have to keep our control of this star system firm. We want ours to be the *last* revolt in this star system."

Iceni had obviously thought about the questions that Malin had raised about what to do after the snakes were dead. Drakon hoped that Iceni's ideas were ones he could live with. He also hoped they didn't involve getting rid of the one other CEO, Drakon, who would be able to challenge her authority here after Hardrad was taken care of.

Iceni closed out her displays, then stood up and walked toward the door. "Any other questions?"

Drakon nodded, eyeing her again. "Yeah. Why are you really doing this?"

She stopped and gazed back at him. "You don't think it's self-interest?"

"I think that self-interest could have led in other directions. Getting me to sign off on rebellion, then turning me in to the snakes might have satisfied them that you were a good little loyal CEO and provided you with a cover for your own actions."

Iceni smiled very briefly and humorlessly. "Then I'll tell you that my motivation is to protect myself, this star system, and surrounding star systems. I need a safe place to maintain power and influence. Midway is the best place in this region to do that because we have the hypernet gate and also jump points to so many surrounding star systems. The Syndic system failed. That system started the war, failed to win it, and ultimately lost it. That system stripped the Reserve Flotilla from the Midway Star System, the only thing holding off the alien enigma race, and left us almost totally defenseless when the enigmas attacked us. The *Alliance* fleet had to save us. The Alliance, which we have always been taught is weak, disorganized, and corrupt because they let the citizens have a voice in who rules. You and I both know all too well how disorganized and corrupt the Syndicate system can be, and now it has proven to be weak as well.

"We need to try something else, and we can't depend on anyone else. Maybe we'll die trying, but I might well die anyway if I tried to cut and run with whatever wealth I could stuff onto a ship while this star system is threatened by the enigmas and by the chaos in some star systems that is following the collapse of Syndicate Worlds' authority. So, I'm a pragmatist, Artur Drakon. Those are my reasons. Do you believe me?"

"No." Drakon returned the same kind of smile that Iceni had given him. "Why didn't you run when the enigmas threatened to attack if you're so pragmatic?"

She paused as if deciding how to reply. "Because I was responsible for everyone in this star system, and I wouldn't run when they were all trapped here."

"You're an idealist as well as a pragmatist?" Drakon asked, letting some sarcasm into his own tone now.

"You might say that, as long as you're not being insulting." Iceni gave him a smile which was mocking this time. "Don't you believe I can be part idealist?"

"Not if it's a very big part. Nobody survives as a CEO if they're in any way an idealist."

"Oh? And how did you end up at Midway?"

Drakon smiled sardonically at her. "I'm sure you already know that. The snakes tried to arrest one of my sub-CEOs, but someone tipped her off and she disappeared before they could grab her. I got blamed, but no one could prove anything, so I got exiled rather than shot."

Iceni looked back at him steadily. "You don't call some-one willing to run those risks to protect a subordinate an idealist? What would you call a leader whose subordinates and soldiers were so loyal to him that the Syndicate sent them all here to get them isolated?"

"I do what I think is . . . appropriate," Drakon said. "I can't control how others see my actions or react to them. And whether or not I survive is still an open-ended question. I'll do what I have to do, and I know the sort of things you've done in the past to maintain your power. But if you want to pretend those are your reasons, I'm willing to go along."

"Fine. As long as you don't double-cross me. If you do—"

"I'll die?" Drakon asked, doing his best to sound non-chalant even though he was itching to rejoin his soldiers.

Iceni's voice was just as relaxed as Drakon's as she answered. "You'll *wish* that you had died." She opened the door and walked out, then waited for Drakon to exit as well before closing and alarming the entrance. "Good luck." With that, Iceni headed off at a quick pace, her bodyguards taking up positions on all sides.

AN hour and a half later, Artur Drakon knelt inside another building, only a single, hair-thin recon probe sticking out from his shoulder and over the edge of the nearby window, scanning the outer sections of the ISS headquarters complex through the sensors on his combat armor. The civilians who normally occupied this office were under guard in the basement, along with everyone else who worked in the building. In their place, soldiers in combat armor huddled in the halls and inner rooms, waiting for the assault on the ISS complex to begin. High on one wall, an ISS surveillance camera stared blankly into the room. Somewhere in the headquarters complex, systems were reviewing the feed supposedly coming from that camera and seeing only routine activity by the civilians who normally worked here. "Report," Drakon ordered.

About one-third of the way around the perimeter, Malin's voice came from his position. "Everything looks routine. No problem."

On the other side of the perimeter, Morgan responded in a tone that mimicked Malin. "Everything looks routine. We've got a problem."

"What's the problem?" Drakon asked. They were speaking over a shielded comm line run overland through every obstacle. A major pain in the neck, but the only way to minimize the chances of any ISS surveillance gear that hadn't been sabotaged picking up some of the transmissions. *Two tin cans on a string. Millennia of communication advances and in the end we're still depending on two tin cans on a string to make sure no one else hears us.*

"The problem," Morgan insisted, "is that everything looks normal. Even though we've spoofed the surveillance networks, the snakes must have picked up *something* from all of their other distributed monitoring gear. But they haven't reacted at all that we can see. No messages to you or anyone else about the troop movements or anything. Routine security around the complex as far as we can tell. It stinks."

"They could be uncertain," Malin argued. "Trying to decipher the fragments that they're seeing. We can't afford to blow the element of surprise."

"It's already blown, moron."

"That's enough." Drakon thought about Morgan's argument as he studied the ISS complex again. "I haven't had any messages from the snake brass today. They usually jump on me every day about what my troops are doing just to let me know I'm being watched. I think Morgan's right. Has anyone seen any vipers moving around?"

"No," Malin said.

"No," Morgan added with a touch of triumph.

"Then everything isn't routine. There are usually a couple of vipers outside running laps or exercising some other way, aren't there?" Drakon blew out an angry breath. The ISS special forces, nicknamed vipers, had an ugly reputation for brutality and for fighting ability. An independent combat force, answering only to Internal Security, and thus doubly hated by the military of the Syndicate Worlds.

"You think the vipers are activated?" Malin asked, then answered himself. "We have to assume they are."

"Right. Armored and ready to fight. This screws up the assault plan."

Morgan came back on. "We need to hit them with everything we've got. If we go in piecemeal like we planned we'll get cut to ribbons by those vipers."

"If we go in all out we blow our chances of surprise!" Malin said. "The sooner the snakes realize we're actually launching an all-out assault on their headquarters complex, the longer they'll have to activate any doomsday retaliation devices they still have control over. They're going to be overconfident, certain that they can handle whatever we've snuck in to hit them here. We have to take them out before they realize we have enough force on hand to take the complex."

They were both right, Drakon realized. "We need to modify the assault plan. Infiltration to clear our way inside isn't going to work now even with scouts in full stealth gear, but we can't send in everything at once without presenting massed targets and panicking CEO Hardrad into setting off his dead-man retaliation devices. Instead of sneaking in by squads, we'll go in by platoons around the entire perimeter at once and shoot our way in. The first barrage is to include the full range of concealment rounds. Sequence the platoons as they jump off to keep from clustering too many personnel in one spot and to keep the snakes from spotting how many soldiers we have here before we've knocked out their external surveillance. Once inside, every platoon is to advance as fast as it can toward the snake operations center. The vipers will be able to block some of the routes, but there aren't enough vipers to stop platoons coming in along every possible approach. How long to get the revised plan uploaded and everyone ready to jump off?"

"Twenty minutes," Morgan replied.

"Make it half an hour," Drakon ordered before Malin could suggest something longer. Morgan always tended to push time constraints a bit too closely. "That will shove the assault time back fifteen minutes. I'll notify the other commanders to move their assaults back fifteen minutes as well and let them know the snakes are prepared here. Let me know when everyone is ready to go."

Drakon linked in to another landline, this one leading back to his headquarters complex. "Sub-CEO Kai, I've been held up at an appointment. They were waiting for someone but only partially prepared for me, so our briefing later this afternoon will be delayed fifteen minutes. Acknowledge." The message went by the landline to his headquarters, then was transmitted along normal channels so it appeared to have originated at the headquarters. Kai replied within moments, then Drakon called Sub-CEOs Rogero and Gaiene with the same message.

He had barely finished when his comm system alerted him to a call from CEO Hardrad. Drakon blew out a long breath, settling his nerves and settling his expression and posture into the appearance of routine activity. It helped his display of confidence to know that his five subordinates who knew everything, who could have betrayed him, were all loyal. Malin, Morgan, Rogero, Gaiene, and Kai had all been with Drakon a long time. He didn't hesitate to share his secrets with any of them, and he was certain none of them would have told Hardrad anything.

Activating a digital background to make it appear he was answering from his office, Drakon accepted the call.

Hardrad look mildly annoyed. That expression alone was enough to make nearly every inhabitant of this star system tremble. "I need to discuss something with you,

Artur." The ISS CEO routinely used first names with other CEOs. It wasn't a gesture of comradeship but rather a lessening of their status compared to him and a not-so-subtle reminder of the power he wielded over them.

"Go ahead."

"First, tell me why there's a false background on your image," Hardrad said. Of course, the snake systems had spotted that.

"I just got out of the shower."

"An odd time of day for a shower," Hardrad observed.

"Not if you work out. What is it you need to discuss?"

"A message in the comm system. It was high priority, intended for me, and yet held up within this star system for several days."

Drakon frowned. "It came through military channels?"

"No."

That only left one alternative, the comm systems controlled ultimately by Iceni, as both Drakon and Hardrad knew though neither named her. Avoiding saying names in conversations like this was a precaution so elementary that CEOs followed it automatically, since security bots scanning transmissions for information and warnings keyed on names first and foremost. "Good," Drakon said. "Heads would roll if my systems suffered that kind of failure."

Hardrad paused again, eyeing Drakon. "I'd like to speak with you in person, CEO Drakon, regarding the reasons for that failure. Here at my headquarters. The subject is sensitive enough that I wouldn't want to entrust the conversation to any form of transmission."

Smooth. Drakon found himself admiring the skills of Hardrad despite his hatred of what the man stood for and his anger at what Hardrad had done in the past. Hardrad had led the conversation in such a way that it seemed he suspected only Iceni of wrongdoing and wanted to coordinate with Drakon before taking action.

But even if Hardrad didn't suspect Drakon of involvement with the delay in that order from Prime being received, he certainly intended to carry out those orders, which meant getting Drakon into ISS headquarters for a full security screen and interrogation.

Drakon pretended to be thinking through his schedule. "All right. How big a rush is this?"

"The sooner the better. I'll send an escort."

Sure he would. A platoon of vipers in full combat armor. "I don't want to do anything that attracts anyone's attention. You understand. I don't need an escort. My bodyguards can handle anything that might come up." He said it with calm arrogance, a CEO sure of his status and power, and Drakon saw Hardrad relax slightly, like a cat who saw a mouse strolling closer and oblivious to danger. "How about if I start over there in about . . . half an hour?"

A long pause this time, while Drakon wondered if he were starting to sweat and whether or not Hardrad could tell, then the ISS CEO nodded and smiled thinly. "Half an hour. If you're delayed, I'll be . . . concerned."

"Understood. You'll be seeing me soon." If Hardrad had a deception analyzer on this circuit he wouldn't spot any falsity in Drakon's voice because Drakon fully intended to be entering the ISS headquarters complex less than half an hour from now.

Should he warn Iceni that Hardrad had finally received the orders to do a security screen on all CEOs? But with Iceni already well on her way toward that heavy cruiser there wasn't any means to safely pass on such a warning, not without Hardrad's very likely detecting the transmission. And Hardrad would be watching for exactly that, for co-conspirators to begin panicking and sending out warnings that the ISS was closing in. "Malin, Morgan, the snakes are gearing up not because they know what we're doing but because Hardrad finally got that message and he's anticipating trouble after he arrests me. He's expecting me to show up at ISS headquarters in half an hour."

Morgan sounded like she was almost choking with mirth. "Oh, yeah. We'll all be knocking on that door in half an hour. Boom, boom, baby."

"Can you communicate the delay in our jump-off to CEO Iceni, sir?" Malin asked. "She might be worried when we don't attack as scheduled."

"She won't like the delay. I don't like the delay. But it's necessary. If you can figure out a way to tell Iceni about the delay that doesn't run a serious risk of being intercepted by the snakes, let me know."

Iceni was going to have to trust him. That was a hell of a lot for one Syndicate Worlds' CEO to expect of another CEO.

He thought about the mobile forces overhead. For the first time in a long while, he wished there was something to ask for help, something that would listen to a prayer that the delay wouldn't cause problems for Iceni and her plans to deal with those mobile forces.

Between the pitiless, ironfisted facts of life under Syndicate rules and the apparent randomness of life and death on the many battlefields he had seen, Drakon had long ago stopped having faith that anything cared about what happened to him. At times like this, he missed the comfort that might have brought and couldn't help hoping that he was wrong.

ICENI walked briskly through the tube mating the shuttle to Mobile Forces Unit C-448/Cruiser/Heavy/Combat, trying to reveal no signs of concern but frowning around slightly in the usual manner of a CEO, which was calculated to immediately put subordinates onto the worried defensive.

The commanding officer of C-448 saluted in the Syndicate manner, bringing his right fist across to lightly rap his left breast. "Welcome to my unit, CEO Iceni. We are honored and surprised by your personal visit."

Iceni sketched a very brief smile back at him. "Thank you, Sub-CEO Akiri. I've long believed that not every inspection should be announced in advance. Are you prepared to storm the gates of hell?"

Akiri blinked at the code phrase, took a deep breath, then tried to nod calmly. "We are ready to follow you, CEO Iceni." Turning to the woman standing beside him, Akiri gestured aft. "Make all necessary preparations."

Her smile a little too tense and eager, the woman saluted him. "Five minutes."

Iceni watched her walk off, not fearing betrayal from that source. Executive Marphissa, the second-in-command of C-448, had once had a brother. That brother hadn't been killed fighting the Alliance but had been arrested by Internal Security before dying during interrogation of what the snakes always called "heart failure." Having done her homework, Iceni knew how badly Marphissa wanted to avenge that death. *Find the tools and use the tools,* the voice of one of her old mentors came back to Iceni. *We're artisans, Gwen, who use people to shape outcomes. Just pick the right people, point them in directions they already want to go, and they'll do your work for you. And they won't leave any of* your *fingerprints showing after the deed is done, unless of course you want to take credit for it.*

"She's capable," Akiri murmured to Iceni as Marphissa left. "But you have to watch her very closely."

Cutting down subordinates wasn't all that unusual (after all, every executive needed someone to blame if anything went wrong), but that Akiri had done it in such a blunt and clumsy way lowered Iceni's opinion of him a bit more. *Have you wondered yet, Sub-CEO Akiri, why out of all the mobile forces unit commanders who pledged loyalty to me, I chose your cruiser to personally command from? Do you think that was a compliment? I know when a subordinate needs to be closely watched, and Marphissa isn't the one I'll be watching.*

Akiri started to say something else, but Iceni held up a restraining hand as her high-priority comm alert sounded. She didn't have to entirely fake a look of irritation as she thumbed the accept command, seeing the image of her all-purpose personal assistant and occasional hired gun, Mehmet Togo.

"We have received a summons from ISS headquarters," Togo began in an emotionless voice. "They are in receipt of a message from CEO Kolani claiming that you intentionally delayed her receipt of orders from the government at Prime."

Damn. The order to Hardrad had already been impeded to the limit they could expect to delay it, but the order to Kolani should have been stuck in the comm system for days yet. Some comm tech too smart for his or her own good must have spotted it and pried it loose from the code hobbles that were supposed to keep the message hung up inside the message-processing software.

Despite all of the security codes and scrambling protecting this conversation on her private line, Iceni knew better than to assume the conversation was private. Those who didn't assume that Internal Security was always listening tended to pay very high prices for their carelessness. So Iceni put on a look of puzzled anger. "Orders? What orders?"

Togo spread his hands, pretending bafflement as well. "I do not know."

"How are we supposed to respond to the ISS without knowing what orders were allegedly delayed?" Iceni demanded. "Military orders? Shouldn't those have come through those channels?"

"I would think so, Madam CEO. Should I contact the CEO with responsibilities for that area?"

Which would be Drakon, of course. "No. Not yet. I'm shocked to hear of this, but I can't confront anyone else when I know so little. Contact CEO Hardrad and tell him that I need to know what this is about so I can take any necessary action."

The screen blanked and Iceni glanced at Akiri. "Have you seen those orders?"

He nodded. "CEO Kolani forwarded them to all ships. We received our copy a few minutes ago. All mobile forces in this star system are to proceed to Prime Star System to operate under direct control of the supreme council of the

Syndicate Worlds. I'm surprised that you were able to hold up a command directive like that in the communications system without alerting anyone."

"It's not easy." Had someone in Drakon's camp let the message out? Had Drakon done it? If he planned on betraying her, he would regret it. She hadn't been bluffing about that. "Did CEO Kolani also give you movement orders when she forwarded the message to you?"

"No, Madam CEO. We're supposed to prepare for departure, but that's all we've been told."

Iceni smiled, willing herself into calmness. "CEO Kolani doubtless wants to hang around here to watch me get hauled into ISS headquarters and torn into very little pieces." She checked the time. "In a few minutes things will begin happening on the surface."

Another chime on her private channel, the notes different this time, and given an ominous aspect from knowing whose call they announced. Iceni took an extra moment to compose herself, then answered again, this time seeing the deceptively bland features of the head of the Internal Security Service forces in this star system. "CEO Hardrad, I'm glad you called. What's this about some orders being held up?"

Iceni had never thought that Hardrad looked the part of a snake, which might have helped his rise through their ranks. Bland-featured, his hair, skin, and clothing all shades of beige, Hardrad seemed even after detailed study to be a perfect colorless bureaucrat. Even his eyes rarely revealed anything but mild disinterest. Iceni, who had studied not only Hardrad's looks but also his career, had not been fooled by the outer ordinariness of the man. Judging by his actions, inside he was a very ruthless snake indeed. Now Hardrad pursed his lips in the mildest of reactions to Iceni's question. "A command directive from Prime, Gwen," he said.

"I should have seen that," Iceni protested. "I am responsible for the overall defense of this star system. Why didn't I see it?"

"It was directed to CEO Kolani." Iceni hadn't expected

Hardrad to appear tense, but it was still unnerving to see him regard her as if she were a piece in a game with an ending that was foreordained. "Why are you in orbit?" he asked her.

"As senior CEO in this star system, I'm responsible for all Syndicate Worlds' assets." Iceni waved one negligent hand around to indicate the ship. "I'm conducting an inspection."

"No inspection was on your schedule."

"I prefer surprises," Iceni said. "You accomplish more that way."

"That is true," Hardrad agreed. A lesser man would have betrayed some feeling then, some darkly humorous acknowledgment that they were both speaking primarily about the ISS and its tactics. But not Hardrad. His expression didn't even flicker. "However, your inspection will have to take place on another day. I need to see you in person. Right away."

She put on her best expression of affronted dignity. "Because CEO Kolani, who commands the most deadly forces in this star system, is accusing *me* of doing something which is probably the fault of her own communications staff? I don't control military communications."

"No. You don't. We need to talk about who does. You understand?"

So Hardrad suspected Drakon? That was reasonable under these circumstances, and yet . . . *If he's also finally received his own orders, Hardrad wants me in his headquarters so he can find out every disloyal thought I've ever had. What better way to get me into that building than by implying that we're going to act jointly against Drakon?*

Assuming that Drakon hasn't really betrayed me.

"We should discuss this right away, Gwen," Hardrad continued. She had never liked the way he used her first name in conversations like this, implying not only familiarity but also inferiority compared to him. "I've notified the ISS representatives on C-448. Some of them will escort you back down to the planet."

Iceni spent a long moment looking at the blank screen after Hardrad's image had vanished. For all his power, Hardrad knew that he had to at least feign respect for senior CEOs. He was acting far too confident by making such an open move against her now. *What does he know?* She checked the time, and her breath caught. Drakon's attack should have started two minutes ago.

"Your orders?" Akiri asked softly.

Strike now at the ISS representatives on this warship and the other warships as well? But if Drakon's move had just been delayed, if he hadn't outright betrayed her to the snakes, then starting her own move now would betray Drakon's impending assault which *had* to succeed. Hardrad would know almost immediately if the status feed from his representatives aboard C-448 was broken. At that point, Iceni might as well broadcast the news that she would be assuming command of all of the mobile forces and her demand that Kolani submit to Iceni's authority. Without Drakon's actions on the surface triggering her agents on other ships she would have to do that, before the snakes on those other ships could strike at the regular unit officers or activate disabling worms that Internal Security was known to plant in every critical system.

Akiri took a message on his own comm unit, then faced Iceni. "The ISS representatives aboard this unit will arrive in five minutes to escort you back to the surface."

What the hell is Drakon up to? How much longer does he need? Or has he already backstabbed me? In which case, I need to act now to try to save my own skin.

"Your orders?" Akiri repeated, his own tone growing not just urgent but also anxious.

CHAPTER TWO

TIME crawled for Drakon as the assault troops made minor changes to their prepositioning, every movement careful as they worked to always remain concealed from the ISS headquarters. Drakon kept his eyes on the ISS complex, seeing nothing at all out of the ordinary across all passive visual spectrums and comm frequencies, but now viewing the ordinary as menacing.

"Assault Force Three is ready," Morgan reported.

"Good. Watch out for those vipers when we go in, Roh. They're tough."

"We're tougher. And every soldier with us hates them. Who doesn't know someone who got hauled off to a labor camp or worse by vipers or other snakes?"

Drakon nodded to himself, thinking of the worries he had lived with for decades, wondering day by day no matter where he was if a door would come crashing open, followed by a squad of vipers with orders from Internal Security to take him off for interrogation about crimes he might or might not have contemplated but would surely confess to after enough physical and mental duress. He wondered if anyone in the Syndicate Worlds had ever been safe from that worry. Snakes. The common nickname for ISS personnel spoke to the general attitude toward them, but the ISS had been vicious and efficient enough to keep dissent down nonetheless.

Until now.

Morgan spoke again, sounding annoyed. "The unit leaders want to know what the policy is on prisoners. Do we take any vipers alive?"

That one was easy. "They won't know anything worth sweating out of them, assuming they aren't conditioned to suicide once captured. It doesn't matter anyway. Do you think any vipers will try to surrender, knowing how the soldiers feel about them?"

Morgan chuckled, her voice delighted this time. "No. They'll fight to the death because they know what'll happen if they're captured alive. I hope we do capture a few."

About a minute later, Malin reported in. "Assault Force Two ready."

"How do your people look?" Drakon asked him. "Any signs of wavering?"

"No, sir. These are the cream of our forces. They've been waiting for this day. And you're not just another CEO. You're the only CEO who ever showed any concern for their personal welfare. They're loyal to you. You're going into battle with them, and how many CEOs do that? It may take time to get all the rest of the planetary troops behind you, but you've got a good reputation among them."

A reputation based on actions that had resulted in his being exiled to Midway, Drakon thought ruefully, along with Morgan and Malin, who had chosen to follow him here. "It hasn't done much for my promotion potential in the past, but maybe that's about to change." Assuming he won, and survived, he would go from being a rather low-level military-specialist CEO within the sprawling bureaucracy of the Syndicate Worlds to being the seniormost military commander in an independent star system.

Tense from waiting, stuck waiting six more minutes for

the new time line to run out and looking for something to distract part of his mind, Drakon seized on the idea of change. Iceni wanted to go back to calling mobile forces "warships." Maybe some other changes were worth considering. "What do you two think about going back to the old rank structure? Dropping the CEO and civilian pay scale stuff and using military titles again?"

"We've been doing it this way for about a hundred and fifty years," Malin said. "It's what the troops and everyone are used to."

Unsurprisingly, that made Morgan jump in on the other side. "I think it'd be a great idea to go back to the old ranks, *General* Drakon."

He liked the sound of that. General Drakon. And uniforms for high-ranking military leaders again instead of corporate suits. Something besides an executive specialty and assignment code to indicate what he was. And not just *what* he was but, in a lot of ways, *who* he was. "We need to break with the past, and maybe the best way to do that is to go even farther into the past." Just decide it and get it done. Don't go through a hundred layers of corporate bureaucracy, then wait for years before a decision finally wends its way back down saying no, and why the hell are you thinking instead of doing what you're told? Was it that bad in the Alliance? They hadn't been able to beat the Syndicate Worlds in a century of fighting, not until Black Jack reappeared, so the Alliance probably didn't offer any perfect world, either.

But he had never cared for identifying himself as CEO Drakon on those rare occasions when he sent transmissions to Alliance military leaders. They were generals and admirals, and wasn't he, too? "I'm a soldier, dammit."

"Yes, sir," Malin agreed. "Maybe the new titles would help establish a new spirit in the troops."

An alert chimed with deceptive gentleness and Drakon checked the incoming message. "CEO-level comms have been picked up between one of the mobile forces cruisers and the ISS headquarters."

Morgan cursed. "That bitch is trying to roll us! She knows we can't back out now!"

"We know Hardrad has received his orders," Malin countered. "He's probably questioning Iceni about it, too."

"It doesn't matter which of you is right. We have no choice now but to go in." No choice but to face the potential for horrendous disaster. The ISS had nuclear weapons buried in the major population centers on this planet, but detonating those nukes required the use of codes held by Iceni. The snakes could blow the nukes anyway, but it would take a lot longer to trigger them without Iceni's cooperation. If she was cooperating with the snakes, the ground forces attack might end in glowing craters rather than victory, but it was impossible to halt the attack at this point without surrendering to the snakes. "We go in."

The timer on his heads-up display scrolled rapidly toward zero, meaning it was time to focus on that and forget the distractions. "All assault forces stand by. Jump-off at zero minute." As the green "go" alert flashed, Drakon sent a command that was instantly relayed to transmitters that bounced the message out beyond the planet's atmosphere, to every orbiting station and facility and every base on every moon where both ground forces and snakes were present. The order could only travel at light speed, meaning it would take minutes and sometimes hours to reach the farthest facilities, but any reports of his attacks on the planet would come in behind it. His people would get the order to attack seconds before the snakes at their locations knew anything had happened back on the planetary surface.

With the next motion, he switched his circuit to the frequency linking the portion of the attack force he was personally leading in. Half-terrified and half-exhilarated, he felt adrenaline surging, while visions of a hundred earlier battles and engagements flashed through his memory as he began yet another. "Assault Force One, fire and move!"

A one-hundred-meter-wide area free of obstacles or cover, grass- and marble- and stone-surfaced, separated the ISS complex from surrounding buildings. Against civilian rioters, that offered plenty of free-fire zone, and even a small number of regular troops trying to assault the ISS building faced formidable defenses. But no complex could be designed to withstand a massed assault by so many troops, so close to their target, armed with so many heavy weapons.

Drakon heard a roar of mingled rage and defiance surge across the comm circuit as his soldiers opened fire on the hated snakes. The breaching teams fired clearing rounds into the double-layered fence around the complex, blowing huge holes in the fences, detonating the mines placed between the fences and destroying the sensors. Other teams fired antiarmor rounds straight into the security towers set at intervals around the complex, most of the towers automated but some occupied by ISS snakes who never knew what hit them.

As the outer rings of defenses were simultaneously blown apart, other weapons teams dropped screening rounds nearer the walls of the ISS complex, generating dense clouds of smoke mixed with floating infrared decoys and radar-defeating chaff.

In every attack he had participated in, Drakon never remembered actually starting to move. This time, like every other time, he went from crouched under cover to realizing that he was charging forward across the open area toward the complex, moving in the low, fast leaps that the power assists in combat armor made easy. His soldiers followed, dim shapes to either side of him. Despite Malin's reassurance, he had wondered if his soldiers would obey him when it came to this. But on the heads-up display of his helmet Drakon could see every soldier moving to the attack.

Fire flashed by, the complex's defenses firing blind in hopes of scoring hits. Electromagnetic pulse charges went off all over the area, but the EMPs which would have fried electronic circuits in civilian gear or standard survival suits couldn't harm the shielded combat-armor circuitry. Drakon's soldiers paused to return fire, their armor's combat systems pinpointing origins for the defensive shots, then rushed onward as the building's outer defenses were rapidly silenced under an avalanche of attacks.

Drakon reached a stout wall, knowing that it had layers of dead space and synthetic armor beneath the stone exterior. Schematics for the ISS complex had been highly classified, but that hadn't prevented Malin from acquiring copies through some inspired hacking. Now more of Drakon's troops reached the wall to place breaching charges specially formulated to blow through that armor. "Take cover!"

The assault troops nearest the wall huddled back as the charges detonated, directing a series of blasts against the fortified exterior to tear two-meter-wide and -high holes in the walls. On the heels of the detonations, the assault troops poured through the gap, knowing that any defenses right behind the wall would have been taken out along with the wall itself.

Drakon went with the troops, knowing that if he were alone he might have trouble nerving himself to leap into the face of the enemy defenses, but he was able to overcome his dread by staying in a group. Once through the hole, Drakon hurled himself to one side as a volley of high-intensity fire ripped down the hallway the gap opened into. *That's not any internal automated defense. We must have run into a viper strongpoint.* Fear forgotten for the moment under the demands of decision-making, Drakon checked the IDs of the soldiers closest to him. The symbols representing those soldiers glowed on the display that projected information onto the faceplate of his armor, showing exactly where they were on a schematic of this floor of the ISS complex. "Second squad, take cover and return fire to keep those vipers busy. Everyone else, head north with me."

There wasn't time to worry now. Drakon had attention only for the map on his helmet display and the glimpses he could catch of the actual building around him through the dust and smoke thrown up by the breaching charges and the fighting. He and the soldiers with him had barely entered the next passage when barrages of defensive fire began raking it as well. Drakon hit the floor, fuming with anger at the holdup, then checked the floor plan on his helmet display again before calling out orders. "Fire some conceal-ment rounds and EMP charges toward those defenders. Combat engineer team sigma, blow a hole in the floor just around the corner."

The concealment charges turned the area between Dra-kon and the vipers into a fog impenetrable by sensors, and a few moments later that area of the building shook as the combat engineers blasted the hole. Drakon and the troops with him crawled back and around the corner, then as the vipers continued to pour fire down the now-empty corridor, he and the others dropped through the new access to the next lower level.

That level felt oddly quiet, even though the building was shuddering as firefights raged throughout other sections. Doctrine called for Drakon to pause now and evaluate his entire force posture before ordering coordinated attacks, but he had trained his soldiers to operate without detailed orders even though such an approach was discouraged by a Syndicate hierarchy which rightly feared independent thinking. Drakon's approach to training paid off, as indi-vidual platoons and squads from the attacking force spread through the building along every open path, like water flooding an area without adequate protection.

The snakes seemed to be reacting slowly, though, wait-ing for orders before they shifted position. The delays were often fatal, as soldiers surrounded and wiped out pockets of defenders.

Drakon's helmet display kept fuzzing and sputtering as the jamming systems inside the ISS building as well as the building's structure blocked signals. But so many soldiers were inside the building, each of the combat armor suits relaying signals to every other suit of armor within range, that Drakon still got a halfway-decent picture of events. "This way," he ordered the soldiers with him, diverting to the south along a short corridor as the roar of battle grew in intensity again. Fear had become a distant thing, lost in the need to concentrate on developments and keep moving fast.

A sudden alert pierced the pounding of the gunfire. Drakon paused to eye the symbol, which told him that this message had to be from one of two people in this star system. He ordered the soldiers with him to halt movement and accepted the transmission.

The image of CEO Hardrad was fuzzy, breaking up into pixilated static before partially re-forming. "Drakon, break off your attack now, or I will detonate the nuclear charges under every major city on this planet."

"You don't have the codes."

"Yes, I do." The interference made it impossible to read Hardrad's expression or get any feel for emotion in the other CEO's voice, not that Hardrad ever showed much feeling in either face or tone. "Iceni betrayed you in exchange for limited immunity. I have the codes, and I will destroy this world before I let you overthrow lawful authority. But, if you stop now, we can reach an agreement. Iceni got some immunity. So can you. The alternative is to die along with everyone else."

In the middle of a battle, and despite his long experience with the cold-bloodedness that often characterized Internal Security, it felt odd to hear Hardrad making such an apocalyptic threat in the same manner as if he were suggesting that forms had been filled out improperly.

But does he have the codes? Did Iceni turn on me to protect herself? Can Hardrad carry out his threat right now? How much longer before my troops can get to Hardrad's office in the heavily fortified command center?

Drakon's eyes rested on the display depicting his soldiers storming deeper into the ISS headquarters building. He could hear orders being passed, and other cries across the comm circuits as his soldiers exulted in finally striking back at an enemy they might have come to hate more than anything in the Alliance. And he wondered if, despite the brutal discipline exercised within Syndicate forces, it would be possible to get his troops to withdraw or if, no matter what he said, they would keep attacking until every snake was dead.

Or until this city, and numerous others, saw nuclear blooms blossom in their centers.

ICENI stood perfectly still as her mind raced. Five minutes until the snakes on this cruiser got here. What if nothing had happened on the surface by then? Did she continue to trust Drakon?

She called Togo, her signal this time having to weave its way around several blocks set up in the comm system, requiring minute after minute before a clear path was finally located. "Have you heard from the ISS?" Iceni asked.

Togo nodded. "We have been told to freeze all systems and prepare for a security sweep. I can no longer make outgoing calls."

"What is the situation in the city?" The question was too blunt, too likely to tip off the snakes that something might be expected to happen, but she had no alternative.

"Quiet."

"I want you to—" Iceni stopped speaking as the call connection broke. ISS must have spotted her penetration and sealed off the access her own systems had located.

"Drakon." Akiri made the name into a curse, his eyes reflecting growing uneasiness.

Iceni could feel the unsteadiness in the man, as if he were a satellite in an increasingly unstable orbit. "Stay with me, or yours will be the first name I tell them," Iceni warned Akiri in a low voice.

Akiri glanced at the sole bodyguard who had followed Iceni through the tube and was standing well back but with his eyes watching everything. Akiri was smart enough to know his odds against that man and experienced enough to know that the snakes would roll up anyone even slightly suspected of disloyalty if Iceni called out that charge, so the cruiser commander licked his lips nervously, then nodded.

Iceni looked down the passageway to see four snakes approaching, their casual arrogance as unmistakable as their ISS suits. Five more minutes had passed, making it ten minutes since Drakon had promised his attack on the surface would begin.

She had a source very close to Drakon, and she had heard nothing from that source. Was it because Drakon had discovered that person was feeding Iceni information? Or because any comms now would be impossible to send to her? Even Togo didn't know that source existed, so he couldn't have relayed any information.

Behind the snakes came Executive Marphissa and several other crew, their paths apparently aimed at Akiri. Iceni could easily tell how nervous a couple of those crew members were, but fortunately the attention of the snakes was centered on her and not on those behind them. Despite what had happened in other star systems in the last few months, the snakes hadn't really absorbed the idea that open revolt could occur. They had been the feared guardians of order for so long and so successfully that a group of them didn't worry as much as they should have about citizens at their backs.

Marphissa and Akiri were both watching Iceni, the executive calm, the sub-CEO visibly tense, questions in their eyes.

The senior snake stopped before Iceni, smiling slightly. Iceni realized that she was effectively under arrest, but the snakes would pretend otherwise, acting as if they were simply escorting her to a meeting to coordinate action against Drakon. Until she was inside the walls of the ISS complex the snakes would follow polite form, treating her with respect. Paying no attention to Iceni's bodyguard, the senior snake gestured toward the access tube. "If CEO Iceni would lead the way?"

Iceni smiled back, deciding to stall for a few more minutes. *If Drakon doesn't do something before they order me onto that shuttle, I'll have to act.* "The shuttle operator hasn't been informed of our departure. I was supposed to be aboard this unit much longer than this."

The senior snake turned to one of his subordinates. "Call the shuttle operator." The call and response took perhaps another minute. "The shuttle is ready to depart. Honored CEO, please lead the way."

Iceni nodded but did not move. "Sub-CEO Akiri, my inspection will take place at another time. Since I appear to be having communications difficulties, inform CEO Kolani of that."

"It will be done," Akiri replied.

"And, Sub-CEO Akiri, ensure that—"

"Honored CEO," the senior snake broke in, now openly frowning, "it is necessary to depart."

"CEO Hardrad did not indicate haste was necessary," Iceni said, playing a card that might gain more time.

"There may have been some misunderstanding, CEO Iceni. Our orders were that your safety would be imperiled if we did not get you into a secure area as soon as possible."

Her safety would be imperiled? There was more than one possible way to interpret that statement. Iceni looked back at the snake as if she hadn't heard him clearly, stretching out a few more seconds, then glanced back at her bodyguard. Alone, he wouldn't stand a chance, face-to-face against four snakes.

"GO to hell, Hardrad."

For the first time in Drakon's experience, he saw Hardrad's composure crack. "You will be the one who dies when I destroy this rebellious city! You and everyone with you!"

"Then I'll personally kick you through the gates when we both get to hell," Drakon said with a laugh. "Since when have you made deals with people? You never bargain, you just bring the hammer down. Offering me a deal means you don't really have those codes."

"I have them! I'll use them!"

"CEO Hardrad, if you had those codes, you'd just use them. No threats. No deals. Just take everyone else down with you because dying to you is a lot less important than making sure no one else ever wins. You gave me too much of a chance to watch you work, too many opportunities to see how you do things. But I guess you didn't spend as much time learning how I do things." Maybe he had made the wrong assessment about Hardrad's being more willing to die than to lose, but Drakon knew with absolute confidence that Hardrad couldn't be trusted to keep any deal. For Drakon and for Iceni, it was a matter of winning or dying.

Drakon broke the connection so that he could focus on the fight once more. If he spoke to Hardrad again before either of them died, it would be face-to-face in the snake command center.

Perhaps the distraction had helped him. Checking the display after not looking at it for a few moments, Drakon could now see an opening that he could exploit in the movements and fighting among soldiers and snakes. Drakon ordered the soldiers with him into motion again, down one hallway, through a door, past another hall, then to a corner. They came out behind two viper fire teams blocking attackers coming from the other direction. Drakon leveled his own weapon as his soldiers hit the vipers from the rear. His targeting sight glowed as it registered a good shot, the weapon jerked as an energy pulse blasted out, and a viper in the act of turning lurched against the nearest wall. Two more hits from other weapons tore the viper in half.

As expected, the vipers fought to the death, the last one turning her weapon on herself to avoid being taken alive by those she had helped torment.

"That way!" Drakon ordered the other platoon, then led the platoon still with him deeper into the complex, following his helmet display's directions toward the ISS command center.

"—floor clear!" he heard Morgan call, then the connection broke.

"Morgan! If you can hear me, send a few platoons up to clear the top floors and get the rest down here!" According to their information, the upper floors had very little in the way of defenses, being regarded as too vulnerable to attack and bombardment compared to those floors going below ground level where Drakon was. Naturally, that meant those upper floors also held the lowest-ranking members of the ISS, who could be rounded up at leisure once the lower floors had been cleared.

He didn't know if Morgan had received the command, but his display showed patches of assault troops streaming through passageways above and to the sides, some penetrating to the next floor down, while clusters of defenders blinked in and out of contact, sometimes disappearing as attackers rolled over them.

Something hit Drakon's shoulder, knocking him back, then the soldiers near him were firing down the hall at another viper strongpoint. One of the soldiers aimed a squat tube down the hall and fired, followed by a terrific concussion that knocked the soldiers with Drakon off their feet.

Drakon lay blinking for a moment in confusion, his armor blaring alarms about damage and a near breach where the viper shot had hit home. His focus on what was happening had broken completely this time, and for that instant he could see and feel nothing but chaos. Drakon clamped down on his nerves, concentrating fiercely until the muddle on his display resolved once again into a recognizable flow of events, then struggled back to his feet. His soldiers were already up and racing to the end of the hallway, where stunned vipers were still trying to gather their wits, only to be slaughtered by close-in fire before they could stand. As Drakon watched them die, he experienced a curious lack of feeling, elation and vengeance also locked away inside him for the moment.

Another soldier loomed through the smoke, stepping out of a hole blown by the concussion charge. "Are you all right, sir?" Malin asked.

"Yeah." Drakon's display showed that they were not far from the command center, which was still one more floor down. "What have you got with you?"

"Two squads."

"I've got most of three squads. Head over that way and try to blow an access into the command center from overhead. That may make the snakes think we're only trying to get in that way. I'll take mine down and through here, and hit them from the east."

"Yes, sir." Malin vanished into the countermeasure-created murk, then Drakon took his small force down some stairs that stretched unnaturally long for a flight only going down one level. But that told him the stolen schematics which had revealed a substantial layer of armor above the ISS command center had been proven right again. The lead soldier in the group finally hit a landing, only to be thrown back and to the side as the explosion of a mine rocked the stairwell. Leaping over the new hole in the landing, Drakon followed as his soldiers pounded down another passageway.

More heavy fire came down the corridor, lashing at the assaulting soldiers. Drakon huddled against one wall, breathing heavily, feeling the sweat coating his face under the helmet and face shield of his armor, wishing that he could wipe off the sweat and wishing that he had another concussion weapon at hand.

A subsection leader dropped to the floor near Drakon. "We think this is automated, sir. Last-ditch defenses for the command center and survival citadel."

"Pretty damned heavy for last-ditch defenses," Drakon mumbled, scrolling through his display. As far as he could tell through the interference, Malin's force hadn't yet been able to punch through the command center's massive overhead armor. That was mainly intended as a diversion, though, and other assault forces were converging on the command center. *How long do we have left until the snakes activate whatever doomsday defenses they have? Iceni swore that without the codes she held as system CEO the snakes would need extra time to engage the override codes, but she didn't know how much extra time.*

The entire complex shook from a prolonged explosion so heavy that Drakon wondered if the structure overhead was about to collapse. In the wake of the big explosion, the building shuddered again, a prolonged and diffuse trembling as if parts of it were indeed caving in. He felt a chill inside, almost frozen by fear that Hardrad had gotten the codes from Iceni or managed the work-around and carried out his threat to nuke the city.

But his suit hadn't registered any radiation burst, and the shock had seemed to come from within the building rather than hitting the outside in the kind of seismic blow that would have been felt when the subsurface nuke created a massive ground shock in the center of the city.

Drakon realized that the defensive fire from ahead had faltered substantially. His display had fuzzed out almost completely except for the floor-plan schematics, but then it flickered to show assault forces streaming into the command center from the side opposite him. Red symbols marking snakes and vipers were melting away from the assault, some winking out as they were destroyed and others moving fast toward the hallway he was in. "Hold positions!" Drakon yelled, readying his weapon. "Snakes on the way!"

Armored figures appeared ahead, mixed with others wearing only survival suits, all of them fleeing toward Drakon's position. He and the soldiers with him opened fire, cutting down the snakes trying to escape from the trap their own command center had become.

The last one of the routed snakes stopped and held out hands in surrender, then slammed backward and down as a shot went dead center into the snake's chest. "Oops," one of the soldiers said without emotion. "My finger slipped."

Drakon didn't bother getting the soldier's identity. He had known going in that no mercy would be shown the snakes; but then the snakes had never to his knowledge shown mercy to the general populace.

A momentary pause came, Drakon cursing as his display fluttered and blurred again. Green symbols popped up at the other end of the hallway, and the automated defenses ceased firing completely. Moments later, Drakon's display cleared as the last snake active countermeasures were shut down and clean links were established with soldiers throughout the ruin of the ISS complex.

He got up and moved to meet the soldiers coming his way, hearing their cheers and those of the other soldiers. For the moment, comm discipline seemed to have fallen apart completely as the soldiers celebrated the deaths of the feared snakes and a sense of freedom they had never before known.

That sense of freedom might cause problems later, probably *would* cause problems later, but he would deal with that.

Drakon entered the command center, which was still filled with drifts of smoke and floating countermeasures that hadn't yet settled. The equipment consoles and desks he could see had been ripped open with close-range fire and clearing charges. Bodies of dead snakes and a few soldiers lay scattered about where they had fallen. He could see across the large space to the opposite wall, where a huge hole gaped.

Morgan stepped out of the murk, her armor pitted from several hits that hadn't penetrated, and rapped her right fist against her left breast in salute. "All resistance has been neutralized, sir."

"What the hell blew that hole through the command center's armor?" Drakon demanded.

He couldn't see Morgan's grin through her armor, but he could hear it. "The engineers rigged up six wall-breaching charges to fire in tandem at the same point, sir."

"Six? How did you know that wouldn't bring the building down on top of us?"

"The engineers said it should be safe, sir. That is, they were fairly confident the building wouldn't collapse."

Fairly confident. He knew who had ordered the engineers to rig that breaching charge that way. "Good work, Morgan."

Malin appeared, too, his armor mostly unmarred but his weapon still glowing with waste heat from frequent firing. "I talked to a prisoner before he died. They were trying to activate hidden nukes buried in a dozen locations, one of them centered in this city, but were still about three minutes from final firing approval."

"Three minutes?" Hardrad had lied, then. Iceni hadn't betrayed them. "If they'd had the codes, we never would have made it this far in time."

"Yes, sir. Good thing CEO Iceni really did withhold those activation codes."

"Where's CEO Hardrad?" Drakon asked, looking around at the shattered command center.

"Dead," Morgan replied.

"That's *what* he is. *Where* is he?"

"What's left of him is in his personal office." Morgan pointed off to one side. "He was working away at activating those detonation codes when his brains got turned into a wall decoration."

Drakon didn't have to wonder exactly who had blown out Hardrad's brains. But he couldn't fault her for the action given what the ISS leader had been trying to accomplish. For all Morgan had known, Hardrad could have been a couple of seconds from detonating those nukes. "Have a team go through that office, checking for traps and anything still operating. Some important files might have survived, and I want anything our people can recover."

Malin passed on the order, listened, then waved about in a grand gesture. "The assault forces in the other cities have reported in. Sub-CEOs Kai, Rogero, and Gaiene say the three ISS subcomplexes have been taken. Neighborhood ISS stations everywhere else are being overrun. They're helpless without backup from the subcomplexes and this place. The planet is under your control, sir."

That left the orbiting facilities, but at worst those would be mop-up work if the attacks there failed. Drakon smiled, his breathing slowing as his body began coming down from its hyped-up battle state. He once again looked around the smoking wreckage that had been the ISS command center, and one of the centers for the authority of the Syndicate Worlds in this star system. That authority was now broken. "Then my first official action is to reinstate the old military-rank system in the ground forces. I am now General Drakon, not CEO Drakon. Do you approve, Colonel Morgan?"

"Yes, sir!" Morgan crowed. "I assume *Major* Malin also approves."

"Bran is a colonel, too, Roh."

Malin pointed toward Morgan. "I'd think she'd be more worried about herself being promoted beyond her level of competence. Oh, wait, that's already happened long before this."

"You're both colonels," Drakon said. "End of discussion. Colonel Malin, please inform Sub-CEOs Kai, Rogero, and Gaiene that they're also colonels now. Colonel Morgan, please have this entire complex swept to ensure no snakes got away or are still holed up anywhere inside." He gazed at broken and shattered equipment consoles, thinking about how long this planet, this star system, had been effectively ruled from this room. "Any loyalist resistance to our attack, or anyone else wanting to rebel against *us*, will require time to organize. All we have to worry about for the moment is those warships out there."

"Warships? We are going retro, aren't we? No matter what we call them, we don't have any way to stop an orbital bombardment," Morgan pointed out.

"CEO Iceni has some space-combat experience. We'd better hope that's enough."

"We'd also better hope that she's still allied with us and isn't planning to get rid of all of her competition in this star system," Morgan added as she turned to carry out her orders. "Otherwise, all hell is going to start dropping onto this planet in a few hours."

ABOARD the heavy cruiser C-448, in orbit about the primary world of the Midway Star System, the senior snake opened his mouth to say something to Iceni, then paused with a startled look as his own comm unit blared an alarm. In that moment, as the snakes took a few precious instants to absorb the fact that something serious was happening, Iceni made a quick gesture to Akiri and Marphissa.

Snake suits had built-in defenses against attack, but the suits left their upper necks bare. The knife Executive Marphissa suddenly produced came around from behind the senior snake and sliced so deeply into his neck that the blade disappeared for a moment. Only one of the other snakes had time to even try to react before all of them were lying on the deck, their blood forming a rapidly spreading pool. Iceni's bodyguard had twitched forward when the knives appeared, then returned to silent watching as the snakes died.

Marphissa listened to a message on a comm unit, then nodded to Akiri. "The last snake, in their snoop room, is also dead."

"How did you get someone in there?" Iceni asked, knowing how carefully the snakes protected their little citadels within units.

"The snake left on duty fancied one of the crew," Marphissa explained, "who offered a liaison while the other snakes were busy. But the climax was a bit more intense than the snake was prepared for."

"The old tricks are the best," Iceni said dryly. "Sub-CEO Akiri, my agents on the other ships whose commanders have pledged loyalty would have acted when the attack on the surface began. Now I need to formally tell every ship, and CEO Kolani, that I am assuming command."

"How many are with you?" Akiri asked.

"With *us*, Sub-CEO Akiri. We're all in this together." Akiri didn't seem entirely convinced of that as Iceni waved around her. "Most of the mobile forces, the warships, are committed to me. Perhaps enough of them to convince Kolani not to fight. But we'll see. Let's get to your bridge."

Iceni looked down at the bodies on the deck, moving her feet slightly to avoid a broad, slow-moving river of blood angling toward her. Despite her feelings about the snakes, and even though this act had been necessary, Iceni found her stomach knotting at the sight and smell. But this was no time to betray squeamishness or irresolution, especially when the citizens around her had already smelled the blood of one set of dead masters. During her difficult climb into the ranks of CEOs, Iceni had gotten very good at pretending not to be bothered in the least by anything she had to do. "Have someone clean up this mess."

With her bodyguard and Marphissa following, Iceni followed Akiri toward the cruiser's bridge, feeling oddly deflated for someone in the midst of a rebellion. There was very little chance that Kolani would accept Iceni's authority, which meant there would be a fight up here as well as on the surface of the planet, and Iceni was already sick of death this day.

CHAPTER THREE

ICENI felt a sense of familiarity as she walked through the passageways of the cruiser. One of her first junior-executive assignments had been on such a warship, and there hadn't been any major design changes in the years since then. That C-333 had been destroyed in a battle (to be seamlessly replaced by another C-333) two months after Iceni had transferred to another assignment, continuing on her path upward through executive ranks, cultivating mentors and connections, discrediting and outmaneuvering rivals. Eventually, she had briefly commanded flotillas of mobile forces, surviving a few bloody battles with Alliance warships whose crews had an ugly yet admirable tendency to fight to the bitter end, before a snake loyalty sweep had left a star system without a senior CEO, and one of Iceni's mentors had rigged the replacement process in her favor.

She laughed very softly at the memory, drawing a brief glance from Executive Marphissa walking beside her. "What would you do, Executive, if you stumbled across a major smuggling and tax-evasion scheme that seemed to have no senior CEO involvement?"

Marphissa frowned. "I'd report it, of course. There'd be rewards for whoever did that."

"You would think so," Iceni replied, "except that in fact a very senior CEO at Prime had her fingers deeply into that scheme, and she wasn't happy at all to lose the income it had generated."

"That's how you ended up at Midway, Madam CEO?" Marphissa asked.

"That's how I ended up at Midway. Promoted to senior CEO of a star system facing an unknown foe and as far from anything as any star in Syndicate space as a 'reward,' while the other CEO went on to bigger and better things on Prime." Iceni grinned. "She was there when Black Jack showed up again with the Alliance fleet."

"How tragic for her," Marphissa commented. "I ended up here because I had a brother who was accused of treason by a sub-CEO who wanted his position."

Iceni had already known that, of course, but the records available to her had left one gap. "Did the sub-CEO also encounter Black Jack's fleet?"

"No. He died just before I transferred. An unfortunate accident."

Iceni raised one eyebrow at her. "How tragic for him. And just before you left. An accident, you say?"

Executive Marphissa's expression remained professionally detached. "The official investigation determined that his death had been accidental."

"Accidents do happen." So Marphissa had managed to avenge herself without being caught, which implied that the executive had some skill sets that could be very useful for Iceni. Marphissa had also made a point of subtly letting Iceni know that. *I need to keep my eye on this one. She has a lot of promise.* "But I don't like being surprised by accidents."

"If I know of any accidents that might occur, I will be sure to inform the CEO in a timely manner." Marphissa glanced at her. "There are many uncertainties in battles fought with mobile forces, though, and sometimes surprises.

How much command experience do you have in space, Madam CEO?"

"Some time with the mobile forces. Perhaps seven years total. It's been five years since I commanded a flotilla, though." Her control of this ship, of the entire situation, rested on her ability to appear to be the best, most competent, and most believable leader in this star system. But something told Iceni that Marphissa was not the sort of subordinate to be easily fooled by a confident demeanor.

"That's something," Marphissa said. "Enough to know what to expect. And you will not be alone on the bridge." She faded back as they reached the bridge, letting Akiri and Iceni enter before her.

The cruiser's bridge felt a bit cramped after the D-class battle cruiser she had last employed as a flagship. Sub-CEO Akiri rapped out orders as he walked to his command seat. "Assume modified battle-alert status. CEO Iceni has assumed direct command of all mobile forces."

"Do we have status reports from the rest of the mobile forces?" Iceni demanded, taking her seat in the position next to the commanding officer's place as her bodyguard assumed a station near the entrance to the bridge. It had taken considerable effort to accumulate the flotilla in this star system even though it was but a pale shadow of the old Reserve Flotilla that had once protected the region. But she had concocted plausible reasons to hang on to mobile forces that were supposed to go to missions elsewhere, had convinced a few mobile forces passing through to remain, and had ceased using Hunter-Killers as couriers back to Prime once it became clear that Prime wasn't returning any mobile forces the central government got its hands on. It had taken a combination of ruthless use of her authority, more than a little bluffing, and occasional orders "lost" after they arrived in the star system but before they reached the mobile forces. But once the recall order for the entire flotilla came through, something impossible to lose the way lesser communications had been made to vanish, both she and Drakon had realized that they had to move before Kolani became aware of it even if the other orders for Hardrad hadn't already forced their hands.

The fruits of her labors were six heavy cruisers including the one she was now aboard, five light cruisers, and a pitiful twelve Hunter-Killers. That entire flotilla would have been lost in the fleet Black Jack had once again brought through this star system not long ago. But measured against what was available to the Syndicate government or any other local authorities in this region of space, the flotilla might be enough to protect this star system.

If she could both win a fight against Kolani and not lose too many of those warships in the process.

On the display that came to life before her, Iceni could see the orbits of all of those mobile forces. So far, none of them had started to move out of its assigned orbit. The units close to Kolani's flagship were ten light-minutes distant from the planet, so they would not have heard or seen any signs of trouble until ten minutes after Drakon's attack went in. At least the lack of reaction before those ten minutes had elapsed meant that they hadn't received any tip-offs that Drakon and Iceni were about to act. Kolani had wanted to keep the flotilla concentrated together, but Iceni had been able to use her own authority and some plausible-enough reasons to divide the flotilla into three portions.

One group, in orbit near the planet because Iceni had insisted she needed an easily visible deterrent to rebellion, held three of the heavy cruisers but only one of the light cruisers and four of the HuKs. A second group, with two heavy cruisers including C-990 which Kolani herself was riding as well as three of the light cruisers and four more of the HuKs, orbited ten light-minutes farther out from the star. The last group, consisting of only one heavy cruiser, one light cruiser, and the remaining four HuKs, was parked near the main mobile forces facility, a massive space station that orbited a gas-giant planet one light-hour out from the star. At the closest point of approach in their orbits, that would put the gas giant roughly fifty light-minutes distant from the habitable world where Iceni was. With the gas giant actually well behind the habitable world in its orbit, at almost its maximum distance away, the gas giant was almost one and a half light-hours from where Iceni's force was. By the time that last, small group could reach them, Iceni and Kolani might well have already decided the issue of who would be in command of the flotilla.

"Data feeds from all other mobile forces in this star system show readiness state three," Akiri said. "Regular cruising readiness, no preparations for battle." He paused. "Of course, they could be falsifying their data feeds to us just as we're presently falsifying our own readiness state to them."

Iceni gave him a hard smile. "That's worth considering. Did you report my presence aboard this unit in your data feed to the other units?"

"Yes, Madam CEO."

All of the units that were accepting her authority should be reporting in to her, then, as soon as they had taken care of the snakes they had aboard. Her eyes rested on the display again. If the unit commanders who had already pledged to support her carried through on their commitments then half of the heavy cruisers were hers, and two of the light cruisers, as well as five of the Hunter-Killers. Unfortunately, one of those light cruisers and one of the HuKs were a light-hour and a half distant.

Akiri was watching his own display with a morose expression. "C-818 will follow CEO Kolani. She's still using C-990 as her flagship, and I believe that unit's commander is also loyal to Kolani."

"That was expected," Iceni replied. "Kolani kept the two cruisers she was surest of with her."

"C-555 and C-413," Akiri began, naming the other two heavy cruisers in this group.

"Are loyal to me." Iceni raised one finger slightly toward her display. "But C-625, out there by the gas giant. That's a question."

"I . . . cannot make an estimate," Akiri said.

"Neither could I. I expect that C-625's commanding

officer will make every effort to avoid committing to either me or CEO Kolani until she sees which one of us wins. The light cruiser with C-625 would support me if it were alone, but if surrounded by mobile forces that stay loyal to CEO Kolani that light cruiser's status is also problematic. Two of the HuKs in the group at the gas giant are newly arrived in this star system, so I have no idea what they might do."

Marphissa nodded. "I haven't even spoken to anyone on those HuKs. They've reported in to CEO Kolani, but we haven't worked with them at all."

"But, Madam CEO," Akiri said hesitantly, "why if you doubted the actions those mobile forces would take did you let them be so far from where you could influence them? I ask so I can learn," he added quickly.

Iceni didn't answer him directly. "Did you review the reports we received of the fighting at Prime, Sub-CEO Akiri?"

Akiri hesitated again, clearly trying to recall the information, then Marphissa answered from her own place on the bridge. "When the new council declared itself, some of the mobile forces there tried to join with them, but because all of the units were close together, the loyalists to the old council destroyed every one of them."

Sub-CEO Akiri nodded, with an annoyed glance at Executive Marphissa. "Yes."

"Then you understand why I didn't want everything within range of CEO Kolani and the mobile forces loyal to her," Iceni said. "I want to make sure that if we fight, I have some chance to decide when and where."

A comm window opened before Iceni, showing the commanding officer of heavy cruiser C-555. "We await your orders, CEO Iceni. All ISS personnel aboard my unit have been neutralized."

"Something is being ejected from C-413," one of the line workers on the bridge reported.

C-413's commanding officer called in moments later, looking oddly serene. "We have just disposed of the last snake, CEO Iceni."

"Out of an air lock?" Iceni asked.

"That particular ISS agent delighted in undermining my authority with my crew, CEO Iceni."

"I see. In the future, avoid theatrics in carrying out your instructions." For all her sympathy with C-413's commanding officer, Iceni didn't want the crews of any of these ships getting used to tossing authority figures out of air locks. If that ever became a habit, it might be entirely too hard to break.

The light cruiser and the four HuKs with Iceni's group also reported in, pledging their allegiance. With the warships around her accounted for, Iceni called the doubtless wavering C-625. "The majority of the mobile forces in the flotilla have already sworn to obey my orders. You would be advised to follow their example as quickly as possible." She would have to wait almost three hours for an answer even if C-625 replied as soon as it heard from her. "What's happening on the surface?" she asked Akiri.

Akiri frowned toward the current operations line worker, who seemed slightly stunned by events as he recited a report in a steady but bewildered voice. "Major fighting can be seen at the main ISS headquarters and the three ISS subcomplexes. Communications from the surface indicate that all ISS substations are also being attacked. We received a fragmentary message from ISS CEO Hardrad, but it was cut off before any orders or information could be received."

"Good. The ground forces are taking care of the snakes on the surface," Iceni announced for the benefit of everyone within earshot. "CEO Drakon is doing his part." It made Drakon sound like a junior partner of hers, but cultivating that impression in the mobile forces might be useful. She paused, blew out a steadying breath, then called Kolani. "CEO Kolani, this is CEO Iceni. I have assumed direct command of all mobile forces within this star system. You are to acknowledge my authority and pledge personal loyalty to me. I await your immediate reply."

Another message, this one directly to every other ship in Kolani's group. "I have assumed direct command of all mobile forces within this star system. You are to acknowledge my authority and pledge personal loyalty to me. I expect your immediate reply."

The earliest she would hear a response from Kolani or any of the ships with her was twenty minutes. "Let me know the instant any of the mobile forces with Kolani begin to alter their movement," she ordered Akiri.

Akiri shook his head. "All of the light cruisers and HuKs with Kolani are under the guns of those two heavy cruisers. They won't be able to bolt without fighting their way out."

"Correct," Iceni agreed, her tone implying that she had already taken that into account.

"But if any of them turn on Kolani," Executive Marphissa pointed out, "their weapons will be within easy range of those heavy cruisers. A sudden, surprise volley could inflict crippling damage."

Iceni smiled. "Yes."

"But won't Kolani be watching for that?" Akiri asked.

Having subordinates who identified problems instead of ignoring them (or worse, being oblivious to them) usually pleased Iceni. But subordinates who raised every possible difficulty without identifying positive aspects or solutions were another matter. This time Iceni raised an eyebrow at Akiri. She could do that in a way that inspired real fear in those junior to her, and now Akiri paled slightly. "Yes," Iceni repeated. "She will have to watch the mobile forces with her and worry about fighting us at the same time."

"I see," Akiri agreed hastily, then busied himself working with his display.

From the corner of her eye, Iceni could see a well-concealed but still-apparent look of disdain on Marphissa. None of the line workers on the bridge betrayed any signs of noticing what had happened, however, which implied that this sort of scene had played out before, most likely when CEO Kolani browbeat Akiri. When Iceni had heard that Kolani had more than once publicly raked Akiri over the coals, she had known that would make Akiri easy to recruit. But Iceni also found herself sympathetic to why Kolani would have chewed out Akiri and wondering why Kolani hadn't already replaced him. Kolani wasn't known for a high degree of tolerance for workers who didn't do their jobs to her standards. And there wasn't anything in Akiri's personal record that should have inhibited Kolani from sacking him. There was an inconsistency in her treatment of Akiri, a problem that Iceni bookmarked in her brain to come back to and investigate when time permitted.

At the moment, though, she had to endure a forced period of waiting while still staying alert and focused. Waiting until replies came from Kolani and the other mobile forces ten light-minutes distant. Waiting until she knew how well Drakon's attacks had succeeded. Or failed. Iceni found her eyes resting on the portion of her display showing the surface of the planet below this cruiser. ISS facilities were highlighted because of the fighting at those locations. If she received information that one or more of Drakon's attacks had failed, it wouldn't be hard at all to designate one or more of those facilities as a bombardment target. Point, assign, launch. Simple. And part of a city, and everyone living in that area, would be destroyed.

I launched bombardments at Alliance worlds. That wasn't hard. I didn't think about the citizens under those aiming points. Are people in the Alliance called citizens? Why don't I know the answer to that? I killed them, and I don't even know what they called themselves.

Of course, that made it easier to kill them.

I never had to participate in an internal stability operation, dropping a bombardment on one of our own worlds to quell rebellion or riot. I was lucky. But here I am potentially facing the same decision.

Was Black Jack really sent by the living stars to stop us? He also stopped the Alliance from bombarding civilians. Was he meant to? My father told me of the stars that watch over us all, but it has been so long, and I'm no longer sure how much of that I accept. I've seen that the men and women who gained the most power in the Syndicate Worlds were the ones who would stop at nothing. Why weren't they stopped? I've seen the aftermath of Alliance bombardments of our worlds. I didn't see many signs there of something caring about the helpless or the weak. You had to stay strong, or you got hurt. Why would something that cared about us wait so long to do anything?

But we did lose, and the Alliance won. And right now, the meanest, most unforgiving part of the Syndicate Worlds, the snakes of the ISS, are dying inside their own fortresses.

Her eyes were locked on one of the ISS symbols, one of the spots where she could order a bombardment to fall. *All right, living stars. My father said you were supposed to guide us as to right or wrong. You told Black Jack what to do? Tell me. Should I ensure that nest of snakes is cleaned out even if it costs the city and citizens around it? Or should I avoid doing the most practical and easiest thing because it would hurt those citizens that I'm responsible for even though those citizens can always be replaced?*

Go ahead. If really you're out there somewhere, tell me.

"Madam CEO," the operations line worker reported. "The mobile forces with CEO Kolani have been seen to alter vector. They appear to be coming around to close on our position."

Executive Marphissa nodded. "Based on the timing, they reacted when they saw the attacks against the ISS on the surface."

Iceni's own answering nod was sharp. Why hadn't she heard from Drakon on how things were going? She couldn't—

It took her a moment to realize what she was seeing. The symbol for the ISS facility that Iceni had been watching had altered in the last few seconds. Instead of beaconing an ISS identification, it now glowed with an indicator saying that it belonged to the ground forces.

Other ISS facilities were changing as she watched, changing from poisonous yellow to bold green. "Try to get comms to CEO Drakon," she ordered. "He—"

At that point, Iceni abruptly remembered her last

thoughts before the line worker had interrupted them. She stared at those symbols for a second, then two. *Was I answered? It's probably just coincidence. Surely just . . .*

"Madam CEO?" Marphissa asked.

"Drakon should be at the main ISS headquarters. Try to get in touch with him there," Iceni ordered, putting extra snap in her command to cover up her momentary loss of self-possession.

Two minutes passed, while Iceni's glower deepened and Akiri began looking desperate again, himself glaring at the comm line worker.

Fortunately for the line worker, another message came in.

CEO Kolani hadn't looked so unhappy since the Alliance fleet had last waltzed unhindered through this star system. She stared at Iceni so viciously that it was as if she were actually seeing Iceni before her. It took Iceni a moment to recall that this message had been sent ten minutes ago. "Former CEO Iceni, you are hereby relieved of all authority and ordered to surrender yourself to loyal representatives of the Syndicate Worlds. I am assuming full authority in this star system until the unlawful actions of the ground forces have been halted and their leaders, including former CEO Drakon, have been dealt with."

"She sent this five minutes after the ISS facilities on the surface were attacked?" Iceni asked.

"Yes, Madam CEO."

For some reason that made Iceni want to laugh, so she did. "CEO Kolani didn't even give me a chance to rebel before she tried to take over." But then Kolani had been talking to Hardrad about that delayed order and implicating Iceni in that matter, if Hardrad could be trusted on that count. *Hardrad can't be trusted on any count, but in this case telling me the truth about Kolani's suspicions would have served his purposes, and I already knew how Kolani feels about me.*

She looked at Akiri. "Tell the mobile forces with us to bring themselves to full combat alert, and make sure their true readiness status is sent onward to Kolani's group."

An alarm sounded, followed by a rippling of Iceni's display before the virtual images solidified again. "What happened?"

"A virus," Marphissa reported. "Delivered in the net connecting us to the rest of the flotilla. It tried to activate the worms planted by the snakes, but we'd already purged them."

Damn. "Can we put filters between us and the mobile forces loyal to Kolani?"

"That's what stopped the virus, Madam CEO. I can't guarantee that the filters will stop the next one."

Double damn. "Break the net connections to Kolani's warships."

"War—?" Marphissa started to ask, then caught herself. "Yes, Madam CEO. What about the . . . warships at the main facility? Anything they tried to send would take an hour and a half to get here, and anything CEO Kolani tried to relay through them would take more than three hours."

"Keep them in the link for now." Iceni gave her display an irate look. Instead of getting accurate updates from those other warships, she would now have to depend on the sensors on the cruisers to know what was really happening.

Accurate updates? "They were already falsifying their data feeds to us, weren't they?" Iceni asked.

The operations line worker nodded. "The movements we're seeing don't match what their updates were telling us. It was . . ." His voice trailed off.

"Say it." Iceni's own voice wasn't loud, but it carried very well to the line worker and everyone else on the bridge.

"Yes, Madam CEO. It was clumsy." Now that he had voiced a criticism of superiors, even though they were on other units, the line worker seemed defiantly eager to keep talking. "They could have matched their false feeds to their actual maneuvers, knowing that we would see any discrepancy; instead, they just kept sending us data saying nothing had changed."

Iceni watched the line worker, who had flushed as he

returned her gaze with worried eyes. She wondered if any line workers on Kolani's units had realized the need to tailor the false data feeds but hesitated to appear to question or contradict superiors. "That's a good assessment," she finally said, drawing a hastily concealed look of disbelief from the line worker. "We need to think of things like that before we give away any information to CEO Kolani. What is your rating?"

"Senior line worker class two, Madam CEO."

"You're now a senior line worker class one. Keep thinking, and tell me what I need to know." Iceni turned back to face Akiri. "Make that promotion happen. I am pleased to see that your crew is well trained and knowledgeable."

Akiri, who had been on the verge of scowling, perked up and bestowed an approving look on the line worker.

"I . . . I have a connection with CEO Drakon," the comm line worker cried with relief.

The window that opened before Iceni showed Drakon in combat armor, smoking wreckage in the background. It took her a moment to realize that the wreckage had once been the ISS command center. She had toured that facility once, but only once, feeling half a prisoner already until safely outside the ISS headquarters again.

Drakon's eyes seemed to hold more weariness than triumph, but he waved around in a casual gesture. "We've got it. There are individual snakes still running loose, but the heads are all dead, and we'll catch the rest pretty quick."

"Where's Hardrad?"

"That's sort of a metaphysical question now."

Iceni had to pause to realize what that meant. "I didn't know you had such a dark sense of humor, CEO Drakon."

"It's now General Drakon. Like you said, we need to cast off Syndicate ways of doing things."

"I see." A unilateral decision on Drakon's part. Not a decision she could protest, but still a worrisome move. "Make sure you examine whatever remains of Hardrad carefully before disposing of it. There may be tiny data-storage devices hidden within him."

"There were," Drakon said. "But they were all dead-manned to his metabolism. When he died, they autowiped."

"Pity. Since I now know that you have the planetary surface under control, I must focus on my own task. There's a battle to fight up here."

"Maybe Kolani will rethink that once she learns the snakes on the planet have been wiped out."

"I'll make sure that she knows," Iceni said. "I will contact you again once the battle is over."

But Drakon shook his head. "What's to keep Kolani from dropping rocks on us during your fight?"

"She'll want an intact planet to offer to her masters," Iceni replied. "Restoring a battered ruin to their control will not impress them. If she did that, she would be blamed for the losses far more than she'd get credit for any success. I am certain of that."

"I'm glad that you're certain of it," Drakon replied, "seeing as how you don't have to worry about any of those rocks hitting you on the head. Have a nice battle."

"Thank you." The window closed, and Iceni gazed morosely at the place where Drakon's image had been. Working with him was going to be challenging, but positioning herself to eliminate him would be a very long-term project.

Assuming that she wanted to eliminate him. She had noticed that CEOs who concentrated on getting rid of anyone who could be competition ended up getting rid of those who could do their jobs well, and that always produced long-term disaster.

Iceni's eyes moved slightly to her display, where the representations of Kolani's forces were steadying out on a direct intercept with the path of the units with Iceni. "She's coming straight at us."

Akiri nodded morosely. "CEO Kolani will focus her fire on this cruiser. She will want to kill you, thinking that will cause the other units to surrender."

"Just as I need to kill her, so I won't have to destroy all of the units following her." Iceni scowled at the display, where automated calculations were summing up projections for an engagement. She had three heavy cruisers to Kolani's two, but Kolani had more smaller warships. In a straight head-to-head exchange of blows, the firepower ratios would be very nearly equal. Victory or defeat would rest on chance, on how many hits went home on the primary targets, on where those hits struck, on which vital systems got knocked out.

She hated depending on chance. "How can we knock out the heavy cruiser carrying CEO Kolani without facing an equal chance of losing this one?" she asked Akiri and Marphissa.

Both looked back at her with puzzled expressions. "We go in hard and fast," Marphissa finally said. "A clean, straight-on firing run. That will give us the best chance."

"Black Jack never uses clean, straight-on firing runs," Iceni said.

Akiri spoke cautiously. "The actions of Geary and the results of his engagements with Syndicate Worlds forces have been classified. We have not seen any official reports on those matters."

Of course not. Stupid, mindless Syndicate Worlds security classification, keeping essential information from its own personnel rather than from the enemy. "To put it bluntly, Black Jack repeatedly inflicted horrendous losses on Syndicate Worlds flotillas, while suffering much smaller losses in exchange. He used tactics that we're still trying to analyze but which seemed to me to vary by situation."

"The rumors were true?" Marphissa asked, appalled.

"Yes. The mobile forces of the Syndicate Worlds have been decimated. There's very little left. You've seen what the Alliance still has."

"Can you also—?"

"No." *I'm not Black Jack. I've studied what we know about those engagements, and I still don't understand why he did things the way he did, how he timed his movements, how . . .*

Can I pretend to be Black Jack? What would he do? Not slam straight into the opposing force with the odds so even.

He would . . . change the odds. "But I do have an idea." She called up a maneuvering recommendation for intercepting Kolani's force, a simple maneuver since Kolani was coming right at them, aiming to intercept the spot where they would be if Iceni's force remained in orbit about this planet as it continued along its own track around the star. "All units, accelerate to point one light speed, alter course to port three two degrees at time one four."

"CEO Kolani's force has also steadied out at point one light speed," Marphissa said. "Forty-seven minutes to contact if she adjusts vectors when she sees our own maneuver."

"We are to concentrate fire on Cruiser 990?" Akiri asked, his hands already moving to set that priority in the targeting systems.

"You will await my command on targeting priority." Everyone was eyeing her with surprise. "I will enter targeting priority at the last moment to ensure that there is no way the information can somehow be provided to CEO Kolani's force." The extra strength in her voice this time made it clear that no one was to question her decision, and they all obediently turned back to their tasks. CEOs were arbitrary, they were doubtless telling themselves, and CEOs loved to micromanage. *Let her enter the order herself when she wants if that is her desire. Oh, but it's not that simple. I may not be Black Jack, but I can try something unexpected.*

Forty-seven minutes. Forty-six, now. She had done this before, the long lead-in to a fight, charging an opponent who could be seen many minutes, or hours, or even days before you could actually exchange fire. Iceni had always thought that it felt like one of those falling dreams, the drop prolonged beyond all reason, watching death come closer and closer. But unlike those dreams, which ended before the impact, battles always brought the crash of contact.

How can I do what Black Jack has done? I don't know enough. All I can do is a crude approximation. But that may be all I need against Kolani, who will be expecting me to follow doctrine since my experience is limited and not recent.

"CEO Iceni," Akiri said, breaking into her thoughts. His own worries were clear enough to see. "I've fought in engagements like this. Fairly evenly matched. There's not much left when the fighting ends."

Iceni nodded. "Are you advising some other course of action, Sub-CEO Akiri?"

Akiri hesitated before speaking. "Let them go. Instead of trying to defeat them, just let them head to Prime."

"And come back with reinforcements?" Marphissa asked.

"We have been told that there aren't any reinforcements!" Akiri insisted, flushing with anger. "CEO Iceni told us there is nothing left!"

Iceni raised one finger, which was sufficient to halt the debate. Executives who didn't learn to watch for and obey the smallest gestures from CEOs didn't last very long. "I understand your concerns, Sub-CEO Akiri. However, we will not have an option on whether or not to fight. CEO Kolani must fight and win. I am certain that she will not flee for Prime to seek assistance because that would be an admission of failure on her part. She would be reporting the loss of this star system despite her own presence here, and the loss of more than half her own flotilla. I doubt that the new government of the Syndicate Worlds is much more merciful than the one it replaced when it comes to CEOs who fail. No. CEO Kolani will not simply leave this star system even if we promise her a free path. She will fight to reestablish Syndicate control here, or die trying, because she will see that as preferable to her likely fate if she fails."

"Would there be any reinforcements at Prime?" Marphissa asked. "That might change her calculations."

"Your commander is essentially correct," Iceni said, giving Akiri acknowledgment of a small victory in the debate. "There might be more mobile units there, but probably very few that can be spared on short notice. Our knowledge of what mobile forces remain in the hands of the central government is very limited. They have some new construction, surely, but how much we don't know. And they need to keep much of what they do have on hand, able to react and serve as a threat against the star systems near to Prime that they still control."

Akiri was watching her. "The Reserve Flotilla? Do we know . . . ?"

"Those rumors are true as well." Iceni said it bluntly, knowing how those around her would take the confirmation of their worst fears. "The Reserve Flotilla encountered Black Jack. It's gone. It won't be coming back here."

Seeing how Akiri's face fell, Iceni wondered how many close friends he'd once had in that flotilla. He was far from being alone in that.

"Another message from CEO Kolani," the comm line worker announced.

"Let me see it." A window popped open before Iceni, revealing a Kolani whose earlier anger had morphed into cold contempt.

"You will surrender, or you will die. Any fools following your commands will die with you. They should know that you have no talent for command of mobile forces and that your thin experience was long ago. For the sake of the safety of the citizens of the Syndicate Worlds, I am willing to guarantee your life if you transmit your surrender prior to firing upon any mobile unit. Those who followed you, doubtless out of mistaken belief in your authority to command such actions, will not be punished. You have fifteen minutes to reply. For the people, Kolani, out."

Iceni leaned back and glanced at Akiri. "I suppose every supervisor and line worker in these mobile units is already aware of Kolani's offer even though this was sent directly to me?"

Akiri and Marphissa exchanged looks, then Marphissa shrugged. "That is certainly correct, Madam CEO. The offer was plainly intended for their ears."

"Then it's past time I sent a message. Set up a broadcast." Iceni waited impatiently for the few seconds required before the line worker responsible gave a thumbs-up. "Citizens of the Midway Star System, those on the planet nearest to mobile forces loyal to me, those elsewhere, those on my mobile forces or in the ground forces of . . . General Drakon, this is CEO Iceni."

For a few months, she had been practicing for this, going over the wording countless times in her head because she dared not create any written record of it in any device or even using archaic pen and paper. Such a document would have ensured her quick death had it been found by the ISS, and Iceni hadn't survived as long as she had by underestimating the snakes.

"You have lived long enough under the control of the government on Prime. The Syndicate Worlds has asked much from us and given little in return. The one thing they offered was security, and the Syndicate Worlds failed in that. The Syndicate Worlds government took the flotilla that long guarded us and left us defenseless when we were threatened by the alien race that lives beyond the frontier. Yes, I now officially confirm the existence of a species about which we know little except that they have posed a threat to us. We must be able to defend ourselves, and yet now the new and illegitimate government on Prime seeks to take the small flotilla of mobile forces I have managed to accumulate for the defense of this star system.

"The Syndicate Worlds government has long boasted of its superiority. Only it could keep us safe, that government claimed. Yet it lost the war with the Alliance. The Alliance fleet came *here*, flaunting the failure of the Syndicate system.

"I will be candid with you. Fear has kept us loyal to Prime. Fear of the Alliance and fear of the ISS. The snakes." She paused for a moment, knowing how shocking it would be for citizens to hear a CEO openly using that term of contempt for the ISS. "But the snakes in Midway Star System are dead, except upon those mobile forces still following the command of CEO Kolani. The Syndicate Worlds is crumbling. The authority of the central government is falling apart, and many star systems have descended into chaos and civil war. I will prevent that from happening here. I have negotiated an understanding with the Alliance, with Black Jack Geary *personally*, to recognize and support the actions I am now taking."

She wondered how Black Jack would feel about that interpretation of their agreement. He obviously hadn't been enthusiastic about the limited commitment he had really made, to defend this star system against the alien enigma race, and that agreement had been reached only because Iceni had possessed something that Black Jack wanted. Hopefully, he wouldn't reappear in this star system soon enough to pick up her transmission, but even if he did Black Jack had agreed not to publicly deny that his protection of the Midway Star System, and of Iceni herself, extended beyond threats from the enigmas.

"I will soon engage and defeat CEO Kolani," Iceni continued, "with mobile forces that have pledged loyalty to me and to the newly independent star system of Midway. CEO Kolani and the snakes on her mobile units will not be allowed to threaten the citizens of this star system. We will chart our own course from this time forth, a course that will keep us safe and prosperous, without the terror of the ISS to always threaten us. For the people! Iceni, out."

Finished, Iceni waited, both elbows resting on the arms of her chair, her hands clasped under her chin. She felt slightly drained, as if she had just engaged in some strenuous physical act. Any response from the mobile forces with Kolani would take a while to be heard, then she would—

It had taken her a few moments to recognize the sound she heard growing as it vibrated through the hull of the cruiser. Iceni had been present at countless official celebrations and ceremonies, had heard many groups of citizens obediently chanting slogans or shouts, but this was different, a wild cheering and jubilation that both thrilled and alarmed. Some of the line workers on the bridge embraced or exchanged hand slaps. One middle-aged subexecutive stood quietly, tears streaming down his face.

Sub-CEO Akiri sat, his shoulders slightly hunched as if

prepared to defend himself from a mob, a sentiment that Iceni could understand at the moment. But Executive Marphissa smiled wolfishly as the sounds of celebration went on and on.

The noise was one word being chanted over and over. "Iceni! Iceni!" Her name, being voluntarily shouted by citizens. She felt more disoriented than ever at the idea of being acclaimed by those she ruled. *What have I done? There's more going on here than just a change in the titles of the masters of this star system.*

Under some stern looks from Akiri and Marphissa the workers on the bridge dampened their celebrations, returning to their tasks, though Iceni noticed that the atmosphere felt different. The sullenness that seemed to always underlie worker attitudes couldn't be sensed at the moment.

"Twenty minutes until contact," the maneuvering line worker announced, sounding now like he anticipated that moment.

Iceni looked at her display, smiling sardonically. In twenty minutes, she would have her first extremely public chance to screw up. If her idea failed, if Kolani badly hurt the ships following Iceni, then all the star system would see it. All of her life Iceni had been taught to avoid showing any sign of weakness. Her fellow humans, she had been told, would strike the moment they sensed any vulnerability, any ineptitude.

In twenty minutes, she just might learn how true that was. At least Drakon wasn't facing any more problems at the moment.

"WE'VE got a problem," Colonel Rogero said.

Drakon's eyes went to the virtual window next to Rogero, where a video feed displayed a very large crowd gathering in a central park. The noise from the crowd boomed even across the volume-modulated circuit. "The citizens are celebrating."

"Celebrating I don't mind," Rogero said. "But this looks

ugly. That crowd is exploding in size like a sun going nova, and the chatter we're picking up is spinning out of control. My instincts tell me that celebration is going to turn into explosion."

"A mob attack on us?"

"No. There's no direction. We've got a thousand 'leaders' who our software has identified in personal comms so far. It's chaotic. Lots of emotion. Feelings that all traditional controls and restraints are gone. I think you can do the math on where that's going to lead."

Drakon nodded. "Rioting. Looting. Breakdown of order. Where are the police?"

"Forted up inside their stations. They seem to be equally afraid of the mob and of our soldiers."

That was at least understandable on both counts. "City administrators?"

"The same," Rogero said scornfully. "Only much more useless than the police." Technically, officials like mayors and council members had been elected to their posts by popular vote, but those votes had been completely rigged for longer than either Rogero or Drakon had been alive, so the winners tended to be less than popular in fact.

After another searching look at the gathering crowd, Drakon nodded again. "I expect you have the same thing happening elsewhere in the region you control?"

"Everywhere crowds can gather. Even some of the ground forces soldiers started to head out to join the crowds before I locked down the barracks. What are my orders?"

Malin had been listening, and now spoke urgently. "You have to deal with this in a way that makes you seem to be on the side of the crowds. Control the mob by becoming their leader."

Morgan's snort of derision almost rivaled the roar of the crowd in volume. "He *is* their leader. We just have to remind them who's in charge by using enough firepower to end this. Orders to disperse immediately, followed by a few violent examples of what happens to those who don't follow orders, will shut this down."

"We don't have enough firepower to kill every citizen on this planet!" Malin snapped at her.

"We don't have to kill all of them, just enough to make an example of those who don't follow orders from us, their leaders."

Drakon listened to them bicker for a moment, thinking through options, aware that Rogero was still waiting silently for instructions. All of their planning had been focused on getting rid of the snakes without having the planet devastated. He had guessed that there might be some problems with crowds, but this looked far worse than those guesses had suggested. As if keyed by that thought, Colonel Gaiene called in just then, at his back a video of the same kind of growing mob that Rogero was facing. Seconds later, Colonel Kai's image appeared, accompanied by similar pictures.

"The situation is rapidly deteriorating," Kai reported.

CHAPTER FOUR

"FIFTEEN minutes to contact with CEO Kolani's force."

Iceni sat watching her display, trying to figure out how to time what she planned to do. Sunk deep in thought, she kept running into obstacles no matter what idea she considered.

"Ten minutes to contact."

At a combined closing velocity of point two light speed even vast distances could vanish far too quickly. Iceni knew how fast those ten minutes would disappear while she tried to puzzle out a solution. In the records she had seen, Black Jack seemed to have some sort of instinct for timing the kind of actions Iceni wanted to carry out, but she had neither Black Jack's experience nor his talent. Some reports indicated that Black Jack also had a team of officers supporting him, people like that female battle cruiser captain on his flagship. But Iceni didn't have—

A phrase she had heard recently ran across Iceni's memory. *You won't be alone on the bridge.* Marphissa. Was she good enough to call this? Akiri definitely wasn't, but maybe the exec could help. "Executive Marphissa, private conference."

Akiri betrayed a flash of worry and jealousy as Marphissa

hastened to Iceni's side, waiting silently until Iceni activated the privacy field around her seat. "Here is what I want to do. Can you time the maneuver properly?" As Iceni explained, she saw Marphissa's eyes widen, then narrow in thought.

"Yes," Marphissa finally replied.

Did that answer reflect overconfidence or a careful professional judgment? "You're certain?"

"Not absolutely certain, no, Madam CEO. But I am reasonably certain that I can."

"Is there anyone else aboard this cruiser who you believe could do better?"

"Not to my knowledge."

"Then you will execute that maneuver at what you feel is the best moment," Iceni ordered. "Without announcing that fact, I will pass maneuvering control of this cruiser to you when we are one minute from contact. I will handle weapons targeting for all mobile—all warships with us."

"Yes, Madam CEO. I understand and will obey."

Marphissa returned to her station, while Akiri tracked her progress with worried eyes. When promotions and demotions could come at the whim of a CEO, private meetings between a subordinate and a CEO would worry any supervisor.

"Five minutes to contact."

All weapons systems were ready on the heavy cruisers, light cruisers, and HuKs under her control. Iceni itched to prioritize their target now, but waited. If Kolani somehow still had a tap into the comm net tying together those units, she might still have time to learn Iceni's plan.

Akiri and the line workers on the bridge were all pretending not to be watching her, but Akiri's nervousness was once again becoming visible. "Madam CEO," he finally said, "we still require your prioritization orders for the mobile units' combat-system targeting."

"You will get it." Iceni marveled at how calm her voice sounded.

"Three minutes to contact."

Roughly five and a half million kilometers separated the

two forces as they rushed together at a combined velocity of sixty thousand kilometers per second. Iceni shook her head, trying to grasp such distances and such speeds. She couldn't really do it. Maybe even Black Jack couldn't. All any human could do was set the scale on their display so that the distances and speeds had the illusion of being something a human mind could accept and work with.

"Two minutes to contact."

Iceni carefully entered her targeting priorities, pausing to triple-check they were what she wanted, then sent them to the combat systems on not just her cruiser but all of the other mobile forces under her control.

Akiri seemed relieved for an instant as the orders popped up on his own display, then jerked with surprise. "What—?"

But Iceni was already entering the commands to shift maneuvering control to Marphissa. Looking back, she saw Marphissa nod to indicate she was ready.

"One minute to contact."

Iceni took a breath, then keyed her comm circuit. "For the people," she sent out to every listener. Perhaps the old phrase, which seemed to have lost any real meaning long ago, would now hearten her supporters.

Marphissa was rigid before her own display, concentrating, one hand poised over her controls.

Akiri gave Iceni a worried look. "Madam CEO, CEO Kolani's force will be concentrating their fire on *this* cruiser."

"This cruiser may not be where CEO Kolani's force expects it to be," Iceni replied.

"CEO Kolani's force is firing missiles," the operations line worker said.

Another nervous glance from Akiri, but Iceni shook her head. "We will hold fire except for defensive systems."

The final seconds to contact dwindled with astounding speed. Hell-lance particle beams speared out from the warships under Iceni's command, aiming to hit the oncoming missiles. Most of the missiles blew up as the hell lances went home, and a few more detonated when last-ditch barrages of grapeshot, metal ball bearings depending on their kinetic energy and mass to do damage, slammed into the missiles short of their targets. Iceni's cruiser jolted as a couple of missiles detonated against her shields, creating dangerous weak spots.

Iceni felt sudden forces jerk at her as Marphissa activated last-moment maneuvering commands. The drone of the inertial nullifiers, normally too low to notice, rose in pitch as they protested the demands being made upon them.

The cruiser bolted upward, fighting momentum to curve away from the track it had held for more than half an hour.

Just beneath the cruiser, the rest of the two forces tore past each other so quickly that the moment of closest approach came and went far too quickly for human senses to register. The cruiser Iceni rode had already pumped out some last-moment missiles, and the rest of her warships did as well.

But none of those weapons aimed for the cruiser being ridden by Kolani. Instead, every missile, every hell lance, went for the stern of the other cruiser in Kolani's force. C-818 staggered as multiple hits knocked down her stern shields and impacted on her main propulsion units.

Meanwhile, the barrage of hell lances and grapeshot aimed at the spot where Iceni's cruiser should have been tore harmlessly past just beneath, only a few grazing the shields of the heavy cruiser as it steadied out again.

"C-818 has lost all main propulsion," the operations line worker cried. "C-818 can no longer maneuver!"

Iceni smiled. "With CEO Kolani down to one heavy cruiser in her force, the odds are now much in our favor on the next firing pass."

"But—" Akiri was shaking his head, trying to grasp what had happened. "CEO Kolani might just run now. Avoid action."

"That would be the prudent thing to do, in the short run," Iceni agreed. "But you know CEO Kolani's temperament. She isn't thinking prudently right now. She is angry.

She wants to kill me even more now than she did five minutes ago. And in the long run, arriving at Prime with only one heavy cruiser would simply guarantee a swift firing squad for incompetence. No, she's going to attack."

On her display, the crippled C-818 had kept onto the same vector, heading helplessly away from the other warships. But Kolani's other ships were bending into as tight a turn as they could manage. That turn covered a lot of space at the velocity they were traveling, but it was plain that Kolani intended to reengage as soon as possible.

"All units, come up one one zero degrees." Iceni brought the rest of her own force curving upward to join with her cruiser, then continued the upward turn, not trying to match the hull-straining tightness of Kolani's maneuver. "She'll come to us," Iceni said, steadying out her force.

Using the standard human conventions for maneuvering in a star system, up was the direction arbitrarily designated above the plane of the planets orbiting the star while down would be below that. Port meant a turn away from the star while starboard meant a turn toward the star. The conventions were the only way of ensuring that one spacecraft understood directions issued by another spacecraft when they were operating in an environment without any real ups or downs. To an observer on a planet, Iceni's warships would have turned so far "up" that they had passed the vertical and were upside down, angling farther above the plane of the star system. Kolani's force had done the same, so that the tracks of the two forces were coming together at an angle as if aiming to complete two sides of a triangle whose base was the original tracks of the warships before their first encounter.

"This time," Iceni said, "we will target everything on CEO Kolani's cruiser." There was a chance that would destroy cruiser C-990, but there was also a chance that Kolani, if she was desperate enough and convinced that victory was impossible, would still launch a bombardment of the planet. That had to be prevented even if the price was a heavy cruiser that Iceni didn't want to lose.

"Madam CEO," the comm line worker said, "we're getting broadcasts from the planet that you might want to review."

"Is General Drakon still in control?"

"Yes."

"Then I'll deal with that after we've finished with CEO Kolani."

The wait wasn't nearly as long as before as the two forces rushed back together. Akiri seemed resigned to the damage that might still be inflicted on his unit. Marphissa appeared enormously pleased with herself but was keeping it mostly under wraps.

Only twenty seconds from contact, the odds changed again.

Iceni watched an alert pulse on her display as two of the three light cruisers under Kolani's control and three of the four HuKs with her suddenly altered their tracks, pulling away from the rest of Kolani's warships. A last-moment trick to create trouble for Iceni?

"They're pulling away from contact," Marphissa said. "Bolting out of CEO Kolani's force."

Iceni only had time to nod before the remaining warships slashed by each other. All of Kolani's remaining units hurled their fire at the cruiser holding Iceni, but that now amounted to only one heavy cruiser, one light cruiser, and one HuK. On Iceni's side, three heavy cruisers, one light cruiser, and four HuKs concentrated their weaponry on Kolani's flagship as the two sides raced past each other in far less time than the blink of an eye.

Iceni's cruiser C-448 was still shuddering from the hits on her shields when the sensors began reporting on the status of Kolani's cruiser. C-990 had been hit hard. Kolani's flagship tumbled through space, with maneuvering systems knocked out, the bow a total ruin, and numerous hull penetrations marking internal damage. "Try to get communications with C-990," Iceni ordered.

"We could finish off the ship," Marphissa offered. "C-990's shields are completely gone."

"No." They were watching her, clearly wondering at a CEO displaying any sign of mercy. Iceni felt her jaw tighten as her expression hardened, and the crew of her own cruiser hastily turned back to their tasks. "I want to recover and repair that ship if possible. We need every hull we can get." There. That sounded like a nice, pragmatic justification for not slaughtering the helpless crew of C-990. "And send surrender demands to the rest of CEO Kolani's units."

The light cruisers and HuKs, both those that had stuck with Kolani and those that had bolted, accepted Iceni's authority in a staggered series of messages that must have reflected how long it had taken each of them to wipe out the snakes aboard. Last came C-818, the cruiser's executive submitting to Iceni. "I regret to report the death during the engagement of our former commander, Sub-CEO Krasny," the exec reported tonelessly.

Akiri frowned and shook his head. "How could Krasny have been killed by hits on the stern of his cruiser?"

"A freak accident, I suppose," Iceni said.

Marphissa gave Iceni a glance that clearly shared Iceni's real opinion, that Krasny had not desired to yield, and his subordinates had taken matters into their own hands. Being a lot more discreet than Akiri, though, she wasn't about to say that out loud. There wasn't any sense in giving the crews of these warships any more ideas about what they could do to senior execs, and CEOs, aboard their own units.

The comm line worker sighed with frustration. "We can't pick up any signals off C-990, Madam CEO. All comm systems on C-990 may be dead. We may have to send a shuttle over."

"C-990's comm systems may be dead, but surely the entire crew is not," Marphissa objected. "Someone could have reached an air lock by now and be sending flashing light messages."

"An escape capsule just left C-990," the operations line worker announced. "There goes another."

"Only two?" Akiri muttered.

Marphissa gestured in the direction of C-990. "We

could close on the cruiser, get near enough to send a boarding party over and establish control."

"Madam CEO," Akiri said quickly, "I advise against that. Something is not right with C-990. If CEO Kolani is still alive and in charge, some communications should have come to us, even if only defiance. She could try to fire bombardment projectiles at the planet. Something. But there's nothing."

"But if CEO Kolani is dead or prisoner because her crew revolted, they should have established communications as well," Marphissa said.

"Exactly! Something is wrong. I do not recommend closing with C-990 within the danger radius of a core overload."

Iceni regarded Akiri for a long moment, then nodded. "I believe that is a wise suggestion. We can't rule out the chance of a deliberate core overload, or one brought about by fighting among the surviving crew. Get closer, but not within the danger radius, and send over an uncrewed probe to see what's going on."

"ALL right," Drakon finally said, loud and clear, causing Malin and Morgan to stop sniping at each other. They knew when he spoke like that to start listening. "We might well be able to suppress those crowds with firepower, but that's a short-term solution. We learned that on occupied Alliance planets when we tried to maintain order that way. I need a long-term answer, and a long-term answer requires the majority of those citizens to be our allies in maintaining order."

He looked at Rogero, Kai, and Gaiene. "I'm going to pass these same orders to every ground forces commander on the planet. You will contact the local police and order them to get their butts out of their stations and on the streets. Tell them that we will back them up, not threaten them, and deploy platoons of troops to do just that. Not squads. Platoons. We need to ensure that subexecs are in charge of each unit, not senior line workers. Tell the police that I'll be taking other steps to deal with the mobs, but we need their boots on the street because their job hasn't changed."

"What about our own soldiers?" Colonel Gaiene asked. "Discipline is *very* shaky, especially in the local ground forces." Outwardly, Gaiene usually displayed a devil-may-care attitude, so the open concern in his expression underlined the seriousness of the problem.

"Pair the locals with platoons of our people and issue instructions that any soldier who refuses to follow orders will be shot. Any other questions?"

"The local authorities, sir?" Kai asked. "What do we do with them?"

"I'll be giving them orders. If there are any problems getting them to do what they're told, I'll notify you to send troops. Local soldiers can handle that job since none of them have any love for their appointed-elected leaders."

"What about the snakes' housing compounds?" Rogero added. "We've swept up the snakes who were still home, but there are families there. Sooner or later, the crowds of citizens will head for those compounds, and you know what will happen to those families."

"The same thing that's happened to a lot of other people's families for a long time at the hands of the snakes," Gaiene commented. "I won't shed any tears if the citizens take revenge."

Drakon hesitated, then shook his head. "We're not the snakes. I'm not Hardrad. Put guards around the snakes' family compounds. Enough guards to keep the crowds off, and make sure those guards are our people and not local ground troops."

"We're going to be spread thin as it is," Kai said. "We've all seen children die, sir. It's ugly, but . . ."

"I know. We killed some of them in the fighting on Alliance worlds. I hated it then, but I couldn't do anything about it. Now I can, and I don't want to see any more dead kids. Understand?" All three colonels nodded. "Now, get your people and the police moving."

"Yes, sir." Rogero, Kai, and Gaiene chorused, all saluting before their images vanished.

Morgan shrugged. "At least you got that part about shooting anyone who doesn't obey orders right. But the mobs—"

"I'm not done," Drakon said. "How much of the snake comm net still exists? The stuff they used to issue proclamations and propaganda to the populace and give orders to local authorities?"

"It's intact," Malin said with a grin. "Not the control nodes in the headquarters and subsector stations, of course. Those have been destroyed. But we've seized the relay points, so we can modify the software to allow them to broadcast signals from an improvised control node."

"How long?"

"Ten minutes."

"Make it five."

It actually took about six minutes, which gave Drakon time to issue the same orders to the rest of the ground forces on the planet that he had given to Rogero, Kai, and Gaiene, and time to come up with something to tell the growing mobs of citizens that hijacked ISS surveillance systems were spotting everywhere. Exactly what to say had taken a little thought before he realized that the Syndicate Worlds had long provided the perfect rationale in its own propaganda.

"This is General Drakon," he said into the net linking all local officials. "I am in control of all the ground forces on this planet and am operating with CEO Iceni. We are in charge. All local officials are ordered to get onto the streets and calm the situation. You are to help maintain order, you are to reassure the citizens that the snakes have been dealt with, and you are to direct all celebrating into harmless paths. Use your local police to ensure that all liquor stores, bars, and pharmacies are closed and locked down immediately. There will be ground forces detachments visiting your homes to make sure that you are following these directions. Get going."

Malin shook his head. "They'd be a lot more effective if they actually represented the citizens in their areas. Being able to control voting software is a lot easier than controlling voters."

"Shift me to full broadcast," Drakon ordered, waiting as Malin entered the commands. When he spoke next, his words would go out to every phone, vid screen, terminal, speaker, public announcing system, and anything else on and off the planet with the ability to receive messages.

"Citizens," Drakon began, "I am speaking on behalf of myself and CEO Iceni. We have eliminated the ISS on this planet and throughout this star system. Henceforth, Midway will be an independent star system. We will no longer follow orders from the failed Syndicate Worlds.

"It is critical that while we celebrate this day, we also do not forget the importance of protecting our homes and our families. A breakdown of order could too easily result in the destruction of our homes, the places where you work, and loss of life. I have ordered the police onto the streets to ensure that everyone and every place is kept safe from anyone careless or irresponsible enough to threaten the safety and security of all our citizens. Because of the possibility that some ISS personnel might still be hidden among the crowds celebrating today, I am also ordering out ground forces troops to back up our police. Be aware that anyone urging actions that could lead to rioting or looting could be an ISS agent attempting to lure you into danger." Perhaps that would lead the crowds themselves to turn on anyone trying to turn them into mobs.

"Celebrate our independence, but do not forget the enemies who will endanger it." That had always been the mantra of the Syndicate Worlds. Invoke the fear of external and internal enemies, of disorder, to maintain support from the citizens. "Though this has been kept secret up until now by the ISS, other star systems have fallen into anarchy and

massive loss of life and property following the collapse of
Syndicate authority. I will not allow that to happen here.
All citizens are to follow the orders they are given by the
police and ground forces. Peaceful and orderly celebration
is allowed and encouraged, but anyone who riots or loots
will be shot on sight. They will not be allowed to endanger
their fellow citizens or to steal from their fellow citizens.
This is General Drakon, for the people, out."

That last phrase sounded particularly false this time
even though he had said it countless times, the repetition
and lack of sincerity each time rendering the words "for the
people" meaningless to everyone who used it. But this time
he had felt those words and been stung by their lack of real
significance. *We didn't do this for the people. We did it for
ourselves, to survive.*

Drakon turned back to Malin and Morgan. "Get a reporting system set up to consolidate what the automated
systems are seeing. I need to know whether the crowds get
out of control anywhere."

Morgan shrugged. "We can do that, but what will you
do if one of the mobs does start to run amuck? Give them
another stern lecture?"

"I'll send in reinforcements and kill as many as I have
to in order to restore order." He had learned that, too. You
did what was necessary, whether you liked it or not. Maybe
there were other ways of handling out-of-control mobs, but
he didn't have access to any of those ways just then. "I will
not have this planet turned into ruins overrun by rioters."

THE optical sensors on the heavy cruiser holding Iceni
were no match for those on a battle cruiser or battleship, but
they were still good enough to easily spot small objects
across light-hours of distance. So close to the battered
C-990 every surface detail could be made out, and when
holes smashed into the hull came into view the sensors
could catch glimpses inside.

Both of the escape pods which had fled C-990 had been

recovered by forces loyal to Iceni. One was empty, and the other held only dead members of the crew who had been shot at close range and apparently died after they managed to launch the pod. From the outside, the cruiser itself still seemed lifeless.

"Could they have killed everyone?" Akiri asked in sickened tones. "Just kept fighting until the entire crew was dead?"

"That's possible," Iceni replied. "How long until the uncrewed probe enters C-990?"

"Three minutes. The approach is taking longer because C-990 is tumbling and the probe has to match the motion before it can enter."

When the probe finally managed to slip inside through one of the rents in C-990's hull, at first nothing was visible but torn equipment and bulkheads. Then the first bodies came into view.

"These were killed by hell-lance fire," Marphissa said. "They were dead before decompression hit."

Iceni just nodded in reply. *One skill we all learned through experience, how to identify how people had died. Too many people, too much experience. And it hasn't ended.*

The probe made its way past the dead, angling toward the bridge. "Vacuum everywhere," the probe's controller reported. "No signs of patching holes to maintain pressure. That hatch was forced when there was vacuum on this side and pressure on the other. That didn't happen when we fired on the cruiser."

The bodies on the other side of the hatch only reinforced that observation. "Damage to their survival suits from hand weapons."

"How many were attacking and how many defending?" Akiri demanded.

"There's no way to tell."

Iceni suppressed a shudder, imagining the havoc that must have played out aboard C-990. The crew fighting among themselves, surrounded by wreckage, no way to tell one side from the other, so that it would have been as easy to target friends as enemies in the death grapple among the intermittently lit and torn-up passageways and compartments.

"The last two mutineers, or the last two loyalists, could have killed each other, not knowing what they were doing," Marphissa commented, echoing Iceni's thoughts. "If there's anyone still alive, they'll probably be at the bridge or at engineering."

"Send the probe to the bridge first," Iceni ordered. That was where Kolani would surely be.

The probe wended its way though the passageways, dodging wreckage and the dead. The interior of the wrecked cruiser increasingly reminded Iceni of a nightmare, emergency lights eerily bright in some places, only flickering in others, deep patches of darkness looming that might have a single, still hand thrust out into the light, the fingers curled in a last attempt to grasp nothingness. A broken ship carrying a dead crew, like something out of a sinister legend of space.

Finally, the armored hatch leading onto the bridge loomed ahead. "That hatch was forced, too," the probe operator said, her own voice sounding strained.

Iceni looked at the bodies visible around the hatch. "They lost a lot of people doing it." Bridges were meant to be citadels for the officers in the event of a mutiny, thus they had active defenses as well as armor protecting them. Some of those defenses had probably been knocked out during the fight with Iceni's warships, but enough had survived to decimate the attackers.

"The bridge is also in vacuum." The probe approached the hatch cautiously, transmitting the codes that should disarm any surviving defenses, and eventually reached the portal.

From the hatch, the bridge appeared mostly intact, but Iceni could see bodies sprawled around. Had the bridge crew fought among themselves as well? The senior ISS agent aboard would have been there, and armed. Kolani's officers would have been loyal to her. But what about the others, the line workers and executives of C-990's crew?

From the viewing angle they had, it was apparent that Kolani still sat in the command seat, her back to the hatch, wearing a survival suit with her CEO markings clear in the light from the probe. But Kolani didn't move, her body rigid. "No signs of life," the probe operator said. "No life data coming in from any survival suits, no warm spots on infrared. Everyone on the bridge must be dead." The probe began to move onto the bridge, while Iceni readied herself to order it stopped. She had already accumulated enough horrible memories in her life to sometimes trigger night sweats as it was. She did not want to see Kolani's lifeless face to add to those.

But before Iceni could say anything, an alarm blared. "The probe tripped some sort of circuit," the operator said. "Power surge detected. Some sort of command seems to have been—"

Iceni's image from the probe went blank as a much louder alarm shouted for attention.

"C-990's core overloaded," Marphissa reported in a low voice. "There must have been a booby trap set, so when someone entered the bridge it would trigger the overload. We're on the edge of the danger zone, so there's no threat to this unit."

Iceni kept her eyes on the spot where the image from the probe had been. Kolani had done it, she was sure. In her last moments of life, Kolani had set a trap for those who would come to gloat over her defeat. Perhaps in those final moments Kolani had had time to hope that Iceni herself would be part of that team. *Sorry to disappoint you.* "Gather the flotilla and return it to orbit about the planet. Let me know the moment we hear from C-625 or any other unit at the gas giant."

They were about six light-minutes from the planet. Information would be a little time-late, but not too much. Iceni closed her eyes, massaged her forehead with the fingers of one hand, then looked for messages from Drakon.

There were several. As Iceni viewed the first messages, she had a sudden chilling vision in which the fratricide and destruction aboard C-990 had just been a prologue to similar scenes to be played out on the surface of the nearby planet.

"THEY need to see *you*," Malin insisted.

"Going out in those mobs," Morgan shot back, "is a good way to ensure he dies."

As usual, both Malin and Morgan had good points. Drakon eyed the reports streaming in on multiple comm windows, seeing reluctant police forces and far-more-reluctant local administrators filtering in small groups among the massive crowds of celebrants. Moving discreetly behind both were platoons of soldiers, usually with more platoons watching the leading platoons.

Here and there, brief spasms of violence played out as someone tried to break into a liquor store or other business and was repulsed by quick and brutal use of first nonlethal riot-control agents, then direct gunfire on anyone who resisted. But such incidents stayed few as the great majority of those celebrating showed no sympathy for lawbreakers. Generations of conditioning on the need to obey authority could not be shed in a day, not when authority was on the streets and acting only against those who were clearly breaking laws.

But still, there was a sense, something that Drakon felt even if he couldn't quantify it, that the situation was balanced on a knife-edge. The mood of the crowds oscillated around a tipping point, giddy, happy, irresponsible, reckless, an ocean of humanity whose waves could shift the wrong way in a heartbeat.

"They're happy to see the soldiers," Malin said. "They see our troops as liberators because we slew the snakes. You need to personalize that, General Drakon. You need to be the liberator, the man who freed this star system from the grip of the Syndicate Worlds and the fear of the ISS."

"They've seen him," Morgan replied. "Everyone saw him when he made that broadcast."

"It's too remote, too isolated. He needs to be among the citizens."

"Where any nut can decide to take a shot at him!"

Drakon let the sound of their debate subside to a buzzing at the back of his head as he considered his options. Malin and Morgan had a good habit of clearly stating their positions and the rationales behind them right up front, as well as a bad habit of then restating the same points in endless back-and-forth argument. "Here's what we'll do," he finally said, putting an instant stop to the debate.

A couple of minutes later, still wearing his combat-battered armor but with the helmet and face shield open, Drakon strode out of his headquarters and out among the crowds. Malin and Morgan both followed a few paces behind, wearing only their black skin suits but carrying unobtrusive and deadly weapons as they watched the crowds around Drakon. As Drakon had expected, all eyes went to him in his armor, paying little attention to those who followed him. In that armor he loomed a bit taller and wider than the citizens, appearing to be a figure literally larger-than-life.

The first mass of citizens he encountered paused in their celebrating, uncertainty in their eyes, as they realized that a CEO was among them. Drakon smiled at them, the same sort of comradely-but-I'm-in-charge smile he would give his soldiers. "It's a good day!" he called. "This is our star system now, our planet, and we're going to take care of it!"

The crowd cheered, ripples of reaction running away from Drakon like rings in a pond in which a rock has fallen. He walked slowly but deliberately through the crowd, the omnipresent security cameras picking up his image and sending it everywhere on the planet. Citizens reached out tentative hands to touch his armor, some straining to touch the scars of recent combat against the snakes. Drakon felt the power of the mob as if it were a single vast organism, huge and immensely powerful, and fought down his wave of fear. He had seen armored troops pulled down and over-whelmed by masses of civilians on Alliance planets and had a healthy respect for what an aroused mob could do. But he tried not to show any concern, instead holding that smile and maintaining his steady pace as he called out occasional vague words about order and law and safety.

A younger citizen, just coming to draft age by the look of him, eyes afire with emotion, thrust himself before Drakon, heedless of the weapons that Malin and Morgan immediately trained upon him. "When are the elections? When will we truly choose those who govern us?"

"We'll get to that," Drakon replied loudly. "Things have changed." No one spent a lifetime dealing with and working among the Syndicate Worlds bureaucracy without developing a skill at mouthing meaningless reassurances that promised nothing.

The passionate young man looked uncertain, then he was pushed aside by other citizens and lost in the crowd. But Drakon had a bad feeling that his question would not be so easily disposed of in the days to come.

ICENI and the others on the bridge of the heavy cruiser watched video from the surface, showing Drakon's triumphal procession through the streets and the adulation the citizens were heaping upon him. "You'd think that I'd done nothing," she commented to those around her, keeping her tones partly annoyed and partly amused to hide the concerns those images created. *If Drakon becomes the face of the rulers of this star system, he can more easily push me aside. Drakon may have to be dealt with after all.*

CHAPTER FIVE

HER assistant, Mehmet Togo, finally called in as Iceni's cruiser neared orbit about the planet once more. "It took some time to override the locks placed on my systems by the ISS," Togo explained.

"Did any snakes make it to my office complex?"

"No, Madam CEO. Several snakes were approaching our entrance when they encountered some ground forces." Togo's lips didn't smile, but his eyes held wicked amusement. "The snakes got no farther."

"Are there any ground forces in or near my offices?" Iceni asked.

"The nearest ground forces are on the streets outside, engaged in crowd control," Togo replied. If there had been soldiers there, out of sight but with weapons aimed at Togo's head, he could have used a code phrase to indicate duress, but that phrase hadn't been in his reply. *Everything is fine.* A good code phrase to Iceni's mind, since *everything* was never fine. Something would always be a problem.

"I'll be taking a shuttle down in less than half an hour. I want a full report before then of what CEO Drakon is up to, and I want to ensure we have just as much access to the planetwide surveillance and announcing systems as he does."

"Yes, Madam CEO."

"I am streaming you some files of the engagement up here where we defeated CEO Kolani's force. Make sure that those files and the news that *my* force defeated the threat of orbital bombardment are broadcast to the populace. I want the citizens to look upward and realize that it is thanks to me that the warships remaining in this star system are here to protect us, not threaten us."

"A very good phrase, Madam CEO. I will make certain all of the citizens hear it before your shuttle has landed."

Iceni grimaced with exasperation. It had been a long day and was far from over; there were too many variables to deal with and not enough information. At least Togo was still alive, and there weren't soldiers crawling around her own offices. Drakon wasn't being too obvious or brash if he intended taking over completely.

Maybe she should speak with him again before returning to the planet's surface where she would be within reach of Drakon's soldiers. Iceni was reaching for her controls when C-625 finally called in from its position near the gas giant.

The woman sending the message wasn't C-625's commander. She was also wearing a snake suit. Two bad omens whose dire implications were quickly confirmed. "This is ISS Executive Jillan to the traitor Iceni. The former commander of this mobile forces unit and several of her executives have been summarily executed. The ISS has established temporary direct control of this unit and will respond only to the orders of CEO Hardrad and CEO Kolani. For the people, Jillan, out."

Damn. Either the snakes on C-625 had been particularly alert and ready to act, or the commander and executives on the cruiser had been too slow to make up their minds. Iceni hit the reply command. "ISS Executive Jillan and all personnel aboard C-625 and the other mobile forces at the main mobile forces facility, this is CEO Iceni. CEO Hardrad and CEO Kolani are dead. All ISS personnel elsewhere in this star system are also dead. I am in full control of the remaining mobile forces in this star system, and my ally CEO Drakon is in full control of the surface of the inhabited planet. This star system is now independent of the Syndicate Worlds and ISS authority no longer applies. You are to surrender C-625 to me. If you do so, the ISS personnel aboard C-625 and the units accompanying it will be granted safe passage out of this star system. A swift response is expected. For the people, Iceni, out."

Akiri wasn't asking, but he and Marphissa had surely already tapped separately into the message to learn what their superiors were up to.

Iceni faced them, keeping her voice level as she continued the pretence that the others did not know the content of the latest message. "The snakes control C-625."

"Should we plot an intercept?" Marphissa asked.

Akiri shook his head. "They can easily evade us with the amount of distance between us. We'd never catch them."

"Do we have other options?" Iceni asked.

Akiri paused, then looked to Marphissa, who also thought before making a helpless gesture. "We can't catch them," she agreed with Akiri. "Not unless they choose to fight us, and that seems unlikely. The ISS personnel in control of C-625 are not combat experienced. They don't know how to operate that cruiser."

"They could let automated systems on C-625 handle maneuvering and firing weapons," Akiri grumbled. "They must know such an attack would be suicide, but we can't assume they know how futile it would also be."

Iceni nodded slowly. "That's another good point. I've demanded that they surrender, but they won't. They'll head for the hypernet gate." Both Marphissa and Akiri gave her surprised looks. "The snakes in control of C-625 aren't like CEO Kolani. They were not responsible for controlling this entire star system. Their responsibility was to ensure control of C-625, and that they have successfully done. They can run to the central government at Prime and report personal triumph as well as the failures of their superiors. That's what they'll do."

Akiri had quickly entered some data into the maneuvering systems. "If they do head for the hypernet gate, we still can't stop them. They have too much of a head start on us. The civilian transport near the gate to act as a courier can't do anything to stop that cruiser. You could order the defenses around the hypernet gate to engage C-625 when it gets close enough, but that might cause C-625 to fire upon the gate and damage it."

Iceni brooded over that question, then made a helpless gesture. "It's not worth the risk of damage to the gate. Tell the merchant ship courier to remain well clear of C-625 if it heads for the gate. There's no sense in losing that ship."

"Are we certain," Marphissa asked, "that the snakes on C-625 won't also launch a bombardment of the planet? The load-out on a single heavy cruiser isn't huge, but it's enough to seriously damage several targets on the planet."

Targets meaning cities. Iceni thought again, then shook her head. "No. Snakes follow rigid discipline, which teaches them to do exactly what they're told and nothing more. They don't have orders to launch a bombardment, and devastating portions of the planet might be the wrong thing to do. Lacking anyone to tell them that they must bombard the planet, they'll take the safe option of leaving that decision to superiors at Prime."

The slight twist of Marphissa's lips conveyed that she knew the concepts of rigid discipline weren't confined to the snakes. But she was wise enough not to say that out loud.

"Let me know if C-625 leaves the mobile forces facility," Iceni directed. She then checked a certain mailbox and found it still empty. Her source close to Drakon had nothing to report, or in the current rush of events couldn't go through the many convoluted steps necessary to get something into that mailbox so that no one could tell where the message had come from. Or that source had somehow been compromised and cut off by Drakon. Nothing could mean nothing to fear, or it could mean a great deal to worry about.

She called Drakon.

DRAKON'S response took an irritatingly long time. He finally called back, still wearing the combat armor. Was that display meant to send a message to her?

"Good to see you're still around," Drakon began.

"How nice of you to say so. I'm so glad you could take time from demonstrating your control of the planet to speak with me."

Drakon smiled briefly. "There were matters that had to be dealt with. I understand that you've won, too. What happened to Kolani?"

"Dead."

"That simplifies things."

"Yes," Iceni agreed. "With Hardrad dead as well we've cut in half the number of CEOs in this star system."

His expression hardened. "Are you implying that should happen again?"

"That is not my wish."

"I'm well aware that you don't need me anymore now that the snakes are gone from this planet. You cut the deal with Black Jack, and you control the mobile forces here. I can't touch you, but you could drop rocks on me all day. Let's not pretend otherwise."

Iceni regarded Drakon silently for a long moment before replying. "We both had our own reasons for rebellion against the Syndicate Worlds."

"We didn't have any choice when those orders came through for Hardrad to conduct the loyalty sweeps. We had to work together, or this star system would have ended up like all those other places where fighting has broken out. It was pure luck that we were already separately planning on revolting."

"I never underestimate the importance of luck," Iceni

said. "I also don't underestimate the value of people who don't betray me when they have the chance."

Drakon laughed. "We had plenty of levers to use against each other if it came to that."

"There was nothing negative I could prove about you as serious as the deal I cut with Black Jack."

"Yes," Drakon agreed. "Making a deal with the Alliance would look bad to the snakes."

"The deal was with Black Jack, not the Alliance," Iceni said.

"What's the difference?"

"I'm not sure at this point. He may *be* the Alliance." Iceni frowned at Drakon. "The deal was worth the risk. We needed to know that Black Jack wouldn't come charging in here to help enforce Syndicate authority, and I needed to be able to imply his backing for what we're doing. The ability to say that Black Jack knew what we're doing, wouldn't interfere, and won't let anyone else interfere, is invaluable."

"Is that actually what Black Jack agreed to?" Drakon asked.

Iceni smiled without any hesitation at all. "Of course."

"That's quite a few important concessions from him. I've been wondering why he gave that up so easily."

This time Iceni shrugged. She had no intention of admitting to Drakon that she had significantly exaggerated the extent of Black Jack's support for her actions. "Maybe he really needed that mechanism to prevent hypernet gate collapses. Maybe he just wanted to be able to have leverage over us in the future. We'll deal with that when we have to. We've already dealt with our former masters. Anything the government on Prime plans will take time to get together. We've got breathing room now."

"No, we don't." Drakon waved to indicate the area outside where he sat. "The citizens are happy now, but I had one hell of a time keeping things from coming apart. Our own populace is poised to rise up in rebellion against us unless we handle them right. Leading this rebellion ourselves was our only chance, but I don't think 'same leaders, same rules, different titles' is going to work very long. The citizens will figure out that game in no time."

Iceni scowled. "We have the tools and tactics left us by the snakes. We can eliminate anyone we need to if they try to rouse the populace against us."

"That worked for the snakes and the Syndicate Worlds. Until it didn't," Drakon pointed out. "I can ID anyone rabble-rousing. The surveillance software makes it easy to spot any leaders emerging by their communications patterns. And I can nail them as they pop up. But they'll learn. How many different ways do you and I know to avoid snake surveillance?"

"Too many."

"And you and I both know how many underground activities there are, black markets in anything you care to name. If a resistance starts using those techniques, spotting them will be as hard as hell. We need at least passive support from the majority of the citizens so rebellion can't gain any foothold."

"We have the warships," Iceni said. "They're our hammer to help ensure control of this star system."

"Big hammer. Blunt hammer. We can nuke cities when things get out of hand, but that tends to dry up public support, and we don't have an infinite supply of cities." Drakon pointed to a display on one wall of the room where he sat, showing images of a mountain near a lake on some planet a very long way from here. "That's from Baldur Star System."

"I've heard of it but never been there. The beauty of the place is supposed to be breathtaking."

"It is," Drakon said. "But when I look at that picture, I wonder if that mountain and lake are still there, or if some orbital bombardment has turned that landscape into a cratered, lifeless ruin. We know the Syndicate way failed. Any fool could figure that out when the damned Alliance fleet came strolling through this star system and informed us that the war was over." He snorted. "Our own government, the oh-so-efficient and effective Syndicate Worlds, couldn't tell us that they'd lost. No. The enemy had to come here and do it, then the enemy blew away a bunch of those enigma ships that have been invulnerable to us because even though we'd spent decades trying to find out stuff about the enigmas, it only took the Alliance a few months to figure out how to defeat the aliens."

"They had Geary," Iceni said in a soft voice. "Black Jack."

"Black Jack." Drakon shook his head. "I didn't believe the information we were getting about his coming back from the dead."

"He came back," Iceni replied. "I talked to him. It's not a trick. Maybe he did us a favor."

"By knocking the legs out from under the Syndicate Worlds government? Maybe. The corporate autocracy always justified itself by claiming to be superior to every other system, especially the inefficiencies of the Alliance." Drakon gave her a skeptical look. "I'll let the remnants of Syndicate authority on Prime try to come up with reasons why we couldn't win a war despite a century of trying, then got our butts kicked by someone who supposedly died a hundred years ago. Are you sure Black Jack won't be back here, trying to add us to an empire?"

Iceni looked down, her eyes hooded, recalling the messages she had received from Black Jack. "I can't be sure of anything, but he seemed authentic. Just a military officer out to do his job. He's either real, or he's the best fraud I've ever seen."

"He has to be working some angle."

"If he were one of us, he would be." Iceni fixed her eyes on Drakon's. "Speaking of working angles, if I haven't made it clear already, we still need each other. If you try to betray me, you might succeed, but even though the snakes are gone you'll still go down with me. Just so you know."

Drakon smiled at her, his voice and expression betraying nothing. "I already assumed that. I have control of the ground forces on the surface here and elsewhere in the star system"—he used one hand to mime pointing a weapon at her head—"and you have control of the mobile forces."

She mimicked his gesture, pointing her own forefinger at him. "Let's hope neither one of us is foolish enough to force the other to pull the trigger."

"What do I have to promise to make you feel secure returning to the surface?"

"Your promises mean nothing." Iceni watched him again, wishing she knew more about the man. "But I do have control of the mobile forces, and I will tell you that if anything happens to me, dead-man programs within their targeting systems will automatically launch a bombardment of the planet using every kinetic projectile aboard these warships."

"I'd hate to see that happen."

She couldn't tell whether or not Drakon believed her. In fact, she hadn't had the chance to set up such a system. But all that mattered was that Drakon believed she had, or remained uncertain about whether such a system to retaliate for her death existed. "Me, too. I'm glad we understand each other. I'll be taking a shuttle down soon. I believe a face-to-face conference in a secure location as soon as possible is important. Where will we meet?"

Drakon paused to think. She knew what he was concerned about. If he came to her offices, it would feed the impression that she was superior to him. But if she went to his headquarters to meet Drakon, it would imply that Drakon was ultimately in charge.

"There's a set of secure conference rooms the snakes maintained partway between your offices and my headquarters," Drakon finally said. "We already went through them, looking for any snakes hiding out there, but I'll make sure they're swept again for snake surveillance gear and booby traps before you land. Is that acceptable?"

It would mean trusting that Drakon and his people would do a good enough job on that sweep. But she would have her bodyguards with her, and they carried their own hidden gear for spotting danger of many kinds. Iceni considered the idea, then nodded. "All right. I'll notify you when I've landed."

WHEN she stepped off the shuttle Iceni could see Togo and several of her bodyguards waiting at the ramp. Much farther off, soldiers and military vehicles were positioned around the landing area. "Why are they here?" she asked.

Togo made a helpless gesture. "Security and crowd control. They said. They have not attempted to hinder us in any way."

"We'll see if that continues." At least Drakon had shown the courtesy to keep his soldiers at a distance from her rather than placing them so close they might have seemed to be controlling Iceni.

She started walking toward her offices. "How does everything look?"

If Togo had wanted to say *everything is fine*, it was the perfect opening, but he didn't respond that way. "Things could be worse."

As they cleared some of the barriers around the field, Iceni could see the crowds of citizens still filling the streets. The noise from them, which had formed a low-level background hum that Iceni hadn't really noticed, rose in volume as Iceni came into view. After a tense moment she realized that once again she was hearing cheers. "For me?"

"You are one of the liberators, CEO Iceni," Togo replied, his expression deadpan. "The citizens are happy that thanks to you the mobile forces are no longer threats but have become guardians of their safety."

Iceni, moved by a silly impulse, raised one hand to wave and heard the cheers rise a little louder. It felt good, and frightening. "Drakon is calling himself General now. I need a new title. CEO has too many bad connotations, and reeks of the Syndicate Worlds."

Togo pulled out his hand unit as they kept walking, the

bodyguards behind at a discreet distance. He punched in the query and frowned as he read the response. "There are many possible alternatives. Queen?"

"A good job description but that might sound a bit autocratic to the citizens," Iceni said.

"There is no sense in telegraphing your intent," Togo agreed. "Governor?"

"Too subordinate-sounding."

"Prime Minister?"

"First among ministers? No, I need to be first, period."

Togo consulted his unit again. "The Man."

"What?" Iceni asked.

"The Man. Archaic. Very archaic."

"And obviously not me," Iceni said.

"The Big Cheese. The Big . . . Kahuna."

"Are you making these up or actually reading those titles?"

"I am reading them, Madam CEO. How about Czar, Kaiser, or Caesar? The first two were derived from the last." Togo frowned again. "But they all mean absolute ruler. Leader, Khan, Sheik, Pasha, Sultan, She-Who-Must-Be-Obeyed . . ."

"I like that last one."

"And it is fitting," Togo agreed. "But it might cause the citizens to believe that you have simply altered your brand name and intend to rule the same as a CEO."

"We can't have them believing that, can we?" Iceni said.

"How about the President? Or First Citizen?"

"That first one is a possibility. How does one become a president?"

Togo consulted the definition. "President describes the position as preeminent and is nonspecific as to the source of authority. It has been used for leaders of entities ranging from absolute dictatorships to societies so populist that they are only one step removed from total anarchy. Calling you the President may be a good choice."

"President Iceni." She tried out the title, saying it slowly. "*The* President, because there are no others. I do like that."

"May I be the first to congratulate you, President Iceni?" Togo said.

"You may. Let's go see General Drakon."

THE office building holding the secure conference rooms which had once belonged to the ISS had a nondescript façade. It had no sign or other identification beyond the street number and could have hosted any of a thousand kinds of modest businesses. The ISS had always displayed that two-faced approach to the outside universe. On the one hand, omnipresent and obvious surveillance systems, and headquarters or regional command centers that were large and clear signs of the power and presence of the snakes. On the other hand, lesser facilities hidden in places where they would least be expected, and other surveillance systems designed to be undetectable except by the most sophisticated equipment. The citizens of the Syndicate Worlds had always known that the ISS was there, but they had never known just where the ISS was, making for a powerful mix of justified fear and paranoia.

Inside the offices, though, the snakes had spared no expense. Iceni strolled past the plush furnishings to stand before a floor-to-ceiling virtual window giving a view on a gorgeous stretch of beach. She might have actually been standing near the sand, hearing the muffled, rhythmic roar of the surf on the other side of an actual window. The primary world of the Midway Star System, usually also called Midway, had a lot of beaches, but the nearest of those was over twenty kilometers from this building. Iceni doubted that this view was that of the nearest shoreline. The position of the sun appeared to be about an hour off, and the beach had the looks of one of the many archipelagoes that dotted the surface of Midway the planet, perhaps one of the island chains the ISS had declared off-limits to others so that the snakes could enjoy recreation there with privacy. The small continent on which the city was located, and which was the only other landmass boasted by the planet, had plenty of nice beaches, too; but they almost always had visitors on them since that was one of the few recreations for common citizens that the Syndicate Worlds hadn't found a way to limit.

The door opened and Drakon entered, followed by two other soldiers. Togo, already seated at the gleaming conference table, murmured subvocally into his mike, and Iceni heard the words clearly through her own pickup. "Bran Malin and Roh Morgan. General Drakon has converted their sub-CEO ranks to colonel. They are his closest and most trusted advisers."

Drakon nodded to Iceni. "All bodyguards outside? Good. Do you object to my two aides being here?"

"Not if you don't object to my assistant," Iceni replied, moving back to the table and taking a seat next to Togo. She surreptitiously examined Drakon's aides as she did so. Unlike Togo, who at nearly fifty standard years old was both physically fit and very experienced, both Malin and Morgan were relatively young, perhaps in their late twenties or early thirties. They appeared to be about the same age. But both seemed to be confident and comfortable in the unpretentious way of people who really knew their job well.

The door sealed behind Drakon and a string of green lights flashed into life above it, indicating security systems active to prevent any intrusions or surveillance. He took a chair opposite Iceni, one colonel sitting to either side of him. "Here's where we are right now," Drakon began without further preamble. "I've got control of the surface and confirmed control of every important facility off the planet as well. My people are still conducting sweeps to ensure that no snakes are running loose on any of the islands. Until we complete those and make sure the populace is settled, I don't have a lot of personnel to spare. The main mobile forces facility at the gas giant is under my control, but they're afraid to blink because they say the mobile forces there are still controlled by snakes."

"That matches the communications I have received from heavy cruiser C-625," Iceni said. "It is possible that the other warships there, one light cruiser and three Hunter-Killers, are still commanded by their own officers, but the snakes on those units must be alert and will not be easily overcome."

"Will they knock out the facility?"

"I don't think so," Iceni said. "It's a very valuable facility to whoever controls this star system, and they have no orders from superiors to do so. I believe they will soon head for the hypernet gate to report on events here to the government at Prime."

Drakon made a dissatisfied face. "And you lost two other cruisers as well?"

That stung. "I lost *one* other cruiser, Kolani's flagship C-990. She sabotaged it. C-818 took a lot of damage to its main propulsion, but I already have other units en route to take it in tow so we can have repairs done. We will have four heavy cruisers to defend this star system." Not until Iceni had said it did she realize how pathetic that force level really sounded.

But Colonel Malin commented before anyone else could. "That's not much, but compared to what else is available out here now, and to the government on Prime, it's a significant defense force."

"You can't catch the last cruiser? C-625?" Drakon asked.

"It's one and a half light-hours distant, General," Iceni replied. "Do you have any idea how many billions of kilometers that is?"

"I've marched enough kilometers to know how far *one* is," Drakon said, his voice growing sharper. "Maneuvering is a matter of planning ahead and outthinking the opponent."

Iceni smiled humorlessly. "I only wish space combat were as simple as ground combat."

"Simple?" She had apparently touched a nerve. Drakon openly glared at her. "I'm sure everything is all clean and easy and sterile up in space, where you can slam shots at the enemy and never see their faces, let alone the blood and bodies, but it's different and harder in the mud."

Visions of the nightmare images from C-990 flashed into Iceni's memory. To her own surprise, her voice came out fairly steady. "You may be seriously underestimating the impact of war even amid the silence of space."

Something in her tone nonetheless registered on Drakon, whose anger shaded into careful study of Iceni. "Did you lose many people up there?"

"No. Except on C-990."

Togo intervened, speaking emotionlessly. "There were no survivors on C-990. Internal fighting killed everyone."

"Internal." Drakon nodded and sat back. "That must have been ugly. All right. There are four heavy cruisers and some lighter units. I've got enough ground forces to hold the planet easily, especially once I get all the local troops up to speed now that I don't have to worry about stepping on the toes of any CEOs a hundred light-years from here."

Iceni, regaining her own composure, brought up a display of this region of space. "According to the latest information we have, there are a few other mobile forces in nearby star systems. I'm going to send individual HuKs out to those star systems to invite those warships to join with us. The last we heard, there were mobile forces units at Taroa, Kahiki, and Lono."

"Nothing at Kane, Laka, Maui, or Iwa?" Drakon asked, naming the other four Syndicate star systems that could be reached from jump points at Midway. Being able to access such an unusually large number of other stars directly had given Midway its name.

He didn't have to ask about the eighth star that could be reached from Midway. Pele had been abandoned to the alien enigma race a long time ago. Every Syndicate ship sent there since that time had vanished without a trace.

"Not to our knowledge," Iceni replied. "The warships we send to Taroa, Kahiki, and Lono will also give us current information on what is happening in those star systems and anything they know about other places. Once they report back here I'll send another wave out to check the remaining neighboring star systems."

"Good plan," Drakon approved.

Iceni watched him, judging her next move. Despite the fact that they had launched a rebellion together, they knew very little about each other as persons. Their coordination had of necessity been through the briefest possible means, all communications and the rare personal meeting in the course of their Syndicate duties carried out with official faces on. Anything else might have compromised their co-operation and plans to the ever-watchful snakes. Their official records were well-known to each other, but the things not in those records remained ambiguous. She knew Drakon's face, but what lay behind it was another matter, and he surely felt the same regarding her.

Making up her mind to confront a volatile issue, Iceni leaned forward. "Now that you've agreed with my plans for the mobile forces, I'd like some input on what your assets are doing. I understand that there are ground forces guarding the snakes' family complexes."

"That's right." Drakon met her gaze without flinching. "All snakes have been pulled from the complexes. All that's left are families."

"What do you intend doing with them, General?"

Drakon paused, then blew out a long breath. "I'm still considering options."

To his left, Colonel Morgan managed to convey disapproval without moving a muscle or making a sound.

Togo spoke into the silence that followed. "They will never be welcome, or safe, within this star system."

Once again, Drakon displayed simmering anger. "Then what are you proposing?"

"It is too late to let the citizens resolve the issue for us—"

"*I* don't let someone else resolve issues in order to make it easier for me," Drakon snapped at Togo.

Iceni kept her expression unrevealing as she watched Drakon. "They can't stay here, and neither you nor I is willing to murder families en masse. That leaves one option. We put them on a ship and send them somewhere else. Back to Prime, perhaps."

Morgan finally spoke. "Waste a ship on that? We'd never see it again."

"That is likely," Togo said. "It is not a cost-free option."

"They're all going to want vengeance," Morgan insisted. "When you kill a nest of snakes, you kill them *all*. Otherwise, the young and the others will come after you someday."

"That option," Drakon said, "is not under consideration."

Iceni nodded. "I agree."

"General—" Morgan began.

"That is all," Drakon said.

As Morgan sat back, her expression gone impassive, Colonel Malin nodded toward Iceni. "I believe that the ship suggestion may be our best option, especially if we contrive to impress the snake families with our military strength before they depart. C-625 will carry news of the forces here when it left. If we wait until C-625 departs, we could fool the snake family members into believing that our mobile forces have received new reinforcements and are far stronger than they are. That is what Prime would believe."

"Planted disinformation?" Iceni said. "Under cover of a humanitarian action? I like the way that you think, Colonel."

Togo made a small gesture of agreement. "One merchant ship would be a small price to pay for misleading the Syndicate government as to our strength."

Left unsaid was something they all knew. With so many star systems spinning out of Syndicate control, the government on Prime had to choose which ones were marked for reconquest. Midway, with its hypernet gate, its access to multiple star systems, and its connection to space controlled by the enigma race, would be a priority for such a counterattack. It wasn't a matter of whether or not Prime would send an attack force to try to reassert its authority, but when that would happen.

"It sounds like we're agreed, then. Work with CEO Iceni's staff on that plan," Drakon ordered Malin.

"President Iceni," she corrected with a small smile.

"President?" Drakon's mouth twisted in a half smile in return. "What exactly does that mean?"

"Whatever I want it to mean."

His smile grew slightly. "Good. Get rid of the Syndicate baggage once and for all."

Colonel Malin rested his arms on the table, gazing at Iceni and Drakon. "That raises a topic I think we must address before it is forced upon us. We have all seen the crowds. They are happy today. The measures we have taken have maintained order. But tomorrow, they will wake up with hangovers, squint at the rising sun, and wonder what under that sun has changed."

Morgan was now displaying disdain with the same lack of sound or movement.

"What are you suggesting?" Iceni asked.

Malin swept one arm to encompass the outside. "We all know how bad things were under the Syndicate Worlds. Only the highest echelons really benefited. For the vast majority of citizens, there was no sense of ownership. The need for security drove compliance with the government more than anything else, but that compliance went only as far as it had to go. Do I need to cite the estimated numbers for losses due to corruption and waste? How inefficient and unproductive our manufacturing and fabrication facilities often are? If this star system is to prosper, we need to get the citizens believing that they have a stake in that prosperity."

Iceni gave him a polite but cool smile. "I have no intention of surrendering power to the mob." That earned her another impossibly subtle reaction from Colonel Morgan, this one of approval.

"We have to stay in control," Malin agreed. "But there are many levels below us. The lowest levels, the ward officers, council members, even mayors could be offered as truly elected positions."

Drakon appeared as uncertain about that as Iceni felt.

But Togo nodded. "I felt the power of the crowds. They will not accept business as usual. We need to throw them a bone. One with real meat on it. Or perhaps a synthetic substitute that they will accept as real meat."

"Low-level positions?" Drakon asked.

"And where would you draw the line?" Morgan demanded. "Give them council members, and they'll demand the right to choose their own mayors, then regional controllers, then generals and presidents! Do we want some citizens off the streets rummaging through the files of what we've done in the past?"

"We cannot control the crowds using only force—" Malin began.

"I can! Give me the authority and the troops, and I'll have the streets cleared and every citizen saying 'yes, sir, yes, sir, three bags full' before sundown!"

After a pause in which Iceni tried not to stare at Morgan, General Drakon spoke. "That's an option, but it has significant downsides. One of them is that if our troops are tied up garrisoning our own population, that means we can't use them elsewhere."

That argument seemed to get through to Colonel Morgan where others had not. "That's true. But we could end up facing the same garrisoning problem if the citizens are allowed too much latitude and start thinking they don't need to do as they're told."

"Yeah. That's a problem. How do we give them enough to keep them happy but not too much so that they think they can demand more?"

Malin answered. "We can't satisfy all of the citizens. Some, a few, will demand total democracy tomorrow. We can highlight the problems that would bring and offer enough evidence of change to keep the great majority of the citizens on our side."

"Just enough evidence of change?" Togo asked.

"And how do we determine what that is?" Morgan asked. "Give too little, in *their* eyes, and they'll demand more. If you give in then, they'll think you'll keep giving in."

Bloodthirsty she might be, but Morgan had some good

arguments. Iceni glanced at Togo. "General Drakon has already played the security card. Keep your homes and families safe. What else can we use to put the brakes on citizen desires to rule themselves?"

Togo looked upward, frowning in thought. "Divide and conquer. A very ancient tactic but very effective. What happens if the citizens can vote what they want? Will the cities take all for themselves since they have more voters? Will the cities be denied what they wish because power blocs of other voters seize control of elected positions out of proportion to their numbers? Change must be careful to ensure that no one is hurt. By keeping the individuals in upper-level positions appointed by President Iceni with the full advice and consent of General Drakon, who all can trust to work in the interests of the citizens since they expelled the snakes from Midway, we will ensure that everyone's interests are protected."

Drakon smiled crookedly. "Damn. You almost make me believe that you're sincere."

"The best propaganda is always anchored on a seed of truth that offers stability and the illusion of legitimacy to the arguments attached to that seed."

Even Morgan looked impressed this time.

"However," Drakon added, "I want an even split on who nominates people for positions. President Iceni can nominate half, with my advice and consent, and I'll nominate the other half, with her advice and consent."

"Fair enough," Iceni agreed.

"The low-level election process will require preparation," Togo continued. "The software must be confirmed to be reliable at actually counting votes instead of simply producing the desired vote totals. Back doors into the software that could allow manipulation of results must be blocked. Except for those hidden back doors that President Iceni and General Drakon wish to continue to exist, of course. Candidates must be found, campaigns must be waged. The process cannot be rushed without denying prospective candidates the opportunity to compete. It will be a long process."

Iceni nodded, smiling outwardly, and wondering why inside she felt a strange sense of discontent. *Wasn't this the solution I wanted? It seems like it. But the Syndicate system* failed, *and isn't this just an attempt to perpetuate it?*

I need time to think. Togo's solution will give me that time, but I will think.

She looked across the table at Drakon. Did his eyes mirror the same dissatisfaction? Or was she imagining that? "Let's do it," Iceni said, and no one objected.

AS he reentered his headquarters complex, Drakon felt himself relaxing for the first time in a very long time. It had been a hard day, but he had done it. He and Iceni had done it.

He had learned a bit more about her, too. Unless Iceni was an excellent actress, she had been genuinely rattled by the losses suffered in the mobile forces engagement. That was reassuring. Leaders who simply wrote off human losses as the cost of doing business were also, in Drakon's experience, fully capable of writing off allies in the same way.

He still hadn't decided whether to contact her again later, just the two of them, to explain about the four snake sentries and their families who were being given new identities and new homes. It didn't seem likely that Iceni would demand their blood, but you never knew. The alternative was sticking them on the same transport as the other snake families, but how would those four snakes explain their survival when all the rest of their comrades were dead? No, that would be a betrayal of his promise to them. Without their aid, he couldn't have gotten to that main surveillance node. He paid his debts.

Which also meant he owed Iceni, but it would be best not to make that too clear in case she saw an acknowledgment of debt as a sign of dependency.

Malin's comm unit buzzed urgently. Malin consulted it, his face losing emotion as he read. "General."

So much for relaxation. "What is it?"

"We'll have to modify what we told President Iceni regarding your control of all important off-planet facilities."

CHAPTER SIX

"WHO and where?" Drakon asked.

"Colonel Dun."

Drakon glanced upward without thinking, even though he was inside a building and couldn't have actually seen the main orbiting facility for this world even if it had been nighttime. "What's she doing? The last report we had from her said that the snakes on that station had all been neutralized, she had firm control, and she accepted my authority."

"I'm afraid that Colonel Dun's firm control may now be the problem. I passed on some of your earlier instructions and just received a reply. Instead of indicating that she would carry out those orders, Colonel Dun said, 'I will consider my options.'"

"Her options?" Dun wasn't one of the subordinates Drakon had brought to Midway. She had come from another place, for a reason he didn't know. "Remind me why Dun was still in command of that facility instead of someone we knew we could trust."

Morgan shrugged. "She had ties to the snakes. She was giving reports to them though supposedly only under duress. That's why she wasn't part of our planning. And trying to ease Dun out of command of the station couldn't be done without attracting a lot of attention and raising warning flags with the ISS. Of course, Dun *could* have been assassinated, opening a way for us to get someone better up there, but no one else wanted to pursue *that* option."

"Maybe I should have let you do that." Drakon walked into his office, Morgan and Malin following. *This isn't their fault,* he told himself. The ISS had plenty of experience with spotting excessively ambitious CEOs who were maneuvering too many followers into too many critical positions. Moving against Dun would have been too obvious.

Morgan stopped just inside the doorway, leaning against one wall with her arms crossed. "Dun is smart enough to know what kind of leverage control of that station gives her. She can threaten to drop large, heavy objects on this planet and do what the snakes didn't manage to accomplish. She's also stupid enough to try blackmailing you."

"I agree with Colonel Morgan's assessment as to Colonel Dun's smarts and Colonel Dun's stupidity," Malin said.

Drakon brought up data on the facility Dun controlled, seeing bad news that confirmed what he remembered. The orbiting facility contained extensive manufacturing plants, fed by ore brought in from asteroids, and those stockpiles of ore would make simple, impossible to stop, and horribly destructive bombs if just dropped onto the planet from orbit. The soldiers under Dun's command were up there to ensure no rebellious crazies did that, but now Dun herself was the rebellious crazy. He imagined the impacts of tons of ore falling from orbit. As Morgan said, the devastation would easily equal that of the nukes the snakes had sought to detonate. "Options? Can we get to her soldiers? Get them to turn on her?"

"They'd all have to turn at once," Morgan replied. "If half turned, and the other half didn't, that gives someone plenty of time to drop rocks. I don't think that option has much chance of success."

"I suggest we talk to her," Malin said. "She'll make demands. Keep talking, give in on a few, small things, while we plan and execute an operation to take her out."

Morgan grinned. "Even idiots get it right sometimes."

"Neither of you think that Dun herself can be co-opted? Turned into a loyal subordinate?" Drakon asked.

Malin shook his head.

Morgan laughed. "Dun will be safe when she's dead."

"Then I'll talk to her, make her think that I'm willing to play along. Meanwhile, you two get started on a plan to take that station. I need a good one, and I need it fast. First priority, ensure nothing gets dropped from that facility onto the planet. Second priority, remove Colonel Dun on a permanent basis. Oh, one other thing. Check the snake files we captured and see if any of the intact ones provide the reason why Dun got exiled here."

"Why does that matter?" Morgan asked.

"I won't know if it does matter until I know the reason. See if you can find it, and get that plan done."

Malin looked resigned, and Morgan rolled her eyes, but they went off together. Despite their mutual antagonism, Morgan and Malin could work well together when it came to producing plans. Drakon had never been able to figure that out, wondering if it was the product of some bizarre love-hate relationship, even though the idea of Morgan and Malin hooking up seemed to be not just impossible but also somehow indecent.

His first look at Colonel Dun when his call to her went through didn't cause Drakon to second-guess his decision.

Dun sat at ease, smiling like a cat that had just cleaned out a fish tank. "Congratulations, Artur," she began.

Using his first name meant that Dun intended treating this as a conversation among equals. But since he had no means at hand to slap her down, he would have to live with that attitude for a little while. "What's this I hear about you giving Colonel Malin a hard time . . . Sira?"

Dun grinned a little wider. "I see no need to submit to

an inferior position in this new setup. Not when I'm literally looking down on you."

"You're not looking down at the mobile forces controlled by President Iceni."

"President? Interesting. You're right. But if those mobile forces try anything, I'll see it long enough before it gets here that I can launch a doomsday barrage. And if I see anybody suspicious coming close, I'll do the same thing. I assume you'd like to avoid that."

"What is it you're looking for?" Drakon asked.

"It looks like you and Iceni are planning to run things as a pair. I want that to become a triumvirate."

You just made a big mistake by giving me the perfect excuse to stall. Maybe a fatal mistake. Outwardly, Drakon made a noncommittal shrug. "I can't decide that alone. I need to talk to Iceni."

"Take your time. I'm not going anywhere. Geosynchronous orbit, you know." Dun laughed outright. "Talk to you later."

Drakon mimed punching the air where the comm window had been, then called Iceni. He couldn't discuss his plans, not when Dun might be able to intercept the conversation, but he could use certain phrases known to CEOs that would indicate that he wanted the response process strung out as long as possible.

Two hours later, Malin and Morgan returned, entering together but immediately going to opposite corners of the room. Malin bobbed his head slightly up and to the side, indicating the general direction of the orbiting station. "We based the plan on the fact that Colonel Dun has spent most of her time in industrial assignments. That was the justification for giving her command of the station. Her military time has been with strategic systems."

"Nukes?" Drakon asked.

"For the most part. Planning and design."

Morgan smiled lazily. "She's going to be looking for a big attack. Missiles, large assault ships, something on that order. Colonel Dun doesn't have any experience with ground ops, special ops, or really, any ops."

"How many stealth suits do we still have operational after the attacks on the ISS?" Drakon asked.

"Enough." Morgan's grin widened. "They're in the plan."

Drakon called it up. One talent he had worked hard to acquire was the ability to quickly review and absorb the essentials of an operational plan. Getting bogged down in details could cause a commander to miss the bigger picture, and even whether the overall plan made any sense.

This one did, but he had expected nothing less. "Two assault forces."

Malin nodded. "One to go after any troops loyal to Dun and take her out by whatever means necessary, and the other to make sure nothing gets launched from that facility by securing and overriding all controls that could do that. We think Colonel Kai—"

"Kai's not doing it. Neither is Gaiene or Rogero. Dun may be overconfident, but we can't assume she's careless enough not to have someone tracking where my top field commanders are and where I am. If I or any of those three colonels heads for orbit, or can't be spotted down here conducting business as usual, Dun will know."

Morgan's eyebrows rose. "Does that leave who I think it does?"

"Yes. You two. Malin will command one assault force and you take the other."

"Dun may be watching us, too," Malin said.

"Maybe, but she doesn't have infinite resources to devote to surveilling people down here, and she probably thinks she can safely assume that wherever I am, you two are also."

"Sweet." Morgan slowly flexed the fingers of one hand as if preparing to go into action right then and there. "I want the force that goes after Dun."

Malin shrugged. "Fine by me. General, you asked about the reason for Dun's assignment to this star system."

"Yeah. What did she do?"

"We found her ISS files. There's nothing about the reason for exile."

Drakon peered at him. "Nothing?"

"Yes, sir. Very unusual. I'm beginning to wonder if Dun isn't a snake herself, operating under deep cover."

"She doesn't match the usual profiles for someone like that," Morgan added, "but we can't rule it out, and if it's true then Dun could be more dangerous than we think. There's too much detail we could check on her career to doubt any of that, so we know her experience, but she might also be operating right now on fail-safe contingency orders from the snakes."

"How long before you can nail her?"

"We can hide the troop movements in routine lifts to the facility and other orbital sites near there, but it will take time. Twenty-four hours. I wanted to push that until we found the blank spots in Dun's ISS records. Now I want to make very sure we don't tip her off."

When Morgan advised caution, it was uncharacteristic enough to emphasize how important it was to listen to that opinion. "All right. Twenty-four hours. President Iceni and I will spin out discussions with Dun to help keep her distracted. I don't want to hear from either one of you again until you're in control of that facility and calling in to tell me."

"I can run you a tight-beam link to the assault-force data feeds," Malin offered. "Slightly time-delayed because it'll have to run through relays to keep Dun's people from spotting it, but we need to do that anyway for team coordination, and the link should be safe from any intercept."

That was tempting, especially since he would have to sit here while they faced danger without him. Drakon nodded. "Thanks. Make that happen."

ICENI had proven adept at stringing along Colonel Dun, dangling major concessions continually just out of reach. Drakon had found himself increasingly admiring her skills.

That didn't equate to trusting her, of course. In fact, watching how well she spun Dun made Drakon wonder how well he was being spun or could be spun if Iceni decided that was necessary.

He hadn't been able to monitor the forces going up piecemeal in shuttles and boosters, packed in with normal shipments. If Dun was tracking anything, it would be whatever Drakon was watching.

It wasn't a major assault by any means. Colonel Dun only had about forty soldiers under her command on the facility, and those were locals whose experience and training were both limited. Against that, Malin and Morgan were leading two assault teams of fifteen commandos each, all the soldiers highly trained veterans. If not for the risk of something heavy being dropped on the planet, Drakon wouldn't have had any concerns about the outcome. But that one concern was a huge one.

An alert signal pulsed on his desk. Taking a long, slow breath, Drakon linked to the incoming signals and a multipaned window opened before him with views from the assault force.

He concentrated, blocking out all else, focusing only on the vids before him which portrayed the images seen from the stealth suits being used by the commandos. Twelve panes in the window. Two of those panes were from Malin and Morgan. The other ten marked section leaders, each controlling a team of two other commandos plus themselves.

About half of the commandos were already on the facility, some popping open specially designed crates to emerge inside warehouse compartments, others on the outside of the facility in the cold emptiness of space, the remainder coming in on long leaps from neighboring orbital locations, their stealth suits keeping them as invisible as the ingenuity of humans could devise. Malin's head turned, his range of vision sweeping across a stretch of utilitarian fixtures that marked one section of the outer shell of the facility. Though invisible to others in their suits, the links to their fellows allowed the commandos to be "seen" by Malin as ghostly images painted on the exterior view.

Morgan's group had also reached the facility and spread out along other portions, phantoms flitting carefully toward their targets. One of the section leaders passed a security camera watching that part of the exterior, the camera blindly tracking across the commando without pause.

The sections had reached accesses leading into the facility at different points. Some were air locks for maintenance workers to use when repairs were done, some were vents and tunnels never intended for human use. In some cases, commandos already inside cracked the air locks for their fellows. Everywhere else, the small, complex devices still known as skeleton keys after some sort of ancient means of opening locked doors were placed against key points and began breaking access codes and manipulating security bolts until barriers swung open.

Commandos began entering, each covering the others with ready weapons, some now in lighted passageways within the facility, others in still-darkened areas cluttered with canisters and boxes where only the occasional robotic minion trundled past with single-minded focus on its particular task.

It had all been silent up to now, almost unreal, as the phantom figures barely seen on the helmet displays of their fellow commandos moved without a word through the plan they had memorized and uploaded into their suits' tactical systems. But the commandos in the passageways could now hear the sounds of human activity, while those in maintenance and storage areas could detect dull thuds and thumps being transmitted through the structure of the facility.

A supervisor whose head was bent over her personal unit came walking around a corner and right past one section of commandos who silently parted to make way for her. She paused, raised her head with a puzzled expression, then concentrated on the unit in her hand again as she walked on down the passage.

Watching it happen, Drakon remembered the strange

feeling of exhilaration that came with being invisible in a stealth suit, an elation that had to be carefully controlled because it could so easily lead to mistakes that would reveal your presence. Bumping against something, or someone bumping against you, a misstep that created too much noise and vibration, even the faint breeze created by your movement that could alert age-old instincts in humans. Defensive training for sentries emphasized paying attention to such almost subliminal alerts. *If you feel a faint wind when there shouldn't be a wind, it may be the last thing you feel.* And if sentries or others were alerted inside an installation like this, defenses could flood important passageways and rooms with mists designed to make it easy to spot the shapes of anyone wearing even the best stealth suits.

But these commandos were experienced and careful, and the people they encountered did not seem to be concerned about attack. Had Colonel Dun told them what she was doing? Perhaps not. More than one sub-CEO and CEO operated on the philosophy that it was easier to keep workers in the dark. *Once you start explaining things,* one of them had once admonished Drakon after catching him briefing his unit, *they'll start expecting reasons for whatever they're told to do instead of just doing it.*

His eyes flicked from virtual window to virtual window in a constant dance, seeing the commandos' progress in a dozen different areas. One section had already reached the primary load control center, fanning out to take positions from which they could instantly disable every bulk transport system. Another was inside a room holding emergency backup controls and circuits, the room completely automated so that the commandos could load in software that blocked functions without alerting the control-system software guardians.

As Morgan slowly turned a corner, the view from her suit showed a small hallway where a soldier stood on bored sentry at an access panel. On one arm he wore a metabolic cuff, designed to automatically sound alarms if it were removed without the proper codes or if the sentry's metabolism showed signs of severe stress. Drakon had never forgotten the sentry in his unit who had arranged a hookup during a late-night shift, not realizing that the metabolic excitement generated by sex could set off his cuff. That sentry had doubtless never forgotten it either; but then, he had been lucky he hadn't been shot the next day.

The section with her followed as Morgan took several quick strides to the sentry, who just had time to glance around with a perplexed look before one of the commandos slammed a disabler into his arm. The soldier's body spasmed, his voluntary muscle control abruptly cut off while involuntary functions like breathing and heartbeat continued unhindered. The cuff produced no warning as the sentry was gently lowered to the floor, then the commandos were going through into the secure area containing the facility's command center and Colonel Dun's offices.

Most of Malin's sections were in position and he was leading the rest in a rush toward the rear of the secure area to cut off any attempt at escape. Morgan's sections were spreading fast through the secure area, dropping the occasional roving sentry before the guards knew they faced any danger. The lucky sentries, those wearing metabolic cuffs, were left helpless but alive. The unlucky ones died silently and swiftly.

Drakon's eyes went to stress monitors, seeing that the commandos were feeling the strain of the quick movement, of the long approach, of the unnatural gliding stride necessary to reduce the sounds of steps while in a stealth suit. It all wore out anyone pretty fast, even someone as well conditioned as these troops.

But everything was going perfectly.

Until one of the stealth suits failed.

To the workers kicking back as they watched equipment readouts in the transport control center, it was if a soldier in light combat armor suddenly appeared in their midst. The smart ones froze, even their breathing coming to a temporary halt, prehistoric instinct telling them that the only way to survive the attack of a predator was to remain absolutely motionless.

But one of the workers was either brave, or she panicked, slamming the emergency-alert button next to her hand before any of the soldiers could react. An instant later her head rocked under a brutal blow from a weapon's butt end and she collapsed, still alive only because Drakon had ordered the commandos to kill workers only if there was no alternative.

Red lights pulsed and alarms thundered, bringing everyone on the facility to full alert. "Move!" Morgan shouted, and her commandos broke into full runs, no longer using the concealment stride.

Malin's section blew open the rear exit, firing as they came through at a guard running toward them. The guard jerked backward under multiple hits before spinning to hit the wall and flop to the floor lifeless.

Soldiers started to pour out of one of the barracks rooms, only to meet a barrage of fire that dropped the first ones through the door. At least one soldier in the barracks tried the emergency exit and found out the hard way about the explosive charge placed there by the commandos.

Someone had figured out that stealth suits were being employed, and at critical areas inside the facility passageways and rooms filled with a fine mist. But the commandos already controlled every important point in the civilian side of the facility, and before the mist had fully deployed one of Morgan's sections got into the military command center and wiped out the soldiers on watch there.

Morgan moved with reckless speed, killing two soldiers near the entrance to Dun's quarters so fast that they were both still falling as she reached the door. A commando put a breaching charge in place, then they all went to either side as the charge tore the door off its hinges and fried automated defenses just inside the doorway.

Drakon could see Malin coming along fast, closing on

Morgan's position as she led her section into Dun's quarters. He was pushing the pace, too. Why? Did he want Dun dead? Or did he want to save Dun for interrogation before Morgan reached her?

The inner door protecting Dun's personal area blew inward as another breaching charge went off, then Morgan was inside the last barrier, her weapon questing for targets.

Malin had reached the back of Dun's area, his own section blasting its way inside from that direction.

Morgan put a round into the center of Dun's bed, then centered shots in each closet door before the commandos with her yanked open the doors. "Not here," a commando reported.

The image from Morgan's suit swung wildly as she surveyed Dun's bedroom, then centered on a wall panel that betrayed signs of being newer than the panels to either side of it. "There!" Two shots failed to penetrate, but a final breaching charge shattered the concealed armored door.

Morgan, who had been against the wall next to the last door as it was blown, was still coming around to face that door when Dun stepped into view, weapon leveled at her. Drakon could see it all from several points of view at once, but he could do nothing. For a few instants, time seemed to slow down as Morgan tried to bring her weapon to bear, as Dun's hand tightened on the trigger of her weapon, as the commandos with Morgan found their lines of fire blocked by her, and as Malin burst into the room with his commandos, Malin's weapon already pointed at Morgan's back.

"No!" was still coming out of Drakon's throat when Malin fired.

"WHY?" Drakon's gaze was centered on Malin, who stood at rigid attention.

"Dun had to be stopped before she activated any failsafes," Malin reported, his tone as emotionless as his expression.

"That was Morgan's primary duty. You knew that."

"It was my assessment, on the scene, that she needed backup."

"Do you think that excuse is ironclad?" Drakon almost shouted.

"Sir, you have always encouraged us to act based on our assessments—"

"Dammit, Malin, if your shot had been aimed a fraction of a millimeter different it would have blown off Morgan's head instead of Dun's! Why the hell did you take that kind of chance? Or was it a chance? You knew that after Dun shot Morgan she wouldn't have gotten off a second shot before the commandos with Morgan nailed her. Was this just a perfect opportunity to end your quarrels with Morgan by 'accidentally' blowing her away during a firefight?" Drakon was shouting now. "If you wanted her dead that bad, why not let Dun do it? Or were you afraid that Dun would miss?"

Malin had paled, but he kept his voice steady. "I . . . General Drakon . . ."

"Yes or no! Did you try to kill Morgan?"

"No!" His voice cracking, Malin stared at Drakon. "No," he repeated in a lower but still-strained voice. "She . . . I knew Morgan wanted to get Dun. I thought . . . she would . . . need help."

Drakon moved back and sat down heavily, glaring at Malin. "Dammit to hell, Bran. *You* were worried about *Morgan's* getting hurt? That's your defense?"

"Yes, sir."

"If I didn't know you, if I hadn't seen a thousand times just how professional and dependable you are, I wouldn't believe you. I still have trouble believing you." He blew out an angry breath. "Your shot could easily have killed her. But Morgan would probably be dead if you hadn't fired. I hope you're not expecting her to thank you."

"Colonel Morgan has already made clear her feelings in that regard," Malin said.

"Yeah. You're damned lucky I was tied into the command circuit and could activate overrides to freeze her suit. Otherwise, she would have killed you then and there. *Why*, Bran?"

"I did not try to kill Morgan, sir. You can put me in the highest level interrogation room you desire, and I will repeat that statement as many times and ways as you wish."

Drakon locked eyes with Malin. "If I put you in that room, and asked you why you worked so hard to catch up to Morgan, what would your answer be?"

Malin hesitated. "To . . . keep her from being killed. Sir."

"You two hate each other."

"Yes, sir."

"So? Do you have some kind of sick thing going on with Morgan?"

Paling again, Malin shook his head, looking revolted. "I have *nothing* like that going on with Morgan."

After several seconds, Drakon made an angry gesture. "I have to believe you. Or have you shot. I prefer to believe you. The official story from this moment forward is that you acted to save Morgan, even though no one who knows you two will believe it. But if anything like this happens again, I don't care whether or not Morgan gets hit, understand? You'll be toast."

Malin appeared briefly disconcerted. "You . . . will let me continue working on your staff?"

"You and Morgan. Yes. She's all right with that. Once Morgan calmed down, she was impressed that you'd tried to nail her yourself under the only circumstances where you might have succeeded and could have gotten away with it. That's the sort of thing Morgan admires in people. She still won't turn her back on you again, but now she seems to think you're worth killing."

Taking a deep breath, Malin nodded. "I guess I should watch my back."

"Yeah. That would be a real good idea even though I told Morgan that I needed both of you. And I'm telling you the same thing. If either of you kills the other, I'm going to make sure the survivor wishes they'd been the one who died. Is that *absolutely*, *completely*, *totally* clear, Colonel Malin?"

"Yes, sir."

ICENI sat in her office, wondering why Drakon hadn't called yet, when he finally did. The virtual image of her co-ruler appeared seated across the desk from her. "The orbital facility is completely secured," Drakon said. "We swept it down to the quark level and except for Colonel Dun's surprises we found nothing that shouldn't be there except the usual contraband, pornography, and recreational drugs. The bad news is that we are now certain that Colonel Dun was working for the ISS."

"Dun? An ISS agent?" Iceni asked, projecting surprise. She didn't want Drakon to know that she had already learned of that from her source close to him.

"There's no doubt at all. Dun had a secondary, small office hidden next to her bedroom. Heavy armor, shielded from detection, and tied in to all the systems on the facility. Only the snakes could have put that sort of thing in place without anyone's spotting it."

"Yet there was no indication prior to that Dun was in the employ of the ISS?"

Drakon shook his head. "No. The snakes had even misled us by leaking information that she was an occasional informant of theirs. Lots of people were occasional informants of the snakes because when they came asking not many citizens could say no. Dun was under really deep cover. She must have been recruited decades ago. And I'll admit that worries me. If Dun could be so carefully hidden, who else in this star system might be a deep-cover agent for the snakes?"

"One of the strongest weapons of the ISS was sowing distrust among everyone," Iceni commented. "Not that we didn't work on doing that to ourselves as well. So, deep-cover snakes and other hidden agents of the ISS must be added to our list of concerns. Thank you, General Drakon. Is there anything else?"

"No. Not at this time."

After Drakon's image vanished, Iceni turned to Togo, who had been standing off to one side, rendered unseeable to Drakon by Iceni's communications software. "What didn't he tell me?"

Togo consulted his own reader. "Just prior to Colonel Dun's hidden office's being broken into, she sent a burst transmission to C-625. The cruiser would have received it half an hour before it entered the hypernet gate."

"Do we have any idea what the message was?"

"No," Togo replied. "Colonel Dun's equipment self-erased and -destructed. I have been unable to determine whether or not General Drakon's people have been able to recover anything from it at all."

"I see. Anything else?"

"There are widespread rumors that during the attack on the facility, one of General Drakon's closest aides, Colonel Malin, attempted to murder the other, Colonel Morgan. I believe this actually occurred, or something like it that could be interpreted as an attempt by Malin to kill Morgan."

"Interesting." Iceni had believed that Drakon kept that sort of thing under control. "From what I have seen of them, I would have thought Morgan would have tried to kill Malin, not vice versa." She drummed the fingers of one hand on her desk, frowning in thought. "Take another look at Colonel Morgan. Dig for whatever you can find now that we also have access to the snake files. I need to know more about her."

"As far as we can determine, she is not sleeping with General Drakon."

Which gave Drakon a few points for common sense, Iceni thought, as well as possibly some credit for ethics. Technically, superiors in the Syndicate Worlds were required to avoid having subordinates as sex partners since it was far too easy to abuse power that way. But in reality it had long been common practice, and almost every other

CEO turned blind eyes to the abuse because they didn't want to give anyone reasons to check them for their own violations of the law. "One of the reasons I trusted Drakon enough to work with him was because he's not sleeping with anyone who works for him. But Morgan is attractive enough in many ways to have been able to attach herself to some CEO more powerful than Drakon, especially after he got exiled here. She chose to come here with him. All my instincts tell me that Morgan intends playing a deeper game than simply sleeping her way to the top."

"There is a widespread belief that a few of her rivals have vanished in the past," Togo noted.

"Yes. Get into every file, check every source, find out what you can. I need to know what she might do."

"And Colonel Malin?"

"Him, too." Iceni paused in thought again. "My impression has been that Malin is careful, controlled, and wants to leave behind Syndicate ways of doing things. But if he tried to kill Colonel Morgan during that military action, it would have been a hasty, impulsive act, and one fully in keeping with Syndicate ways of doing business. See if you can find out who the real Malin is."

After Togo had left, Iceni sat looking at some documents on her screen but not really reading them. *Why didn't Drakon tell me about the message Dun sent? I wonder what was in it? My source says Drakon's workers haven't been able to get anything out of Dun's equipment. The failure to inform me about internal problems with his staff is another matter and more understandable. No CEO ever admits to that kind of thing going on even if there are dead executives littering all of the conference rooms and the survivors are busy trying to wash the blood off their hands. But I've always thought it was a sloppy way of doing business. Only the boss should be deciding who gets the axe.*

That was a joke, wasn't it? Sort of a pun. Too bad there's no one else in this star system who would find it funny.

Another incoming message arrived, from Sub-CEO Akiri on C-448. "Madam C—excuse me, Madam President, there has been an unexpected development." Akiri paused, plainly reveling in being the bearer of important news, while Iceni seethed at the small delay in actually hearing that news. "One of the Hunter-Killers with C-625 did not enter the hypernet gate with the other mobile forces. It remained, and we have just received a transmission from HuK-6336 saying that they have overcome the ISS agents and those loyal to the Syndicate Worlds and will be joining us. HuK-6336 reports substantial personnel casualties in overcoming the snakes and loyalists, but says all equipment is operational."

"Good," Iceni said. "What about the three HuKs loyal to me that were shadowing C-625?"

"They are still about a light-hour from the hypernet gate, awaiting further orders."

"Tell them to proceed on their missions to the other star systems. I need to know what's going on at Lono, Taroa, and Kahiki. Make sure the commanders of those HuKs know that anyone who recruits more warships for our star system can expect to receive suitable rewards."

"Yes, Madam President." Akiri looked a bit disappointed because he had no chance at those rewards, but there was no way she was going to let one of her heavy cruisers go wandering off. They were needed right here.

Well, that news wasn't planet-shaking. A single HuK didn't have much capability. But it was a small piece of good news, so she wouldn't turn her nose up at it, and she desperately needed every warship she could get her hands on. *I've put up a good front. I wonder if Drakon suspects how much I haven't told him, especially about how worried I am with such a small flotilla to stave off any attempt at reconquest by the Syndicate Worlds government. They say the stars help those who help themselves, but the shipyards here can only produce warships up to the size of heavy cruisers, and that only one or two at a time if I order them to build nothing else. The government on Prime would have heard about the revolt here eventually, but C-625 will bring word to them much faster than I'd hoped. Thanks to*

Black Jack, Prime doesn't have much, but it won't take much to brush aside a flotilla built around four heavy cruisers. It will take my own HuKs a while to reach the jump points for the stars they're visiting, and then a while for the jump transits. Time I don't have to spare.

If we don't find more warships soon, this may be a very short-lived revolution.

CHAPTER SEVEN

THREE days without a disaster. That made it three good days.

Drakon sat going over the latest reports. The citizens were suitably enthusiastic about real elections for low-level local officials, and the propaganda about taking it all slow seemed to be working to keep all but the hotheads happy. The hotheads themselves were being monitored by the police, and if they got too warm, they would find themselves being cooled off the hard way.

He paused, watching a vid of snake families being lifted to the merchant ship that would haul them to Prime. Crowds of citizens watched the shuttles lift, cheering wildly. Having spilled the blood of the actual snakes, the people seemed satisfied with expulsion from the star system for the family members. As the shuttles closed on the merchant ship, the virtual windows in their passenger compartments would show a dozen heavy cruisers and numerous smaller warships approaching the planet or orbiting nearby. The majority of those warships were illusions, but hopefully the deception would fool the families, who would surely be interrogated when they reached Prime. *Win/win. Iceni had a good idea there. I just wish we could be sure we have eliminated or found every snake in this star system.*

I'm actually certain that we haven't. There are more out there somewhere. If those four turned snakes I'm hiding try anything or contact anyone, I'll know it the instant it happens, but I doubt that they were tied into anything like deep-cover programs. That's not how the snakes worked. They kept as many secrets from their own lower-level workers as they did from the rest of us.

Everything seemed to be going well, but Iceni had been increasingly moody and irritable as the days went by. "Malin," he called over the command circuit, "do we have anything new on what President Iceni is doing?"

"I learned a short time ago," Malin offered, "that the commander of one of the heavy cruisers, someone named Akiri, has been transferred to an assignment on the surface of the planet. His new title will be Adviser to the President on mobile forces issues."

"Adviser to the President, huh? Which entails what?"

"We have no specifics on the job, General," Malin replied.

A job with no defined purpose? Ha. I've seen that maneuver before. Iceni wanted Akiri out of where he was but didn't want to raise any fuss over it, so she "promoted" him to a meaningless job. "What do we know about Akiri?"

"An undistinguished record, no known mentor or sponsor. Command of that unit was the highest he would ever go."

That fit. After a few months, when no one was any longer paying attention, Iceni would probably slide Akiri into some obscure job suitable to his limited talents. "Who took over command of the cruiser?" Drakon asked.

"An executive named Asima Marphissa who was second-in-command. She's been promoted to sub-CEO. There were a number of more senior executives bypassed in favor of Marphissa."

"Hmmm. It sounds like President Iceni is grooming this Marphissa for bigger things."

Malin nodded, his eyes distant with thought. "The new flotilla commander?"

"Could be, though Iceni will probably wait a month or so before doing that for the sake of appearances since Marphissa is being boosted over people with more seniority. See what you can learn about why Iceni has taken an interest in this Marphissa and whether it's going to be a full-bore patron relationship."

"Yes, sir. Is there anything else?"

Drakon hesitated. "President Iceni strikes me as being increasingly temperamental over the last few days. Do we have any indications of what might be making her unhappy?"

"She has encountered Morgan, sir."

"Very funny. I already have to deal with one volatile female in the form of Morgan. I don't need another in President Iceni, and it's not like what I know of her. I think something has her seriously worried. See if you can find out what."

Malin spoke carefully. "We are maintaining troops at a higher state of alert than called for by the situation, General."

"You know why that is. I need to be ready to react fast if we learn that President Iceni is getting ready to move against me."

"She is very likely worried that the heightened alert status means that you intend moving against her unilaterally, sir."

"Are you advocating that I stand down? That would give her a lot more room to maneuver."

"You know my assessment, sir," Malin said. "I am confident that President Iceni is willing to accept partnership with you and will only strike at you if she believes that you are preparing to strike at her."

"You've been wrong in your assessments sometimes. I'll think about it. I'm also worried about more Colonel Duns popping up. I know we can trust Colonels Kai, Rogero, and Gaiene, but the locals are another matter."

"Colonel Morgan is investigating all of them as you

directed," Malin said. "She *is* thorough, as well as highly distrustful. It is unlikely that anything will get past her."

And that assignment kept her and Malin from interacting too much for a while. Drakon nodded. "When I get Morgan's report, I'll make a decision. Did we ever learn anything that would tell us what was in the transmission Colonel Dun sent right before she died?"

"No, sir. There wasn't anything recoverable in Dun's equipment. We do know that it went to the cruiser that was taken over by the ISS agents aboard and not to anyone else in the star system. The cruiser does not appear to have relayed that message back into the star system to anyone on this planet before it entered the hypernet gate."

What had Dun wanted to tell the snakes on that warship? What had been important enough to be what Dun surely suspected would be her last transmission to anyone? But thinking about that led back into memories of seeing Malin aiming at Morgan's back, and Drakon didn't want to go there. "Let me know if we get any clues as to what the message was."

"Perhaps President Iceni might have some ideas of what the message could have been," Malin suggested. "She is in constant contact with the mobile forces and has experience in commanding them."

"That's possible." Drakon sat back, rubbing his eyes. "I didn't see any sense in telling her about it until I had some idea what it meant. And I don't entirely trust the mobile forces anyway. Maybe that's what's giving President Iceni problems. Is she concerned about the loyalty of those warships? If more of them went the way of that cruiser, it could be real bad for us and weaken her own position relative to me."

"I will see what I can learn," Malin said.

"What about that assistant of hers? Togo? Could she be worried about him?"

"He is very loyal to her as well as very dangerous, sir. Extremely valuable to President Iceni, and he is also one of her most effective weapons."

"Really?" Togo had seemed distinctly unthreatening at the meetings where Drakon had seen him, but then a real pro would maintain that sort of low profile. "Can he be bought?"

"I doubt it, but I can make some discreet inquiries through third parties."

If Togo couldn't be bought, and he was both deadly and important to Iceni, he would have to be dealt with too if Drakon was forced to move against her. "Is he anything you and Morgan couldn't handle if it came to that?"

"I would be hesitant to take him on myself. Morgan could probably do the job, but it would be a challenge even for her. However, I strongly advise against such a move. Taking out Togo would be a declaration of war against President Iceni and might spur her to make some rash actions against whoever she thought was responsible."

"Is there anything going on between them?"

"No, sir. Purely business, subordinate and CEO."

"You know how much ground that can cover, Bran." After the call ended, Drakon found his thoughts fixed on Iceni and Togo. What did it matter to him if she did use Togo to satisfy her physical needs? It happened all the time in CEO ranks. But he had never been comfortable with the idea, a stance that only seemed to lead to frustration since nearly every woman he met worked for him, and those who didn't work for him could too easily be assassins working for someone else. It had been far too long, and that just made the pressures of his job a bit harder. *Maybe that's what's bothering Iceni, too. Maybe it's been a while for her. Too bad she and I couldn't . . . Yeah, right. Two CEOs in bed together? Who decides who gets to be on top?*

But even though he dismissed the idea, it kept lingering in the back of his mind until he gave up in disgust and got up to work out.

Before he left his office, though, Drakon paused, thinking. He made another call. "Colonel Malin, inform all ground forces unit commanders they are to stand down to alert status four effective immediately."

He had sent her a clear peace offering. It would be interesting to see how Iceni responded.

"GENERAL Drakon, we have received authorization codes from President Iceni's office allowing us to link to the mobile forces units in this star system. We can now monitor their readiness states."

So, she had returned his gesture in kind. Both of them still had their weapons, but both of those weapons had been powered down. Drakon started to relax, but he tensed a bit again at Malin's next words. "I also should inform you that Colonel Morgan has returned from her latest inspection and investigation," Malin reported, his voice and face extremely neutral. "I believe that you can expect to see her in the very near future," he added before ending the call.

Great. Now what has Morgan's pants in a twist? Maybe she found another Colonel Dun situation, but if she did, why wait to tell me until she got back? That's the sort of problem Morgan would want to address right away and with some form of lethal weapon. Sighing, Drakon waited for her to show up.

As Malin had predicted, he didn't have to wait long.

Morgan didn't quite slam open the door to his office, but that was because she knew better than to pull that sort of drama with Drakon. "How long had Rogero been working with the snakes?"

So that was what this was about. Even Morgan knew that she couldn't go after Colonel Rogero, or Kai or Gaiene, without clearing it first. And apparently she had also learned that Drakon already knew all about Rogero's situation. Only Malin could have told her that, and he had probably enjoyed watching her reaction.

Drakon leaned back, deliberately casual, as he answered. "Colonel Rogero had been working for the ISS for a few years."

"And you didn't tell me?" Morgan was seething, looking dangerous as well as angry.

"I figured you'd find out."

"But you told Malin?"

"He figured it out, too," Drakon replied, being careful not to add *before you did.* When that message had come for Rogero while the Alliance fleet was transiting through this star system, it had made it all but inevitable that both Morgan and Malin would eventually follow that thread to its source.

Morgan leaned forward, her hands resting on the front of his desk, still angry but also curious. "Why? Why is Rogero still alive? He's been a source for the snakes. He could have ratted us all out before we took down the snakes."

"No." Drakon kept his calm demeanor. "I knew from the first day that Rogero had been approached by the snakes and told to cooperate or else. He told them nothing about me that I didn't want him to say. Rogero helped lull the snakes into thinking I wasn't planning anything."

"He was your agent? Doubled against the snakes? But what about the Alliance, General? What about the fact that Rogero's loyalty is so far compromised that he's involved with some enemy bitch?"

"I knew all about that, too. I knew about it when I got Rogero transferred back to my command, and that took some string-pulling. The government wanted Rogero stuck on a labor-camp staff on some hellhole world until he died. That's where he and the Alliance officer got involved with each other, at the labor camp where Rogero had been transferred for using his head in a crisis instead of just following procedure." Drakon reached out and grabbed his drink, taking a long slug of caff. "I gave some snake exec the idea of using him as a source against the Alliance, so the ISS helped me get it done. The snakes set things up for the Alliance woman to get liberated and Rogero to send and receive messages with her. I knew that they'd also tell him to report on me, but that way I knew who one of the snake spies was."

"You worked with the snakes to put a spy on your own staff?" Morgan stared for a moment, then laughed. "You're crazy!" Something in her voice made it sound as if that made Drakon the most desirable man in the galaxy.

He couldn't help grinning. "Like a fox."

"Yes! So the ISS got Rogero's Alliance bitch freed and back in their fleet? Where's she right now? I know she's with Black Jack's fleet, but what is she doing?"

"She's in command of one of the Alliance battle cruisers."

Morgan paused, a smile growing. "A battle cruiser commander? In Black Jack's fleet? And she's hot for Rogero? Forgive me, General. You're not just crazy. You're crazy brilliant."

"Thanks." Drakon shrugged. "Whether she's still hot for him is an open question. The message she sent Rogero when Black Jack's fleet passed through here last time could be summed up as 'Hi, how's it going?' It subtly asked for information on the situation here but doesn't give any clues to her current feelings."

Flopping onto a sofa, Morgan sprawled out, a leg cocked over one end of the sofa. "What did our lover boy reply?"

"Rogero didn't send a reply. Iceni managed to get him the message without the snakes finding out, but anything he sent in answer might have been spotted by the snakes and he was only supposed to communicate with the Alliance woman through them. That would have attracted attention from the snakes that could have been deadly for all of us."

"Yeah." Morgan gazed thoughtfully toward the opposite wall, one hand absently stroking the hand weapon holstered at her hip. "But how does Rogero feel? Does he want to run off with this bitch?"

Drakon hitched forward a bit, speaking more forcefully. "Rogero's feelings are up to him as long as he stays loyal to me, and I strongly advise that you not describe the Alliance woman in that way if there is any chance of Rogero's hearing you."

Morgan grinned. "He's in looooove, huh? Men are so damned easy. He's probably dreaming about taking a shuttle out to meet his sweetheart when that fleet comes back, so they can both have some happily-ever-after on some Alliance hick world. But, boss, you can't let someone who knows as much as Rogero does go over to the Alliance."

She sounded relaxed and casual, but her hand, as if of its own accord, tightened about the grip of her hand weapon.

"If Rogero makes that decision, it's his to make. He's earned that from me, and I know he won't tell the Alliance anything that would hurt me."

"Sir, seriously, you're crazy brilliant, but you don't always want to do what you need to do." Morgan smiled wider. "That's why you need me."

Drakon kept his own expression somber. "I also need Rogero. Nothing is to happen to him unless I say so."

"General—"

"I mean it, Morgan. I want to see what Rogero tells this battle cruiser commander of Black Jack's when that fleet gets back here."

"*If* it gets back here, you mean," Morgan said. "They went diving deep into enigma space. Nothing we sent in has ever come back from there."

"Nothing of ours," Drakon agreed. "Except you."

The catlike assurance vanished and her eyes went cold for a moment, as if endless space itself were looking out through them. "They sent in someone else. She had my name, she looked like me. But she died. I came back." The coldness faded, replaced by Morgan's usual steely intensity. "Black Jack may have bitten off too much this time."

"Maybe. But then, we never beat the enigmas. He did."

Morgan's eyes flashed again at that, this time with heat, and Drakon understood exactly why. It grated on him, too, that this Alliance officer, a man who by all rights should have died a hundred years ago, had not only crushed the mobile forces of the Syndicate Worlds but also smashed an enigma fleet attacking Midway Star System. The Syndicate Worlds had been in arm's-length contact with the alien enigma race for more than a century but had learned less in that time than the Alliance had somehow figured out in a much shorter period. They had all been saved by Black Jack, but mingled with their thankfulness were very strong feelings of envy and resentment.

Black Jack must have been in survival sleep for that century, Drakon thought. He didn't seem to have aged much if at all. Had the Alliance actually lost him after the battle at Grendel? There were unconfirmed intelligence reports that that might have been the case, that Black Jack had been in a damaged survival pod. Or had the Alliance deliberately kept their hero in cold storage for decade after decade until they decided things were desperate enough to thaw him out? That was what the Syndicate government would have done with a hero who was big enough to possibly challenge them. The Alliance government claimed to be different from the Syndicate government, but was it?

Morgan sat silent before looking back at Drakon and smiling again. "I could get to him. Like Rogero got to that Alliance battle cruiser commander. When Black Jack gets back, I'll send him some messages. Hero-worship stuff. Adoring-female attention. He'll bite."

Drakon returned her gaze, seeing how she was draped across the sofa, her tight skin suit emphasizing every curve. Beautiful and dangerous, a combination that set the little monkey that all men carried in their heads to jumping up and down with excitement. And Morgan knew it. "Black Jack might already have a woman. There are some rumors."

"Not a woman like me." Morgan winked and stood up. "It's worth trying, right?"

He tried to weigh the idea dispassionately, feeling a spark of jealousy at the thought of Morgan with Black Jack, and doing his best to bury that feeling. Leverage over Black Jack. Inside information on what he intended. It was impossible to overstate how valuable those things could be. "Maybe. Did you discover anything else?"

"Nope. If there are any more snake sleepers out there, none of them are in command positions in the ground forces," Morgan declared confidently.

That was good news. If anyone could have found those sleepers, it would have been Morgan.

SUB-CEO Akiri never knew what killed him.

The assassin who entered his room through bypassed alarms and locks stabbed a nerve paralyzer into Akiri's neck, waited a moment to confirm that Akiri was dead, then headed for the next target.

Mehmet Togo, blessed with keener instincts or perhaps the protection of guardian ancestors that he had secretly continued to revere despite official Syndicate discouragement of such "superstition," awoke as the assassin entered his bedroom. Grabbing his weapon, rolling off the bed, and firing as he dropped to the floor, Togo watched dispassionately as the killer fell backward and lay unmoving. In his haste, he had aimed a killing shot rather than an incapacitating one, an inexcusable failure which meant the assassin would be answering no questions.

SUB-CEO Marphissa's life was saved by an unauthorized secondary hatch alarm that she had rigged up and bribed the cruiser's electrical officer to ignore. The silent alarm woke her in time for Marphissa to seize the hand weapon that every prudent Syndicate CEO, sub-CEO, and executive kept near at hand in the event that someone else sought improved promotion opportunities. As the assassin finished bypassing the regular alarm and entered her stateroom Marphissa put a shot into his chest, then, despite strict regulations to capture intruders so they could be subjected to exhaustive interrogation, slammed three more shots into him as he hit the far bulkhead.

Regulations be damned; she had no intention of letting the killer get back up again.

SUB-CEO Marphissa's call came in as Iceni was receiving Togo's report. "I have alerted all mobile forces, but it appears that there was only one assassin," Marphissa said. "No others have been detected, and no one was killed, so I was either the first target or the only target. I do not think this was a . . . routine . . . assassination attempt."

"I agree," said Iceni. "We also had an assassin strike down here. Sub-CEO Akiri was not as fortunate as you. He and the assassin are both dead."

"Someone struck at both me and Sub-CEO Akiri?"

"That's correct. In the same night." Iceni looked at Togo. "Have my bodyguards found anyone else inside the complex?"

"No, Madam President. I have analyzed how the assassin penetrated the complex, and it does not appear that she could have reached your living area. The means she had to penetrate security were not good enough to overcome those defenses."

"Good. Have you identified the assassin on your cruiser, Sub-CEO Marphissa?"

Marphissa made an angry noise before she answered. "He is a blank. Not part of the crew, not listed on any mobile forces registry. But we're nowhere near any occupied orbiting facilities. No one could have reached this unit from a distant location without being detected!"

Togo's voice stayed unperturbed. "The assassin here is also a blank. No identity files match her, not ground forces, or mobile forces, or any citizen files."

"How is that possible?" Marphissa asked. "ISS surveillance software would have spotted the presence of someone who wasn't in the files even if they were never seen. I know that. Someone like that leaves a hole, a place where someone is doing things but that has no one apparently in it, that's obvious to the software."

"The assassin here could have come from many places," Iceni said.

"Sub-CEO Marphissa is correct, though, that the killer would have needed assistance to remain undetected on the planet," Togo said. "Someone in a high position."

Iceni eyed him. "Are you prepared to name that person?"

"I note only that General Drakon has not notified us of an assassin striking his staff this night, Madam President.

There have been no alarms or unusual activity from any ground forces location."

That could be a damning bit of evidence, except that Iceni was certain Drakon knew how to do things like this right. Identify someone expendable on your own staff, someone you didn't mind getting rid of, and off them at the same time as assassins hit your opponent. It provided cover and helped get rid of deadwood on your own staff. That was basic CEO tactics. If she had judged Drakon even remotely right, he couldn't have been stupid enough to leave himself unmarked if he had targeted Iceni's people this night. "How could General Drakon have gotten a killer onto Sub-CEO Marphissa's cruiser? Sub-CEO, you say the assassin on your cruiser could only have come from one of the warships near you?"

"Yes, Madam President."

"What if he used one of those ground forces stealth suits?"

"We would have found it after we killed him," Marphissa said. "We did find a standard survival suit in a waste receptacle that hadn't been purged, but it could have come off any unit."

"The killer disposed of his survival suit?" Iceni asked. "Then it was a suicide mission, not just an assassination."

"Yes, Madam President. I would have to agree."

A suicide mission. That didn't sound like Drakon's ground forces. It sounded like—"ISS."

Marphissa gazed at Iceni uncomprehendingly. "You think there were still snakes among the crews on our mobile units? But every one of these units has purged Syndicate loyalists from the crews, and no one could have left a unit, even just in a survival suit, to come over to this cruiser without someone on that unit detecting the departure."

Iceni glanced at Togo. "These purges were thorough?"

"Yes!" Marphissa insisted. "Look what happened on HuK-6336 when they left the other loyalist units. Two-thirds of that crew died in the fighting!"

"That would seem to—" Iceni stopped speaking, recalling that when she had first heard that HuK-6336 had left the other loyalist warships, she had recently finished talking to Drakon.

About the discovery of a deep-cover agent for the ISS. Someone who did not seem to be ISS.

"Sub-CEO Marphissa," Iceni said, trying to keep her voice calm, "did you not tell me once that you never spoke with the officers aboard HuK-6336 prior to the overthrow of the snakes?"

"Yes, Madam President," Marphissa replied, plainly surprised at the question. "They had arrived in this star system only a week prior to our operation and spoken only with CEO Kolani."

"Then your first personal knowledge of the officers on HuK-6336 came after they said they had killed all of the snakes aboard as well as all Syndicate loyalists?"

"Yes."

"Did you know any of the officers on HuK-6336 prior to that? Did anyone on any of the other units with you?"

"No, Madam President, but that's far from impossible. The mobile forces have many officers in them."

Togo understood. He had realized what Iceni was driving at and had tensed.

"How," Iceni asked, "do you know that the men and women you have spoken with actually are mobile forces officers?"

"I . . . we looked at the crew roster they provided when they joined up . . . but what—" The sub-CEO's mouth fell open. "Do you mean . . . ?"

"I mean, perhaps what actually happened was that the snakes and firmest Syndicate Worlds loyalists aboard HuK-6336 slaughtered the real officers and any of the crew whose loyalty was in any way doubted, then replaced the actual crew roster with one showing the snakes as the officers and identifying the real officers as the dead snakes. HuK-6336 didn't surprise C-625 by staying behind when the cruiser took the hypernet gate. That was an act to fool us. The snakes on HuK-6336 had orders to stay behind."

"A Trojan horse full of snakes," Marphissa whispered, her eyes wide. "And they're positioned near the other mobile forces now. Madam President, I don't have any means of boarding HuK-6336 and taking it over. Not by surprise, and not by assault. We have no special forces on any of my units."

That was something she should have already arranged with Drakon, Iceni thought irritably, and there was no time to get those special forces sent up there now. "What else can you do?"

Marphissa paused, eyes intent. "I can cut HuK-6336 out of the command net without its being known to that unit. They'll think they're still linked in. Then I can order the rest of my warships to power up their shields and their hell lances."

"Won't HuK-6336 be able to spot that?"

"They will, after the process is well under way on the other units. If I see that HuK is starting to get its own shields up and weapons readied, I'll order them to stop. If we can get full combat preparations on the other warships and the HuK hasn't matched them, they'll be helpless."

Iceni looked for holes in what of necessity had to be a quickly improvised plan. "What if the HuK keeps preparing for combat despite your orders?"

"Then, with your permission, I will have all other units fire upon HuK-6336. That will be the only option that will prevent HuK-6336 from either escaping or inflicting damage on other units."

"That seems an extreme solution given that we are only operating on suspicion as of yet," Iceni said.

"Madam President, if those on HuK-6336 are mobile forces officers, they will obey my orders not to prepare for action. They would not be insane enough to go against those orders, knowing that I could destroy them."

After a long moment, Iceni nodded. "You make a good argument, and I agree that we have no other choice. Can you knock out the HuK and leave it able to be boarded later?"

"It will be difficult . . ."

"Concentrate on knocking it out. If there's anything left, that will be a bonus. Hopefully, they'll surrender when they realize that it's hopeless." But Iceni saw the looks in both Togo's and Marphissa's eyes and knew they were thinking the same thing that she was, that the snakes hadn't shown any willingness yet to surrender.

"Once the crews of these other ships realize what was done to most of the crew on the HuK," Marphissa cautioned, "there will be little chance of the snakes' being allowed to surrender even if they attempt it."

"I understand. Can you keep me linked in while you carry out this operation?" The mobile forces flotilla was still in orbit, close enough that the time lag between Marphissa and Iceni was too small to be a problem.

"Yes," Marphissa replied immediately though her eyes had grown distant as she focused on other matters.

Iceni watched, silent, as Marphissa entered commands, waited, checked, called orders to her line workers on the bridge of the cruiser, paused, then began calling the other warships with the exception of HuK-6336. "At time two zero, you are to begin bringing shields to full strength and powering up all hell lances. The target will be HuK-6336 if it resists following orders."

Another pause, then Iceni heard a question coming in. "Sub-CEO, can you tell us why HuK-6336 is being targeted?"

"The officers and crew we have dealt with on HuK-6336 are probably actually snakes. President Iceni and I believe that the snakes assigned to that HuK killed the actual officers and most of the crew. Those crew members remaining are the ones who were willing to assist the snakes in their slaughter of their companions. Are there further questions?"

Togo nodded approvingly. "A clear and strongly motivating response," he commented to Iceni.

"She will make a good commander of my mobile forces," Iceni agreed. But something was still bothering her, something besides the snakes on HuK-6336. Why had

Akiri been the assassin's first target? Akiri's skills as an executive had seemed marginal at best, yet Kolani had kept Akiri in command despite her reputation for relieving anyone who displeased her, and now an assassin had made him a primary target. Unfortunately, it was too late to stick Akiri in an interrogation cell to see what might be learned from him. "I want Akiri's room and belongings thoroughly searched for anything out of the ordinary," she told Togo.

"May I ask if there is a particular focus for the search, Madam President?"

"There are pieces in Akiri's puzzle that do not fit. I want to know why. Find *anything* that doesn't fit what we know about him."

A few minutes remained until twenty after the hour; then, as the other warships began preparing for battle, Iceni waited to see what would happen as she watched the activity around Marphissa. "Do you think the snakes on the HuK will immediately try to prepare for combat when they realize what is happening?" Iceni asked Togo.

"I do not think so. Actual mobile forces executives probably would do that, but if these are ISS, trained to ask directions before they act?" Togo's tiny smile flickered briefly to life. "They will call Sub-CEO Marphissa and ask what they are supposed to do."

Moments later, Togo's prediction was confirmed. "Sub-CEO, this is HuK-6336. Are we supposed to be making combat preparations?"

"No," Marphissa replied.

A pause. "The other mobile forces are preparing for combat."

"Yes. But you are to refrain from strengthening your shields and you are not to power up weapons. Do you understand, HuK-6336?"

"No."

Whether that was a reply to Marphissa's question or a denial of the orders was unclear. "HuK-6336 is powering weapons," a line worker on Marphissa's cruiser warned.

"Are you certain?" Marphissa asked.

"One hundred percent certainty, Sub-CEO. Shields are beginning to come up in strength as well."

"HuK-6336, cease strengthening shields and powering up weapons immediately. Power down shields and weapons. This is your final warning." Marphissa paused for only a moment, then looked over to the line worker.

"No change, Sub-CEO. HuK-6336 is continuing to prepare for combat."

Iceni saw Marphissa's face harden, then she reached one finger to tap a preset command.

Far above Iceni, in high orbit about the planet, particle beams shot out from three heavy cruisers, four light cruisers, and five Hunter-Killers, their fire concentrated on nearby HuK-6336.

The single volley was all that was required. HuK-6336 was close and at a dead stop relative to the other warships, so it had been impossible to miss. Hunter-Killers had very little armor, HuK-6336's shields hadn't even been at half strength, and on a unit of such small size almost every square meter contained critical equipment. The undersized warship was so badly torn up by that single volley that Iceni, watching the damage reports flashing onto Marphissa's display, wondered why the HuK hadn't broken into several pieces.

Marphissa sat gazing angrily at the wreck for a moment, then jerked into sudden action. "All units! Accelerate at best available velocity away from HuK-6336! Rear shields at maximum! Do it now!"

Togo gave Iceni a questioning glance. Iceni hesitated, then the reason for Marphissa's order hit her. "The power core. She thinks HuK-6336 will suffer a power-core overload."

"But how can there be any survivors to order such an action?"

"There don't have to be. Not if the snakes loaded deadman instructions into the core control systems. And that's exactly the sort of action we've seen them employing."

An instant later, HuK-6336 vanished as its power core exploded.

Iceni saw the cruiser that Marphissa was riding rock under the impact of the shock wave. "Only minor damage because the HuK's power core was relatively weak, our shields were at full strength, and we were accelerating away like bats out of hell," Marphissa reported to Iceni a short time later.

"That was a good call," Iceni replied. "You handled that entire situation very well, Sub-CEO. I am impressed by your ability."

It was about the strongest praise a CEO could provide, and Marphissa flushed with pleasure.

Before Iceni could say anything else, Togo cleared his throat apologetically. "General Drakon is calling, Madam President. He wishes to know why mobile forces in orbit about this planet are firing upon one another."

"I'll talk to him. Sub-CEO Marphissa, we'll speak again in the morning."

But Iceni stopped as she began to turn away, looking at Marphissa's display until the connection broke. On the display was portrayed a rapidly spreading cloud of dust that had once been a Hunter-Killer warship and perhaps twenty human beings. She could muster no sympathy for the humans, who had slain so many of their comrades, but she regretted losing that small warship.

DRAKON had appeared to be shocked by the news of the assassination attempts and Akiri's death, as well as satisfied with her explanations last night, but the next morning he sought to speak with her privately, not depending on comm circuits but instead showing up outside her office complex without any bodyguards, without even either Colonel Morgan or Colonel Malin who usually accompanied him. Disturbed by that unusual behavior, Iceni ensured that her office defenses were all active and working properly before she instructed her bodyguards to allow Drakon access. "What is this about?" she asked as he entered.

Drakon stood looking at her, scowled, looked away, then

finally spoke in a low, rough voice. "Thank you for not accusing me of involvement in last night's activities."

"I think more highly of you than that, General," Iceni said. "If you had planned those attacks, more of my people would have died."

He bared his teeth in a pained smile. "I'll take that as a compliment. I came over here, alone, for two reasons. The first to demonstrate my willingness to put myself on the line as a sign that I should have nothing to fear from you. Because I had nothing to do with those hits. Do you want me to say that again in another part of your office complex?"

She shook her head. "No, General Drakon. You need not submit yourself to interrogation to convince me. You wouldn't have made the offer unless you knew you could pass such a test. What is the second reason for your visit?"

He swallowed, chewed his lip, then spoke abruptly. "I want to apologize to you."

"You . . . what?"

"Apologize." He seemed to be having trouble getting the word out.

Small wonder. Iceni was having trouble believing that she had heard right. Apologies among CEOs were rare enough that Iceni couldn't remember ever having received one. Or even heard of one. Was "rare" even the right term for something that had never happened to her knowledge? "You . . . have you done something to me?"

"Not on purpose." Drakon took a deep breath and finally looked directly at her again. "I neglected to tell you something that might have helped you figure out that HuK was a problem. Back when we took out Colonel Dun, she managed to get off a message to that snake-controlled cruiser before it bolted through the hypernet gate. We haven't been able to find any clues to what the message was. Just some update, I figured. Maybe word to her snake bosses that Dun had been nailed and they should let her family go, or something like that. I was advised to tell you, but I didn't think it was important."

Iceni gave him a quizzical look. "But now you think you know what it was about?"

"I think it was word to that cruiser that Dun had been found out, that she was being taken down, and they needed someone else to take over the hidden-among-the-ranks-of-this-star-system's-defenders job."

"Oh." That did make sense. "The snakes on the cruiser then ordered the ones on the HuK to wipe out the officers and disloyal crew members, so they could pretend to escape from the other units controlled by the snakes, move here, and be part of our plans and deliberations? You're right. It could well have happened that way."

"And you might have thought of that," Drakon continued heavily, "if I'd told you about the message. So . . . I am . . . sorry."

"For . . . ?"

"I should have kept you fully informed, not decided what you needed to know. I don't want someone else deciding what I need to know, and I should give you the same courtesy." Drakon shook his head, looking angry, but the emotion clearly wasn't aimed at her. "I'll try not to slip up that way again."

Iceni stared at him. Drakon really had just apologized to her. And done so unambiguously, not some halfhearted *too bad if I made you screw up.* What was she supposed to say? It had been so long since anyone had said "I'm sorry" except subordinates who were groveling before her, and the accepted responses to that ranged from "you're fired" to "you're going to be shot" to "if it happens again, you'll be fired or shot." None of those phrases seemed appropriate now, though. "I . . . understand."

"You do?" Drakon seemed as uncertain as she did of the proper protocol.

"Yes. It . . . was . . . a . . . reasonable . . . error. I . . . Damn. Why don't we have words for this?"

"We haven't needed them," Drakon said, sounding bitter and amused at the same time.

"Perhaps we will need them in the future. I will say this, I am not at all certain that I would have made the connection between Dun's message and what HuK-6336 did. I'm fairly certain that I wouldn't have. But I do wish to know anything like that that comes up from now on."

"You will."

It sounded like a promise. If so, there would be no better time to test it. "Is there anything else?"

Drakon hesitated, and she could easily imagine the thoughts running through his mind. "I've had all the ground forces commanders screened to see if any others were like Colonel Dun. As far as I can tell, none of them are."

"That's good to hear." She waited.

"Um . . . Colonel Rogero. You already know about him."

"Yes."

"And I know of four surviving snakes and their families who are still on this planet."

Iceni stared at him. "Explain, please."

He did, and when Drakon had finished Iceni spent a moment rubbing her chin to give her time to think. Why hadn't Togo spotted that information before Drakon had told her? "These snakes are under constant observation?"

"Constant and complete."

"What if I insisted that they be shot?"

Drakon glared at her. "I promised them they wouldn't be killed."

"I see." She let alternatives tumble through her mind before looking back at him. "All right, General. They're your responsibility. If they do anything, if they contact anyone, I expect to be informed."

"I'll do that."

"Are there any more surprises for me, General?" Iceni asked.

Another pause as Drakon frowned in thought. Would he tell her about Malin's apparent assassination attempt against Morgan? Her source had already given her all the details of that, but would Drakon say anything at all?

"Yeah, one more thing. I had a serious incident on my staff. But it's been resolved."

That was something. More than she had expected. "Good. I will also try to keep you informed in the future. If the hits had been only against your workers last night, I'm certain that your suspicion would have turned my way."

He gave her that crooked smile of his. "If you'd planned hits against me, I probably wouldn't have survived to register any complaints."

"How nice of you to say so. But now we will have no secrets from each other."

"Of course not." Drakon mimicked her own sarcasm in a shared joke about how untrustworthy CEOs actually were. Neither she nor he would really believe the other wasn't withholding some secrets.

Drakon gave a gruff farewell and left, leaving Iceni looking at her door after he had closed it. An apology and a promise, both of which appeared to be at least partly sincere. *Damn you, General, you're providing far too powerful a good example for me.*

Is it just an act?

DRAKON walked steadily back toward his headquarters, hardly noticing the citizens who were hastily clearing a path for him, now with every sign of enthusiasm rather than fear. He wished he could believe that the emotions the citizens showed him were genuine, but over the centuries people at every level of Syndicate society had gotten very good at hiding their true feelings, instead projecting whatever they thought they were expected to show.

Just like CEOs. He wished he could believe that Iceni was sincere.

Why did I tell her about Malin and Morgan? I didn't tell her much, but I still revealed that my staff had a serious problem with dissension, and that's exactly the sort of thing CEOs always want to know so they can try to exploit that dissension. Why did I tell Iceni that there was a possible crack in my defenses that she could exploit?

Of course, she might think that was a trap, designed to see if she would make a move in that direction.

I did intend to say I was sorry for not doing my job well enough. I made a mistake. The one thing I hated most in my bosses over the years has been their failure to admit when they screwed up. That was one of the pillars of the Syndicate Worlds, I guess. Never admit a mistake. I can't remember the government ever doing that. Hell, even when Black Jack was knocking on their door with a fleet the previous Syndicate supreme council would rather have died than admit they had made any errors. And so they did die. But I doubt the new bunch at Prime is any better.

They're CEOs, aren't they?

But, then, so is Iceni. And so am I.

Can you teach old dogs new tricks? But I never learned the old tricks. That's how I got here, exiled for not being self-focused enough, for not being willing to write off the lives of subordinates as the cost of my own promotions. And Iceni was exiled, too, for reporting on illegal activity instead of just trying to grab a piece of it for herself. Neither one of us fit properly into the Syndicate system.

Malin is right when he says the failure to admit mistakes means you can't learn from them. I have plenty of experience to prove that.

Maybe it's a good thing I told Iceni a bit about the mess between Malin and Morgan. Even though I wasn't intending to set a trap, not consciously anyway, that's what it is. If Iceni tries to contact either Malin or Morgan without my knowledge, I'm certain that they'll tell me.

And then I'll know something more about Iceni, and I'll have to decide what to do next.

CHAPTER EIGHT

A display showing nearby stars floated above the center of the conference table. Iceni wasn't looking at it, though. She seemed to be lost in thought, staring at the virtual window and its peaceful beach as if she wasn't really focused on it.

"What's up?" Drakon finally asked. "You wanted to meet on neutral ground, no aides or assistants, just you and me."

She inhaled slowly, as if coming back to full alertness, then gazed at him. "Yes. We have some very interesting news from Taroa. The HuK I sent there returned several hours ago. Have you seen its report yet?"

"Yes." Drakon glanced at the star display, where Taroa glowed brighter for extra emphasis, as did the star Kane for some reason. "Three-way civil war. They didn't have that many troops on hand, so the fighting isn't too severe, but it's widespread. Since Taroa doesn't have a hypernet gate, there weren't nearly as many snakes or Syndicate troops there, so the loyalists can't put down the other two factions."

Iceni nodded, and he noticed that now she was looking toward not the depiction of Taroa, but that of Kane. "There was another item reported to me by the commander of the HuK. It's not even in the classified report. He managed a face-to-face meeting with the commander of the light cruiser at Taroa, which so far has remained neutral in the struggle and may join us here."

"That's nice." One light cruiser, more or less, hardly seemed that critical an issue to have Iceni so distracted.

"It's what else that light cruiser commander told us that's important. You know the shipyards at Taroa engaged in some significant construction for the Syndicate Worlds. Nothing compared to the major shipyards at places like Sancere, but still large projects. Taroa's shipyards are much better than ours since the Syndicate government judged that they weren't in as much danger from direct enigma attack and put more money into them." Iceni's eyes locked on his, and she leaned forward. "Taroa's shipyards have nearly completed construction of a battleship. It only has a skeleton crew and is still fitting out."

Drakon stopped breathing for a moment. "A battleship?" he finally said. "You told me there were only light mobile forces at nearby stars."

"Yes. That's what I believed to be true. The official story was that the battleship had been sent to another star system much closer to Prime for final fitting out so the Syndicate government could ensure control of it. But what actually happened was that the CEO on Taroa sent it to Kane, thinking that he might really need a battleship someday and thinking that he could get away with pocketing the battleship in the chaos following Black Jack's victory at Prime."

"Good guesses on his part."

"Weren't they? But we need that battleship more than he does. If we gain control of that battleship, we will have enough firepower to have a decent chance of fighting off any attacks on this star system."

"Can we finish the work on it here?"

"Yes."

His eyes went back to the star display. "And it's at Kane. How are they hiding a battleship at Kane? It's not a heavily populated star system, but there are plenty of citizens there and merchant ships coming and going."

"I asked myself that same question." Iceni zoomed the display in on Kane, and soon enough that star system floated above the table, its planets visible. "The main mobile forces facility there is like the one here, out near one of the gas giants. See these large moons? If the battleship was positioned in the right place around the curve of the gas giant and relative to the two moons, it wouldn't be visible from inhabited locations in the star system or from the normal shipping routes. You couldn't find it unless someone went to the gas giant looking for it."

Drakon nodded slowly, trying to put the concept within his own experience with ground operations. "Hide it where no one would think to look. Surely, someone in Kane knows about it."

"The light cruiser commander believes that local authorities in Kane are playing along and keeping the battleship's presence quiet in exchange for a promise that it will be used to defend them as well as Taroa."

He pondered the news, out of habit running through the planning implications. "If that information is accurate, we can't afford to take time to send a scouting mission. We need to get to the battleship before the weapons are active or the people fighting on Taroa send for it to tip the scales. That means going in blind."

"I know." Iceni ran one hand through her hair. "It could also be a trap, with mines set to hit anything coming out of the jump point at Kane. But I don't see any alternative. The prize is just too big. We cannot afford to hesitate."

Drakon eyed her. "So what's the problem?"

"There are two." Her eyes were on his again. "I'll have to take almost every warship that we've got. I'll leave one HuK as a courier to let me know if disaster strikes here while I'm gone. You'll be practically defenseless if any other mobile forces show up. And I need to command this mission personally. I think I can trust Sub-CEO Marphissa, but the stakes are too high to risk that she might be tempted to make her own use of that battleship, and she has never commanded a flotilla in action."

"You need to go personally." So that was it. "Meaning, you leave me alone here in this star system."

"Exactly."

Drakon shrugged. "If you come back with a battleship, then it doesn't matter what games I might have played in your absence. You'll have the winning hand."

"And if there's no battleship there? Or if it has already got enough weapons active that I can't take it and come back only with what I took, or even less if I lose some warships, then what?"

He leaned back, rubbing his lower face with one hand. "You'll just have to trust me."

Iceni exhaled heavily. "Let's go over that last statement of yours again, General Drakon, so you can let me know if there's any portion of it that would give you pause if I had said it to you."

"That 'trust' word might give me some trouble." Drakon spread his hands. "I can't give you any hostages that you would think tied my hands. I could promise to not betray you, but what's the promise of a CEO worth? Mine is actually good, which is why I rarely give it, but I know you have no reason to accept that. I have played straight with you."

"As far as I know."

"What's the alternative, Madam President? We both sit here in this star system, holding guns on each other, until a big enough flotilla from Prime shows up to screw both of us? That's assuming whoever wins at Taroa doesn't decide it would be nice to control a hypernet gate and sends that battleship to take over here before the Syndicate Worlds government can get around to it."

Iceni looked at her hands where they rested on the table's surface, then back at him. "What do you want for this star system, General Drakon?"

There were many possible answers, most of which would be lies or misdirection. He looked back at her, deciding to answer with as close to the truth as he himself understood it. "Something better than I grew up with. Something worth dying for if it comes to that."

"I know your record. There have been many times that you could have died for the Syndicate Worlds."

"And that would have annoyed me. Seriously. Hell, I didn't care about the Syndicate Worlds. I was trying to protect people I cared about even if they were dozens or hundreds of light-years distant. I didn't have any choice." Drakon made an angry and helpless gesture, remembering those years. "Now I do. I want to care about what I'm fighting for. I don't know exactly what that is. Getting rid of the snakes and the rest of the Syndicate control was an immediate necessity, something I could plan and do, but after that . . . I'm still figuring that out."

She watched him silently for so long that he wondered about saying something else. "I am afraid of you, General Drakon," Iceni finally said. "I am afraid of what you might make me do. I don't want to see this star system destroyed."

"I don't either." Drakon tapped the table surface for emphasis as he spoke. "Do you think I'm stupid?"

"No."

"Then, as long as there's any chance of your coming back with a battleship under your control, why would I be dumb enough to try taking over in your absence? Let's be totally pragmatic here. If I wanted to take over, the first thing I'd have to do is kill you. That way, I have a chance to get the mobile forces, the warships, on my side. Without them, my position is untenable."

Iceni smiled. "You've obviously thought about how to get rid of me."

"Are you trying to claim that you haven't thought about what it would take to eliminate me as a rival? The point is, once you leave this star system, I can't touch you. That means the best way for you to ensure that I don't take over is to leave. It doesn't make you vulnerable, it makes you invulnerable as far as I'm concerned."

She stared at him, then laughed. "General, your logic cannot be faulted."

"When do you leave? And do we let the citizens know?"

"As soon as possible, and . . . there are good arguments for telling them and good arguments for keeping them in the dark." Iceni's eyes were back on the star display. "If I can't be found, too many people will conclude that General Drakon might have disposed of the competition. Once my flotilla jumps for Kane, I will have my own staff tell the citizens that I am leaving on a special mission to . . ."

"Try to bring peace to our neighbors?" Drakon asked mockingly.

"Oh, that's good. Yes. A mission of mercy."

"I wasn't serious. What happens when you get back, and they learn that you were actually on a snatch-and-grab mission for a battleship?"

Iceni smiled at him again. "I'll have a battleship. Why should I care how anyone feels?"

This time, Drakon didn't return the smile. "Anyone? Including me? You'll have a huge amount of firepower under your control."

"Yes. You'll just have to trust me."

At least she didn't use a derisive tone when she quoted him. "What are you going to use to capture it? Assault parties from the crews of the mobile forces?"

"What can you give me?" Iceni asked.

"A lot more than you can use. Can you bring up the current status on your mobile forces?" Drakon studied the information as it popped up on the display. "Very limited free berthing capacity, and you'll only be able to haul three shuttles with you. I recommend providing you with three squads of special forces. That's way too few to tackle the crew of a fully operational battleship, but if this one is still working with a skeleton crew it should be enough."

"I will accept your recommendation," Iceni said. "Who will command your special forces?"

"Normally a force that small would be commanded by a lieutenant or a captain at the most." He saw her uncertainty at the new titles. "That would be subexecutive or junior-executive rank. But you need someone senior enough to be in control of a battleship, someone we have no doubt of in terms of loyalty and reliability, and the more experienced the better."

Drakon paused to think again. Normally, he would be considering sending either Morgan or Malin, but Morgan was still acting too much like a loose cannon at the moment, and after Malin's actions during the assault on the orbital facility Drakon didn't feel comfortable having him out of sight for a while. "Colonel Rogero. He's the best for this. Aggressive and capable, as reliable as they come, and his subordinates won't have any problems handling his area of responsibility down here until he gets back."

"Rogero?" Iceni questioned. "Reliable?"

She knew about the Alliance battle cruiser commander. Drakon had briefed Iceni on that when the message had come for Rogero while Black Jack's fleet was here. "Absolutely."

"What about your other senior commanders?"

"Kai is solid but can be slow. He prefers to plan things out, then go by the plan. You need someone who will move fast and be more agile. Gaiene is aggressive enough, too much so sometimes, but on his own he can get a little wild. You don't need someone willing to take too many chances when you've only got three squads to play with. I'm also not comfortable with how well Gaiene's subordinates are set up to operate without his oversight."

Another long look at him, as if she were trying to read his mind, then Iceni nodded once. "All right. I need your soldiers and Colonel Rogero in orbit as soon as possible."

Drakon did some quick estimating in his head. "Two hours."

"Can you make it one?"

"No. Besides, a two-hour scramble I can pass off as being part of a training exercise. A one-hour panic party will arouse way too much attention."

"Then I agree. Two hours. I will see you again when I return, General Drakon."

EVEN though Iceni had decided that she had no alternative to going to Kane, the idea of trusting Drakon not to stab her in the back in her absence left her in an even worse mood than before as she hastily prepared to take a shuttle up to C-448. She would be risking her control of the star system and putting herself back at the mercy of the crews of the warships. They had sworn loyalty to her, but they had also made similar oaths to the Syndicate Worlds. Every CEO knew that inconvenient oaths were easily disposed of, but now those crews certainly knew it, too.

Those crews had also learned how easy it was to dispose of authority figures. The workers were becoming privy to the same rules that the higher levels had followed for generations, and that could not be a good thing for those in the higher levels.

Nor could she take any bodyguards along on an extended voyage on something as small as a heavy cruiser. There was no room for them, and the potential for a misunderstanding and violence in the cramped quarters of a warship too high.

Her imagination filled with an image of being shoved out of an air lock by laughing workers, Iceni jerked nervously when the door to her office announced a visitor. Togo. Him she shouldn't have to fear, but the fact that she had overreacted didn't help her disposition. Wonderful. She hadn't even boarded a shuttle or left her own office yet and she was already unnerved.

"What is it?" Iceni snapped as Togo entered.

"You asked for whatever I could discover about Colonel Malin and Colonel Morgan," Togo said, imperturbable in the face of her grumpiness. "I thought I should provide you with what I knew before you left. Forgive me if I was in error."

"No. You aren't mistaken. I'd like to know more about Drakon's team before I leave this star system in their hands." Iceni closed her eyes, calming herself, then looked at him. "Take a seat. What did you find?"

Togo sat down, not relaxing in the chair but keeping his back erect. He hadn't lasted this long as personal assistant to a CEO by presuming on his acquaintance with those of high rank. Bringing out his reader, Togo cleared his throat, then began reciting his report. "Colonel Malin is the child of an unmarried officer in the medical service who was widowed four years before his birth when her husband died fighting the Alliance."

"Frozen embryo or a fling?" Iceni asked.

"Apparently a fling. The identity of the father is unknown."

There wasn't anything unusual about that, not after so many years of war. So many husbands and wives had died, so many men and women had sought someone to help them bear heirs of their bodies, no questions asked.

"Bran Malin's mother helped him get into the subexecutive ranks," Togo continued. "She reached the rank of sub-CEO before retiring, but died several years ago as the result of long-term ailments contracted while working at a classified medical research facility. After a few assignments in a variety of support and frontline positions, Bran Malin asked to be assigned to the ground force commanded by Drakon. He is now twenty-eight years old and has served with Drakon for seven years, first commanding ground units directly and eventually becoming a close and trusted adviser to Drakon." Togo lowered the reader. "That is all there is though I can recite his assignments prior to Drakon's command. Your earlier assessment, that Malin is controlled and careful, is borne out by every source I could find. Since he is both controlled and careful, there is nothing in Malin's record indicating that he has ever expressed any unhappiness with Syndicate rule."

Iceni pondered that, then nodded. "And Morgan?"

"Her history is much more interesting."

"Somehow, I thought that it would be."

That earned Iceni a small smile from Togo before he resumed his usual unrevealing expression. "Roh Morgan's parents died in action when she was very young, and she was raised in a succession of official-duty orphanages. She joined the ground forces as soon as legally old enough at seventeen and volunteered for the commando branch. Her training for that was cut short, and it took considerable digging to find out what happened after that."

Iceni leaned forward, intrigued. "Some secret assignment?"

"Extremely secret, Madam President. So secret that the code name itself has apparently been wiped from the records. But I was able to piece together the concept with what remained in ISS files. It was an operation aimed at the enigma race."

"The enigmas?" She hadn't expected that. "Every operation the Syndicate Worlds has staged over the last century to try to learn more about the enigmas has been a total failure."

"As was that involving Roh Morgan," Togo confirmed. "I was able to determine that the plan involved the use of small, natural asteroids, which would be hollowed out to each hold a single commando frozen into survival sleep along with just enough equipment to maintain that state. The asteroids were launched from a ship outside an enigma-held star system, pushed inward toward the planets at velocities low enough to seem normal."

"No wonder they put the commandos into survival sleep! At those velocities, it would be decades before the asteroids reached any planets."

"Yes." Togo paused, then shook his head. "When close enough to a planet, the commandos would be awakened, and were then expected to land and send out any information they could before being hunted down and killed by the enigmas."

Iceni stared at him. "A suicide mission lasting for decades and no guarantee that it would actually accomplish anything. Morgan volunteered for that?"

"Yes," Togo said again. "As you know, the Syndicate government was desperate for any information about the enigmas. For the first couple of decades, the enigmas gave no sign that they were aware of the operation, but when some of the asteroids began approaching the inner system, the enigmas started to target and destroy them, one by one. A decision was made to attempt a recovery of any surviving commandos, and two, including Morgan, were picked up by a special automated craft that, for some unknown reason, the enigmas did not destroy."

"That's odd," Iceni said. "That the enigmas let two commandos be recovered, yes, but mostly that some CEO approved risking those kinds of resources to save the lives of two junior workers."

Togo made an apologetic gesture. "The intent was not to save the workers. It was desired to recover their asteroids intact so they could be carefully examined for whatever might have betrayed their special characteristics to the enigmas. That Morgan and the other commando survived was simply a by-product of the recovery."

"Oh. Naturally." She didn't bother asking whether the examination had found anything, because she knew it couldn't have. The asteroids, like every other Syndicate Worlds action in connection with the enigmas, had failed because of quantum-level worms the aliens had successfully seeded into every Syndicate automated system. Thanks to those worms, the enigmas had always known exactly what the Syndicate Worlds was doing and could even spoof Syndicate sensors in invisible ways. The Syndicate Worlds had never found those worms, undetectable by normal computer-security means. No, it had been the Alliance that had done that. Black Jack, to be specific, then he had given the secret of finding and neutralizing those worms to the Syndicate Worlds. The embarrassment of that Syndicate failure had been the final blow for Iceni, the last straw that had led her to begin planning for revolt.

Togo tapped his reader. "There were some problems with the awakening of Morgan and the other surviving commando. While their period in survival sleep was roughly twenty years, that should not have been long enough to cause difficulties. I could find no details of what the problems were, just vague references. Some of those references led me to believe that there may have been some special mental conditioning of Morgan and the others before the mission."

"Special mental conditioning?" That could mean many things, many of them very ugly.

"I do not know for certain, Madam President. Morgan's psych evals after awakening rated her within acceptable limits, but erratically so. She was rejected for further duty with the commandos. Morgan was eventually released for duty in the regular ground forces. This happened just as the ground forces were facing a serious shortage of junior officers as a result of some failed major offensive operations that had resulted in an even higher-than-usual rate of casualties among junior officers. A large number of worker-level ground forces personnel were designated for immediate promotion to junior subexecutive, and one of those was Morgan."

Iceni eyed Togo skeptically. "She was chosen for promotion to subexecutive rank despite her history and evaluations?"

"I could not determine why, Madam President. There is a medical evaluation declaring her fit for immediate promotion, but no explanation for it. Morgan herself could not have been in any position to bribe or influence anyone with authority to make that call, but there is no trace of any patron who would have intervened on her behalf and no room in her history for such a patron to have been acquired."

"When you said that Colonel Morgan's history was interesting, I didn't expect it to be quite this interesting," Iceni commented.

"Unfortunately for Sub-Executive Roh Morgan, no ground forces commander would accept her assignment to their command because of the oddities in her record and the less-than-standard psych evals. Finally, Drakon accepted her in his command on the grounds that she deserved a chance."

Iceni raised an eyebrow at Togo. "Is that your assessment, or do you have firm evidence that was his reasoning?"

"Drakon's acceptance message said, 'This officer deserves a chance to succeed.' His decision to give her that opportunity formed the foundation for Morgan's intense loyalty to him, though my sources say she is also now very admiring of Drakon's skills as a leader and a combat commander."

That was indeed intriguing. "So Colonel Morgan is actually your age?"

"She was just short of eighteen when she volunteered for the suicide mission. Chronologically, she is now older than me, Madam President. Physically, because she did not age during survival sleep, she is twenty-seven years old. She has served with Drakon for eight years now."

What would have motivated a girl not yet eighteen years old to volunteer for a suicide mission? Iceni sighed, wondering how many girls, and boys, of similar age had died during the century of war with the Alliance. "So Morgan was already working with Drakon when Malin arrived?"

"Yes. All accounts indicate that they disliked each other intensely from the moment they first met."

"Hate at first sight?" Yet they had both stayed with Drakon. Was he that inspiring a leader? It didn't seem like enough of an explanation. "How are Morgan's psych evals now?"

"Close enough to standard deviation to be judged acceptable," Togo said.

That wasn't exactly a ringing endorsement of someone's stability. "Interesting. That's more than I knew, but it leaves a lot of unanswered questions. Keep an eye out for anything else you can learn. Those two are very close to General Drakon, and understanding the why of that will help me understand General Drakon. Do you have any questions about how to handle matters while I'm gone?"

Togo hesitated. "I ask that I be permitted to accompany you, Madam President. As we have recently seen, even mobile forces units are not immune to the threat of assassins, and if someone in the military wished you ill, having you struck down while outside this star system might be seen as a means to deflect attention from the guilty party."

She gave him an intent look. "Do you have any intelligence that something like that is planned?"

"No."

"I have no reason to believe that anything like that is under way." Not quite true. Not true at all, actually. But her source close to Drakon was in a position to know if Drakon made use of an in-place asset to order such a strike against her. Even Togo didn't know about that source, though, because it was simply too important to risk compromise.

"Madam President, I do not know what General Drakon has told you—"

"I am not fool enough to base my security on what I am told by those who could threaten it," Iceni said. "Do you have solid information, or good intelligence, indicating an active threat from that direction?"

Togo paused, then shook his head. "No, Madam President."

"It's your job to watch for danger to me, and you do it well. Keep doing it while I'm gone. The best service you can render me is to stay here, monitor the actions of potential threats, and help keep things running smoothly until I return."

"Yes, Madam President."

Something else occurred to her then, along with a measure of surprise that Togo himself hadn't already brought it up sometime ago. "What about the search of Sub-CEO Akiri's room and belongings? What did you find?"

Togo shook his head. "Nothing inconsistent with what was known of him, Madam President."

"No clues as to why he was the assassin's first target? No indication of why CEO Kolani kept him in command despite her low opinion of him?"

"No, Madam President. There was nothing to offer any explanation of either. Perhaps there was no link between those things. CEO Kolani may have enjoyed bullying Sub-CEO Akiri, and he was designated a special adviser to you, which would explain the assassin's interest."

Plausible. Yet . . . But she had no time to focus on that now. "All right. That's all."

After Togo had left, Iceni took a few moments that she couldn't spare to think about his report. *Drakon gave Morgan a chance when no one else would. A young woman, little more than a girl, with considerable physical and mental trauma in her recent past. I wouldn't have given her a chance. Who would take such a risk? But Drakon did. No wonder she's so loyal to him. No wonder his soldiers are loyal to him. He seems to care about people despite all the CEO training that he went through.*

I wish I could trust that man. I think if I could ever trust Artur Drakon, I might actually come to like him.

And then he might stick a knife in my back. I'm glad Togo will be keeping an eye on him.

SUB-CEO Marphissa seemed happy to see her, but then Iceni couldn't remember the last time one of her subordinates had been foolish enough to look unhappy at her appearance. *Yes, I do. It was that executive who was skimming funds. He looked very unhappy. Not as unhappy then as he did when he was punished by being given a uniform and sent off to help in the hopeless defense of that star system near Alliance territory. Where was that again? It doesn't matter now. All the defenders died, the Syndicate Worlds recaptured the star system eventually, and in the end the Syndicate Worlds lost the war, so it meant nothing. Something worth dying for, Drakon said. Yes. We all need that.*

"You said we'd be conducting exercises, Madam President?" Marphissa asked.

"That's correct. Are all of the ground forces soldiers aboard?"

"Yes. One squad on each of the three heavy cruisers,

and the three shuttles are stowed on the exteriors of the cruisers as well. They brought a lot of equipment and supplies with them."

"Good. We'll head out toward one of the jump points and put the warships and soldiers through their paces to make sure everyone is still sharp and practice coordinated actions." That was the sort of thing CEOs routinely did, making people run in circles to show they could, so no one would question it.

"Which jump point?"

Iceni settled herself in her seat on the cruiser's bridge. Midway had a lot of jump points for other stars, eight to be exact. It was that and not population or wealth or industrial capability that gave Midway its name and made Midway a valuable and important star system. It had also earned the star system a hypernet gate, which in turn made the system even more valuable.

One of those jump points led to a star named Pele. That was the jump point the Alliance fleet had used not too long ago on its way to learn more about the alien enigma race. Except for occasional futile attempts to gain information about the enigmas, no Syndicate Worlds ships had made that jump for more than half a century. When the enigmas had attacked the Midway Star System, they had appeared at that jump point.

As she looked at the representation on her display of the jump point for Pele, Iceni remembered what Togo had told her concerning Colonel Morgan. Which star system had it been, she wondered, where Morgan had almost died? It struck Iceni then that Morgan's life had been shadowed by terrible events, yet at the same time Morgan had repeatedly been so fortunate that luck alone didn't seem enough to explain her survival until now, let alone her status with Drakon.

Have the living stars looked out for you, Colonel Morgan? But, then, why have they also been so cruel to you?

There were no answers to those questions—there were never any answers to questions like that—and Sub-CEO

Marphissa was awaiting instructions. Iceni pretended to study her display for a moment, then waved in the general direction of two of the jump points, one of which led to Taroa and the other to Kane. "Head that way."

The closest of those two jump points, that for Kane, was out past the orbit of the last planet in the star system, a frozen ball of gas and rock mockingly nicknamed Hotel for the abandoned research facility sitting vacant on it. That put it almost six and a half light-hours distant from where Iceni's flotilla sat. At point one light, they could cover that distance in sixty-five hours, or almost three days. But charging toward the jump point at that velocity would attract attention. Was it riskier to attract that attention or to spend twice as long getting there at a more routine point zero five speed? Put that way, it didn't seem wise to loiter on the way to the jump point. Every minute might count.

"All warships are at maximum fuel state?" Iceni asked. Her flotilla status readout showed that they were, but no one could trust those figures. Unit commanders routinely gundecked the real numbers in order to look better. A good flotilla commander found ways to keep track of the actual data despite that.

"Yes. Ninety-eight to ninety-nine percent fuel status for all units," Marphissa replied immediately.

"Then let's see how well these units can sustain acceleration," Iceni announced. "Bring formation velocity to point one light and hold it there."

The small flotilla surged into motion as their main propulsion units lit off. Iceni watched them accelerate, her attention mainly for C-818. That heavy cruiser's main propulsion units, badly damaged during the battle with Kolani, had just recently been declared fully repaired.

They weren't.

"What's the matter with C-818?" Iceni asked in a deceptively mild voice as the heavy cruiser lagged farther and farther behind the other warships.

Marphissa had already been checking the same thing. "C-818's commander says the propulsion units are only putting out sixty percent of maximum. They were all supposedly tested at one hundred percent when repaired."

At least they were still near the planet. Iceni called Togo. "Whoever certified the repairs on the main propulsion units on C-818 is either incompetent or corrupt. Find out who that individual was and make an example of that person."

"How strong an example? Should I have them shot?"

She really hated finding out someone had failed totally in their responsibilities. "If it was a matter of corruption, yes. If it was incompetence, bust that person down to the lowest-level dirt sweeper."

"Those speaking for the citizens have been agitating for the courts and legal system to become a functioning justice system," Togo pointed out. "A summary execution might help them win wider support for that idea among the other citizens."

Why did the simplest things have to be made difficult? "Fine. Incompetence is an internal disciplinary issue and not subject to the courts by Syndicate law, which we have yet to alter. If your investigation finds corruption instead, give the individual a quick trial, *then* have them shot."

That took care of that aspect of the problem, but it didn't help C-818. "Sub-CEO Marphissa, order C-818 to return to orbit about the planet and respond to orders from . . . General Drakon until I return."

"General Drakon?" Spotting an already-annoyed Iceni's reaction to the question, Marphissa quickly saluted. "I shall inform them of your orders immediately, Madam President."

"And tell them to get those propulsion units fixed properly!"

"Yes, Madam President."

Iceni glowered at her display, letting her bad mood settle around her like a dark halo. Without C-818, she had only three heavy cruisers left. There were also the four light cruisers and seven of the Hunter-Killers, but that made for a ridiculously small force to assault a battleship that might have substantial defenses and armaments already activated.

At least the HuKs sent to Taroa and Kahiki had returned in time to accompany her. If nothing else, they might provide targets for the battleship long enough for some of the other warships to get in damaging shots.

But the HuK she had sent to Lono hadn't made it back yet, and it should have. What had happened at Lono? One more thing to worry about.

"Madam President?"

Iceni swiveled her head like a gun turret to focus on Sub-CEO Marphissa. "What?"

"Can I provide our units with an estimate for the duration of this activity?" Marphissa asked carefully.

"Is there any problem with supplies on any of the units?"

"No, Madam President. All units are prepared for extended operations." Marphissa eyed her before adding one more thing. "All weapons are also at maximum."

"Good." In that respect, things were as good as they could be. And she had Marphissa to thank for keeping the warships in readiness. "You've done well. Effective immediately, you are confirmed as flotilla commander until further notice."

"I—thank you, Madam President."

Iceni found herself smiling thinly at Marphissa. "Don't thank me until you learn what I'm going to expect of you in that position."

MORGAN strode into Drakon's office, looking suspiciously cheerful. Before the door could close, Malin followed her. That caused Morgan's jovial mood to dim for a moment, but then she turned a grin on Drakon. "Give the word and she's dead."

Drakon leaned back in his seat, taking his time replying. "President Iceni, you mean."

"Yes, sir. I've got someone right next to her ready to move. We've even got deniability built into this. It's sweet."

Instead of answering her, Drakon looked at Malin.

"You need to ask yourself two questions, General,"

Malin said. "First, do you trust the agent who claims to be ready to act on our behalf—"

"That agent has every reason to carry out the action!" Morgan interjected.

"—and, second but most importantly, do you want Iceni dead? What would you gain from that, and what would you lose?"

Morgan shook her head in disgust. "What would he gain? Anybody but you would already know the answer to that."

Holding up one hand slightly to stop the arguing, Drakon shifted his gaze back to Morgan. "How certain are we of this agent?"

"I sent out feelers, the agent responded, and we did the usual dance around each other to see if our interests coincided. The agent can get right next to Iceni," Morgan emphasized, "and if the agent was able to arrange things properly, the hit does not have to be in this star system."

"The agent is new," Malin said. "We don't have much track record to go on."

"How did you—?" Morgan glared at him. "If we wait for everything to be perfect, we'll never move. But Iceni will. General, you know we can't screw around indefinitely waiting for a one hundred percent chance of success."

"That's true," Drakon agreed. "But the bigger question is whether I want to, and if I did want to, whether now would be the right time. I told both of you, and no one else, where Iceni is going and why. You know how important it is that the mission be successful."

"That sub-CEO knows her job," Morgan said. "She can do it without Iceni."

"That is not a certainty, and Iceni has not targeted you, General," Malin said.

"That we have determined," Morgan snapped back at him.

"I have more confidence in you than that," Malin told her with a cold smile. "If someone was trying to get at General Drakon, you would know."

That compliment took Morgan aback for a moment, but

she rallied quickly. "I'm not perfect. General Drakon knows better than to put total trust in *anyone*," she added with a look that made it clear that the jab was aimed at Malin.

"Then why should he trust this agent? It's an old ISS trick, General. Dangle an opportunity in front of someone, and when they take the bait, you have them. How do we know that President Iceni doesn't want you to send that order? If you do, and this is a setup, you'll be playing right into her hands."

Morgan's eyes blazed. "Are you implying that I'm working with Iceni?"

"I would not imply a charge like that. I'd make it outright if I had proof."

"Only if my back was turned! General, I know my job. I know what the agent will do."

Drakon closed his eyes, trying to sort out options. *The bottom line is, I don't want to kill her. Not unless I'm forced to. She's doing a good job running her half of things and hasn't been working to undermine me in any obvious ways. Whether she's working in less obvious ways is another question.* "No," he finally said. "I don't think this is the right time, the solution isn't one I want to pursue unless it is clearly required, and I would like to have a better track record on the agent before I entrust that person with such a critical move."

Malin tried not to look triumphant while Morgan suppressed a scowl. "But the option isn't off the table?" she asked.

"It doesn't hurt to have someone in that position ready to act if necessary. The capability might be very important at some point." The identity of that individual might also prove useful if Drakon ever had to sacrifice anyone to keep Iceni convinced he was working with her. "But I'll make the decision on whether and when it's necessary."

HER stateroom on the heavy cruiser was far from spacious or luxurious. Iceni sat looking around its confines, remembering her own days as a junior executive, living in quarters much smaller and more Spartan than this. *You've become spoiled, Gwen.*

Having ensured that the defenses and antisurveillance equipment built into her outfit were all working properly, Iceni called Sub-CEO Marphissa. "I need to see you."

Marphissa arrived with gratifying haste. "Yes, Madam President?"

"Close the hatch and sit down." Iceni waited, watching Marphissa intently, her equipment remotely analyzing the sub-CEO's physiological status for signs of not just nervousness but also fear or outright deception. The tiny, portable equipment wasn't nearly as effective as that inside an interrogation cell, but it provided helpful inputs to regular observations of someone. "Have you heard from General Drakon?"

The signs of nervousness shot up, but no clear signs of deception registered as Marphissa answered. "Not since we left orbit."

"You heard from him before then?"

"Not from him. Just expanded instructions from whoever is in contact with me. I already had a code phrase that would order me to kill you at the first good opportunity. The expanded instructions added a second phrase, which would order me to wait to kill you until we were outside the star system."

"I see."

"I take it," Marphissa said cautiously, "that means our current trip toward the jump points means we will actually jump for another star."

Iceni made a noncommittal sound in reply. "But you haven't received either code phrase?"

"No."

Did Drakon want to kill her or not? Using Marphissa as a double agent had seemed a good way to establish Drakon's intent, but perhaps he was just waiting for a better time. The addition of a code for killing Iceni outside the star system was particularly disturbing in light of one of

Drakon's arguments when she had spoken with him about this mission. At least the use of Marphissa ensured that Iceni would gain advance notice if an assassination was ordered while she was on a warship.

Assuming that Marphissa, who had been told to respond to the feelers from someone very close to Drakon, and to pretend to be ready to assassinate Iceni, had not turned a third time and decided to actually try to follow orders to kill. Eliminating Iceni would leave a very large vacancy in a position vastly more senior than the one Marphissa now had and would leave Marphissa in control of the mobile forces that could give her the power to claim that position. This was a delicate business, a tricky business, a confusing business. She would hate to have to order Marphissa killed. The woman had proven to be a very capable subordinate. Having to deal with such issues gave Iceni headaches at times. "Notify me immediately if you hear from General Drakon's contact again."

"Yes, Madam President."

"What about Colonel Rogero? Any problems?" Rogero would make an excellent backup for Drakon if Iceni's assassination was ordered and Marphissa didn't succeed. An experienced soldier, loyal to Drakon, with a squad of special forces at his back. And Drakon had the perfect blackmail to use against Rogero as well.

"No problems," Marphissa said. "He's in one of the staterooms formerly used by the snakes, and he's keeping to himself, but I've told my officers to monitor him and the ship's systems keep me informed of his location. He's been fairly stiff with me every time we've talked. I don't think he likes mobile forces unit commanders."

Iceni managed not to look amused. *The problem is that he likes one mobile forces unit commander far too much, and she's an* enemy *mobile forces unit commander. Would you kill me, Colonel Rogero, if Drakon ordered it and threatened to tell everyone about that if you didn't?* "Keep a very close eye on Colonel Rogero."

"The ship's systems will automatically alert you if

Colonel Rogero comes within ten meters of you," Marphissa said.

"Excellent." On something as small as a heavy cruiser that might produce too many false alarms, but if so she could have the alert parameters changed. "Then there's one other thing." Iceni smiled to lower the tension. "General Drakon has suggested that I look at changing the rank titles within the mobile forces. That would make clear our break with the failed Syndicate system."

Marphissa nodded. "No one has any love for the Syndicate command structure. We're not working in business jobs. We're mobile forces."

"Exactly. I did not want to use the same titles that Drakon has adopted for his ground forces. You're not ground forces."

Marphissa nodded again, emphatically this time.

"I looked for a rank structure from earlier times, but not one that was the same as the Alliance now uses," Iceni said. "I believe we need to avoid that as well."

A third nod, very strong. "We are not a . . . minor subset of the Alliance."

"I agree. Someday . . . well, here." Iceni brought up a file and pivoted the display floating above her desk so that Marphissa could see it. "This is a rank structure that was once used in part of the Syndicate Worlds before all forces were unified under a single corporate system."

Marphissa gazed at Iceni in disbelief. "The Syndicate Worlds once allowed local variations in how things were done?"

"It is hard to believe, isn't it? That was more than a hundred and fifty years ago. These were star systems that, back then, had been absorbed into the Syndicate Worlds recently enough that they still retained some individuality." "Absorbed" was a nice way to describe what had actually been a conquest without combat of a small group of star systems next to both Syndicate and Alliance space that had foolishly tried to stand apart from both powers. Neutrals had been low-hanging fruit in those days, and the Alliance had been eager to avoid outright fighting. If the idiots running the Syndicate Worlds hadn't attacked the Alliance they might have been able, over time, to similarly acquire control of minor coalitions like the Rift Federation and the Callas Republic. Instead, both had ended up associating actively with the Alliance during the war. *What will happen to their supposed independence now?* Iceni wondered. *Will the Alliance formally take them over? Surely, they wouldn't just let them go back to acting on their own. I should ask Black Jack about that when his fleet returns. He must be the one making that decision.*

Iceni raised her forefinger to point to parts of the display. "As flotilla commander, you will be Kommodor Marphissa. Depending on their seniority, their sub-CEO or executive rank, individual warship commanders will be Kapitan First, Second, or Third rank, and below that the lower executives and subexecutives will be Kapitan-Leytenant, then Leytenant, and Leytenant Second rank, and, finally, the most junior will be Ships Officers."

"I think this change will be welcomed," Marphissa said. "It's good that it's not the same as that of the Alliance and is also different from the structure put into place by General Drakon. The mobile forces, I mean the warships, will like being distinct in that way."

"Is any part of the new rank structure unclear?" Iceni asked.

"Is there no rank above Kommodor?"

Iceni laughed. "You're already worried about that? Atmiral."

"Atmiral," Marphissa murmured, as if trying on the title.

"We need a few more warships before there will be any call for an Atmiral, Kommodor Marphissa."

THEY were thirty light-minutes from the jump point for Kane. Iceni, seated on the bridge of the heavy cruiser, turned to Marphissa. "Kommodor, take the flotilla to the jump point for Kane and order all units to be prepared for action upon exit at Kane."

"Kane?" Marphissa asked, plainly having expected Taroa. "Is there an estimate of what we may face there?"

"I will brief you when we have entered jump."

That left five hours at point one light speed. Iceni stayed on the bridge, watching her display where the warships, moving at about thirty thousand kilometers a second, crawled across the vast distances inside a star system. At the same velocity, a journey to the nearest star, Laka, would require nearly twenty-five years.

The old and proven jump technology would allow the flotilla to reach Kane in about six days, though, taking a shortcut through a still-poorly-understood dimension in which distances were much shorter.

As they finally approached the jump point, Marphissa looked at Iceni. "Permission to proceed with jump to Kane?"

"Permission granted. All units are to be at combat readiness status one when we exit at Kane."

"Yes, Madam President." Marphissa passed along those orders to the other warships with them, then ordered the jump.

Iceni felt the odd twisting as the endless bright stars against an eternity of black space vanished. In their place, the outside views now showed the monotonous, dull nothingness of jump space. Though human ships had been transiting jump space for centuries, it had never been explored because there was no known way to explore it. Ships could not deviate from their paths between the small areas in space called jump points where jump space could be accessed from normal space. Human sensors could detect nothing except the gray void.

And the lights. As Iceni watched, one of the mysterious lights of jump space bloomed ahead. No one had ever learned what those lights were, what caused them, or what they meant, if anything. There were rumors and superstitions, of course. When Iceni was in normal space or on a planet, she inwardly mocked those who thought the lights were signs of some powerful otherness watching humanity. But when in jump space, a region where no human really belonged, Iceni always felt a chill inside when she saw one, as if she were gazing on something whose face could not be comprehended by the human mind. At such times her father's old stories of the living stars seemed to have extra force.

There was also no way to send messages between warships, or any means of communication with the regular universe. Secrets could not be compromised. "Kommodor, it is time to discuss our mission."

To her credit, the new kommodor took the news without flinching. "A battleship?"

"Yes."

Marphissa made an uncertain gesture. "This should be . . . interesting."

"Yes," Iceni repeated, hoping that it wouldn't be too interesting.

Six days later, the heavy cruiser at full combat alert and Marphissa looking fiercely determined, the flotilla prepared to exit at Kane. "If the battleship is combat ready and anywhere near that jump point," she commented to Iceni, "then the result will be a short battle indeed."

"Are you ready to find out, Kommodor?" Iceni asked, trying to look and sound completely confident.

"Yes, Madam President."

The gray nothingness of jump space was replaced by stars and blackness, Iceni struggling to overcome the effects of exiting jump so she could focus eyes and mind on her display and learn what awaited them at Kane.

CHAPTER NINE

ALARMS sounded on the cruiser, targeting systems that hadn't been impacted by the transition from jump space locking on to the large ship near the jump exit but waiting for human approval before they fired. Using tricks she had learned long ago, Iceni managed to fight off the disorientation caused by jump exit and grimly focused on her display.

There was something big there, all right.

Nervous laughter erupted on the bridge as everyone else recovered enough to view their own displays.

"A freighter," Marphissa said. The huge, boxy merchant ship loomed within less than a light-minute of the jump point, clearly headed outward with its cargo. The Syndicate Worlds might be collapsing, violence and economic uncertainty might be breaking out everywhere, but business was still business. "Should we intercept it?"

"No," Iceni replied. "We need trade to continue in this region. We need to encourage people to trade with us. Wish the freighter's crew well and assure them that Midway remains safe for everyone who wishes to do business there."

While Marphissa did that, Iceni studied her display. They had arrived at a jump point only five light-hours out

from the star Kane, whose solar system was smaller in di-
ameter than that of Midway's. The nearest planet to the flotilla was only twenty light-minutes away, far enough from
the star's warmth to be very cold indeed. Closer in to the
star were two gas giants, one at three light-hours from
the star and another one and a half light-hours out. Beyond
them, close enough to Kane to benefit from the heat of the
star, were three inner planets, one a bit too cold for comfortable human habitation, one a bit too hot, and the third, at
only seven light-minutes from Kane, just right in human
terms. It was that planet that held the bulk of the human
presence in the star system, in towns and cities clinging to
the edges of continents that remained mostly unsettled.

But it was that gas giant one and a half light-hours from
the star that held Iceni's attention. She could see the mobile
forces facility orbiting that gas giant and see one of the
large moons that also orbited the planet, but there was no
sign of the battleship. Either it truly was hidden behind the
curve of the planet, or her information had been false and
the mission a fool's errand.

It would be nearly five hours before the people on Kane's
main inhabited world saw the arrival of the flotilla, but
Iceni knew she should send them a message to arrive at
about the same time as the light showing the arrival of the
warships. What the message should be had depended on
what she found when they arrived here.

"No fighting apparent anywhere in the star system,"
Kommodor Marphissa commented. "Only peaceful communications and movement detected." She pointed. "But
we do have opposition to worry about."

About four light-hours from the flotilla, orbiting Kane
close to where the gas giant swung about the same star,
were several warships. "One heavy cruiser, three light
cruisers, and six Hunter-Killers," the operations specialist
confirmed with unusual speed. Since Iceni had ordered
their line worker ratings changed to specialist designations,
the morale of the crew had shot upward remarkably.

Iceni rubbed her chin, trying to read significance in the

positioning of those forces. "Can we tell if the Syndicate Worlds still controls this star system, or has someone else taken over?" Midway, with its hypernet gate and strategic importance, had also gained a more substantial ISS presence than less important star systems had to deal with. Some, like Kane, which had a decent world for humanity but nothing otherwise special to distinguish them, were backwaters that since the discovery of the hypernet had seen little interest from the Syndicate Worlds. While that had kept Kane from receiving much investment, it had also kept the numbers of snakes and their facilities to much lower levels. Until recently, if Kane had bucked Syndicate authority, it would have been only a matter of time before the central government sent mobile forces in either to accept unconditional subservience or pound the planet into surrender, a much more cost-efficient solution than stationing a large ISS presence in the star system.

But who did the mobile forces here now answer to? Are they still enforcing Syndicate rule? Not knowing that made it hard for Iceni to decide who to present herself as.

"All of the communications we're seeing reflect Syndicate Worlds' procedures and use their nomenclature," the communications specialist said.

"Which might just mean they haven't changed anything yet," Iceni muttered. *I have to go with my gut on this, and my instincts tell me that so far the Syndicate Worlds is still running things here. Maybe the authorities in Kane are just paying lip service to the Syndicate Worlds, but I don't think that they've formally abandoned Syndicate rule.*

She tabbed her own communication controls, placing a real-appearing avatar of a woman who didn't look like her to appear as the sender when the message went out. "This is CEO Janusa, operating on orders from the Syndicate Worlds' government on Prime. We have just arrived from Midway, having reestablished Syndicate control in that star system, and will proceed to your mobile forces facility for resupply and refitting. For the people, Janusa, out."

Kommodor Marphissa gave her a slight smile. "I suppose if you want someone to impersonate a Syndicate CEO, using a real CEO is the way to go."

"Former CEO," Iceni corrected, but smiled back. "There is a certain attitude, a way of talking, that becomes habit. They won't have any files on a CEO Janusa here, but Kane doesn't get all that much traffic from elsewhere in Syndicate space, so their news was always far behind developments elsewhere. If they ask who I am, I'll tell them that I was recently promoted by the new government on Prime."

"Do you believe they will let us proceed to their mobile forces facility?"

"If they do without any objection, it may well mean that our intelligence was faulty or that the battleship has already left. But if they object and attempt to delay our going there, it will be a strong sign that our prey is indeed present. We won't wait for their reply, Kommodor. Order the flotilla on a vector to intercept the mobile forces facility."

"At what velocity . . . CEO Janusa?"

Iceni only pondered that for a moment. "Point one light speed. I am a brash, new CEO. I have no time to waste plodding through an unimportant star system. I have important business elsewhere, and I want everyone watching to know that I am important and have important business to conduct."

"I will keep your importance in all matters in mind, CEO Janusa," Marphissa replied.

"That's how you have always dealt with CEOs, isn't it?" Iceni asked, her earlier mockery shifting to an unpleasant self-appraisal. "We are all so important."

Marphissa was bold enough to answer truthfully. "Not all CEOs were alike, but all had to be treated the same way."

"OBSTLT," Iceni added sardonically.

"Or Be Subject to Life Termination," Marphissa agreed. "I chose to back you, all of the commanders of these warships chose to back you, because we believed you were different enough in important ways."

"You backed me because you saw an opportunity for greater advancement."

"That was not the only reason, and in some cases not the reason at all." Kommodor Marphissa grinned. "I have just contradicted a CEO to her face."

"You obviously haven't made a habit of that in the past." Iceni regarded her carefully. "What is it you want, Kommodor? You and the others?"

"We want you to care as much about what happens to us as you do about what happens to you."

"You don't believe in asking for small things, do you?" Iceni looked back at her display. "I have a responsibility to those who work for me. Don't assume that makes me some sort of . . . *humanitarian*."

"I would not presume to accuse you of such a thing, Madam President."

"Good." Iceni let her gaze rest on the inhabited planet. Nearly five light-hours distant, so her message would not be received there until that time had elapsed, and any reply would take at least as long even if sent immediately. At least ten hours before she received any answer, and she had slept poorly earlier due to worries about what they would find here at Kane. "I am going to get some rest. Notify Colonel Rogero that it will be approximately forty hours before we expect to employ his ground forces. And notify me of any significant changes in the situation."

"Yes, Madam President," Marphissa said, all business again. "What about the readiness state of the warships? Do you wish them maintained at condition one?"

"No." There had been times when Iceni had been under the command of CEOs who kept their crews at maximum combat readiness for days at a time so they would be "ready for anything." The actual result had been that the crews were totally exhausted when they finally encountered the enemy, and thus far from being ready. She would not repeat that mistake. "Bring the warships back to standard cruising readiness state. Make sure every unit commander knows that I want the crews well rested when we get close to that gas giant." There wasn't anything *humanitarian* about that, either. It was simply good planning.

Nonetheless, the wave of relief that swept through the junior officers and specialists on the bridge was so strong that it almost felt like a physical thing. Iceni suppressed a smile, recalling the days when she had resigned herself to indefinite time on a bridge duty station while the enemy was still several light-hours distant. Everyone on the bridge knew that their target was a battleship, yet all of them seemed confident and cheerful. She could not understand it.

As Iceni closed the hatch on her stateroom, she felt the sense of respite that came from being behind a locked barrier. How long had it been since she could go out among others without worrying about who was at her back?

She felt more confident about Marphissa, though. The woman showed every sign of being smart, capable, loyal, and willing to speak truth to power. That last was often regarded by CEOs and sub-CEOs as an annoyance at best, but Iceni knew the value of that quality in a subordinate when married with the other virtues. Assuming that Marphissa really was all of those things, particularly loyal.

Did they really decide to back me because they thought I would care what happened to them? I suppose I do care, to the extent that I wouldn't abandon them to the enigmas when things seemed hopeless. That was my responsibility as the CEO in charge of the star system. That's how I operate—I do my job right—and not taking care of them now, when my fate rests on how well they perform in battle, would be foolish.

She lay on her bunk, gazing upward, wondering why the memory of the cheerful confidence in the crew made her feel rewarded. Their opinions didn't matter. They didn't matter. She had been taught that all of her professional life.

But, then, she had rebelled against what she had been taught, hadn't she?

Because that system had failed.

"CEO Janusa." The man sending the message seemed to be cautiously welcoming. Iceni didn't recognize him. "I am

CEO Reynard. Welcome to Kane. I congratulate you on your victory in the Midway Star System and would be appreciative if you would forward me the details of the fighting there so that I can learn from your example."

He's not a CEO. He's talking like a sub-CEO, trying to flatter me as a way of gaining information. Interesting.

"CEO Reynard" had taken on a concerned look. "I must inform you that our mobile forces facility orbiting the fourth planet was recently picked clean of supplies by another Syndicate flotilla. If you will instead proceed to the second planet, I will ensure that your flotilla receives any support that it requires. That will allow you to resupply as quickly as possible so you can proceed with your assignment. For the people, Reynard, out."

So, "Reynard," what is your real name and what is your real game? Have the Syndicate Worlds been overthrown here? What happened to CEO Chan, who was in control here the last I heard? He could have been swept up by the snakes, in which case you could be a Syndicate replacement, promoted rapidly after the ISS cleaned out the CEO ranks in this star system.

He also seems eager for us to leave. One thing I can be certain of is that "Reynard" doesn't want us going to the gas giant. That's a good sign. "Maintain course for the mobile forces facility about the gas giant," Iceni ordered Marphissa.

She thought about her next step, then activated her comms.

"This is CEO Janusa responding to CEO Reynard. Unfortunately, I lack the time for a diversion to the second planet of this star system. My flotilla will proceed to the mobile forces facility, where I am certain I will be able to acquire whatever I need. For the people, Janusa, out."

Another message. "This is CEO Janusa to the commander of the flotilla located near the fourth planet of this star system. I am here under direct orders from the government at Prime. I wish to be contacted by your commander as soon as possible. There are urgent requirements that necessitate changing your tasking." *Those requirements being the need to get you farther away from that mobile forces facility so I can have a free hand there.*

"CEO Janusa is really throwing her weight around," Kommodor Marphissa commented after Iceni finished sending the second message.

"She's a real bitch," Iceni agreed. "That will ensure that no one questions whether she's a real CEO. Have you had any luck informally contacting the commanders of any of the warships in that other flotilla?"

"I've sent them some feelers via the unauthorized back channels in the comm system, but no replies yet."

"Let me know the instant there are. I'd much rather collect those warships as additions to my flotilla than have to fight them."

They were twenty-eight hours' travel time from the mobile forces facility.

The next message came seven hours later, from the facility orbiting the gas giant rather than the inhabited planet. "CEO Janusa, please alter vector and proceed to the second planet. I regret to inform you that we have had an outbreak of serious illness following the last flotilla's visit to this facility. We have yet to identify a successful treatment. More than half of our personnel are already incapacitated. For the people, this is acting facility commander Sub-CEO Petrov, out."

"She looks in good health for someone overseeing a plague-struck facility," Iceni commented. "Kommodor Marphissa, I want your ship's physician to evaluate the appearance in this message of Sub-CEO Petrov, if that is indeed her real name."

Marphissa passed on the order, then turned to Iceni. "If they are suffering from possible plague conditions, then regulations call for the facility to have already been broadcasting a standard warn-off when we arrived in this star system. Instead, this message comes at a time delay consistent with having received orders to send it from the authorities on the second planet after those authorities had heard your reply to their request that you divert there."

"What an astounding coincidence."

Listening to an internal message, Marphissa nodded. "Understood," she said. "Madam President, my unit's physician says that Sub-CEO Petrov was clearly under stress when she sent the message but showed no signs of illness or long-term stress outside normal parameters for a sub-CEO."

Iceni watched the slow changes in the positions of objects on her display as her flotilla raced steadily toward the gas giant, and as the planets, moons, asteroids, and comets in the Kane Star System swung much more slowly about their sun or each other. "The flotilla near the gas giant still hasn't moved. How long can they wait to move and still be able to intercept us before we reach a position where we can see behind the curve of that planet?"

"Approximately . . ." Marphissa shrugged. "Three hours before we reach the gas giant. It depends on just where behind the curve the battleship is located."

Something didn't feel right, and Iceni finally knew what it was. "They're trying to warn us off. We've ignored the warn-offs. You know how things work. If the first admonition or threat doesn't work, you escalate until you find something that the other side has to pay attention to. What do they have that we would have to pay attention to?"

Marphissa's frown only lasted a moment. "A battleship."

"Yes. If they swing out that battleship and say 'Stay out, this is a restricted area,' even CEO Janusa would have to listen. They haven't done that yet, though." Neither had the flotilla commander replied to her direct order to contact her. That was also odd. "Still not a word from any unit in that other flotilla?"

"No, Madam President. Nothing."

Iceni frowned. "When I was executive rank and even sub-CEO, that would have been very unusual. We always contacted by back channel other units we encountered to pick up the latest unauthorized information so we could anticipate events or prepare personal defenses against negative actions." But no one in their right mind would ever have admitted to a superior that they did it. She had sometimes wondered how much more the Syndicate Worlds might have accomplished if its executives didn't expend so much effort working internal politics. The war had often seemed to take a backseat to inner power struggles.

"Really?" Kommodor Marphissa asked, trying to project surprised innocence. "If that sort of thing still happened, and of course I'm not saying it ever does, but if it somehow did, I would expect it to happen under these circumstances. But it hasn't."

"Somebody has even the back doors locked down," Iceni mused. "Have the snakes slaughtered the crews on those warships like they did on HuK-6336?"

"If they did, they could be at a disadvantage in a battle. They'll only be able to operate the units using automatic controls since they might lack the crew to do the jobs otherwise." Marphissa eyed her display. "Or there could have been a revolution, and the crews of those units don't want to give themselves away to us since we have superior numbers."

"All possibilities." Iceni stabbed an internal comm control. "Colonel Rogero, have you been monitoring ground forces communications in this star system?"

"Yes, Madam President."

From the way he always carried himself and spoke, Rogero seemed to be even more professional than Drakon's praise had indicated. It made all the more mysterious his lapse in getting emotionally involved with an enemy officer. Unless that enemy officer was something truly exceptional herself. *And there's no sense asking Rogero that question because if he's in love, he'll think she's the only woman like her that has ever been or will ever be. Love has far too negative an impact on anyone's ability to think clearly.* "Is there anything out of the ordinary at all?"

"Only one thing. All communications appear to be routine."

"And that is out of the ordinary?" Iceni asked.

"It is when we're here, Madam President. There should have been some reaction, some discussion, something to reflect our presence. There has been nothing."

"Can you tell me what that means, Colonel?"

"No. It is unexpected and unusual. That's all I can say. Wait." Rogero had turned and was talking to someone else, then faced Iceni again. "My comm analyst has found no signs of comms with any ground forces that might indicate those forces are aboard a battleship near the gas giant. They wouldn't be communicating directly with such forces if they wanted to hide their presence from us, but there are always leaks in other comms where someone references supplies or a personnel movement or something else that compromises the secret. We haven't seen anything like that."

"So all we will face are crew members?" That was good news.

"Madam President, it appears unlikely that there are any ground forces aboard that mobile unit, but if a force of vipers or other snakes is on that battleship, we wouldn't be able to tell. The ISS is very good at concealing information within apparently routine communications."

Perhaps not good news after all, then. "I appreciate your assessment, Colonel. We will be at the gas giant in twenty hours. How long will it take your soldiers to board the shuttles when I order an assault on the battleship?"

"Two minutes. We will be armored up and ready." Rogero hesitated. "You do realize that if a major portion of the battleship's weaponry is active, our shuttles will not survive to reach the mobile unit. A shuttle's survival time on that kind of an approach is measured in seconds."

"I understand." She hadn't realized the odds against the shuttles would be that bad, but it probably depended upon just how much of the battleship's weaponry had been activated.

After Rogero had signed off, Iceni considered her remaining options. There weren't many other things that she could do to influence events right now, but there was one big thing remaining in her arsenal of surprises. "When we're closer to the gas giant," she told Marphissa, "I will drop the disguise, tell them who I am and what we represent. If they are snakes, that will bring them out of hiding. If they aren't, they'll know they can avoid a fight." Twenty hours left until they reached the facility, and likely seventeen hours until the other flotilla moved.

Iceni gazed at the representation on her display of her own flotilla. The warships were in the standard Syndicate mobile forces formation, a box with the three heavy cruisers side by side in the middle, the four light cruisers posted at the rear corners of the box, four of the HuKs at the front corners, and the other three HuKs just below the heavy cruisers in the center of the box. A simple arrangement, with firepower concentrated in the center, and easy to shift direction without changing the configuration of units because all the warships had to do was swing together onto new vectors. It had worked for decades against the Alliance, if by "worked" one meant that it allowed the Syndicate Worlds' flotillas to slug it out with Alliance fleets until the survivors on whichever side prevailed could claim victory.

And then Black Jack had shown up, and massive flotillas started disappearing, wiped out in battles with the fleet led by him. *I've seen what records we have of the battles. He used all kinds of different formations, swinging them all over in every direction, somehow bringing them all together at the right moment to hammer our flotillas. What I wouldn't give for lessons from Black Jack on how to control a force of warships in battle. But what do I have that he would want? Access to our star system? I can't deny him that. He has a fleet that dwarfs anything I could muster.*

Is he the sort of man who craves conquering every woman he meets? If so, that would give me one thing to offer. He can't have had many Syndicate CEOs. But that doesn't match what I've heard of him, or how he acted when we spoke, and . . . and I really don't want to do that. If it was mutual desire, that would be one thing, but if it was for some gain then I would be selling myself, and for all my sins that is one thing I have avoided. Perhaps my rivals would define my actions differently, but that's what I believe.

"Madam President, is something wrong?" Marphissa asked.

Aware that some of her inner turmoil must have been showing, Iceni put on a mask of straightforward thoughtfulness. "I was just contemplating our formation and whether I should change it if we have to fight."

"I think that depends on the status of the battleship," Marphissa suggested.

She was right. Iceni nodded. "I'll make the decision when I have the necessary information."

So far, though, necessary information seemed to be in short supply in the Kane Star System.

THIS time, "CEO Reynard" had on a more aggressive front, perhaps because Iceni's flotilla was only five hours' travel time from the mobile forces facility by the time the message from him was received. "CEO Janusa, access to the mobile forces facility has been restricted by order of the Syndicate Worlds. You are required to divert your flotilla from its current course and proceed to the second planet, where your supply needs will be met, after which you can proceed on your missions outside this star system. Failure to comply with this direction will constitute disobedience to a directive of the Syndicate Worlds. For the people, Reynard, out."

Iceni considered her reply. Events were reaching the point at which decisions would take on momentum that would be hard to alter in the time remaining. What would most likely produce the reactions she needed from the people in Kane, and in particular those in the warships in the other flotilla?

"It is time to announce our true colors," Iceni said to the others on the bridge before she triggered her own comm controls to broadcast. This time, she deactivated the avatar so that everyone would see her true appearance.

"People of the Kane Star System, this is President Iceni of the independent star system of Midway. Midway has thrown off the yoke of the Syndicate Worlds and no longer answers to the CEOs of the weak, corrupt, and incompetent government on Prime. As the Syndicate Worlds crumbles, it is time for the star systems of this region to join together for mutual protection and support, so we can follow those courses of action in our best interests rather than the orders of distant masters who represent a failed approach. Distant rulers who would take our wealth, demand our obedience in all things, and give nothing in return. Only we can defend ourselves. Only we can ensure the safety of our homes.

"The ISS at Midway has been wiped out. We are no longer forced to bow to the snakes. I urge you to join us. My flotilla will support your struggle. To any who still wish to follow the decrees issued by the dead hand of the Syndicate Worlds, I tell you not to seek to hinder our movements or actions. We will fight, and we will win. For the people, Iceni, out."

She turned to Marphissa. "Contact the other flotilla again. You personally. I want them to hear from someone else in a mobile forces command role talking directly to them."

"Yes, Madam President." Marphissa sat silent for several seconds, then activated her own comms. "Warships of the Kane flotilla, this is Kommodor Marphissa of the Midway flotilla. Join with us to defend this region against aggression and disorder, join with us to defend all that we hold dear. We truly fight for our people now. If you choose not to join with forces of the independent star system of Midway, you must avoid any fight with us, or we will annihilate you. For the people, Marphissa, out."

The messages were going out at the speed of light, but it would take them a while to reach their destinations. "In about half an hour, when our messages reach the other flotilla, all hell is going to start breaking loose in this star system," Marphissa predicted.

"I wish I could see the reaction on the second planet when the messages get there," Iceni replied. "The important thing is that it will take an hour and a half for my message to reach that planet, and another hour and a half for any response from the planetary authorities to reach the warships in the other flotilla. They'll have nearly three hours to make up their own minds on what to do before they receive orders from their bosses on the second planet."

There was nothing left to do then but sit and watch. Iceni didn't want to be distracted when something finally did happen, so she avoided the urge to pull up some work documents or a novel or a twitch-and-move game and instead just stared at her display. She discovered that hitting one command produced an expanding sphere image that represented the message she had sent, spreading at the speed of light through the star system. On a display covering such a wide area, the bubble appeared to move slowly but steadily, sweeping across installations, planets, warships, and merchant ships. Iceni got a kick out of seeing when her message actually arrived at each location.

But she wouldn't have any idea what their reactions would be until the light from those movements reached her. Iceni found she could activate reaction bubbles, showing how long it would take her to see such activity, but the swarm of expanding bubbles quickly merged into a welter of foam in which it was too hard to make out individual expansion waves. She wiped out that option, couldn't seem to locate a simpler one, and glowered at the display. *I will not be one of those clueless CEOs who can't carry out simple functions without some lowest-level untrained worker showing me how to enter the commands. I'll just work it out in my head. Thirty light-minutes to the other flotilla. That means thirty minutes until they received the messages from us, during which time we get three light-minutes closer to them at point one light speed. Then the light showing their reaction needs to come back to us, which will take . . . about twenty-five, twenty-six minutes as we keep closing on them. Close to an hour, even if those other warships react immediately.*

Space is too damned big.

"VECTOR changes on the other flotilla."

The announcement by the maneuvering specialist jerked Iceni out of the light nap she had dropped into without realizing it. Blinking away sleep, she tried to make out the movement on her display.

"Coming around toward an intercept on us," Marphissa commented. "We'll have to see where they steady out, but I'd bet that they're coming toward us."

"But *why* are they coming toward us?" Iceni demanded. Everything had once been easy. If they were Alliance warships and they came toward you, it meant they wanted to fight. If they were Syndicate warships, they wanted to join up. But now Alliance warships might be friendly, Syndicate warships were likely to be hostile, and she didn't even know who these warships were answering to, let alone if they were readying for a fight. "Kommodor Marphissa, if we have not heard anything from that other flotilla within the next five minutes, you are to inform them that we will destroy them as soon as they enter weapons range."

"The Kane flotilla is steadying out at point one light speed, on a direct intercept with us," the maneuvering watch reported. "Time to contact, two hours and twenty-one minutes."

"Still no battleship," Iceni muttered.

"They may not have one," Marphissa said.

"Then why do they want to keep us away from that gas giant?"

The warning went out, but still no reply. Iceni sat watching the distance close, her irritation rising with every second that passed without any communication from the other flotilla. *Even if they say they want to join us now, I think I'll still order them to be blown away.*

"Incoming message." The comms specialist paused. "It's not from the flotilla."

"Show me," Iceni ordered.

A window opened to show a junior officer standing on what was clearly the bridge of a battleship. If the sub-CEO on the mobile forces facility had shown only normal levels of stress, this executive was clearly in far worse straits. His uniform showed signs of having been worn for days or weeks, his face was lean in a way that evoked thoughts of very limited rations, and his eyes held an almost feverish intensity. "This is Sub-Executive Kontos, acting commander of the mobile forces unit B-78, to . . . to . . . President Iceni." Kontos paused to lick his lips and clear his throat as if speaking distinctly was an effort.

"A subexecutive commanding a battleship?" Marphissa commented. "Has that ever happened?"

"During battles, when a crew was almost wiped out," Iceni replied.

Kontos started speaking again. "We are barricaded within the primary citadels. We are the . . . survivors of the outfitting crew. Myself and . . . a number of line workers. We control the bridge, engineering, and the primary fire-control center." Kontos was clearly doing his best to recite a correct report but occasionally stumbled over the words. "We . . . have been able to hold out because of the internal armor and the . . . antimutiny defenses."

"Who are you holding out against?" Iceni mumbled angrily.

"The ISS," Kontos said, as if answering her question. "We . . . don't know how many. They overran some locations . . . My last order received was to . . . seal ourselves inside critical control areas and . . . wait for relief. We have not heard anything since . . . except demands . . . from the ISS . . . that we surrender. External comms have . . . been . . . blocked, but we managed a work-around in time to . . . hear your message."

"The snakes have taken over here," Marphissa said, her voice hardening.

"That explains it all, doesn't it?" Iceni said. "The snakes wiped out the officers and who knows how much of the crews on those warships. The only thing I don't understand is why they didn't order CEO Janusa to assist them."

"Perhaps they actually knew who you were despite the avatar and have known you were playing them. If you'd gone to the second planet and docked our warships at one of their facilities for resupply, we might have been over-whelmed by boarding parties before we could get away."

"Oh, damn. You're likely right. That's where they'd have access to enough personnel to do that."

"We request assistance," Sub-Executive Kontos asked. His voice cracked on the last word, and Kontos sagged a moment before straightening to attention again. "We know they're bringing . . . breaching gear strong enough to get into the citadels. Request . . . assistance."

The message began to repeat, then abruptly cut off.

"The snakes found their work-around and blocked it," Marphissa commented.

"Sub-CEO—" The operations specialist caught herself. "Kommodor, we've been tracking a freighter moving at a good clip toward that gas giant. It fit the profile of a rush resupply mission, so we haven't paid much attention to it, but it might be bringing the breaching gear for the snakes."

"As well as more snakes, no doubt. Can we get there before it does?" Marphissa asked.

"It will beat us by about ten minutes if we hold our vector."

Iceni nodded slowly. *We charge in at best speed, brake hard, blow away that freighter, and get our ground forces on that battleship. Simple. As well as incredibly compli-cated to carry out.*

"It could be a trap," Marphissa cautioned. "To get us in there close to the battleship. If its armament is operational, we could sustain enough damage that the flotilla here could finish us off."

"It could be," Iceni agreed. "But if so, that subexecutive is the best actor I've ever seen. Certainly a lot better than

'CEO Reynard' or 'Sub-CEO Petrov.' Are you bringing up a possibility, or do you believe this is a trap?"

Marphissa sat watching her display for a moment before answering. "Only a possibility. If it were a trap, they could have sent us a message from Sub-Executive Kontos a long time ago to see what we would do. I think the snakes had been willing to starve out the survivors from the outfitting crew. That would cause less damage to the battleship than breaking into the antimutiny citadels. When we showed up, the snakes knew they had to get the breaching equipment there and crack open the bridge. But because we came in this quickly and straight for the gas giant, they haven't had enough time."

"Then let's go save Sub-Executive Kontos and his brave line workers, Kommodor."

CHAPTER TEN

"SUB-EXECUTIVE Kontos, this is President Iceni. We are on our way to relieve you. Hold out as long as you can. We wiped out the snakes at Midway, and we will do the same here. If you manage to get comms working again, keep us apprised of your status." Odds were that Kontos wouldn't be able to receive her message, let alone reply, but if they could hear any of it that might inspire the surviving crew to hold out long enough.

Marphissa raised one finger toward her display. "How do we take down the other flotilla quickly enough to get our ground forces to that battleship? We don't have enough of a firepower advantage to knock out all of those other warships in a single pass."

"We're not going to try." Iceni settled back in her seat, feeling a surge of confidence. She had viewed the records of Black Jack's battles over and over again in the last few months, trying to spot patterns, and suddenly one of those patterns had come clear to her. Whenever possible, Black Jack had avoided doing what his opponent wanted. It seemed so simple a thing. If the enemy wanted you to attack in such a way at such a place, then if you could you did

something else. That hadn't been how war had been fought
for . . . how long? Kill the enemy, destroy the enemy's
forces, slam head-to-head until one side gave way. That's
how it had been since those who knew how to fight in other
ways had died in the first decades of the war, those they had
partly trained dying soon afterward. But Black Jack had
come from that earlier time. And he never did what his opponents wanted.

"Madam President?" Kommodor Marphissa waved at
her display again. "We need to destroy that flotilla."

"No, we don't. We need to defeat it. What do they want?
To slow us down. To inflict damage on us. To keep us occupied long enough for the snakes to gain full control of
that battleship. We won't let them do any of those things."

Marphissa nodded in the manner of someone who wanted
to acknowledge she understood what had been said but not
necessarily what it meant. "What will we do instead?"

"We will get past that oncoming flotilla without engaging it, brake our velocity far enough to release the shuttles
carrying our ground forces assault team close to the battleship, then accelerate again and engage and defeat the other
flotilla as it returns to fight us."

Another nod of partial understanding. "How will we do
that, Madam President?"

Iceni smiled. "I have established our goals and objectives, Kommodor. As you are the flotilla commander and
experienced operator of mobile forces, I will leave it up to
you to find the best means of accomplishing those goals
and objectives."

"I . . . see." Marphissa stared at her display for a little
while. "Thank you for this opportunity to excel, Madam
President." Remarkably, not a bit of sarcasm came through
when she said that.

"I have every confidence in you, Kommodor."

Marphissa sat for long minutes, just looking at her display, saying nothing, her eyes intent. Finally, her hands
moved, tracing out possible actions so that the ship's maneuvering systems could produce predictions.

"Kommodor?"

Jerking out of her absorption in her planning, Marphissa turned an annoyed scowl on the operations specialist. "What is it?"

"Kommodor," the specialist said with a nervous swallow, "I was thinking, if the ISS is controlling the other flotilla's mobile forces, and if they are running them on automatic controls because the officers are dead or under arrest, then those are the same automated systems as our own mobile units use."

"Your point?" Marphissa snapped.

"If we run a simulation in which our automated systems are controlling the actions of the other flotilla, it will tell us what the automated systems on the other flotilla will actually do in response to anything. We can predict their reactions."

The annoyance dropped from Marphissa's face. "That is an excellent observation. The limitations of simulations are always the inability to know what the other side will actually do, but in this case we could know that precisely. Set up the simulation."

"Yes, Kommodor!"

Iceni leaned closer to Marphissa. "Why isn't he a sub-executive? I mean, a ships officer or leytenant?"

"I will look into that," Marphissa replied.

As the simulation went online in part of her display, Marphissa went back to work, her expression gradually going from tense to a sort of qualified satisfaction. "It can be done, Madam President. I will have to download commands to the other units in the flotilla to ensure the timing is right. The hardest part will be the braking maneuver to reach the battleship. That will stress our units the most."

"But we can do it? It is within the capabilities of our warships?"

"Yeeessss." The affirmative reply was drawn out enough, tentative enough, to inspire some worry.

"Show me." Iceni ran the plan through her display, watching the motions play out in accelerated time. Some of the maneuvers would push the strain on the warships very close to the red zone, where a ship would literally come apart under the stress, but none of them actually pushed into the red. In theory. In practice, the plan would create strains that might spike too high for individual units. "We'll need to override the automated maneuvering safeties," Iceni commented.

"Yes, Madam President. The safeties wouldn't let us do this."

Play it safe and lose, or risk it and have a chance of winning? Why was she here if she wasn't willing to run risks? "Well done, Kommodor. I approve your plan. When do you intend downloading the plan to the rest of the flotilla?"

"Eleven minutes prior to contact. We're all within a light-second of each other, so that allows plenty of time for ship systems to accept the plan and be ready to execute it at ten minutes prior to contact."

"But not very much time for the commanders of those warships to realize what they're going to do." Iceni regarded the plan again. "That may be a good thing. If they have time to study this, they may start thinking and decide there's mistakes."

"Even the Syndicate system couldn't manage to get us to completely stop thinking," Marphissa replied.

"Some people never needed any encouragement to stop thinking, Kommodor, and some never started thinking at all. Send this to Colonel Rogero now, so he can prepare for loading his soldiers. We'll be under some serious g-forces while his people are getting into the shuttles, and even with combat armor that will make things difficult for them."

THREE light-minutes separated the two flotillas, each racing toward the other at point one light speed, for a combined closing rate of point two light speed. That meant fifteen minutes until the two forces came into very brief contact.

Very brief, but long enough for their weapons to hurt the other.

Iceni reviewed her flotilla's readiness for at least the hundredth time in the last several minutes. Every unit at combat readiness state one, every weapon ready to fire, targeting systems locked on to the approaching flotilla. She had left her flotilla in the box formation, deciding that messing with that would be one change too many and probably more than she could handle anyway. *Just because you may have figured out one thing about Black Jack doesn't mean you're anything close to being him.*

"Here go the automated commands," Marphissa reported as she tapped her controls. "Beginning countdown to activation."

Thirty seconds later, the commanding officer of C-413 called in. "What kind of plan is this?"

"A plan ordered by President Iceni," Marphissa replied. "Activation in twenty-five seconds. Failure to activate will have to be explained to her."

"I— We'll speak of this later!"

"Ten seconds to activation." Marphissa gave a sudden look of alarm to Iceni. "Are you prone to motion sickness?"

"I hope not."

"Activation!" the maneuvering specialist announced.

Heavy cruiser C-448 and every other warship in Iceni's flotilla jerked into sudden maximum acceleration as the inertial nullifiers groaned in protest. Iceni kept her eyes on her display, trying to breathe slowly and deeply despite the pressure. It would be only a few more seconds until the other flotilla saw her flotilla altering velocity. Since any combined velocity above point two light speed complicated targeting solutions and started reducing chances of hits at an increasing rate, the automated systems on the other flotilla's ships would respond by pivoting their units around and firing off the main drives to brake their velocity.

The force on Iceni halted abruptly as the main drives in her flotilla cut off. Other pressures jerked at her as thrusters pivoted her flotilla's warships up and over, then the main drives kicked in again at maximum, shedding velocity as hard as they could.

Within seconds, the other flotilla saw the moves, kicking off its own drives, pivoting its ships again, then accelerating at maximum to once more try to compensate for the maneuvers of Iceni's flotilla.

"Three minutes to contact," the maneuvering specialist gasped as the main drives in Iceni's flotilla cut off again. Once more, thrusters fired, swinging the warships up and over again toward the other flotilla, main drives lighting off at maximum before the warships had even steadied out.

"They are going to be hating us over there," Marphissa got out with a strained laugh as they saw the automated systems on the other warships react again. Trained human crews would have seen the small time remaining until contact and known the need to override the attempts of the automated systems to match the maneuvers of Iceni's flotilla.

The snakes controlling that other flotilla were not trained crews, and right about now would be feeling very disoriented.

The other warships cut off accelerating and started swinging again, this time down, at the same moments as the two forces rushed toward contact. The bows of the opposing flotilla, where most armaments and the strongest armor and shields were clustered, were actually swinging away from Iceni's warships. She could imagine the curses that the humans on the other flotilla were uttering as their weaponry passed out of engagement envelopes just as Iceni's warships flashed through that moment of close contact.

Iceni's own ships were better aligned to fire, but far from perfectly because of the jumble of maneuvers. She felt the cruiser under her tremble slightly as hell lances and grapeshot tore out toward the other warships, her senses not really registering any of that until her flotilla had raced past the others. Iceni's flotilla was adjusting vectors to aim straight for the increasingly close gas giant, while the other flotilla flailed around, the two forces diverging at something close to point two light speed.

Laughter broke out on the bridge, startling Iceni. "Can

you imagine their faces right now?" she heard one of the specialists say to another.

"Quiet on the bridge," Marphissa called, but not harshly since she was grinning, too. "Too bad we couldn't score many hits ourselves."

"We hurt them a little," Iceni observed, watching her display update as the sensors of her flotilla coordinated their readings and produced a single analysis of damage to the other ships. "But, mainly, we got past them without being hit ourselves." The only hits on her own warships had been a few glancing blows, easily deflected by even the weak shields on the Hunter-Killers.

Battles were supposed to be about inflicting as much damage as possible on the enemy. Her orders and Marphissa's plan had turned that on its head, instead turning the engagement into avoiding damage. Since the other flotilla hadn't expected that, and had been controlled by snakes with little experience at mobile commands, it had worked exactly as intended. So when the commanders of the other ships began calling in, expressing frustration and dismay over the odd engagement, Iceni answered them instead of letting Marphissa handle it. "Our goal in that engagement was to get through to the battleship with minimum delay. That we achieved. Review the rest of the plan. Once we drop off the shuttles carrying the ground forces, we are going back to hurt that other flotilla because by then it is going to be trying to get past *us*. Does anyone have any problems with *my* decisions?"

Unsurprisingly, no one expressed such concerns to her. Everyone also stopped complaining to Marphissa, who nonetheless looked dissatisfied. "They should respect my decisions, too."

"They will. Or I'll get rid of them and find commanders who do." That statement, Iceni was sure, would also find its way around the flotilla by informal means.

The gas giant loomed ever larger before them. Off to one side, the bulk of the mobile forces facility, slightly smaller than Midway's, hung in a geostationary orbit which ensured it would always be within line of sight of the second planet except for a single brief window each year when the star blocked it as the second planet orbited Kane. Swinging in past the facility was the merchant ship they had been tracking, ponderously braking itself as it began to pass out of sight around the curve of the gas giant. Unlike the warships, the merchant ship could only change velocity slowly.

"We can divert a HuK or a light cruiser out of our formation to intercept and take out that merchant ship," Marphissa said suddenly.

"Do it. Make it a light cruiser. I want the snakes on that freighter to know a little fear as they see it coming for them."

"This is Kommodor Marphissa to light cruiser CL-773. Detach from formation, intercept as soon as possible and destroy the freighter tagged by my targeting system."

"This is CL-773. Understand detach and destroy. Confirm we are not to accept surrender of the merchant?"

Marphissa looked to Iceni, who shook her head. "Confirm destroy, do not accept surrender, CL-773."

"Yes, Kommodor."

"We couldn't trust that they would actually abide by a surrender offer," Iceni commented, annoyed with herself that she was justifying her decision to her subordinates.

"They would not," Marphissa agreed. "It would be a trick to buy them time to reach the battleship."

The flotilla had begun bending around the curve of the gas giant, the maneuvering systems pivoting the warships again so that they could brake velocity down once more, this time for a sustained period, and arc onto a vector that would, for a while, match a partial orbit about the gas giant. As they did so, CL-773 angled away, its vector aiming in a tight curve for an intercept with the frantically decelerating freighter.

"There it is!" Marphissa cried as part of the battleship finally appeared, its bulk hanging in a low orbit. "Communications, we're a lot closer and in line of sight. Try to punch a message through to Sub-Executive Kontos and let him know we're almost there."

Iceni inhaled deeply, feeling relief flood her. If the snakes hadn't broken through to Kontos yet, then success might be very close indeed. "Colonel Rogero, are your forces ready?"

"Yes, Madam President." Like the rest of the ground forces, Rogero wore full combat armor, the mass of it looming in the passageway where the special forces waited to run through the access tube and into the shuttle mated to the outside of the heavy cruiser. Iceni checked the other heavy cruisers, seeing their status reports indicating their shuttles preparing for separation.

The strain on the warships grew as they swung closer to the gas giant and the battleship while simultaneously trying to reduce their velocity so that it would be slow enough to safely release the shuttles for their assault on the battleship. Normally, this kind of maneuver, a close swing by a planet or star, was made to use their gravity to accelerate ships. Iceni's flotilla was instead fighting that, and she could hear the hull of the heavy cruiser creak alarmingly as it protested the forces wrenching at it. The moan of the inertial nullifiers rose to a higher-pitched shriek as they maxed out. Iceni's display flashed red, frenzied warnings blinking for attention.

Reengage maneuvering safeties immediately.
Exceeding maximum stress conditions.
Hull failure possible.
Inertial nullifiers overstressing.
System failures imminent.

"Kom . . . mo . . . dor," Iceni struggled to say over the strain of the g-forces.

"Forces . . . are . . . passing . . . maximum . . . now," Marphissa got out, and as she finished Iceni could feel the pressure on her body ease and hear the pitch of the nullifiers begin to descend.

The battleship was growing in size at alarming speed

while the warships kept slowing as fast as their main propulsion units and hull structures could manage. "Go, Colonel," Iceni said, but Rogero already had his soldiers in motion, the hulking figures in their armor stumbling down the access tube into the shuttle and latching into the seats there. Without the power assist from their armor, the soldiers couldn't have moved under such conditions.

"Forty seconds to shuttle launch," the operations specialist announced.

Iceni watched the last soldiers hurling themselves onto the shuttle as the seconds scrolled down. "We're still going too fast," she said to Marphissa.

"We'll be within acceptable parameters when we launch the shuttles," Marphissa replied, her eyes locked on her display.

Iceni could see the velocity markers edging down steadily, dropping to meet the safety margins for shuttle launch, and wondered if they would make that. The battleship appeared to be right on top of them, so huge compared to even the heavy cruisers that it seemed to be more a moon shaped like a massive pregnant shark rather than something made by the hands of humanity.

"Ten seconds to launch."

"We're not there, Kommodor!" Iceni said.

"We will be." Marphissa didn't take her eyes off of her display, one hand hovering over the command for the shuttle launch.

Off to one side, light cruiser CL-773 tore past the merchant ship, pumping out hell-lance fire and slamming two grapeshot bundles into the ship's command deck, the impacts knocking the merchant ship off course. Rolling slightly, the merchant ship wobbled onto a descent toward the gas giant.

"Five seconds."

The velocity markers and launch margins were coming together as Marphissa's hand swept down a small distance. "Launch!"

Iceni watched the symbol of the shuttle detach from her

heavy cruiser, the other two shuttles breaking free of their own cruisers within a couple of seconds and following the first in a dive toward the battleship which now seemed to fill space before them.

"We're coming under fire," the combat specialist exclaimed. "Hell lances from the battleship."

"How many?" Marphissa demanded.

"One . . . three . . . four hell-lance projectors. They're not firing in a volley. They must be under local control."

"The snakes," Marphissa said. "Sub-Exec Kontos's people still command the fire-control center, so the snakes can only employ as many hell lances as they can manually aim and fire."

"Four hell-lance projectors is still too many when we only have three shuttles!" Iceni retorted.

"C-555 is taking hits," the operations specialist said. "They're targeting the heavy cruisers."

Iceni laughed in sudden relief. "Idiots. They probably haven't even noticed the shuttles yet." Her heavy cruiser, like the other warships, was pivoting again, turning to continue around the curve of the gas giant, gratefully accepting the gravity assist from the huge planet as the flotilla began accelerating once more.

The battleship was there, then behind them, still heart-stoppingly close. But the shuttles were almost in contact with the hull now. "Make sure you drop relays," Iceni ordered. "I want to be able to monitor the special forces once we're out of line of sight. Have you managed to contact Sub-Exec Kontos?"

"No, Madam President. We'll drop two relays as we come around the planet."

"Shuttles have made contact," the operations specialist said. "Reporting solid locks on the hull at targeted locations."

"They're inside the firing zones of the hell lances," the weapons specialist added. "The shuttles are safe from defensive fire."

On her display, Iceni's eyes held for a moment on an

image of the crippled merchant ship, its control gone, gliding past the battleship and sliding inexorably closer to the gas giant's atmosphere. Anyone still alive on that ship wouldn't be alive much longer. *There's nothing I can do about it. They're too far behind us now for any of my ships to get back there in time even if I wanted to rescue snakes from that fate.*

But it's still an awful way to die.

"Give me a display linked to the ground forces assault teams," Iceni ordered. Moments later the display popped up next to her. All she had to do was turn her head and touch individual screens to see exactly where the team leaders were and what they were doing. The screens flickered, then steadied. "What was that?"

"Something on the battleship tried to jam the connection," the comms specialist said. "We powered through it."

"Give me the— Where's the—" Iceni finally hit the right touch spot, and the view from Rogero's armor expanded while his comms became audible to her.

The view felt odd, looking through the vacuum of space at an angle along a slightly curving wall where other suits of combat armor clung. "Get the lock open," she heard Rogero order.

One of the soldiers placed a palm-sized device with care, then waited while information scrolled across the readout on the device. "Access code broken," the soldier near the device reported. "Override code blocked. Auto-lock overridden. Local lock disengaged."

A large section of wall faded back, then slid sideways. From Rogero's position, Iceni could see the outer layer of armor on the battleship forming a thick bar on the side of the lock. "Inside," Rogero ordered. "Full combat footing, weapons free to fire."

CHAPTER ELEVEN

SHE had read Rogero's plan and knew that each team of special forces had an objective. One would head for the engineering control center to rescue the surviving crew there. The second for the weapons fire-control center. And the third, with Rogero, for the bridge.

They had to get through two more air locks to reach the interior of the battleship, passing successive layers of heavy armor and leaving tiny comm relays in their wake to keep the signals clear even when the air-lock hatches sealed behind them. The soldiers encountered no one as they cleared the last lock and stood within the passageways of the battleship, stretching eerily empty in all directions.

One soldier raised an arm to point. "Surveillance cam up there watching the lock exit. That's not on standard battleship schematics."

"Snake gear," Rogero said. "They know we're inside now. Get going."

Rogero moved in the middle of his group as the three sets of soldiers scattered, heading for their respective goals. "Sub-Executive Kontos, this is Colonel Rogero of the independent Midway Star System. We are inside the hull and heading for your location. Can you hear me?"

No answer.

Iceni saw a swarm of symbols swim across Rogero's heads-up display. "Team Two has encountered resistance," someone reported to him, her voice slightly distant across the comm system tying the suits into one network whose every piece was mobile. "Not, repeat not, vipers."

"Try to get one alive," Rogero ordered, "so they can tell us how many of them are aboard and whether there are vipers anywhere on this thing."

"Negative. All dead." The other team leader didn't sound too regretful. "Proceeding to objective."

"How big are these damned things?" one of the soldiers muttered into the comm as they rounded a corner and headed down another long passageway broken at intervals by bulkheads with armored survival hatches set into them.

"You can get lost for days," another soldier remarked. "How come none of the internal hatches are being sealed on us, Colonel?"

"Controlled from the bridge," Rogero replied. "Part of the antimutiny system. The snakes can only override one hatch at a time. Left here," he ordered as they reached an intersection of passageways.

"But the plan in our suits—"

"Is a straight shot to the bridge. Guess where the snakes will be waiting for us?"

"Team Three meeting resistance. One soldier down."

"Team Two has hit an ambush. Four, five snakes. Got one still alive."

"Make the snake talk," Rogero said, his voice toneless despite the exertion in it as his team trotted down another stretch of passageway.

"Team Three through resistance. Four snakes dead."

"Team Two reporting prisoner died before talking. Looks like conditioning-driven suicide."

"That is sick," a soldier grumbled.

"They're damned snakes; what do you expect?"

"Keep it down," Rogero ordered. "Right here and up that ramp."

Iceni pulled her attention away from the soldiers for a moment, refocusing on the bridge of her heavy cruiser. "How does it look?" she asked Marphissa.

"The other flotilla is coming back, heading straight for the battleship. We're twenty minutes from intercept. How are the dirt eaters doing?"

"So far, so good. Get my attention when we're ten minutes from intercept. I want fire concentrated on the heavy cruiser and the light cruisers. Those HuKs could pound the battleship all day and hardly scratch it."

"Yes, Madam President."

Back to Rogero, who was in yet another long passageway but moving more slowly, his soldiers moving in groups of two which rushed forward while others covered their movement with their weapons. The bridge was located deep inside the hull, well protected and linked to exterior sensors so that it had as good a view as if it were on the outside of the hull in a compartment lined with picture windows. *Windows on a warship. What a funny idea,* Iceni thought. *Who would put actual windows on any spaceship instead of using virtual ones and keeping the hull as strong as possible everywhere?*

"Ten meters to the bridge citadel boundaries," one of the soldiers said. "Where the hell are they?"

"Hopefully not in—" The soldier who had spoken flung himself backward as weapons fire lashed the passageway.

"We found 'em!" someone yelled as Rogero's team all fired, the crisscrossing patterns of fire in the passageway momentarily intense enough to cause Rogero's face shield to protectively darken nearly to black.

"Move!" Rogero yelled. The soldiers charged forward, the fire from the light weaponry of the snakes glancing off their armor and staggering the soldiers as they ran straight at the defenders.

Iceni couldn't grasp what was happening for the next few moments as images flashed by too quickly to interpret.

Rogero was with his soldiers, firing, shapes in lighter armor were falling, springing up, trying to run, only to fall, sometimes in pieces as more than one hit from the soldiers' weapons literally tore apart some of the snakes.

"Area clear."

"Spread out and check for more," Rogero ordered, stepping over one of the dead snakes to peer around a corner. Down a short passageway sat the heavily armored main hatch leading onto the bridge. Scars on the armor told of attempts to break through it, and damage to the nearby bulkheads and overhead marked active defenses for the bridge that had been destroyed by the snakes so they could gain access to the hatch.

The plug-in for the local comm net was still fine, though. Rogero shoved a wireless link into it. "On the bridge, this is Colonel Rogero. The snakes out here are dead."

The reply took a moment. "Colonel?"

"Sub-CEO. We've changed our rank titles now that we're no longer subject to Syndicate rule. Do you have control of the internal monitoring system? We don't know how many snakes are aboard or where they are."

Another voice broke in on Rogero. "Team Three has reached the fire-control center. Contacting occupants now."

"Team Two is engaging another snake strongpoint just short of engineering control."

The voice from the bridge came on, loud and stressed. "Main propulsion! You need to get to main propulsion!"

"We've got people almost to engineering control—" Rogero began.

"No! Main propulsion. The snakes couldn't run the main drives, but they could rig the fuel cells to blow! They threatened to do that if we didn't surrender."

"Now you tell us," Rogero growled. "Team Two, Team Three, new orders. Leave sections to protect the fire-control center and engineering control, and the rest of you get down to the fuel-cell bunkers as fast as you can and look for sabotage. The snakes have threatened to blow the cells."

"What are we looking for, Colonel?"

"Explosive charges, det cord, timers, nuclear weapons, anything that doesn't belong."

"Sir, we don't know what belongs in fuel-cell bunkers—"

Iceni broke in, speaking to both Rogero and Marphissa. "We're setting up a link to engineers on the warships for your soldiers. By the time they get down there, we can have engineer eyes to assist their search."

"Understood," Rogero called back. "The sooner the better."

"I've got a battle to fight here!" Marphissa snarled as she frantically hit some commands. "We're eleven minutes from contact with the other flotilla . . . ten minutes now. Comms, get engineers on the heavy cruisers linked to the ground forces net. Everyone else, eyes on the other flotilla!"

Ten minutes. Iceni checked her display, where the two flotillas were coming together at a slight angle this time since the other force was aiming for the battleship rather than trying to hit Iceni's flotilla. That didn't make them any less dangerous, though, and her own CL-773 light cruiser was still trying to claw back into formation but a bit behind.

Well behind them, but angling around the curve of the planet, the doomed merchant ship was glowing with heat as it coasted through the upper layers of the gas giant's atmosphere. Part of the merchant ship broke free, spinning deeper into the atmosphere to form a trail of bright fire before it vanished. Iceni tore her eyes from the sight, hoping that no one on the freighter was still alive to suffer through its destruction.

Marphissa was chewing her lip as she eyed the oncoming flotilla. "With CL-773 lagging, we're tied with them for light cruisers and only have a superiority of one Hunter-Killer, seven to six. Our advantage is in having three heavy cruisers to their one."

"What is your argument?" Iceni asked.

"You ordered me to target the light cruisers and heavy cruiser. That will disperse our fire and make it unlikely we can achieve any kills on this pass. I want to either concentrate fire on the lone heavy cruiser, or on the three light cruisers."

"I don't like that. Either way, you would be letting some significant firepower get past us."

"If I try to engage all of them, Madam President, *all* of their significant firepower will get past us."

Subordinates didn't argue with CEOs very often, knowing the futility of it and not wanting to risk the consequences. Iceni gave Marphissa a cross look. "I don't like either alternative."

"There are no other alternatives. We don't have enough warships to stop all of them in one pass."

"Then which do you recommend?" Iceni asked, knowing how she sounded from the way the specialists on the bridge were taking care to avoid doing anything that might attract her attention. "The light cruisers or the heavy?"

Marphissa stabbed one finger at her display. "The heavy. Whoever is in charge of the snakes will be on the heavy. If we decapitate the snake force, the others may take some time deciding who is in charge, or even call superiors elsewhere for instructions."

"Or they may go on and hit the battleship in some vital spots while it can't defend itself."

"Yes, Madam President."

A frustrated pause. "Get the heavy cruiser."

"Yes, Madam President."

Of course, if the snakes had rigged the fuel cells on the battleship to explode, and the soldiers couldn't disarm the sabotage in time, the battleship was going to be blown apart regardless of how the engagement between flotillas went. And she couldn't dive back into watching how the soldiers were doing, not when her flotilla was less than five minutes from clashing again with the other warships.

The box formation of Iceni's flotilla was actually coming in from slightly above and to the side of the other formation and would cut at a diagonal through the other flotilla during the firing pass. Marphissa was aiming straight for the heavy cruiser at the center of the other formation, and Iceni could see the units in the other flotilla beginning to pivot a bit so they would be bow on to the attack while continuing in the same direction toward the battleship. "Combined closing speed of point one six light this time," Marphissa commented. "And only a small deflection on the targets. We should have good hits."

"So should they," Iceni replied.

There was nothing else to do but wait and watch the other flotilla rapidly swell in size, then in an instant be right there and in the next instant be gone, the heavy cruiser Iceni was riding rocking from impacts and alarms warning of damage. "All units come starboard one three zero degrees, up zero seven degrees, immediate execute," Marphissa was ordering.

The flotilla began curving around to try to catch the other force again. Most of the flotilla, anyway. "CL-924 and HuK-2061 have suffered propulsion damage," the operations specialist was saying.

At the same time, the combat specialist was reporting on damage to their own ship. "Hell lance battery one is inactive. Missile launcher three disabled. Several hull penetrations, no critical systems lost."

"Get the penetrations sealed," Marphissa ordered. "I need that missile launcher back online."

"We don't have the means to repair it," the combat specialist replied hesitantly. "Damage is too extensive. We'll need repair support."

Marphissa clenched one fist, shaking her head. "If this were an Alliance warship, we'd have enough people and parts aboard to fix damage like that. Damn the Syndicate bureaucrats and their cost-cutting 'efficiencies.'"

Iceni remembered the same frustration from her time in the mobile forces, having to wait to repair any significant damage until civilian contractors could arrive. "We can change that, but it won't happen overnight."

"Thank you, Madam President. The other flotilla must have concentrated their fire on this cruiser. It's a good thing they had fewer heavy cruisers than we did."

Reports were also coming in on damage to the other side as the sensors on Iceni's warships spotted and evaluated whatever could be observed, and Iceni could see damage markers blinking into existence on the symbol of the lone heavy cruiser in the other flotilla. "At least we hurt him worse than he did us."

The extra firepower of Iceni's three heavy cruisers had made a difference, inflicting serious damage on the enemy cruiser. "He's completely lost maneuvering, drifting away from the rest of his formation," the operations specialist said.

"But he's not dead yet."

"No. It looks like he still has comms to the rest of his force, and there are some weapons assessed still operational."

Iceni turned a narrow-eyed look on Marphissa, who was frowning in thought. "I think we should go for the kill on the heavy cruiser," Marphissa said.

"Why?"

"Because we can't catch the rest of the other flotilla before it reaches the battleship. But if the commander on that heavy cruiser gets scared enough, they will be yelling for help and may order back their own units to save them."

Another set of bad choices to choose from. "There's no way of catching the light cruisers?"

"Not unless they turn back toward us."

"A possibility that you didn't mention when asking me to concentrate our fire on the heavy cruiser!" Iceni tried to suppress anger and frustration, knowing that she had to make the decision quickly and still worried about what might be happening on the battleship. *Go for the head. When dealing with snakes, always go for the head.* "Get the heavy cruiser. This time I want it destroyed."

"Yes, Madam President!" Kommodor Marphissa adjusted the course of her units, curving away from a stern chase of the light cruisers and HuKs remaining in the other flotilla, and aiming for the crippled heavy cruiser. "Twelve minutes to intercept."

"Get my attention at five minutes." Iceni turned to focus on the display showing the soldiers again.

Many of them still showed empty passageways. A few revealed worn-looking mobile forces personnel in the engineering and fire-control citadels, their faces still reflecting disbelief and joy at the arrival of rescuers. Rogero and some soldiers with him were still stalled outside the bridge.

But roughly half showed engineering spaces, most of them with ranks of fuel cells looming nearby, the soldiers' points of view swinging as they hastily examined the area for evidence of sabotage.

"I can't see anything here that shouldn't be," an unfamiliar voice complained, probably one of the engineers on one of Iceni's heavy cruisers. "Try to find something that doesn't belong," the engineer instructed the soldiers.

"How can I find something that doesn't belong when I don't know what does belong?" one of the soldiers replied in exasperated tones.

"Look for something that looks like it could explode."

"I thought everything down here could explode!"

"It can! You want to find the things that could explode but aren't supposed to be there, so they don't blow up the things that could explode but are supposed to be there!"

"What?"

Rogero's voice broke in. "Just scan as much as you can as fast as you can. Engineers, tell me what the most effective means of setting off the fuel cells would be. That might help us narrow our search."

A pause, while the images of the fuel cells continued to stream past, then another voice came on. "Actually, if you want to make sure they all blew, you'd want to ensure the cells didn't just rupture but were hit hard enough to detonate."

"What would that take?" Rogero asked.

"Umm . . . ten-kiloton nuclear device or larger."

"We can detect nukes. There aren't any down there."

"Then . . . oh. It's not in the fuel cell area at all."

Another engineer's voice. "You don't mean sympathetic ignition?"

"Yes, that would do it."

A third engineer's voice. "That's obvious, isn't it? If you work the calculations—"

Rogero, almost shouting this time. *"Where. Is. It?"*

"Primary feed for the fuel cells. If you rig the feed to release all energy in a single event instead of a controlled release into the power core, you'd get a blowback into the fuel-cell storage area, which would detonate the rest of the cells in storage, and the entire stern of the battleship would be blown to atoms. That's assuming the power core didn't also overload—"

"Get to that feed," Rogero ordered his soldiers. "You in engineering control, I need a software check to see if any snake viruses are in the propulsion-regulation systems or power-core-regulation systems."

"But, Colonel," one of the soldiers protested, "the snakes said the fuel cells—"

"Run that statement by one more time and see what's wrong with it! 'The snakes said'? Doesn't that mean the truth is going to be anything but that?"

"Five minutes, Madam President."

Iceni jolted her attention back to the bridge of the heavy cruiser. Drakon had apparently been right about Rogero's virtues as a leader. "We may save the battleship after all."

"What?" Marphissa asked with an appalled look. "Something—?"

"Never mind. Where's the rest of the other flotilla?"

"Here." The other flotilla glowed brighter on Iceni's display, the vector from it leading inexorably to the battleship. "Fourteen minutes before they can open fire on the battleship. I've warned the shuttles to get on the opposite side of the battleship so they can't be targeted."

"Good." The course of their own formation was bending just as relentlessly toward the damaged heavy cruiser.

"The damaged heavy cruiser is putting out escape pods," the operations specialist said. "One . . . two . . . three."

Marphissa frowned at the display. "Only three? We can't have killed that much of the crew already." Red danger markers flashed on the displays. "The cruiser is firing its still-operational hell lances? We're still far too— Damn. They're firing on their own pods."

"Who's in the pods?" Iceni demanded. "Snakes or crew members trying to escape the snakes?"

"Three more escape pods just ejected."

"We've got comms from one of the pods," the communications specialist cried. "Kommodor, they say they're crew, trying to escape and surrender. The snakes control the bridge."

Marphissa looked at Iceni. "Are they really crew? Or escaping snakes? What do we target?"

"The cruiser. If the snakes turn out to be in the escape pods, we can easily run them down later."

"But if the cruiser is already controlled by what's left of the crew—"

"Then they waited too damned long before taking over." Iceni kept her tone cold to hide the sick feeling in her gut. *I have to decide now. I hope I'm right.*

"One minute to intercept."

Marphissa tapped a control. "All weapons target the cruiser. We want a kill this time," she ordered in a flat voice.

The flotilla flashed by the heavy cruiser, hell lances and grapeshot slamming into the crippled unit, and as they curved away, Iceni watched the display light up. "We blew their power core. Did the escape pods get far enough clear to survive the core explosion?"

"Yes. They took some damage, though."

"They'll have to live with it for a while. No. Send that damaged light cruiser and HuK to intercept the escape pods," Iceni ordered. "They can handle that. Get the rest of us back to the battleship."

The remainder of the other flotilla was still aiming for

the battleship, but they would see the fate of the heavy cruiser at any moment. Iceni, trying to guess how much damage the light escorts could do a battleship without operational shields, touched her comm control. "All units in the flotilla approaching the battleship, this is President Iceni. Be aware that my forces have seized and now control that battleship and everything on it. A portion of its weapons are operational." Almost pure bluff since the soldiers probably couldn't get to any of the few working hell lances in time to fire them at the approaching warships. "All the snakes aboard it are dead. Your flagship has been destroyed. Any unit that ceases attacking my forces will be granted mercy. Stop fighting for the Syndicate system. It failed. Fight for yourselves. For the people, Iceni, out."

And she waited. Waited for the light-speed message to reach the other flotilla, itself only a couple of minutes from reaching the battleship, and for the light from any reaction to come back to her.

And saw one of the other formation's light cruisers suddenly peel away, bending toward empty space.

"That got their attention," Marphissa commented with a grin. "There goes another."

"Three HuKs taking evasive action away from their formation," the operations specialist said. "Because of time variations, the actions don't seem to have been coordinated."

The remaining two light cruisers and three HuKs in the other formation abruptly altered their own vectors, curving upward to avoid the firing envelope of the battleship and cross above the gas giant. As they cleared the gas giant, one more light cruiser and another HuK lurched away from their comrades, leaving the formation down to one light cruiser and two HuKs, which seemed to be aiming toward Kane. "Second planet," Marphissa predicted. "That will be their objective."

"Why run back there?" Iceni asked.

"Because there are probably some high-ranking snakes on that planet who are going to want to be evacuated.

Comms, see if we can get into contact with any of those light cruisers or HuKs that left their formation. Are we to continue toward the battleship, Madam President?"

"Yes. Make sure the light cruiser and HuK picking up the escape pods are ready for anything. I want to know who is really in those escape pods. If they're occupied by snakes, those snakes may be armed." She turned to look at Rogero's view, seeing the still-sealed bridge hatch. "Colonel, status report."

"We found the sabotage to the fuel-cell-feed system. If we'd tried to move the battleship it would have blown its own butt off, if you'll pardon the phrase."

"But it's not a danger now?"

"There's no imminent threat of the battleship's blowing up, Madam President. But we don't have control because the bridge is still sealed against us. They won't open up for me. They think it's a snake trick. They know you from your transmission, and say if you show up they'll know we've really cleaned out the snakes and it's safe to open up."

That was annoying, but . . . "Is it safe for me to come aboard?"

"Not entirely. The internal monitoring system is a mess, and what does work runs through the bridge. But if there are any snakes still lurking in the underbrush, we will be able to protect you from them."

"All right. We'll bring C-448 to a relative stop near the battleship and have a shuttle take me over to you."

IT was very hard to believe that the danger was over. The other flotilla had been defeated, most of its units refusing to fight her anymore as their surviving officers and crews sent out feelers to discover what Iceni intended here at Kane. She would have to let Marphissa handle those for a little while because it was more important to get the bridge on the battleship opened up.

Iceni walked from the shuttle, through the air lock, and onto the decks of the battleship. Her battleship. The shuttle dock on board wasn't functional yet, so access tubes and air locks would have to do. As warships went, the battleship was a bit of a fixer-upper, but as warships went, it was also the finest defensive unit she could hope for.

Colonel Rogero was waiting for her, standing and looking down the passageway toward her as she walked out of the air lock and turned to face him. He began to salute, then his weapon came up and he fired.

CHAPTER TWELVE

ICENI thought that her heart had stopped, only slowly realizing that Rogero had only fired once and that the shot had gone past her. She turned her head, seeing a snake still standing several meters behind her, swaying, a large hole in his chest. The snake's weapon fell from hands that had lost life and strength, then he collapsed to the deck.

Rogero jogged past her to examine the snake and confirm that he was dead.

She swallowed, her heart pounding back into life. "I thought you said your soldiers would provide security for my visit to this unit, Colonel Rogero."

"I have guards posted—"

"Then *whichever* guard is posted on *that* hallway is either already dead or soon will be—"

"Madam President." Rogero's voice halted her in midsentencing to a firing squad. "I left that passageway unguarded."

She could either order him shot immediately or learn Rogero's reasons. *"Why?"* Iceni asked with what she thought was admirable control.

"Because we knew that the snakes had seeded this unit with surveillance gear, but we couldn't find all of it in the time we've had to work. Any surviving snakes would have known where I had guards on watch, would have known a shuttle was coming in, implying that a VIP was on the way, and would have seen that passageway unwatched. We also know these snakes had been conditioned to fight to the death rather than surrender. A surviving snake, seeing a path 'accidentally' left open, would have taken the opportunity to get the VIP using that opening rather than risk an ambush later on, an ambush that could have come at us at any time, from any direction."

"And just *how* did this contribute to my security, Colonel Rogero?"

"It meant I knew exactly where and when to watch for anyone trying to attack you, Madam President."

She stared at Rogero, still angry but realizing the logic of what he had done. "Very good. *Don't* do that again."

"Yes, Madam President."

"Is that the sort of thing that General Drakon rewards in his subordinates?"

"Yes, Madam President."

"I am different, Colonel Rogero. You'd be advised not to forget that. Lead me to the bridge."

The short passageway in front of the bridge hatch felt menacing to Iceni as she walked partway down it, knowing that the eyes of the surviving crew on the bridge, and any surviving internal defenses, were focused on her. "This is President Iceni. This mobile forces unit is now under the control of the forces of the independent star system of Midway. I promise you safety. Now open up for us."

The wait that followed seemed far too long. She was wondering if she should say more when Iceni heard gears hum into life and the soft hiss of massive bolts being withdrawn. There came a thunk, then the hatch swung inward with the ponderous movements of something that carried a lot of mass.

Iceni walked forward as Colonel Rogero and the nearby soldiers followed.

The bridge didn't smell too good, which wasn't surprising since its life support had been running on emergency local isolation mode for some time and the crew members inside the bridge clearly didn't smell too good, either. Sub-Executive Kontos was forming the survivors on the bridge into two short ranks facing the entrance.

As Iceni halted, Kontos turned, the movement causing him to stagger dizzily against the nearest equipment. She waited while he straightened and saluted with an arm that wavered before Kontos's fist hit his breast. "Sub-Executive Kontos, acting commanding officer of the outfitting crew on B-78."

Iceni returned the salute with a solemn expression, seeing how the line workers standing in ranks swayed on their feet, their gaunt faces reflecting deprivation. "You've been on short rations?"

"The emergency supplies were not yet fully stocked since the unit is not operational," Kontos replied in a clear, strong voice. "We have rationed supplies as necessary to hold our position until relieved." Then he fell sideways again against another console and struggled to stand up.

"Everyone relax," Iceni ordered. "Including you, Sub-Executive Kontos. Sit down, lie down, whatever you need. Colonel Rogero, get food and water up here. Kommodor Marphissa, do we still have a link?"

"Yes, Madam President."

"Get that shuttle back to you. I want C-448's physician and her assistant on this battleship as soon as possible. These crew members need attention. I don't know what medical supplies are aboard this unit, so make sure she brings an emergency field pack."

Rogero, who had finally opened his armor's face shield, knelt to help Kontos sit back against a console. Straightening up again, he came to stand by Iceni and speak in a low voice. "He held them together. They've been slowly starving in here, isolated with no comms except when they managed to get around the snake blocks for brief periods, but he kept them from giving in. Pretty impressive for a junior subexecutive."

"Do you think that I'd judge him harshly because he collapsed?"

"He is not at his best now," Rogero said diplomatically.

"I can tell when someone has taken himself to the limit, Colonel Rogero, and I realize what it must have required to keep the rest of the crew effectively resisting." Iceni nodded as she looked at Kontos where he sat slackly against the console. "If Sub-Executive Kontos wishes to remain with us, he will be more than welcome as one of our mobile forces officers."

Rogero smiled. "I was going to say that if you didn't want him, I was certain that General Drakon would."

"Too bad. I've got dibs on him, Colonel."

"You're already getting the battleship, Madam President."

Iceni stared at him. Rogero had a sense of humor. Who would have thought it? "I heard that one of your soldiers was injured."

"Wounded. Not seriously. The snakes were equipped to slaughter unprepared mobile forces crew members, not to fight combat-armored troops."

"How very unfortunate for them."

"President Iceni?"

"Yes, Kommodor."

"Light cruiser CL-924 has picked up the first escape pod from the heavy cruiser. They confirm that the occupants are crew, not snakes."

Iceni fought down a sense of relief as suspicion rose in counterpoint to it. "They have identification as crew members or they are crew members?"

"They are, Madam President. I sent their images around the flotilla, and one of them is known to someone on C-413."

"Good." Iceni looked at the exhausted survivors of the outfitting crew around her as some soldiers arrived bearing ration packs. "Get that doctor over here."

SHE spent a while touring the battleship under the watchful eyes of two of Rogero's soldiers, who were along just in case any more snakes were lurking in the tremendous number of compartments and passageways inside the ship. The fire-control citadel and the engineering control citadel both had fewer survivors in them than the bridge had, but the crew there reported that Sub-Executive Kontos had managed to stay in communication with them despite snake efforts to break the links.

There was considerable irony in that, Iceni realized. The citadels existed because of fear the line workers in the crew might mutiny, or that the ship would be boarded by Alliance Marines. The citadels were designed and intended as places where the officers and ISS agents could hold out for a long time until the unit could be retaken by Syndicate forces. But the measures intended to make certain of Syndicate control had instead been used to save a good portion of the outfitting crew from the snakes and had ensured that Iceni could wrest control of the battleship from the Syndicate Worlds.

"Madam President, Colonel Rogero asked us to inform you that the crew members from the bridge have been taken to the main sick bay. It's not fully outfitted, but the beds are in, and some of the equipment is working."

"Take me there."

The sick bay was far larger than it felt since the extensive wards and operating rooms were all divided at regular intervals by bulkheads intended to ensure that no single large compartment could be lost to damage or lose air pressure all at once. Like all battleships and battle cruisers, this ship was designed to deal with wounded from not just its own crew but the crews of any smaller escorts, ground forces, and anyone else.

At the moment, most of those half-equipped wards and rooms were silent and empty. The surviving members of the outfitting crew were almost all in a few wards, with just one representative of their teams remaining in each of the citadel locations. "Where is Sub-Executive Kontos?" Iceni asked Rogero when she saw him.

"He insisted on remaining on the bridge until properly relieved. The physician has been to see him, and I've made sure he's got food and water." Rogero gave her a questioning look. "Are you still sure that you want him?"

"Positive. Who's the senior surviving crew member in here?"

"Probably this one." Colonel Rogero led the way, his combat armor large and more menacing than usual in the environment of the sick bay, stopping at a bed holding a middle-aged man in a line worker's uniform. "The food and water, and some meds your physician dealt out, have them all half-conscious right now."

"I know how to wake him." The man lay flat, breathing heavily, his eyes on the ceiling but dazed and out of focus. Iceni came to a stop right by the bed. *"You,"* she said, giving the single word an intonation that only CEOs used, making of it the shorthand question that every worker knew had to be answered quickly and accurately. *Who are you, what is your job title, and what are you doing?*

Reflexes drilled into the worker by a lifetime of experience jolted him into awareness. The eyes snapped into focus and went to her face. "Senior Line Worker Mentasa, systems integration, assigned to the outfitting crew for Mobile Unit B-78." He struggled to sit up until Iceni reached out one hand and gently pushed him back.

"Rest," Iceni said. "What can you tell me about what happened aboard this unit?"

The line worker blinked as if unable to order his thoughts and confused by Iceni's actions, then nodded slowly. "We were working . . . our usual shifts. Our commander was . . . Sub-CEO Tanshivan. He was . . . what . . . supply ship. The supply ship. Priority delivery." Mentasa blinked again. "The sub-CEO . . . went to meet it. We were in . . . in comms with him. Lots of people came out of the lock. Lots. Weapons. Sub-CEO yells 'They're here to kill us.' Don't know how he knew. Yelled it. 'Seal citadels' he ordered. And then . . . and then . . . he died. I mean . . . they shot. And . . . we lost comms."

"You had no warning the snakes were coming? No reasons to think they might come?"

"No. Been . . . demonstar . . . demonstrations on the planet. Heard about that. Big rallies. Before the news feeds cut off. Not our business. Not sure what it was about. I never been here before. To Kane, I mean. A few days later . . . they came."

"So you sealed the citadels?"

"Yes." Line Worker Mentasa blinked back tears. "Not everybody inside. Just our shift. But . . . had to seal the citadels. Damned snakes . . . *killed* the rest. Then tried to get us to open up. Stupid. Killed their hostages. Stupid, damned snakes."

Rogero was nodding. "Their plan counted on surprise. The warning provided by the sub-CEO before he died helped negate that, but the snakes rigidly followed the same plan, killing all members of the outfitting crew as they encountered them. Only when they realized that the citadels had been sealed and couldn't be broken into with what they had did the snakes understand that they should have kept some hostages alive to force the ones in the citadels to open up."

"Yes, sir," Mentasa said, peering at Rogero. "Sorry we wouldn't open for you. We knew the lady, the . . . the CEO would save us."

Iceni shook her head, angry and not certain exactly why. "I'm not a CEO. I am President Iceni."

"I'm sorry, Madam . . . President? I don't know what a president is."

"Better than a CEO," Rogero replied.

"Uh, yes, sir. We saw the ship coming. The freighter. We had enough opticals working to see it come around the planet. We knew it had to have more snakes on it. And then you guys . . . you came around behind it and . . . and we knew the stars would save us—" Mentasa stopped speaking, his eyes widening in alarm.

Iceni smiled down at him. "Relax," she repeated. "I'm not afraid of your beliefs, and the rules of the Syndicate Worlds no longer apply where I am in control. If you want to speak of things like that, you can."

"Do you believe in the stars? In the ancestors?"

That was a question she had never expected to be asked, and it startled an honest reply out of her. "I don't . . . Yes."

"Because," Mentasa continued, his voice firming, "we saw that freighter coming. One more hour and they would have been here and we would have been dead. One more hour. Maybe half an hour. Maybe less. But you came. The stars wouldn't let us die."

Iceni gazed back wordlessly. *Then why didn't they save your comrades? The ones outside the citadels? Show me some reason in who lives and who dies. Why can't the stars do that? It would be much easier to hold to the faith of my father if they would.* "Where are you from?"

"I've been working in Taroa for about fifteen years now. Got a family there." Wariness had returned to the worker's eyes. CEOs had a tendency to draft workers they needed, and he must know that Iceni needed him to help get this battleship operational.

"You and the other survivors of the outfitting crew will be offered the chance to remain on this battleship and come with us," Iceni said. "Or you can take your chances here at Kane. If you come with us, you'll be allowed to continue on to Taroa if you want, but we'll offer good wages for you, and safety for your family from the snakes." *Does this man know what is going on at Taroa? Almost certainly not, and there seems no purpose in bringing it up right now.* "Once you've recovered somewhat, we'll ask you what your choice is."

"Thank you, Madam . . . President. The stars will judge you well for this day."

Turning away, Iceni walked for the exit. *If the stars or something else ever does judge my life, judges everything that I've done, I'm not expecting a happy outcome for myself from that.*

Just outside the exit, Iceni saw the physician from C-448

as she returned from checking the crew at the citadels. "How are they? All of them?"

The physician shrugged. She was an older woman, close to retirement age, who always seemed weighted by the lives she had failed to save in all the years of her service. "They are all malnourished and suffering from severe physical stress." She shrugged again. "When I was just starting out, I spent six months of my medical training as an assistant at a labor camp, so it's nothing I haven't seen before."

Labor camps. The Syndicate Worlds' all-purpose form of punishment short of immediate death. All too often, labor camps had simply been a more extended means of carrying out a death sentence. She had known people sent to labor camps. A few of them had come home when their sentences were up. The others hadn't survived long enough.

Thinking of that, and of what the snakes had tried to do here, and what the line workers had endured to make possible her own success, something inside Iceni fractured. "There will be no more labor camps. Not anywhere that I have authority." She walked away, leaving Rogero and the physician staring in her wake, her footsteps echoing hollowly through the empty passageways of the battleship as the soldiers guarding her hastened to catch up.

"TWO of the light cruisers want to join us," Marphissa reported. C-448 had mated to one side of the battleship, like a lamprey attached to a whale, allowing easy access for crew and supplies. "And two of the HuKs. The other light cruiser and the other two HuKs that left their flotilla want to head for the star systems where most of their crews came from."

"Where are those star systems?" Iceni asked, leaning back in the command seat of the battleship. Few of its controls worked at the moment, but it still felt awesome to sit there. With just her and Marphissa present, it only emphasized how much larger and impressive the battleship's bridge was compared to that of a heavy cruiser.

"The light cruiser wants to get to Cadez. The HuKs are aiming for Dermat and Kylta."

"None of those are close." Iceni sighed, feeling a curiously weary sensation now that the tension of the last several days was relieved by the successes. "But if they're home for those crews, I wish them luck. What about the light cruiser and two HuKs that headed for the second planet?"

"They're in orbit there. We've seen some shuttle activity. There are no signs of trouble on the planet, though, or in comms." Marphissa paused, her gaze wandering across the almost deserted bridge. "I talked with Colonel Rogero about that. We think the citizens here are waiting to see what you do, Madam President, and what the senior snakes do."

"That's a good guess. Citizens who don't learn to wait and see what their superiors are up to tend to pay a big price." Iceni smiled wryly at Marphissa. "Are you and the colonel friends now, Kommodor?"

"Not exactly friends. Mutual respect is probably the best term, I think. And I'm not crazy enough to want to get involved with a dirt eater even if he weren't giving off vibes of already being involved with someone else."

"Really?"

"It's just an impression. You know how some people seem to be wearing a ring even when they're not. Colonel Rogero felt like that to me."

Wearing a ring? With an Alliance officer involved? "Did he make a play for you?"

That brought a laugh from the Kommodor. "No. I'm sure if he intended that, he knew he'd be wasting his time."

"You're committed to someone?" Iceni asked. It never hurt to know little details about people that might be useful in the future.

This time Marphissa smiled, but sadly. "There's only been two men that I might have committed to. One died at Atalia before that happened, fighting the Alliance. The other told me after my brother was arrested by the snakes that associating with me any longer might harm his career."

"How nice," Iceni commented.

"I'm sure once he got out of the hospital, he went on to some other fool woman." Marphissa looked around the bridge again, clearly wanting to change the topic. "Where are we going to get enough people to crew this battleship?"

"We'll have to recruit. Maybe in other star systems, like Taroa. A lot of people there are probably eager to leave right now." Iceni gave Marphissa a half smile. "This battleship is going to need a commander. Any suggestions?"

"I . . . will have to go through personnel files for the other field-grade mobile forces commanders available to us—"

"Kommodor Marphissa, this is where you're supposed to say something like 'I would be honored if you would consider me for such an assignment.'"

Marphissa stared at her. "Two months ago, I hadn't even commanded a heavy cruiser."

"And two months ago, I was a CEO, not a president. The individual in command of this battleship has to be someone I trust, someone who can handle the responsibility, and someone who can serve as my senior mobile forces commander." *And someone who isn't too ambitious. If you had immediately volunteered yourself, you might not have been offered the assignment.* "If you want it, the job's yours."

"I am honored by your trust and confidence in me, Madam President. Yes. I would be pleased to accept such an assignment." She looked around again, this time with a growing sense of ownership visible in her eyes. "B-78. Somehow it seems it should have more of a name than that."

"Oh? Like the Alliance does? The *Inexplicable* or the *Undesirable* or the *Insufferable*?"

Marphissa grinned. "The crews already give the mobile units nicknames."

"I know. When I was a subexecutive, I was on heavy cruiser C-333. The line workers called it the *Cripple Three* when they thought no officer could hear them."

"The crew on C-448 call the cruiser the *Double Eight*.

If our warships are going to have names, don't they deserve better names than that?"

"Like what?" Iceni waved around the bridge. "What should B-78 be called?"

Kommodor Marphissa looked slowly about her, then back at Iceni. "B-78 will be the flagship of the Midway Star System?"

"Of course."

"We could call it the *Midway*. Battleship *Midway*. I'm certain she would proudly represent that name."

"Hmmm." *She?* Give a ship a name, and people immediately started talking about it as if it were a living thing. But, then, the line workers, the crews, had always done that, too. About every ten years or so in the past someone higher up would propose formally naming mobile units, citing intangibles like morale and unit cohesion, but the proposals had always died in the bureaucracy, which cited cost, the lack of proven concrete benefits, and the redundancy of giving a name to something that already had a perfectly good unit number. *One of the few cases where bureaucrats have repeatedly objected to redundancy. And they killed some of my proposals, too, on equally arbitrary grounds. It would be nice to make this happen knowing how unhappy it would make the bean counters.* "I'll consider it."

"Kommodor!"

Marphissa clenched her jaw. "There's never any rest, is there?" she commented, then accepted the call. "Here. I'm on the bridge of the battleship."

"There's something happening on the mobile forces facility."

"Something?"

"Internal and external explosions, Kommodor."

Iceni tapped her own comm unit. "Colonel Rogero, get someone up here fast to watch the bridge. I need to get back over to the C-448."

SETTLING into her seat on the bridge of the heavy cruiser, Iceni called up a close-in look at the mobile forces facility. Though that was orbiting the gas giant just like the battleship, it was distant enough to be almost invisible around the curve of the planet and no threat to the ships with Iceni.

But something was definitely happening there. "We don't have comms that might indicate what's going on?"

"There's fighting taking place," the specialist currently occupying the operations console offered.

"Is there?" Iceni put all the crushing force of a CEO's sarcasm into that reply.

Marphissa turned to face all her specialists. "Find out who is fighting and any indications of why. Someone on there must be talking to someone else."

"President Iceni?"

"Yes, Colonel Rogero."

"I understand there is fighting on the mobile forces facility. Will you require any of my soldiers to conduct operations there?"

That was a very reasonable question. Iceni felt like slapping herself at having forgotten for a moment that she had ground forces available.

But only three squads. And that mobile forces facility might not be large by shipyard standards, but it was damned big by most other criteria. "Do we have any idea how many people are on that facility?"

The operations specialist, perhaps trying to make up for his earlier gaff, answered her quickly. "That design should have a standard base-occupancy level of six hundred, with up to one thousand more possible based on current work under way."

"I'll need more ammunition," Colonel Rogero said. "If that facility actually has that many workers on it."

"There's no sign of other ships being worked on," Marphissa said. "If we could see inside the primary dock—"

"We have a blowout on the primary dock," the operations specialist announced as the information flashed onto their displays. "Something blew up inside. Our systems are estimating a Hunter-Killer with partial core collapse."

"That's as good as a look inside. It means there is nothing inside that dock," Marphissa said to Iceni. "Nothing left, that is. Nothing left of the dock, either."

"Somebody was trying to get away," Iceni guessed. "But who?"

"Madam President, we have a message for you from the facility."

"Show me." Iceni saw the window pop up before her, revealing a stern-looking woman in the uniform of a senior maintenance line worker.

"This is . . . this is Stephani Ivaskova. I am a free worker!"

Oh, damn. That's not good.

"We have taken this facility from the ISS and from the Syndicate Worlds. Our workers' committee is in charge. We want you to . . . to recognize our control!"

Iceni waited a moment longer to see if Free Worker Ivaskova was done, then replied. Since the orbiting mobile forces facility was only a couple of light-seconds distant, the delay in communications wouldn't really be noticeable. "This is President Iceni of the Midway Star System. We have no reason to attack you as long as you refrain from any actions against us."

"You . . . whatever president means, we don't want any more CEOs or executives telling us what to do."

"This isn't my star system," Iceni said. "I have no interest in trying to control anyone here."

"You are holding property belonging to us," Ivaskova declared. "We insist that you turn it over to our workers' committee."

"What property would that be?"

"The battleship."

Iceni shook her head, keeping her expression unrevealing. "We took that battleship from the Syndicate Worlds, not from you. I intend keeping it. As soon as we know it's safe to move, we'll take it to Midway to finish readying it for full operational capability."

Ivaskova turned her head, talking to what seemed to be more than one other person, the off-side conversation rendered deliberately unintelligible by the comm software. Based on the changes in Ivaskova's expression and the way her gestures became more and more emphatic, the talk rapidly escalated into a vigorous argument of some kind.

"Workers' committee?" Marphissa asked Iceni. "What is that?"

"Another word for anarchy. Workers' committees are like a virus, Kommodor. A plague. We need to ensure that plague does not spread to our warships. Get our comm experts to work blocking every means of communicating with that facility except through one channel that you personally control."

"The back doors—"

"Shut them down as fast as new ones open," Iceni ordered. "This is top priority for your comm personnel."

"Yes, Madam President."

"And ensure that someone is watching the comm personnel to make sure that they aren't talking to the workers' committee either."

As Marphissa worked, Ivaskova finally turned back to Iceni. "We demand the battleship."

"Your demand is noted. Are any of your executives still alive?" Iceni asked, fairly sure that she could easily distract the workers' committee.

"Uh, yes, a few. Most died, either fighting the snakes or fighting us, especially when the HuK in the main dock blew while they were trying to get away. We know that Sub-CEO Petrov died there."

"What has been happening on the second planet? It seems very quiet, but so did your facility until recently."

Ivaskova might be a free worker in name, but a lifetime of answering to authority caused her to reply to Iceni without questioning her role. "The snakes took over. They killed a lot of people. There were demonstrations going because the citizens, the workers, demanded more rights. We wanted the CEOs and the snakes to go, so we could govern ourselves. And then the snakes hit, and nobody wanted to do anything for a while since the snakes controlled the mobile forces. But we saw you beat them, so we moved. Those three mobile units orbiting the second planet, they're snake-controlled still, right? As long as they're in orbit, the people on the planet might wait. But maybe not. We're tired of this. Sick of this. We'd rather die than be slaves any longer."

This just kept getting worse. If that kind of thinking spread to Midway . . . Iceni felt sudden gratitude for Colonel Malin's advice to throw a bone to the citizens to keep them from demanding the entire feast. "I appreciate your assistance, Worker Ivaskova. I will be back in touch with you." Iceni ended the call, then let out a heavy sigh.

How to keep this confined to Kane?

And what would those mobile forces units controlled by the snakes do if the planet they orbited broke into full revolt? She knew the answer, and it sickened her to think of the destruction and death that would rain down on the planet from above.

Not that she could afford to worry about that. Nor should she. *It's about protecting my own position at Midway. If I start worrying about the welfare of the citizens . . . All right, I do worry about that.* "It would be useful for Kane to end up allied with us."

"Madam President?" Marphissa asked.

"I was just thinking aloud, Kommodor. Aside from comms, do you think the people on that mobile forces facility can pose any threat to us? They were very insistent on wanting the battleship."

Marphissa's brow furrowed in thought. "If they want it, they won't try to destroy it by improvising mass throwers, but we still should move it beyond their reach. If I mate another heavy cruiser to the battleship we can tow it, slowly, until the planet blocks any view of it from the mobile forces facility."

"Excellent. Do that."

"If they didn't blow up all of their tugs when that HuK was destroyed, they might use some of them to try to reach the battleship. If that happens, we can either destroy the tugs en route or let Colonel Rogero's soldiers deal with the workers when they debark."

"The second approach will be more subtle if it comes to that." Iceni frowned at her display. "We need to send someone after those three warships still controlled by the snakes."

"We can't catch them," Marphissa said. "Not unless they decide to give battle."

"No, but we can chase them away from the second planet. According to the workers on the mobile forces facility, the snakes suppressed earlier mass dissent and are still in charge on that planet, but the population is ready to rise up again. There can't be that many snakes left here, so they're holding the population hostage using those warships."

"If we send a force to drive off the warships . . ."

"The senior snakes will either have to take their chances among the populace or get on those three units and head for the nearest jump exit," Iceni finished. "Two of our heavy cruisers are going to be tied up towing the battleship a short ways."

"That leaves one heavy," Marphissa said. "We send C-555, plus four light cruisers and four HuKs. That will be plenty enough to overwhelm the remaining snake forces if they try to fight, and leave us the two heavy cruisers, two light cruisers, and the remaining five HuKs here in case we have to defend the battleship from a suicidal attack or some other flotilla showing up at an awkward moment."

"Get that going. Notify the commander of C-555 that he will be in command of the detached flotilla. I want to see how he handles that. And one more thing. Detach a single HuK to proceed back to Midway immediately to provide General Drakon with information on what has happened so far. Make sure the HuK has the latest, best estimate for when we can move that battleship under its own power again without worrying about its blowing up."

Iceni looked at her display, trying to think, trying to recall if she had forgotten anything. She had been talking about a single HuK. *Was there another single HuK that had been a concern? Oh.* "Kommodor, did you hear what the workers on the mobile forces facility said happened to that HuK in their primary dock?" she asked Marphissa in a voice pitched low enough that it seemed intended for only the Kommodor, but that the specialists on the bridge would also be able to hear. "They blew it up when those aboard were trying to leave. Everyone aboard died."

"Everyone?" Marphissa eyed her, then understanding dawned. "The entire crew? They didn't just kill the snakes?"

"No. Apparently they think of mobile forces personnel in the same way as they do snakes." Her statement, which would surely be repeated around the flotilla, was a small but hopefully effective inoculation against the infection threatened by the workers' committee on the mobile forces facility. At least it would help ensure that any overtures from those workers were met with suspicion by the crews of her warships.

TWELVE hours later, Iceni watched the shape of the mobile forces facility slowly begin to slide around the curve of the gas giant as heavy cruisers C-448 and C-413 strained to move the mass of the battleship to a new position in orbit. Watching a visual of the mobile forces facility, it was as if the facility was what was moving, not the battleship, creeping a bit at a time out of sight. "We can't accelerate any more than this?" Iceni asked.

Marphissa spread her hands. "We could, Madam President, but we have to slow it down again. The faster we get it going, the more momentum, the longer it will take us to stop it."

"Even presidents have to answer to the laws of physics, I suppose." A comm alert sounded. "I'm being called by the mobile forces facility," Iceni said. "They've probably noticed that the battleship is going away."

"Even a workers' committee should have realized that they don't have any means of making you give it back." Marphissa leaned closer, activating the privacy field around her chair. "There's talk among the crews about what happened at that facility. Little agreement with what they did but what seems to be general agreement with their grievances."

"That's not good."

"On the positive side, some of the things you've done, like changing their titles from line worker to specialist, are viewed as evidence that the workers will be treated with more respect by you than they have grown used to expecting from Syndicate CEOs."

But what did that mean they would expect from her in the future? "How much longer until we can move this battleship under its own power?" Iceni asked for what must have been the twentieth time.

"The latest estimate is another sixteen hours. Madam President, it would be dangerous to get that battleship under way with only the outfitting crew. There's not enough of them to operate that unit safely. I strongly advise cannibalizing the crews of the heavy cruisers for enough personnel to get the battleship to Midway." Marphissa paused, then continued. "I should add that if we did so, the combat capability of the heavy cruisers would be significantly compromised."

Why did I ever become a CEO? Or rather, a president? "I'll consider the suggestion." Keep the battleship safe by taking crew members from the cruisers, which meant the cruisers couldn't adequately defend the battleship, and the reason the cruisers needed to be there was to keep the battleship safe. It would be nice every once in a while to have some good alternatives to choose among.

At least this time she had plenty of opportunity to consider her decision. With the mobile forces facility no longer able to view the battleship, the heavy cruisers had begun pivoting the battleship up and over so they could point it and them in the other direction and begin using their main propulsion units to slow it back down. Iceni watched the perspective of the gas giant on her close-in display shift slowly as the battleship and the two heavy cruisers mated to it gradually brought their noses up and up. It wasn't quite as bad as watching grass grow, but must rank as a close second even though in the visual light spectrum the images of the clouds on the gas giant could be dramatic.

That was the problem with space. On rare occasions, things happened way too fast, with only moments to make crucial decisions and only tiny fractions of a second to engage the enemy, but by far the majority of the time everything happened slowly. Even with the tremendous velocities that modern spacecraft could achieve, it took a long time to cover billions of kilometers, and light itself seemed slow when it took hours to cross the distance between you and another group of ships, or between you and a planet. The flotilla she had sent to the second planet to chase off the snake-controlled warships had left nearly twelve hours ago, but was still nearly three hours from getting there even when traveling at thirty thousand kilometers a second. And whenever the snake-controlled warships reacted to the approach of that flotilla, it would take her about an hour and a half simply to see it.

Simultaneously bored and tense, finding it hard to focus on the decisions that had to be made at some point but not immediately, Iceni thought about Marphissa's proposal to name the battleship. If she named that battleship, then there would have to be names for the other warships as well, the cruisers and the HuKs. Was there supposed to be some kind of system to that?

If there was, the Alliance would use such a system. And naming conventions were the sort of thing Alliance prisoners would have spoken freely about since they didn't involve anything the Syndicate Worlds could have used in the war. Iceni did a search of interrogation results, finding a series of reports on that very topic.

The first answered a question she had actually wondered

about for some time but never gotten around to looking up an answer for. Why didn't the Alliance politicians stroke their egos by naming Alliance battleships and battle cruisers after themselves? The answer involved those same egos, because it turned out they could never agree on who got the honor, instead engaging in endless squabbles. *Which raises the question of why the Syndicate Worlds never named our battleships and battle cruisers after the highest-ranking CEOs. I can't believe the Alliance politicians have bigger egos than the top CEOs that I've encountered. Maybe our CEOs, like their politicians, couldn't agree on whom among them to honor.*

Why not name the battleship after her? The *Iceni*. There was something breathtaking about the idea of a battleship *Iceni*. But something in her felt a little odd at the idea, too, as if she were an incredibly ancient ruler with an incredibly huge ego constructing a massive monument to herself. Like one of those . . . what were they called . . . pyramids back on Old Earth.

Still . . . *All right, say I name it after me. If all goes well, at some point we will find a way to get another battleship or a battle cruiser. I'd have to name it after Drakon. Assuming that something hasn't happened to Drakon before that. But then what about a third? Who gets that name? I've seen how vicious internal fights can get over far smaller issues of ego and precedence and recognition. Do I really want that kind of headache? Do I want my largest warships to be pretentious monuments to living politicians? And what if I named one Drakon, and he and I had a falling-out? Rename it. Maybe rename it again. And again. And the name means nothing to anyone because everyone knows it's just a flavor-of-the-month sort of thing.*

Could the Syndicate bureaucracy's refusal to give warships names have actually been a smart thing to do given the way CEOs are? I suppose even the Syndicate bureaucracy gets things right every once in a while.

But naming it *Midway*, as Marphissa suggested, would avoid those problems. And if she acquired allied star systems, the next battleship or battle cruiser could be, say, *Kane*. That would stroke the egos of an entire star system. A useful thing to be able to do.

What about the smaller warships? The Alliance, it seemed, named its heavy cruisers for armor or fortifications or simply hard substances, like *Diamond*. The light cruisers were named for both offensive and defensive things, and the destroyers, larger than Syndicate HuKs but with the same kinds of missions, were named after weapons.

She needed that kind of category system but couldn't use the Alliance system. No one would like that. What else was there? As she had with the rank system, Iceni called up historical files, searching for ships once associated with the Syndicate Worlds or parts of it that had names. She had to go back a long way, to the period when the star systems in this region were first being colonized, some by very long voyages from Old Earth itself to stake a human claim to as much space as possible at a time when there were worries about quickly encountering another intelligent species.

There were some names in those old historical files. A lot were human names, individuals whose meaning and onetime importance had been long since lost. Perhaps some of those names had belonged to politicians, but if so, their quest for immortality through that means had fallen far short of eternity.

But there were other names. Manticore, Basilisk, Gryphon. She knew some of those. Mythical creatures. Powerful mythical creatures. And the names were also linked to long ago, to the ships used by the ancestors that the crew members had covertly continued to worship despite official disapproval. Good. Very good. That took care of the heavy cruisers.

Phoenix. Iceni kept her eyes focused on that name, thinking about that creature. She had been increasingly bothered by the scorched-earth tactics of the snakes and even non-ISS types like the late CEO Kolani when they were cornered. The thought had already occurred to her that such people wanted to leave behind nothing that Iceni could use, nothing but ashes that would provide no benefit for the citizens of rebelling star systems.

But in mythology, the phoenix rose from ashes. A rebirth. That particular symbol was not for any one ship. No. She would hold that one ready, to symbolize what might become far more than one star system linked by association, ready to work together against their former masters and any other threat. They would build something new from the ashes of the Syndicate Worlds.

But that was a matter for another day. For now, what about names for the light cruisers? Iceni looked at her display in hope of inspiration. On the display, the detached flotilla still hung moving slowly against the image of this part of the star system. The projected vector for the flotilla curved toward the second planet, like the path of a bird of prey swooping down upon its victim.

A bird of prey? Hawk, Eagle, Raven? Was a Raven a bird of prey? Never mind. She liked the imagery.

That left the HuKs. What to signify with them? Something she wanted to encourage. But what? The sort of thing she had seen with Sub-Executive Kontos, standing sentry on the bridge of the battleship until relieved.

Standing sentry.

Sentry.

Sentinel. Defender. Guardian. Scout. Warrior. There were a lot of options there. And crew members who had been happy to be changed from being line workers to being called specialists would surely like the idea of their ships having similarly less generic titles.

Decision made. No bureaucracy to be consulted.

Iceni looked to Marphissa. "So, Kommodor, when do you want to be formally appointed the commanding officer of the battleship *Midway*?"

Marphissa's face lit. "She will get a name?"

"Yes." *She. I guess that I'd better get used to hearing that.*

"Madam President, I am honored beyond measure that—"

"Kommodor!" the operations specialist said. "Activity near the second planet!"

Iceni swiveled her gaze back to her display. An hour and a half ago, the snake-controlled warships had done something. But what?

CHAPTER THIRTEEN

"ACCELERATING and vectoring away from the planet," Marphissa commented after watching for a few minutes.

"What about shuttle activity to them?" Iceni asked. "There wasn't any alert on that before they started moving."

"There have been a lot of shuttle runs to those units ever since they achieved orbit. The half hour before they started moving had plenty, but not an unusual amount compared to the hours before that."

All they could do was sit and watch until the one light cruiser and two HuKs still controlled by the snakes settled out on a clear vector. The bent cone indicating possible courses kept narrowing until it formed a single curving line heading past the star and outward. "The jump point for Kukai," the maneuvering specialist announced.

"That was their only other choice unless they wanted to go to Midway," Marphissa noted, "but they are leaving the star system."

"Make sure," Iceni said, "that our detached flotilla—"

She stopped speaking as an alert sounded, and new symbols flashed on the display.

"They've launched bombardment projectiles," the combat specialist said in a hushed voice.

Damn. How many projectiles did those three units have on board? Enough to devastate the second planet?

"They're headed . . . outward," the combat specialist reported, his voice reflecting bafflement.

"What?" Iceni leaned closer to her display as if that might provide more detail. "They can't hit the battleship from where they're firing. Not with unguided projectiles that would have to whip around the gas giant in a partial orbit before impact."

"That is correct, Madam President, but the projectiles are heading toward the gas giant."

Marphissa spread her hands in bafflement, eyes fixed on her own display. "How long until we can figure out what they're aiming at?"

"Maybe half an hour, Kommodor." The combat specialist hesitated. "They must know that trying to hit any mobile unit with kinetic rounds fired from that distance is hopeless."

"And yet they launched them in this direction."

"Yes, Kommodor, but there is one thing near here, one thing orbiting the gas giant, which is not a mobile unit."

An angry sound came from Marphissa. "The mobile forces facility. But why don't they want to preserve that intact in the expectation that they'll control it again when the Syndicate Worlds sends new forces here?"

"Excuse me, Kommodor, but the facility isn't intact. It was badly damaged during the fighting to control it. We don't know how badly, but we know the main dock has been destroyed. That explosion must have torn apart most of the shipyard capabilities on the facility."

Marphissa turned to Iceni. "The facility is no longer very useful, and the snakes know that the workers' committee took it over. They're sending the strongest possible message to this star system by smashing that facility. What do we do?"

"Why do we have to do anything?" Iceni asked. "The

citizens on the mobile forces facility will see the projectiles coming and they'll evacuate."

"Yes, Madam President. The only mobile unit at the facility was destroyed in the internal fighting, and we destroyed the freighter on its way here with snake reinforcements. They'll have to evacuate in any surviving tugs and escape pods, which are certain to be overloaded."

Oh. Iceni judged the distances involved to reaching safety. "That will be pushing the capabilities of the pods, and probably the tugs."

"We could detach a few of our—"

"No." She might not want the workers' committee and their fellow radicalized workers to suffocate in the cold dark, but that didn't mean she wanted them spreading poison to her crews. "What about that merchant?" She pointed to her display, centering it on one of the merchant ships that had arrived since the fighting or left the second planet, crossing the star system on their way to one or the other of the two jump points that were all Kane had. Prudence might have dictated postponing any voyages, but in the Syndicate Worlds caution alone wasn't accepted as an excuse for failure to carry out ordered tasks. Schedules must be met. As soon as the combat between the flotillas ended, merchant ships had gotten under way. One of those merchant ships was only ten light-minutes from the gas giant though already past the planet's orbit and heading outward.

"Should I contact them?" Marphissa asked.

"No, I'll do it." Composing herself, Iceni tapped her controls. "Merchant ship SWCC-10735, this is President Iceni. The citizens on the mobile forces facility orbiting the fourth planet will soon be forced to evacuate. You are to alter course toward that facility, rendezvous with the tugs and escape pods from that facility, and take the citizens in them safely to the second planet before proceeding on your business. Acknowledge receipt of this message and understanding of your orders. For the people, Iceni, out." Short and to the point. There should be no room for misunderstanding.

But a reply would take about twenty minutes. Ten minutes to get there and ten to get back.

The battleship and two heavy cruisers had finally finished swinging completely about and were slowing again under the thrust of the cruisers' propulsion units when the reply came.

"This is Senior Ship's Controller Hafely." Hafely had the fixed expression characteristic of those executives who couldn't conceive of doing anything contrary to directions. In Iceni's experience, most executives like that couldn't do anything without clear and detailed directions, either. "My ship is owned and operated by the Yegans Syndicate. I am under orders from my Syndicate not to deviate from my assigned transport movements except as required by authorities of the Syndicate Worlds or if threatened by Alliance raiders. I am continuing on my movements as scheduled by my Syndicate."

"Not even a courteous sign-off at the end," Iceni commented.

"Madam President," Marphissa said, looking and sounding angry, "should I take appropriate action?"

"Oh, no, Kommodor. I want to respond to this individual personally. He needs to be motivated." Another moment to prepare, then Iceni hit the transmit command once more and began speaking in a calm voice. "Senior Ship's Controller Hafely, this is President Iceni of the independent Midway Star System. You seem to be under the mistaken impression that I care about your orders from the Yegans Syndicate. You also seem to think that you are not required to obey *my* orders. I will say this once, Senior Ship's Controller Hafely. Listen carefully."

Her voice had hardened and deepened, lowering slightly in volume. "I am in command of three heavy cruisers, six light cruisers, and eight Hunter-Killers. Any one of those units is capable of totally destroying your ship. If I do not as soon as possible receive an acknowledgment of your orders from me to assist the evacuees from the mobile forces facility, as well as your intent to obey those orders, and see your ship begin to carry out those orders, I will send one of my light cruisers to intercept your ship and obliterate it. But that cruiser will be under orders to attempt to ensure that you personally survive the destruction of your ship, so that you can be placed in an escape pod that will be launched on a vector that ensures it cannot be reached by anyone before its life support gives out.

"You have one remaining chance to get this right, Senior Ship's Controller Hafely. You should be extremely grateful that I am giving you that chance rather than immediately ordering your execution for disrespect toward me."

Her voice returned to calmness. "For the people, Iceni, out."

Feeling tired, Iceni stood up. "Let me know if we don't receive a positive reply from Senior Ship's Controller Hafely within half an hour, and if we don't see his ship begin to turn around to meet the citizens who evacuate from the facility. As soon as you see the ship begin to move, contact the mobile forces facility and tell them the merchant is coming to pick them up. Am I forgetting anything?"

"How do we ensure that the merchant actually takes them to the second planet?" Marphissa asked. "That might require detaching a warship to shadow the merchant until it gets there."

She didn't want to do that. It would tie up a warship for even longer than the commitments she was already dealing with. Iceni pointed at another symbol on the display. "That's the light cruiser that wanted to go to, where was it, Cadez? Why haven't they left?"

The comm specialist answered. "I've talked to them, Madam President. They have some people on the second planet that they wanted to pick up before they left, so they've been waiting around to see if the snakes would leave."

"Good. Contact that light cruiser, Kommodor Marphissa. Tell them we chased away the snakes from the second planet, and tell them what I've ordered the merchant to do." Iceni paused. Could she just order the light cruiser to do something? They might refuse, and she had no means of catching them to enforce an order. Giving an order you couldn't enforce was a bad idea. It could make you look very weak, indeed. "Ask them if they will intercept that merchant and escort it to the second planet to ensure that the citizens from the mobile forces facility reach the planet safely."

It all felt very . . . humanitarian. Hopefully, no one would interpret that as a sign of weakness in her. She needed the goodwill of whoever ended up ruling this star system and didn't want to burn any bridges with any factions, that was all. That didn't mean she would return the battleship, but it did mean issuing a few threats to save a few lives to earn the kind of intangible currency that could purchase important dividends in the future. "I'm going to work in my stateroom for a while."

As Iceni left the bridge, with every intention of lying down and trying to rest, she noticed out of the corners of her eyes that the specialists all seemed to be happy for some reason.

GENERAL Artur Drakon eyed the latest intelligence update souriy. Even a few months ago, intelligence updates had been much, much longer and much simpler. In those days, there had been two categories. The Alliance category contained the latest that had been learned about the enemy's intentions and capabilities, as well as information about recent Alliance military operations and losses. The best that could be said about that category was that it usually correctly identified the star systems in which combat had taken place. Intentions were never more than a patchwork of guesses, and capabilities rarely showed any changes that mattered. And, of course, the information was time-late, as much as several months late if you were stationed somewhere like Midway far from the border with the Alliance. Even when you were stationed closer to the front, information about other areas where fighting was taking place could be weeks old at best.

The Syndicate Worlds category was almost always shorter, and almost always even less useful. Actual losses of forces or defeats were never accurately reported and had to be teased out through the grapevine and unofficial contacts. Syndicate Worlds' plans were always subject to deliberate disinformation and sudden, last-minute changes if one influential CEO abruptly lost that influence and their replacement had other plans. And, of course, that was all time-late as well.

Yet everyone of rank was supposed to know what was in the updates, so reading them was mandatory, and in any event they offered important clues as to what your superiors wanted to believe themselves and wanted you to believe.

The intelligence update before Drakon now was far smaller, but with more categories. Midway. Local Star Systems. Syndicate Worlds. Alliance. Other Star Systems. Enigma Race. Much of the information was fragmentary, and the time lags had grown far worse as travel through space once controlled by the Syndicate Worlds had grown more difficult and official networks had collapsed along with Syndicate authority. But at least the information reflected the truth as best they knew it. Or as best Colonel Malin knew it.

Midway. Stable, almost suspiciously so, the citizens enthusiastically embracing the elections for low-level offices. The euphoria from the destruction of the snakes hadn't faded yet, and the Syndicate Worlds hadn't yet retaliated. Trade was weaker than it should be, but it had been trending that way for some time. In some ways, the Syndicate Worlds had been unraveling for years and decades under the pressure of the war, maintaining an image of strength thanks to military power that masked the growing hollowness and dissent behind it.

Taroa. Three factions contesting for control. None strong enough to win. Malin had emphasized that. He wanted Drakon to think about it.

Kane. Critically important, but they still knew nothing. Until some ship arrived bearing news from Iceni, all they could do was wonder what she had found there and whether she had succeeded in her mission.

Syndicate Worlds. Very little new. A recently arriving merchant ship had carried a message from CEO Jason Boyens for Iceni, and Malin had already intercepted that long enough to copy the contents. Unfortunately, Boyens didn't tell them much they didn't already know. The new government was weak, everyone was struggling for position and influence, and star systems continued to break away from Syndicate Worlds authority. The message had been sent well before news would have reached Prime of the rebellion at Midway, so it offered no clues to reactions by the government.

Enigma race. Nothing to report. If Black Jack's fleet had stirred them up again, the aliens must still be busy confronting the Alliance.

Other star systems. This one reported in chaos, that one declaring independence under a strong CEO or a group of them, yet another joining a loose conglomeration of other local star systems for protection that the central government could no longer provide. This information was the oldest and most patchy, and so least reliable.

Alliance. *Personal briefing required.*

"Colonel Malin, I'd like to speak with you." Drakon waited until Malin arrived and closed the door behind him. "What's this item on the Alliance?"

Malin checked the security readouts before replying. "I managed to access some of President Iceni's personal files, General."

"That must have been extremely difficult."

"It was challenging. I couldn't get to everything, not by a long shot, but I did find the records of her conversations with the Alliance fleet, the ones even the snakes never located."

Drakon took a moment to contemplate how history, especially his history, would have been different if Malin were working for the snakes. "Do we have copies now?"

"I couldn't copy them, sir. That would have left clear

footprints because they were locked. I recorded a summary of what I saw, though." Malin brought out his own reader. "What we were told about the conversations between President Iceni and Admiral Geary the first time the Alliance fleet was here, when they defeated the enigma force, seems to have been accurate. President Iceni did not withhold any meaningful details."

"What about the second time? When President Iceni says she made that deal with Black Jack?"

"I found that, General." Malin frowned at his reader. "Admiral Geary did not in fact promise to back the actions of President Iceni. What he promised was to assist in protecting this star system against the enigma race. He also promised not to openly repudiate any claims that Iceni made of more extensive promises of protection, but he did not in fact promise or offer such protection."

"Hah." Was that good news or bad news? "So President Iceni's hand isn't as strong as she's been claiming. She doesn't have major backing for anything she does."

"That's correct, sir. It increases the threat to this star system because we can't count on the Alliance fleet actively opposing a Syndicate attack, but it also means that President Iceni needs your backing all that much more."

"What else did you find?"

"Something odd that I noticed." Malin's frown deepened. "I've questioned what I think I saw, because it doesn't make sense, but I am certain of it. In the messages sent by the Alliance fleet in its first visit here, Geary wore the insignia of an Alliance fleet admiral."

"Is that what he called himself then? We've got records of the broadcasts he made to the whole star system and to the enigmas."

"Yes, General. Fleet Admiral Geary. But in the messages with President Iceni on his latest visit here, I am certain that Geary was wearing the insignia of an admiral."

That took a moment to sink in. "A regular admiral? A lower rank than he displayed the earlier time? Malin, that doesn't make any sense at all. Hell, it's impossible. Who could have busted Black Jack down a rank? He owns the Alliance."

Malin made a baffled gesture. "I have been trying to come up with an explanation, General."

"Why would he pretend to have a lower rank now than he did then? Is it some kind of trick?" That was the only reason that offered any hint of sense.

"Perhaps it was related to their mission into enigma space," Malin suggested. "Something to influence the way the enigmas reacted."

"Who the hell knows enough about the enigmas to predict how they'd react to anything?" Drakon frowned, trying to rationalize this information, but his thoughts ran in circles, going nowhere. "Did you spot any other discrepancies?"

"None that I noticed."

"What did President Iceni think the difference in rank meant? Did you find any sign of that?"

"No, sir. She may not have noticed it since Alliance military command issues haven't been her priority in recent years."

Why would the man who, by all accounts, controlled the Alliance accept a demotion? It had to be a trick, but who was the trick aimed at? Maybe the enigmas. Or . . . "Maybe it's aimed at us. Black Jack must have known that we'd spot the discrepancy sooner or later. Does he want us to think his position is weak? Why? Oh, hell. If we think Black Jack is weaker than he is, then we'll be more likely to provoke him, to offer him a reason to do what he wants. And we know he wants control of this star system."

"A way to fool us into demonstrating our true intentions toward him?" Malin said. "That is a possible explanation. Or perhaps Black Jack is just trying to keep us off-balance. I'm not an expert on mobile forces engagements, but the reports that I have seen said that Black Jack is always doing the unexpected, appearing to be doing one thing when he's actually preparing to do something else."

"So now he appears to have been demoted from Alliance Fleet Admiral to Alliance Admiral." Drakon pounded one fist lightly on his desk. "It's a strategy. We have to figure out the goal of that strategy, but I'd be willing to bet that it's aimed at tricking us into some misstep."

"It could be aimed at the Syndicate Worlds government on Prime," Malin pointed out. "An attempt to fool them into restarting hostilities or simply taking action contrary to the peace agreement. That would give Black Jack the excuse he needed to totally crush them, leaving not even a rump form of the Syndicate Worlds to deal with."

"And leaving lots of weak star systems to be scooped up into his personal empire." Drakon nodded. "You might have it, there. And, of course, we'd be one of the first star systems that Black Jack would want to collect. You didn't spot any other deals with President Iceni? Anything that would mean she intends turning us over to Black Jack's control?"

"No, sir. I am certain no such agreement exists. I am certain that President Iceni does not have any more trust of the Alliance than you do."

"What about her trust of Black Jack?"

Malin paused to think. "My impression is that she sees him as a very powerful rival, sir. Much as she does you."

"She puts me in the same category as Black Jack?" That seemed funny, somehow, being placed alongside someone with as much power and influence as Black Jack. "What about plans to take me down? I assume if you'd found anything like that you would have mentioned it before now."

"I found no plans," Malin confirmed. "She is maintaining files on you and your actions, but it seems to be for contingency purposes, in the event she feels she must take action."

Could he actually trust Iceni? Now that he knew she had, if not lied about, then at least greatly exaggerated the terms of her agreement with Black Jack. And she had withheld some important information about Black Jack, though, as Malin said, that could be because Iceni hadn't recognized something that was staring her in the face. "Your impression is that President Iceni is not a threat to me at this time." Drakon made it a statement.

"Yes, sir," Malin confirmed. "I continue to advise that any action against her would be a mistake."

"You know Colonel Morgan's opinion on that."

"Yes, sir, and you know that I disagree with her in the strongest terms."

Drakon laughed. "Hell, whenever you and Morgan disagree, it's always on the strongest terms. See if you can get back into President Iceni's files and learn more, but be careful to avoid leaving footprints." The door alarm sounded. "And here's Colonel Morgan herself."

"Speak of the devil," Malin murmured.

Morgan swaggered in, apparently ignoring Malin but not turning her back on him, either. "I just got word that there was a firing squad busy earlier today," she announced. "Some supervisor from the primary orbital dockyard got *severely* reprimanded."

"Who ordered the execution?" Drakon demanded, nettled that something like that had happened without his knowledge.

"Supposedly, the orders came from the President," Morgan said. "But those orders all came through her goon."

"That assistant of hers? Togo?"

"Right." Morgan cocked one questioning eyebrow. "I wonder what we might have found out if we'd had a chance to talk to this supervisor?"

Had that supervisor stumbled across something they weren't supposed to know? Drakon glared at the situation display. "We know there was a problem with that one heavy cruiser that the President left behind. Was it related to that? What were the charges against this supervisor?"

"Corruption," Morgan replied. "One of the one-size-fits-all charges. They actually did a show trial, even though that supervisor was too low-ranked for that to make sense. Quick arrest, quick trial, and quick execution. Routine stuff, except for the trial part."

"Routine for snakes," Malin said.

"And CEOs who want to remain in power," Morgan shot back.

"Iceni hasn't even been here for more than a week," Drakon said. "I don't like the idea of this assistant of hers unilaterally ordering executions." *How to get that across to the assistant in the most intimidating way without appearing to elevate the importance of the assistant to that of someone I will deal with directly?* "Colonel Morgan, you are to contact this assistant of the President's directly. Tell him that no further executions are to take place without my specific approval. If I hear of any more such actions, I will take action. Make sure that the assistant is absolutely clear that I mean that."

"I can do that," Morgan said with a smile. "Or I can just get rid of the assistant. That'll send a nice, strong message to his boss and to everyone else."

"Togo is not an easy target," Malin cautioned.

"Neither am I. But even I offer myself as a target sometimes, don't I?" Morgan needled Malin. "General, the President, and everyone else, needs to know who really runs this star system."

"I appreciate the need to be treated with an appropriate level of respect," Drakon said. "But I'm not ready to send that strong a message to the President. Does anyone else need reminding of my status?"

"There are some citizens," Morgan scoffed. "Some of those morons who want to be elected to local councils. There have been statements made in their election materials that deserve some severe reprimands from you."

"They're blowing off pressure," Malin insisted. "It keeps that pressure from building up."

"Or we can just eliminate the source of the pressure," Morgan snapped.

"I'm keeping my options open," Drakon said to stop the latest argument. "From all I see, both I and the President are still regarded by the vast majority of the citizens as the heroes who liberated them from the snakes. If I start offing every citizen who says otherwise, it will dent that image pretty fast. If anyone goes beyond talk, or starts getting too many other citizens listening to them, that will be a different matter."

"General," Malin said, "if you held an honest election tomorrow, the citizens would overwhelmingly vote you and President Iceni as their leaders. No one could claim that your power came from any other source but the people themselves."

"Why the hell would he want to do that?" Morgan demanded. "Why let 'the people' believe for one second that they have any right to pass judgment on whether or not General Drakon is in charge?"

Malin pointed upward. "We don't exist in isolation. There are other powers. We have to worry about them."

Drakon stared at Malin, as did Morgan. She laughed. "Are you invoking fear of ghosts to back up your arguments now? You've been around the workers too long."

"You could read my statement that way, but you could also take it to mean such things as the Syndicate Worlds," Malin said coldly. "They haven't disappeared. We have a pathetically small flotilla to defend ourselves until President Iceni returns. If she has not lost any of the units she took with her, but hasn't gained a battleship, our flotilla will only be pitifully small. With the battleship, it will still be small. And as we all know, the Syndicate Worlds will not attack only with mobile forces and ground forces. They will try to soften us up by any means, create civil unrest, undermine our strength by sabotage, and use every other trick in the Syndicate book to make us an easier target for reconquest. We know this from the inside. We have played this game ourselves. Mobile forces are not our first line of defense. Nor are ground forces. We need the citizens to believe that this is *their* star system, that General Drakon and President Iceni are *their* leaders, that we are the best means to ensure their safety against external forces. And then the citizens will ensure that when our forces defend this star system, they have a firm backing behind them."

"You ensure a firm back by having a firm spine," Morgan said.

"Is there anything else?" Drakon said in a voice that instantly silenced the debate. He didn't feel like going over this again, not when his mind was puzzling over what Black Jack was up to and worried about what might have happened to Iceni.

Malin took a deep breath. "There is one other item I wished to discuss with you, sir. Taroa Star System."

This time, Morgan rolled her eyes. "Are you going to advise General Drakon to go there and tell everyone at Taroa that they should all just get along?"

"No, I'm going to advise General Drakon to go there with troops and intervene in the fighting."

Morgan let surprise show for a moment, then grinned. "I want to hear this."

SHE hadn't slept well for days, and the last several hours had been particularly bad. Iceni finally erupted from her stateroom on the heavy cruiser, crew members scrambling to stay out of her way, and stormed up to the bridge. "Why the hell isn't that battleship ready to move?"

Kommodor Marphissa gulped nervously before she answered. "The engineers and system specialists say one more hour, Madam President."

"That's what they said an hour ago!"

"Madam President."

She spun to see that Sub-Executive Kontos had just entered the bridge as well.

"I was coming to report to you, Madam President," Kontos said. Though still thin, after rest, food, and water, he no longer wavered as he stood, not even when faced by a CEO on the rampage. "One more hour and no more. I personally guarantee it."

The already-hushed bridge seemed to grow deathly quiet. Under the Syndicate system, announcements of personal responsibility could presage rewards, but more often foretold serious punishment.

Iceni eyed Kontos. "Are you aware of what happened to the last person who failed to carry out their work as they had promised me, Sub-Executive Kontos?"

"I need not concern myself with that, Madam President. There will be no failure. Battleship B-78 will be ready for movement under its own power in one hour."

His calm and confidence penetrated even her anger. Either Kontos was very brave and very capable, or he was a total idiot incapable of understanding the fate his own words were creating. "One hour, Sub-Executive Kontos. Or you may find yourself outside without a survival suit trying to push the battleship to the jump point."

"I understand, Madam President." Kontos saluted and left.

Her frustration snuffed out by Kontos's performance, Iceni turned to Marphissa, who was still staring at where Sub-Executive Kontos had stood. "The boy is insane," Marphissa said.

"Would you want him to be one of your officers, Kommodor?" Iceni asked.

"Absolutely. He would be an incredible asset. If I didn't have to kill him."

"Then I'll let you in on something I just decided. If that battleship is under way in one hour or less, Kontos will be your second-in-command when you assume command of the *Midway*."

Marphissa's shocked gaze switched to Iceni. "Second-in-command? That's a sub-CEO or senior executive position."

"He'll have earned it, don't you think?"

A pause, then the Kommodor nodded. "Yes. Yes, I do."

FORTY-SEVEN minutes after Kontos had spoken to her, he called Iceni again. "Battleship B-78 is ready to move at your command, Madam President."

Marphissa, scanning her readouts on the readiness of the battleship, nodded with an amazed look.

Iceni settled back in her seat, looking around the bridge of the heavy cruiser. It felt far less occupied even though every specialist station was in use. With so much of the crew temporarily assigned to working on the battleship, the heavy cruiser had a strange sensation of emptiness. "Ready all units to proceed to the jump point for Midway, Kommodor."

The heavy cruisers mated to the battleship had been loosed, and the light cruisers and HuKs brought in closer to escort the massive warship. They were finally preparing to get back to Midway, hopefully to depart Kane before any strong Syndicate Worlds force showed up at Kane, and hopefully to arrive back at Midway before any Syndicate Worlds attack showed up there. The propulsion problem with heavy cruiser C-818 had been a blessing in disguise. She hadn't needed C-818, and its presence back at Midway offered some protection for the star system until she got back.

Far off, the three snake-controlled warships had jumped for Kukai hours ago. Since then, the detached portion of Iceni's forces that had been shadowing them had turned to rejoin the others. "Tell the subflotilla to alter course to rejoin us just prior to the jump point for Midway," Iceni told Marphissa.

The merchant ship, with its new cargo of evacuees from the mobile forces facility, still had a way to go before it made it back to the second planet; but the light cruiser bound for its crew's home had remained with it, ensuring that Senior Ship's Controller Hafely didn't try to cut his losses by jettisoning evacuees.

Where the mobile forces facility had been there was now scattered junk, most of the debris having been knocked out of orbit, but some spiraling down into the greedy maw of the gas giant to vanish amid the multicolored clouds.

On the second planet itself, crowds could be seen in the streets, but too little in the way of comms could be picked up from the location of Iceni's ships to know who was doing what to whom now that the snakes had run for their lives. Did the fires that could be seen in the streets mark celebration, or rioting, or fighting, or all of the above?

"All units," Marphissa ordered, "come port four three degrees, down zero one degrees, accelerate to point zero three light speed, maintaining station on B-78, execute now."

They were actually moving again. Iceni realized that she was smiling even though the shape of the gas giant receded with painful slowness beneath them. Only part of the battleship's main propulsion units were working, enough to get it moving, but it would accelerate even more sluggishly than usual for a battleship, and getting it up to point zero three light speed would take a while. It would also take a while to get to the jump point at that velocity, but at least they were on their way. Feeling happy indeed, Iceni called the battleship. "Sub-Executive Kontos, do you want to take service in the mobile forces of the Midway Star System?"

Kontos grinned. "Yes, Madam President."

"Then you are promoted to Kapitan-Leytenant, effective immediately, and appointed second-in-command of battleship B-78. Congratulations."

The next call was to Colonel Rogero. "Are your soldiers enjoying the accommodations aboard B-78, Colonel?"

"Yes, Madam President." Rogero wasn't wearing his combat armor, of course, but he still somehow carried the aura of being ready for anything. Iceni found it a dangerously pleasant sensation. "Though in truth there's so much space, and so few crew," Rogero added. "It's a little spooky."

"Is everything in place?"

"We are ready for anything," Rogero affirmed.

That was a code phrase, meaning that, if necessary, Rogero's soldiers would turn on the crew and ensure that the battleship reached Midway. It was ironic, considering her own doubts about Rogero, but she had to count on him to ensure that Kontos or some other members of the battleship's crew didn't decide they wanted some other destination.

In truth, some of the delay in the battleship's being ready had been her own fault. Some of the technicians had covertly installed overrides where overrides were strictly prohibited by Syndicate regulations. Only someone able to get inside the three citadels could have installed the overrides. But now, if anyone chose to try to hole up in those citadels again, Iceni could activate the overrides and quickly gain access to the inside of the three citadels.

Naturally, there was always the chance that the technicians would talk, despite the certainty of what Iceni would do to them if they told anyone. But between fear and the rewards promised for their discretion, the technicians would almost certainly stay quiet. Iceni had long ago learned that, like threats, promises of rewards were best kept. She had once worked for a man who thought the opposite and routinely stiffed his subordinates and workers on things he had pledged for them. Business as usual, until the night an assassin came for that boss, and his guards, employees who had also had promised rewards yanked from them, looked the other way.

She took care of those who worked for her. That was simple self-interest. But even workers who had been treated well could decide to betray those they worked for. Thanks to the heroics of Kontos and the other surviving members of the outfitting crew, she had gained control of this battleship. No one, no matter how heroic, would take that control away from her.

But it was still a long way to the jump point at point zero three light speed.

"SOMETHING is happening at Lono," Colonel Malin reported.

"Dangerous something?" Drakon asked.

"It could be. A merchant ship that came from there said it saw three heavy cruisers and a number of smaller escorts."

Lono. Only one jump away, with enough firepower

mustering there to blow away the single heavy cruiser that Iceni had left at Midway. "Did you find out anything about the HuK that President Iceni sent to Lono?"

"Yes, sir. According to what the merchant ship heard, sometime ago a HuK appeared at the jump point from Midway, took off across the Lono Star System without pausing, and jumped for Milu."

So much for that HuK. Someone had decided to go home or take other independent action. "What can we get to Lono to confirm what that merchant reported about a flotilla?"

"All we could do is requisition another merchant ship, General."

Something slow. "We need scouts out, Colonel Malin. How can we get scouts watching the nearest star systems for trouble?"

"It's a mobile forces issue, General," Malin said.

"And we're damned short of mobile forces."

Malin stiffened as his comm alert sounded and he checked his reader. "A HuK has arrived at the jump point from Kane. There's a message coming in from it. It's eyes only for you."

"Route it to me." Drakon waited impatiently until the message popped up on his queue, then tagged it.

Iceni smiled triumphantly at him. "I am happy to report that I have defeated a snake-controlled flotilla at Kane and gained control of the battleship being outfitted here. As soon as the battleship is ready to move, we will proceed back to Midway." Attached to the message were some files listing detailed events.

Drakon scanned the files quickly. "President Iceni hasn't lost any units. She actually picked up a few more. Plus the battleship."

"How long until she gets back?" Malin asked.

"She didn't say. Call that HuK and tell it to divert to the jump point for Lono. The HuK is to pop in, look around Lono, then head back here." The Syndicate flotilla at Lono might already be on the way to Midway, in which case it would arrive before the HuK even got to Lono to find it empty of threat. That couldn't be helped. "How much chance do you think that heavy cruiser we've got, C-818, would have against a flotilla with three heavy cruisers in it?"

Malin shook his head. "From what I have been able to learn of C-818's commanding officer, she would probably run rather than fight."

"And I can't replace her because of my deal with President Iceni. But C-818's commander could have an accident and need to be replaced. Morgan would take care of that."

"Sir, I advise against that action. C-818's commander is remaining on her unit in orbit. She is wise enough to know that is the safest course of action for her personally. As long as she is on that warship in orbit, reaching her will be hard to achieve, and deniability would be even harder to achieve if something happened to her."

"Damn. Then all we can do is hope that whatever's at Lono doesn't get here before President Iceni gets back."

CHAPTER FOURTEEN

"THIS is Executive Level Two Fon, acting commanding officer of CL-187, for President Iceni."

Iceni rested her head on one hand as she watched the message. Light cruiser CL-187 was about four and a half light-hours distant and nearing the second planet, so this wasn't exactly timely news, but it was also the most recent information she had received from that part of Kane Star System. Her own flotilla, crawling along in company with the battleship, was itself still nearly thirty light-minutes, or sixteen hours' travel time at its current velocity, from the jump point for Midway.

"We will arrive at the second planet in company with the freighter carrying refugees from the mobile forces facility in three hours," Executive Fon continued. "It has been my pleasure to carry out your wishes, President Iceni, and to assist in ensuring the safety of the refugees."

Executive Fon was groveling like a real executive, Iceni thought, something any snake in disguise would have trouble counterfeiting.

"We have been speaking with our people on the second planet," Fon said. "They tell us there has been much celebrating and a few demonstrations over the form of the new government, but no fighting. We anticipate no problems recovering our people from the planet before we head for Cadez."

That was good news. She was tired of watching people kill each other as the iron discipline of the Syndicate system disintegrated. A little break from that violence would be welcome, and perhaps the lack of violence would help restrain the more radical workers from gaining control.

"Once we have completed our escort mission and retrieved our people, CL-187 will return home to Cadez. The use of the hypernet gate at Midway would make this journey much quicker, easier, and less hazardous for us. We hope, in light of the service that we have rendered, that you will permit us the use of the hypernet gate when we arrive at Midway."

Well, of course. They had wanted something from her. No wonder Fon and his light cruiser had done as Iceni had asked. The collapse of the Syndicate Worlds hadn't altered the way people handled business like that.

"When we arrive at Midway, we will be happy to provide you with an update on the latest information we have from Kane," Fon added. "For the people, Fon, out."

Very good. He was smart enough to also dangle that offer as a gesture of goodwill. It would cost the light cruiser nothing to provide Iceni with that valuable update, but they hoped her gratitude would ensure the use of the hypernet gate unhindered.

Iceni straightened herself, checked her appearance, then hit the reply command. "Executive Fon, you and your unit will be welcome at the Midway Star System. I will look forward to hearing the latest information about Kane from you at that time. I anticipate no problems with your free access to the hypernet gate at Midway in light of your service to me and the citizens of Kane. For the people, Iceni, out."

Nearly five hours before CL-187 got her message, and sixteen damnable hours before her flotilla could jump for Midway. Followed by six days in the gray purgatory of jump space. Though the seemingly endless creeping through normal space even to get to the jump must also qualify as a form of purgatory.

But at least this type of purgatory had an end. Iceni sat on the bridge for the last hour as her reunited flotilla approached the jump point. She was returning with a battleship, three heavy cruisers, six light cruisers, and nine Hunter-Killers. Still a small force by the standards of the recent war, but no longer one that could be brushed aside.

Once she got the battleship operational, that is. "You may jump the flotilla for Midway when you are ready, Kommodor Marphissa."

The stars vanished again.

THREE days into their journey through jump space. Three days left to go. By the end of that time, the strangeness of jump space would have begun wearing on them. Iceni remembered the feeling all too well, the sensation that your own skin belonged to a stranger, that you were intruding somewhere not meant for humanity. When it came to that, it wasn't like she wanted to stay in jump space any longer than she had to anyway.

Iceni's hatch alert chimed. She checked her surveillance and security devices, confirming that only Marphissa stood there and that she was unarmed. "Enter, Kommodor."

Marphissa stood for a moment after entering the stateroom, as if uncertain of herself. "Madam President, I wanted to say something to you."

"You're grateful for command of the battleship." Iceni waved her off. "That's understood. I think you can handle it."

"No, Madam President. It's not about me. I wanted to tell you, to thank you, for what you did in Kane. For ensuring that those citizens from the mobile forces facility were saved."

Iceni leaned back and regarded Marphissa curiously. "Did you know any of them?"

"No, Madam President."

"And you surely knew what a threat their ways of thinking posed to you and me personally, as well as to the stability of our home."

"Yes, Madam President."

"And you knew that they had killed everyone on that HuK that tried to escape during the fighting on the facility. Mobile forces personnel like yourself among them. So why did their fate matter to you?"

Marphissa hesitated again. "It is very easy to kill, Madam President. Too easy. Saving a life is harder, and not expected. I wanted you to know that I am grateful that, despite all of the things you have just accurately noted, you still strong-armed that freighter into saving those citizens."

"All right." *What else was there to say?* "I had my reasons. Let me tell you, if those citizens had killed our people, had destroyed one of *my* HuKs, I wouldn't have lifted a finger to save them."

"That would have been justified," Marphissa agreed, "even if it was not just."

"What?" Iceni sat straighter. "Not just?"

"What I mean, Madam President, is that if those citizens had done that, not all of them would have been responsible. The leaders would have given the orders, and some might have followed them, but others might have thought those orders wrong and not participated in the destruction of the HuK at all."

"And what does that have to do with anything?" *What is Marphissa driving at?*

"The entire group would have been punished, Madam President, regardless of their individual actions."

"And what would you have preferred I do differently if that had been the case?" Iceni asked. She could easily use her tone as a whip to indicate displeasure or disagreement, but she kept her voice composed out of curiosity to learn Marphissa's reasoning.

"A trial, Madam President," Marphissa said.

"A trial?" *That again?* "To produce a finding of guilty

that has already been determined? What's the point of that? You sound like those citizens I heard about before we left, the ones who think our justice system needs to be fixed."

Marphissa paused once more before answering. "Do you believe the justice system that we have inherited from the Syndicate Worlds needs to be fixed, Madam President?"

"Offhand, no," Iceni said. "It delivers punishment quickly and surely. The guilty do not escape. What would I fix?"

"The purpose of a justice system isn't to punish the guilty, Madam President. Punishment is easily administered. The reason a justice system exists is to protect the innocent."

Iceni stared at Marphissa in astonishment. "Where did you learn that?"

"The Syndicate Worlds tried to eliminate every document, every book, that didn't match their own beliefs, but it is very hard to destroy every thought that humans have committed to writing."

"The underground library?" No one officially knew such a thing existed, but unofficially everyone had heard of it, and many found ways to access it. Rather than being a single building or process, Iceni had heard the underground library compared by the ISS to an infestation of electronic vermin, springing up in every star system, wriggling into every possible access, popping up someplace else as fast as one way in was sealed off. "You can't believe everything you read. Punishing the guilty is necessary for any system to survive, for anyone to be able to feel safe. That must be our priority."

"The guilty?" Marphissa asked, her breathing getting deeper and faster. "And if an innocent person is instead punished?"

Iceni shook her head. "There are no innocent persons. We are all guilty of something. It's merely a matter of the degree of guilt and the seriousness of our crimes."

"That is what we have been told, Madam President! What if there is another truth?"

"How can we compromise security and say that we are protecting the people?" Iceni demanded.

"Protecting the people? Madam President, the legal system of the Syndicate Worlds protects only those with power and wealth and punishes only those too weak to save themselves! If the goal is to protect the people, then why are the crimes of those who rule us never punished?" Marphissa stood rigidly straight now, her eyes registering defiance and perhaps some fear.

No matter how many thought it, no one was ever supposed to say it. Not to anyone superior in position. It was one of the first rules that everyone in the Syndicate Worlds learned, or they became early casualties of their own lack of discretion. "You presume much based upon our short working relationship," Iceni said in her coldest voice.

"I presume much based upon who I think you are," Marphissa replied. "Madam President, no matter your own motives, no matter how you act, what of the others in authority? You may protect us from injustice and punish only those who deserve it, but what of the others who control our destinies? What controls them?"

Iceni sat watching her silently for a long time, unable to think of an adequate response. The traditional reaction of a CEO to her words would have been to have Marphissa arrested and turned over to the snakes. Unless Marphissa knew something about Iceni that she didn't want the snakes to know, in which case the prisoner would unfortunately die in an accident prior to the snakes' gaining custody. The snakes were gone, but someone else could easily be found to fill the same role if Iceni were the sort to do such a thing to someone who had served her well and shown no disloyalty otherwise. It rankled Iceni that Marphissa had correctly judged that she would not take an action like that. "Kommodor, you should return to your duties," she finally said.

"Yes, Madam President."

"Kommodor."

Marphissa paused in the hatch, turning to face Iceni and

stand at attention, lacking only a blindfold to look like someone already facing a firing squad.

Until she spoke, Iceni wasn't sure what she would say. "I much prefer those who speak their thoughts to my face to those who speak them behind my back. I will think on what you have said."

Wise enough not to offer a reply, Marphissa saluted and left.

Iceni ensured that the hatch was sealed again and all security active, then sat and closed her eyes. *Does that fool think that I've never suffered from the Syndicate so-called justice system? I know its flaws as well as anyone.*

She had never sold her body, but she had been forced to yield it twice, each time to men who were far enough above her in the corporate hierarchy to know that they were safe against any penalty for their actions. Even as young and inexperienced as she had been then, Iceni had known that if she had tried to charge them with crimes she would have been the one convicted of "unjustly defaming" Syndicate officers. She had instead turned her desire for revenge into a climb for power, so she could get into a position to strike back, but both men had died before she could do so, one in an industrial accident and the other during a battle with the Alliance.

How many others had suffered the same way that she had? *She* would not be a victim. *She* would find a means for revenge. But revenge had been denied her by chance.

Marphissa had avenged herself for the death of her brother. A death brought about only by an allegation of wrongdoing. Should only the strongest have a means to justice? And that form of justice had only been vengeance. Nothing that Marphissa, or anyone else, did could have brought her brother back to life after he was executed for the crime of being accused of wrongdoing by someone who profited from that accusation.

Did punishment truly serve a purpose when all knew it was a weapon with no guidance, mowing down low-level criminals but also anyone unfortunate enough to fall under suspicion or to have something someone more powerful desired?

That's the question, isn't it? We talk about the need for safety and security, but how many citizens of the Syndicate Worlds have ever slept feeling safe and secure? No. We spent every day, every night, wondering when the heavy knocks would come on the door, when the door would be broken open, when one of us would be hauled off to answer for crimes whether or not we ever committed those acts. I'm the most powerful person in the Midway Star System, and I hide behind locked doors and security systems even when I have bodyguards on call. Safety and security, hell.

Iceni sighed, leaning back again, her eyes still closed. *How do I fix that and still keep myself, and others, safe? Capturing that battleship may turn out to be one of the easiest things I've had to deal with.*

I hope General Drakon is having an easier time. I ought to be worried about what he's doing, but for some reason I don't understand, I feel safer knowing that he's watching things at Midway. Hopefully he can handle anything that comes up before I get back.

"A flotilla has arrived at the jump point from Lono," Malin reported over the hoot of alarms behind him.

Drakon was in his command center in a heartbeat. Haste was absurd when the enemy had just been sighted six light-hours fifteen light-minutes distant, but it still felt necessary. Human reflexes insisted that an enemy in sight was an imminent threat, and human bodies and brains still responded to that ancient imperative. "Son of a bitch," he muttered as he took in the information.

Two heavy cruisers, three light cruisers, four HuKs. And he had exactly one heavy cruiser to deal with them. It didn't take an expert in mobile forces to know those odds were lousy. "Colonel Malin, inform the commander of

C-818 that President Iceni has concealed a large explosive charge in her unit, and if C-818 doesn't hold its ground and defend this star system, I have the codes to detonate it."

Malin hesitated. "A heavy cruiser isn't so large that she won't be able to eventually discover that there is no such charge, General."

"All I need is for her to have to remain here while she looks for it. We need some defensive presence."

Morgan had also arrived and shook her head. "For a moment I thought our President had actually done something smart."

"If she did," Drakon said, "I don't know about it. We haven't heard anything from that flotilla yet?"

"No, sir," Morgan said. "They didn't send anything the moment they arrived here."

"That's odd. I would have expected an immediate demand that we surrender."

"They're heading . . . for the hypernet gate," Malin reported. "They took up that vector immediately upon leaving the jump point."

Drakon glared at the display. "No Syndicate flotilla would destroy that gate deliberately. They know there's no longer a threat of the gate's wiping out this star system when it collapses, but the Syndicate Worlds needs that gate. Why destroy the primary reason they want control of this star system back?"

Morgan suddenly laughed. "Oh, hell. They didn't come here to attack us. They're supposed to just pass through."

"How long will that buy us?"

"Not long at all, General. Right now, they're picking up lots of comm traffic floating around about General Drakon and President Iceni and the independent Midway Star System, and they're noticing there's nothing on the ISS circuits at all. Maybe they're even picking up comments about the snakes here being dead." Morgan pointed toward the display. "They're deciding what it means, and they're deciding what to do about it. Say you're the commander of a flotilla and have a chance to reconquer a star system that has pulled out of the Syndicate Worlds? And the only mobile forces the rebels have is a single heavy cruiser? What would you decide, General?"

Drakon nodded heavily. "We'll probably get their demand for submission to them within half an hour. I am open to suggestions."

"Talk," Malin said. "Keep them at arm's length as long as possible. President Iceni could return at any moment."

"Tell them you'll collapse the gate if they attack," Morgan suggested.

That sounded potentially useful.

"What would you do if I made that threat, Colonel Morgan?" Malin asked.

She paused, then shrugged. "I'd call your bluff."

"Because it would have to be a bluff, a threat we dare not carry out. If the gate collapses, the value of the infrastructure in this star system shrinks to almost nothing. Control of the star system could be achieved simply by wiping out everyone and everything here by bombardment. They would no longer care what we might do in retaliation for that bombardment."

Morgan scowled but nodded. "That's right."

"Then—" Drakon began, to halt when a comm alert sounded. "Twenty-five minutes for them to evaluate the situation and issue their demands. Let's see what they say."

He didn't recognize the woman sending the message. She looked older, and his first impression was of caution. But first impressions could create later mistakes. Drakon concentrated on what she said and how she said it.

"This is CEO Gathos for the rebels in the Midway Star System. You are to surrender immediately, acknowledging the authority of the Syndicate Worlds, and deliver to me your primary leaders, former CEOs Drakon and Iceni, and their senior staff. If you do not transmit your capitulation within half an hour of your receipt of this message, I will initiate bombardment of noncritical infrastructure. For the people, Gathos, out."

"Do you know her?" Morgan asked.

"No," Drakon said. There were a lot of CEOs in the Syndicate Worlds. Iceni might know her, but if Iceni were here to tell him about Gathos, then Iceni would also be here with more mobile forces. "Assessment?"

"She means it," Morgan replied.

"Agreed," Malin said.

"Half an hour, or she starts throwing rocks. That rules out talking to buy time." He looked at the display again, where the path of the Syndicate flotilla had altered, curving down toward the star and toward this planet. Half an hour to reply. Gathos and her flotilla wouldn't hear that answer for six hours, but he still had to send it within the deadline.

"Pretend to surrender," Morgan said. "The ship that delivers you to them will have commandos aboard, and we'll take one of their heavy cruisers. That'll give us two heavy cruisers to their one, or at worst, they'll have one left, and we'll still have one."

To call that plan desperate was to understate things. "Malin?"

He shook his head. "Colonel Morgan's plan is a very weak reed on which to base our survival, but I can't see any other option that offers better odds. The only other thing I could suggest is prayer."

"Prayer?" Despite his tension, Drakon smiled crookedly. "What would I pray to, Colonel Malin? And what would have any cause to listen to my prayers?"

"Only you could know the answers to those questions, General."

"Then if you are so inclined, feel free to pray to whatever you can think of that we get out of this in one piece. But also get moving on Morgan's plan." He knew it had no chance at all. The moment he surrendered, the locals would start creating trouble, objecting to the return of Syndicate authority and tying down his troops, and the commander of C-818 would have plenty of time to confirm that there were no hidden explosives and either head for distant star systems at high speed or surrender her heavy cruiser to Gathos.

But a very small chance was better than none at all. Drakon's hand hovered over the reply control.

"General?" Morgan sounded baffled. "They've turned."

"What?" He looked back at the display, seeing that six hours ago, CEO Gathos's flotilla had bent its course again, turning away from the star and aiming straight for the hypernet gate. "What the hell is she doing?"

"Maybe she lost her nerve."

"Why? Because she looked up my service record? Somehow, I doubt that."

They kept watching, but the Syndicate flotilla stayed with the vector it had steadied out on. Drakon's eyes went to the time. The half-hour time limit was about to expire. "Maybe Gathos is trying to trick us into not surrendering so she has an excuse for pounding this star system into rubble."

Morgan had been watching the movement of the flotilla with narrowed eyes, and now shook her head. "No. She's running. I'd stake my life on it."

"You are."

"Oh, yeah. I am." Morgan grinned fiercely. "But maybe I can get to Gathos before I die."

A sudden laugh from Malin sounded at the same time as another alert from the display. He pointed. "Now we know why CEO Gathos changed her mind about trying to reconquer this star system."

At the jump point from Kane, another flotilla had appeared. Heavy cruisers, light cruisers, and Hunter-Killers arrayed around the unmistakable bulk of a battleship. "President Iceni's units arrived closer to the jump point from Lono than we are, so the light from their arrival reached CEO Gathos's flotilla before it reached us. She would have seen immediately that Gathos's flotilla was here, and issued a threat that would have reached Gathos at almost the same moment as Gathos saw our reinforcements."

Drakon laughed, too. From the planet, the battleship didn't show any signs of being barely operational. Its huge, threatening, ugly, beautiful hull seemed to gleam wickedly among the much smaller warships surrounding it. "President Iceni, this is General Drakon. I am really happy to see you. Welcome back. For the people, Drakon, out."

"She cut it fine enough," Morgan grumbled.

Turning to Malin, Drakon gave him a questioning look. "Did you get a prayer off, Colonel Malin?" Malin nodded. "Whatever you asked for, something seems to have listened."

Malin showed the ghost of a smile. "I asked that you receive what you deserved, General."

Drakon paused in surprise, then laughed again. "I guess nothing listened to you after all. If I'd gotten what I deserved, I'd have died storming Gathos's flagship. You two can stop worrying about setting up that suicide mission and get back to working on preparations for the Taroa operation."

PRESIDENT Iceni watched him warily from across the table. She looked tired, having taken a heavy cruiser at high speed back to the planet while the rest of her flotilla stayed with the battleship, but her eyes also held a spark of elation. "Neutral ground. Totally secure. No assistants or aides. What is it that you want to talk about? I've already heard that you were unhappy about an execution that I ordered."

Drakon nodded. "Yes. The execution is a minor issue, but I don't want it to be forgotten. I didn't like being surprised to hear that someone had been shot on your orders."

"CEO's prerogative," Iceni replied.

"You're not the only one running things here. I want to have a say in something like that. I want to know what someone has done, and I want a chance to evaluate the circumstances."

Iceni tilted her head slightly as she watched him, tapping one fingernail against the table. "You think that I silenced someone?"

"It's possible. You know what they say. Dead lawyers tell no tales."

"No lawyers were involved in this matter." She paused, eyes hooded in thought. "But you think it might have been something like that."

"How do I know otherwise?"

"A reasonable question." Iceni smiled at him, the expression holding no real feeling. "I will agree to inform you in advance of any more executions, as long as that agreement binds both of us. You also don't order any executions without telling me in advance of their being carried out."

He had expected an offer like that. He had also expected her to offer something that seemed like more than it was. Iceni's proposal left a huge loophole because executions weren't the same as assassinations or neutralizations. Neither of them would be agreeing not to eliminate anyone by purely extralegal means. But that was all right. He was on record with her about his concerns, and she knew that he would be watching for any signs that she was silencing people who knew the wrong things. "Fine."

Iceni's false smile had vanished. "I'm going to be candid with you, General. I've been considering a number of issues about how punishment and other legal matters are dealt with."

"What do you mean?"

"Ensuring that trials really do try to determine guilt and innocence. Ensuring that only those truly guilty are punished."

"Are you joking?" Drakon eyed her for any signs of twisted humor, or perhaps insanity.

"No. I'm very serious. Needless to say, I will not do anything that imperils you and me, or that would create instability among the citizens."

"Fine," Drakon repeated. "I don't have any objections to looking at that kind of thing, as long as we're in agreement on whatever's done, and as long as you and I are looked after in any changes. All right. That was a minor issue. Let's talk about why I wanted this meeting. Taroa."

"Taroa? Has one of the factions there prevailed?"

"No. Not yet." Drakon called up a large display, pointing to a representation of the Taroa Star System. "But we've run everything we know or can reasonably well guess through simulations, and every simulation says the Syndicate loyalists will win. The only variation is how long it will take."

Iceni frowned as she eyed the display. "Simulations are not reality. They can be extremely flawed."

"I agree. But I looked at the data myself, and my gut tells me they're right this time. The loyalists have too many resources, including control of the main orbital docks."

Iceni tapped some controls, zooming in on the primary inhabited world at Taroa. "What happened to the light cruiser that was hanging around there?"

"According to the last we heard, it left."

"Going back to Prime to report to the central government?"

"No. Going home." Drakon gestured vaguely. "Lindanen Star System."

"That's not close, but it's not all the way across Syndicate space, either." Her eyes went to the display again. "Have you thought about what it's like right now, General? All those star systems where Syndicate rule has ended or is shaky, all the mobile forces deciding whether to stay or go home. The ground forces, too, I suppose. They have the means to force someone to send them where they want to go. Everywhere out there, the broken remnants of the Syndicate Worlds' military are making their way to wherever they hope to find safety and survival."

"Or putting down roots where they are. It's strange to think about," Drakon agreed. "And worrisome. Those broken pieces of the Syndicate military could end up in the hands of someone who wants to use them to build a new empire."

"Someone like us?" she asked.

"Could be. But I gather that's not what you want to do."

"We haven't got the strength to build an empire," Iceni said. "Just defending this star system is going to be a full-time job."

"Even with the battleship?" Drakon asked, waiting to see if she would tell the truth about the status of that unit.

Another pause as she watched him. "You've probably already heard about the state of the battleship. It's potentially a huge asset for us. But most of its systems are still not operational, and it has far too few crew members to operate those systems even if they were working."

She had told the truth. That was heartening even if it was driven by the recognition that Drakon's own sources would have learned the truth sooner or later. "How long until the systems are all up and running?"

"With what we have at Midway to work at it? Five to six months. And getting enough crew will take at least that long. Midway isn't the most heavily populated of star systems." Iceni turned her head slightly to smile at him in sudden understanding. "Taroa."

"Yeah. A place with better ship outfitting yards than we have, stuff we can bring here, and a lot more trained workers who could be enticed to join the crew. You and I both know that we can't afford to wait five or six months for that battleship to be ready to fight. We have to get it ready faster, and the means to do that are at Taroa."

"Do *you* want an empire, General Drakon?"

"No." Drakon pointed to the representation of Taroa. "There are three factions fighting for control of Taroa. The Syndicate loyalists including the snakes, some group that sounds like those worker committees you ran into at Kane, and some bunch calling themselves the Free Democratic Star System of Taroa. None are that strong because Taroa doesn't have a hypernet gate. Maybe a third of the Syndicate soldiers went with the Free Taroans, but the rest, and all of the snakes, are in the loyalist camp. Local soldiers mostly went with the Free Taroans though some joined the workers. Our latest information, which is about two weeks old now, confirms that the worker faction is weakening. We got an unconfirmed report that the loyalists put out feelers to the rebel Free Taroans to unify against the workers, but the rebels were smart enough to know they'd be next once the workers were crushed. That just delays the outcome, though. Even if the Syndicate loyalists don't get reinforcements or other support, and they're the only faction with any right to expect that, they'll still win as the workers and the Free Taroans run low on weapons and ammo."

"Leaving one of the nearest star systems controlled by the Syndicate government," Iceni said. "That would not be to our advantage."

"No," Drakon agreed. "And the workers are unlikely to be much better from our point of view though they've got practically no chance of winning. That leaves the Free Taroans."

"Yes. But it sounds like they want elections for every office. Living with that next door might be very difficult. Working with that might be very difficult."

"Maybe. It might also give you and me a test population, a place to see what happens when the citizens rule themselves. I think what we need to focus on is that the Free Taroans are better than the alternatives."

"True," Iceni conceded. "Still, elections at those kinds of levels . . ."

Drakon settled back and smiled. "Elections? We're old hands at elections, aren't we, Madam President? You know what they can be like. Fraud, bribery, vote manipulation . . ."

Iceni returned his smile. "All of which we are veterans at."

"And all of which, my assessments agree, those pure-minded Free Taroans will convince themselves could never happen in whatever system of elections they come up with."

"Meaning we will have substantial influence on the Free Taroans?"

"Bought and paid for," Drakon agreed. "It's the Syndicate Way, isn't it?"

"As much as I detest many things about the Syndicate

Way, those particular methods may prove very useful. So, not a conquest?

"Absolutely not. An intervention, tipping the scales, not a conquest. If we try to impose our will on Taroa with what we have, it'll turn into a quagmire that'll suck this star system dry in no time. We'd be easy meat for the Syndicate Worlds when they came knocking at the hypernet gate demanding to be in control here again. For personal reasons, I'd rather that not happen."

"I'm sure I wouldn't enjoy that outcome, either." Iceni sat back, her eyes hooded in thought. "I believe that I planted some seeds at Kane for what might grow into a formal relationship between our star systems. If we could achieve similar results at Taroa, establish the grounds for creating an alliance of sorts, it could reap very important longer-term benefits. Trade, defense, a bubble of stability and order amid the collapse of the Syndicate Worlds. Three star systems isn't much, but it would be a start toward that, and it's a lot more than one star system."

Drakon nodded. "Humanity only started with one, and look where we've ended up."

"I don't aspire to that degree of success. However, intervening at Taroa will require a significant investment in ground forces and mobile forces. We need those assets here."

"We do. We also needed them here when we heard about the battleship at Kane, but it made more sense to send just about every warship to Kane. Now it makes more sense to send some of those warships to Taroa." He could see that Iceni was convinced yet still reluctant to commit the necessary forces, so Drakon played his last card. "There's something else concerning Taroa's shipyards. The last few ships that went through there reported that the main construction dock is completely concealed. They're at the stage where components of something are being assembled into a hull."

"Something?" Iceni murmured. "Something big if they need to use the main construction dock."

"Something big," Drakon agreed. "And I think we could use that something big more than whoever it's being built for right now. Which would be the Syndicate government on Prime. If we get the docks, we get that hull."

"We get the docks? That could be exceptionally useful." Iceni nodded and gave him a searching look. "What would you require to gain control of those docks and ensure victory for the Free Taroans?"

"I'd want to bring three brigades," Drakon said. "That will require requisitioning some of the civilian merchant ships here. And a decent-sized flotilla of warships to deal with any light mobile forces that might show up there to give us trouble. If there are no mobile forces waiting at Taroa, what we have with us will help overawe the opposition."

"If you want to overawe, the battleship is the way to go, but it's not even close to ready."

"I wouldn't want to come in with the battleship," Drakon said. "It's too big, too threatening. Showing up like that would make it look like a conquest before we said a word. I want to have time to explain that we're there to assist our, uh, friends, the Free Taroans."

Iceni nodded again. "In exchange for control of those docks and what is being built there. All right. Three brigades. All of your soldiers, leaving me with the local troops."

"The locals could handle anything that came up," Drakon said, choosing his words carefully. "But what I intended was to bring two of my brigades and one of the local brigades. That would leave one brigade of absolutely reliable soldiers here."

"Absolutely reliable?" Iceni asked, smiling thinly. "Just in case someone tried something while you were out of this star system?"

He hadn't wanted to put it that bluntly. "If you want to think of that brigade as my insurance against you, then fine. You decided to leave that heavy cruiser here to watch me while you were gone. But that's far from the only reason to leave that brigade here. You know as well as I do that the locals aren't one hundred percent to be counted on."

"But you want to take a brigade of them on this mission?"

Was she subtly taunting him? Or probing for his justifications? Drakon made an open-handed gesture. "My own soldiers can stiffen the locals if necessary, and the locals should be able to handle anything we find at Taroa."

"So we'll *both* feel safer if you leave one of your brigades here?"

"That's right."

"How thoughtful of you, General." Iceni rested her chin on one fist as she regarded him. "Which brigade? Which colonel?"

"Colonel Rogero's brigade."

"Colonel Rogero? Again? Is Colonel Rogero particularly fond of me?"

Drakon laughed briefly. "I don't know his personal feelings about you. I do know he can be trusted here." Gaiene, for all his skills and loyalty, if left alone for an extended period was likely to be shot by an enraged husband or furious father, and Gaiene might well be drunk when the bullet hit if he wasn't worried about Drakon showing up to check on him. Kai wouldn't run out of control, in fact seemed to have no vices at all or any other interests outside of his job, but was too rigid, not flexible enough to react quickly if something unexpected occurred and Drakon wasn't around to give new instructions. "Colonel Rogero also got to lead the force that went to Kane with you. Colonels Gaiene and Kai deserve a chance at action, too."

"And which local brigade?"

"The One Thousand Fifteenth. Colonel Senski's command."

"Colonel Senski. Hmmm." She didn't seem convinced, but Iceni finally nodded a final time. "You will also be taking your two aides?"

"Colonels Malin and Morgan? Yes."

"Then I agree to your proposal. How long will it take before you are ready to go?"

"Normally," Drakon began, "it takes a while to set up a movement of this size, but—"

"But you started preparing well before I got back, anticipating that I would agree to the mission," Iceni finished. She said it not as if guessing, but as if she had known that coming into the meeting.

Either Iceni was trying to rattle him by pretending to know good intelligence, or she really had some very good inside information on Drakon's troops. The best reaction at the moment was probably no particular reaction. He smiled at her as if her foreknowledge was not an issue at all. "That's correct."

Iceni smiled back. "I'll consult with Kommodor Marphissa on the size of the flotilla to accompany you. We will have to resupply those warships, and that will take a while. I'd estimate at least a week for them to get back here and prepare to go out again. I won't mislead you as to my intentions. I will want to hold back enough warships to protect this star system and my battleship while it's being fitted out, but I'm sure whatever we send with you will include at least one heavy cruiser."

Drakon gave her an inquiring look. "*Your* battleship?"

"Did I say that? *Our* battleship, of course."

"And I understand it has a name now." Why not flaunt his own information gathering?

"The *Midway*. Yes."

He had expected her to take the obvious course and name it after herself, which would have been a clear sign of ambition and ego. The fact that she had chosen something else reassured Drakon considerably. "Are you going to name the other warships, too?"

Iceni smiled again. "I already have. The implementing order is going out today. The heavy cruisers will be the *Manticore*, the *Gryphon*, the *Basilisk*, and the *Kraken*. The light cruisers will be named *Falcon*, *Osprey*, *Hawk*, *Harrier*, *Kite*, and *Eagle*. The Hunter-Killers will be *Sentry*,

Sentinel, Scout, Defender, Guardian, Pathfinder, Protector, Patrol, Guide, Vanguard, Picket, and *Watch.*"

"Really? Those are pretty good."

"I'm glad that I surprised you in that respect, General. Obviously, I cannot accompany you on this mission, so command of the mobile forces will be given to Kommodor Marphissa."

Drakon nodded. "I've heard that she's capable."

"She is. She also has an unfortunate tendency to speak her mind. I hope that you can work with that."

"I've got some experience with subordinates like that," Drakon said dryly, thinking of Malin and Morgan. "They can be the best kind of subordinates if they know what they're talking about, and if you're lucky."

Iceni gave him a surprised look. "Yes, General. They can indeed." She paused for a long moment before speaking again. "Will you tell me something?"

"That depends what it is."

"When you were facing the flotilla commanded by CEO Gathos, why didn't you betray me to save yourself? You could have claimed that you had just played along with me in order to get me to expose myself. It might not have saved you, but it would have given you some chance."

Drakon looked back at her for a while before replying. "If you want the truth, and if you want to believe that it's the truth, that never occurred to me." It had never occurred to Malin or Morgan, either. Or if either of them had thought of it, neither had brought it up. Why not? Malin should have seen the possibility, and that kind of opportunity was the sort of thing Morgan usually thought of first. Why had neither of them suggested turning on Iceni to at least buy some time?

"It didn't occur to you?" Iceni sat watching him. "I know a lot about you, but I don't really know you, General Drakon. Trying to predict what you're going to do next can be difficult."

"I have the same problem with myself at times," Drakon said.

"Do you? I know what you *should* do in any given situation, based on what we've been taught and our experiences, but I don't always know what you *will* do."

He shrugged, surprised that she was openly discussing such things. "There are a lot of situations where being a bit unpredictable can be an advantage."

"Of course," Iceni agreed. "But . . ." She studied him again. "Do you intentionally do it as a tactic, or is it part of you? Something you would do even if it didn't bring you an advantage?"

His own defenses were automatically rising, trying to keep him from betraying too much of what he thought. Drakon shrugged again. "Why would a CEO do something that didn't bring an advantage?"

"That's a good question. Yet here you are. You were exiled to Midway, and unlike me, who got sent here for bad luck as much as anything, you were sent here for doing something that had no possibility of benefiting you personally."

Drakon met her eyes. "That depends what you consider a benefit. I did what I considered to be the . . . correct thing."

"As opposed to the right thing?"

"The right thing? You mean like morally right? Nobody does that."

"Nobody admits to it," Iceni corrected him. "We know what the Syndicate Worlds looks like on the outside, and how a lot of it really works on the inside. And we know how the people around us look on the outside, but not what's really inside because we all learn to hide that."

"Yes." Despite his wariness, Drakon felt his internal barriers lowering. What she was saying matched his own thoughts, the sort of thing you couldn't discuss because you never knew who might use it against you. "I don't know you, either. I don't know who you are inside. I didn't know that you thought about stuff like that."

Iceni smiled in a self-mocking way. "I just spent a while traveling. You know what that's like. All the books and movies you could ask for at your fingertips, but also a lot of time to think if you want to spend your time doing that. Especially in jump space. Nothing is happening outside, so inside you can . . . think."

"What else did you think about?" he asked, and realized genuine interest had prompted the question.

"Have you ever wondered who you would be if you hadn't grown up in the Syndicate Worlds?"

"You mean, if I'd been born on some Alliance planet?"

"Perhaps," Iceni said. "Or perhaps somewhere else. Some star system far away, where they've never heard of the Alliance or the Syndicate Worlds or the war. Suppose you had grown up there? Who would you be?"

He could have laughed off the question, but Drakon thought about it. "You mean who would I be if I wasn't me?"

"Not exactly."

"Who would you be?" he asked her.

"I don't know," Iceni answered. "And that bothers me. Who would I be? I've spent my life, as you have, being careful, being afraid, toeing the line, playing the system, sometimes being a victim and sometimes being a victor. When we stuck our necks out, those necks, and the rest of us, ended up here in exile. Which was lucky because those necks could have been chopped off. Now the system is ours. We could make it what we want."

"Like that thing about the trials?"

"Like that."

Drakon felt himself really smiling, not just faking the gesture. "I guess that is nice to think about."

"At least when none of our aides or assistants or guards are around to keep us on guard. It's like living in a strait-jacket sometimes, isn't it?"

"It is," Drakon agreed. "Freedom is, well, frightening in some ways. But we've never really had it, so we don't know what it could be."

"If you could do anything, absolutely anything, *right now*, what would you do?" Iceni asked.

"Um . . ." He didn't want to answer that honestly,

because he had always found women with that kind of curiosity, that kind of intellect, to be extremely attractive. But he doubted that Iceni would be flattered by an expression of physical desire, *right now*, for her, even if the desire was generated by her brain and not the other parts of her. "I don't know. Run naked into the woods, I guess."

Iceni laughed. "Really? What an interesting idea. What made you say that?"

"It was the craziest thing I could think of," Drakon said.

"It sounds like fun. Let me know if you ever decide to do it."

If only he could trust her.

CHAPTER FIFTEEN

DRAKON preferred simple plans. They had fewer things that could go wrong. Even the simple parts could turn into a total goat rope, but if you kept the parts limited in number, that at least offered a chance to limit the number of goat ropes you would have to deal with when the plan hit reality head-on. "Not bad."

Malin checked his own readout of the plan, and Morgan gave Drakon a surprised look. They knew that "not bad" wasn't the same as "good to go."

"What's wrong with it?" Morgan asked.

"Only one thing." He pointed to the display over his desk where the plan for entering the Taroa Star System played out in three dimensions. "You've got one freighter loaded with half of one brigade coming in early and alone to surprise and capture the primary orbiting docks before the rest of the force shows up. That's good. It's critically important that we capture those docks intact along with whatever is being built there and the skilled workers building it. But your plan calls for you to use part of Gaiene's brigade, with Morgan along to represent me, while Malin and I follow with Kai's brigade, the rest of Gaiene's soldiers, and Senski's local brigade."

"I can handle it," Morgan said, bridling.

"Yes, but in action you and Gaiene are both very aggressive. What's needed there along with Colonel Gaiene is someone to watch the flanks and rear, someone to make sure we get whatever is being built in that main construction dock—"

"I'm just as good at that as Malin, there."

"—and someone who can immediately deal with the Free Taroans before they realize that we stole their primary docking facility. That's me."

It was Malin's turn to object. "Sir, that lead freighter is going in without any escort. If there is even one light mobile unit in the Taroa Star System, and it is under control of the snakes or Syndicate loyalists, then it could choose to intercept that freighter. That would put you at very great risk."

"The last word we had is that there are no Syndicate or snake-controlled mobile units at Taroa," Drakon said. "If one has shown up, it won't be hanging around the jump point for Midway. It'll be at the fourth planet, where most of the population is and the snakes and Syndicate loyalists are fighting the other two factions. Our freighter will be able to evade it for long enough if a warship like that comes for us, and once the rest of the force shows up, we'll have enough firepower to make it run."

"General, you are too important to risk yourself that way. If the loyalists have any nukes emplaced on those docks, they can blow the entire thing to hell if they realize in time what's happening. I can—"

"No," Morgan broke in. "*I* can handle it."

"You're both good," Drakon said, "but this is my job. Morgan, you'll ride with Colonel Kai, and Malin, you'll be with Colonel Senski. End of discussion."

They talked a bit longer about details, working those matters out, then Malin left.

Morgan paused before leaving, however. "If this is

because you think that Gaiene would hit on me if we were on the same ship, you're wrong."

"That's not it." Not that exactly, anyway. The idea of Gaiene and Morgan cooped up together on the freighter for a few days had bothered him, but not for the obvious reasons suggested by Morgan's allure and Gaiene's randiness. They both knew when to rein in those aspects of themselves. Just why having them jointly on that freighter for this mission did concern him, Drakon didn't know, but he had learned to listen to his gut feelings. And he did want to make sure that he, and no one else, was the first one talking to the Free Taroans. "It's about my being in direct contact with the people on the primary inhabited planet at Taroa. Your ideas of diplomacy are a little more aggressive, and involve a little more firepower, than may be appropriate there."

Morgan eyed him, then grinned. "Well, yeah. I am better at breaking things. All right, General."

"You and Malin will be on two different ships. Make sure it stays that way. I don't want my command staff concentrated on one target."

Her grin didn't waver. "You also don't want your command staff being cut in half if I got fed up with Malin and gutted him like a fish. Got it. But there was another thing."

"What's that?"

"Colonel Rogero. Alone here with her royal highness."

"Do you mean President Iceni?" Drakon asked.

"Yes, sir." Her smile fading, Morgan stepped closer. "General, we know Rogero had ties to the snakes, we know he has ties to the Alliance—"

"We've been over this."

"—so how do we know he doesn't have ties to Iceni? How do we know that he's not feeding her stuff that only those closest to you are aware of?"

Drakon considered the question because he had learned to pay attention to Morgan's instincts, too. "From the way you framed the question, I assume that you have no proof of that."

"I can get it."

"Real proof, Morgan. We're not the ISS. We don't find ways to prove someone is guilty by manufacturing evidence."

She shook her head, looking unfazed by the rebuke. "No. I don't have evidence. But I'm looking."

"That's part of your job," Drakon said. "Are you suggesting that I leave you behind to keep an eye on Rogero?"

"No, sir. I'm suggesting that you do something about him before it's too late."

"No. That's all, Colonel Morgan."

TOGO stood before Iceni's desk, his usual impassivity somehow seeming more stern. "I am concerned for your safety, Madam President."

That didn't sound good. Iceni focused her full attention on him. "What have you found?"

"General Drakon will be leaving the star system with most of his senior officers."

"I am aware of that."

"He will be leaving behind Colonel Rogero," Togo continued. "The man who earlier attempted to kill you."

Iceni shook her head. "I've double-checked Rogero's record. He's an excellent shot. If he had wanted to hit me when I stepped onto the battleship, he would have hit me."

"We cannot know that with certainty. We cannot know whether he faltered in carrying out his orders."

"You think that Colonel Rogero is being left behind to see that I am killed? Or to personally kill me?"

Togo nodded sharply. "While General Drakon is outside the star system. He will have perfect deniability."

It was the flip side of the earlier argument. That didn't mean the argument didn't have logic behind it, though. "Do you have any information actually linking Colonel Rogero to an assassination plot aimed at me?"

This time Togo hesitated. "There are some very disturbing rumors concerning Colonel Rogero, Madam President.

They call into question his loyalty and who he truly answers to."

So some form of information about Rogero's contacts with the ISS and that woman in the Alliance fleet had leaked out. "Rumors?" Iceni pressed. "You know how I feel about rumors."

"I have nothing solid, but the nature of the rumors indicate that Colonel Rogero may be extremely dangerous. He should be dealt with before—"

"No." Iceni leaned forward to emphasize her words. "That is not authorized. If you find proof, I want to see it. If all you have is rumors, I will not change my mind."

"But Madam President—"

"Proof."

"With all respect, Madam President, the proof may be your death."

"I don't think so." Iceni sat back again, smiling slightly. "And I think too highly of your own abilities to believe that Colonel Rogero would pose a threat while you are nearby."

Togo stood, irresolute, then nodded. "I will protect you, Madam President."

"Of course."

She watched him leave, then sighed and turned back to her work. Maybe Rogero was a threat, but she had no doubt that, whatever his orders, Rogero had deliberately avoided hitting her with that shot. A shot that had killed a snake whose intentions toward her didn't have to be guessed. For that, Rogero deserved at least a little restraint on her part.

She had told Drakon that she wouldn't order any more executions without informing him. Assassinations didn't count as part of that agreement. Prudence, as exercised by Syndicate Worlds' CEOs, meant erring on the side of ensuring that potential threats were eliminated.

But the words that Kommodor Marphissa had spoken to her, about the need to ensure that only the guilty were punished, still bothered Iceni. And Drakon had seemed to listen when she brought it up. Really listen, as opposed to nodding occasionally to fake interest in what she was saying. Not many people did that, of course, not when she had wielded the power of a CEO and currently the power of a president, but when she was younger, it had happened with discouraging frequency. Nowadays, the fake interest was much more carefully contrived. But Drakon had actually listened. *For a moment there . . . no. You can't afford to think that way. You let your guard down with him because you were so relieved to get back here safe, with the battleship and in time to scare off that flotilla, and to learn that he hadn't moved against you. But that doesn't mean he isn't planning something, or won't do something if you give him a good enough opportunity. Never trust anyone, but especially never trust another CEO. And that's what Artur Drakon is even though he calls himself a general now.*

Keep telling yourself that, Gwen. You can't drop your defenses with him. If he ever got you in bed . . . oh.

Wow.

I wish I hadn't thought about that.

AS Iceni had said, space travel could be very boring even with all the latest entertainment options at your beck and call. Not that a freighter was set up to deal with the entertainment needs of so many soldiers crammed into cargo compartments modified to offer life support and accommodations for half a brigade.

Drakon had the luxury of his own room, a closet-sized affair that offered privacy and little else. Taroa wasn't too far as jumps went, but the journey to the jump point took a while, then there were four and a half days in jump space, followed by a long, tense trip toward the fourth planet in the Taroa Star System.

There weren't any mobile forces units at Taroa, but that didn't mean some couldn't show up at any moment, and even a HuK or a corvette would be more than a freighter could handle. The small fast attack craft that had once served as defenses just outside planetary atmospheres had been swept up in a recall from Prime months ago, sent to some star systems far from here apparently in a harebrained scheme to fight Black Jack's fleet. They hadn't come back and had never been replaced by new units, so even that threat was at least temporarily gone.

Twelve hours' travel time out from the main docks orbiting the fourth planet, Drakon walked through the modified cargo compartments and other habitable parts of the freighter. The civilian crew members were deferential in the manner of people who knew they could die in a heartbeat if they offended him. Drakon had considered telling one of the nervous crew members that their deference offended him just to see how they would react but decided that would be gratuitously cruel. He knew from his own experiences when he was much more junior in rank that jokes like that were only funny to the superior who made them.

Everywhere else he went, his soldiers greeted him with feigned surprise as they worked on equipment, or studied advancement courses or tactics, or worked on virtual trainers. Drakon knew full well that he was being tracked by his soldiers everywhere he went on the freighter, and they were busy keeping each other apprised of where he was headed next. With some work and deceptive movements, he could probably surprise some of his soldiers in the middle of gambling or unauthorized unarmed-combat competitions, but it wasn't worth the trouble, especially since his soldiers knew better than to engage in any wild parties so close to a combat operation. So Drakon kept to an easily forecast path, threading through crowded cargo compartments and along passageways lined sometimes on both sides with soldiers sitting awake or asleep. He gave them a calm, confident demeanor that was only part masquerade and they gave him a professional and prepared appearance that was also only part pretense but would be full reality when it came time to attack.

Finally on his way back to his own room to do some final preparations of his own, Drakon came across the brigade commander. Colonel Gaiene sat in a passageway, back against one bulkhead, facing the bulkhead across from him since no one else sat on that side. If they had to describe Conor Gaiene's appearance in one word, most people would have chosen "dashing." Or maybe "gallant" or perhaps "swashbuckling." Even sitting on the deck, he somehow seemed ready to leap up and lead a charge.

That was how he appeared until you noticed his eyes, dark and weary even though Gaiene was still a few years shy of middle age. Now those eyes looked up as Drakon approached. "Good afternoon, General."

"Good afternoon." There were few other soldiers near the command deck, and those were giving their brigade commander as much room and privacy as current circumstances allowed, so Drakon took a seat next to Gaiene. "How are you doing?"

"I'm sober. And alone. Alas." A female soldier walked by, and Gaiene watched her appreciatively though discreetly. "No sleeping with subordinates. Is that rule really necessary?"

"I'm afraid so."

"Most CEOs don't care. Most CEOs right now would have a drink in one hand and one of their subordinates in the other."

Drakon grinned. "I'm not most CEOs."

"No. You're not." Gaiene looked toward the far bulkhead, his expression pensive. "For which I am smart enough to be grateful."

"You're brilliant in battle, Con."

"And the rest of the time I'm a royal pain in the butt." Gaiene ran one hand through his hair, and Drakon caught a glimpse of the ring on one of his fingers. How long ago had she died? Ever since then, Gaiene had tried to forget her with every woman who was willing and every bottle he could crack open. But he still wore the ring. "I don't know why you keep me around."

"I have my reasons."

"Any other CEO would have had me in a labor camp long before this," Gaiene remarked. "As one of the guards or as one of the inmates."

Drakon nodded. "And that would be a real waste."

"A waste. Yes. We know all about that, don't we? Scarred lives and damaged souls. We're all damned, you know," Gaiene went on in a conversational voice. "Everywhere we've fought, we've left a little piece of ourselves and replaced it with a small piece of the hell we found in that place. Now most of us is scattered in a hundred little pieces in a hundred places where death walked. I see those places. I see them all the time. Usually in my dreams, but sometimes I see them when I'm awake."

Gaiene could be moody when sober, but this was worse than usual. "Are you all right?" Drakon asked. "Can you handle going into another fight?"

"I'm fine. The psychs say I will soon achieve emotional equilibrium again. They've been saying that for a very long time. I will go on, though," Gaiene added, his tone now slightly distant. "I will go on until the day I end; then you will give me a proper warrior's burial, and you will go on."

"Unless we both end together that day," Drakon said.

"Ah, no, General. It's not for you to talk of endings. You still have a future."

"So do you."

But this time Gaiene did not reply. He sat, his eyes on the opposite bulkhead, but looking at another place and time.

There were a great many things that Drakon needed to be doing. But he sat next to Gaiene for a long time without talking, shoulder to shoulder against a future that was uncertain and a past too clearly remembered.

"FIVE minutes to docking," the announcing system on the freighter declared. The operator of this particular freighter had chosen a woman's voice using an odd and strong accent, producing an effect that combined attention-getting for the strangeness and annoyance over the difficulty of understanding some of the words.

"Probably the voice of the owner's mistress," Gaiene

commented. He and all of his soldiers were in combat armor, ready to go when the freighter docked.

"I can't think of any other explanation." Drakon's armor was tied into the freighter's own systems, so he could monitor the approach directly. On visual, the shape of the dock ahead of them stood out brilliantly white against the black of space. "No sign of any special— Wait. Looks like a squad of local troops in armor."

Colonel Gaiene sighed with exasperation. "Now we'll have to waste ammunition on them."

"Maybe. Maybe not. They don't look tense." The troops waiting on the dock were being careless, moving so they were clearly silhouetted against the bright white of the dock walls instead of keeping to shadowed locations or cover. And they stood holding their weapons casually, propped over one shoulder or resting nose first against the deck. He had seen similar carelessness and postures before, when commanding detachments who had felt what these soldiers clearly felt, though he hadn't let them get away with those kinds of behaviors. "Looks more like they've been on alert too long. They're going through the motions, but they're bored by it all. They've probably been doing the same drill when every ship arrives."

"Do you want to try to take them alive?"

Drakon thought for a moment, then nodded. "It's critical that we keep the snakes on this facility from realizing what's happening until it's too late for them to trigger any self-destruct. The sooner we start shooting, the less time we'll have. How do we surprise them with overwhelming force and keep them from sounding an alarm?"

Gaiene smiled. "Contraband in one of the freight compartments. The sort of contraband that bored soldiers would love to get their hands on. They'll have to go check it out in person before anyone in authority confiscates it."

"What kind of contraband?"

"Hmmm . . . happy dust." A mythical drug, undetectable by any means, nonaddictive, no side effects, cheap, and the nearest thing to feeling like a god.

"Happy dust doesn't really exist," Drakon pointed out. "It's an urban legend. Or I guess just a legend since I've never been anywhere that hadn't heard of it."

"Which means we don't actually have to have any," Gaiene pointed out in turn. "Sergeant Shand!"

A stout soldier trotted forward. "Yes, Colonel."

"Get out of your armor and into a survival suit. You are a drug smuggler. You have a cargo of happy dust. You are willing to bribe the squad of local soldiers with some of it as long as they let you keep the rest. Get them all into this freight compartment."

"Yes, Colonel."

By the time the freighter shuddered gently as the grapples locked it into the dock, Sergeant Shand was ready, looking remarkably seedy and dissolute in a grubby survival suit pulled out of the freighter's emergency locker. Shand went to the compartment access, while Gaiene dispersed his troops around the compartment itself, hidden behind anything that would serve.

Drakon watched, keeping his breathing even, his heart rate under control. Gaiene could be trusted to handle the assault, but Drakon had to remain calm and focused, ready to spot problems before they developed and make sure nothing hung up anywhere.

When one of the bored soldiers opened the access to plug in and check the manifest, Shand was there, talking suit to suit with the soldier on the crew circuit as he gestured in alternately enticing and pleading ways.

More soldiers showed up. Sergeant Shand waved invitingly inside.

They followed him. Drakon counted a full squad as the last cleared the access. His outside view showed no one visible on the dock.

A sudden rustle of motion marked a couple of companies of soldiers leveling weapons at the shocked local troops, all of whom were wise enough to freeze into total immobility.

Motion on the dock, a single figure in battle armor coming out, pausing long enough to take in the situation, then heading toward the freighter access like someone who was very unhappy and ready to unload that emotion upon others. "Is their squad leader with them in here?" Drakon asked Gaiene.

The reply took only a moment. "No."

"He or she just figured out that the squad is all inside the freighter and is heading this way, no doubt mad as hell."

A few seconds later the sergeant came storming through the access, then stopped as four of Gaiene's soldiers near the door planted weapons against the sergeant's helmet.

Gaiene clucked a disappointed sound. "The sergeant tried to send an alert. Our jammers blocked it inside the hull. She has an impressive grasp of profanity."

"She can exercise it on her squad while they're all locked up aboard here," Drakon said, as the locals were disarmed and herded away. "We've got a couple of minutes more at best before somebody notices that they're gone from the dock." He switched to the command circuit that went to every one of his soldiers. "Don't forget to let any of the soldiers defending the facility surrender if they don't fight us. We need to move fast, and we don't need any last stands holding up the attack. Move!"

The elements of the brigade exploded from the freighter, using the big cargo-loading hatches. Soldiers swarmed along the dock, heading for objectives loaded into their combat armor. There had been plenty of copies of the layout of the facility available at Midway, and the soldiers had spent a lot of their time on the trip running virtual assaults. Now they didn't hesitate as they attacked the real thing.

Just inside the facility access, a snake sitting at the personnel screening desk died before she knew what was happening, her alarm untouched. A group of civilian workers fled in panic, some huddled against the deck in fright, but the soldiers ignored them until one reached for an alarm panel, only to be knocked sprawling against the nearest wall.

Drakon stayed back, trying to remain near the center of

the mass of soldiers as they spread through the facility. He focused not on the action in the area right around him but on the big picture shown on his helmet display, watching for trouble, especially with any of the units heading for the main construction dock and those charging toward the control compartment for the orbital docks.

Colonel Gaiene seemed to be everywhere, always in the lead, pushing his troops in a race to occupy as much of the facility as possible and overrun as many local soldiers as they could before alarms sounded.

A team of combat engineers locked into the control circuitry of the docks and began downloading software to take over systems and prevent any new commands from being entered by the defenders.

Still no alarm as Gaiene's troops charged through still-open hatches and down undefended passageways. The barracks nearest the docks got swamped by a wave of attackers, the surprised defenders blinking in amazement as they were suddenly confronted by overwhelming numbers of armored soldiers. None were foolish enough to resist.

The attack spread through the facility in a ragged bubble as different sections were overrun. A break room full of off-shift workers was seized. A workshop occupied. "Secondary docks cleared," a battalion commander reported to Gaiene and Drakon. "Heading into the main dock now."

Drakon focused on the displays from unit leaders charging into the dock. The security doors were unmanned, using automated readers that were overridden in instants, then soldiers were swarming into the main construction dock. "Hot damn," one of the unit leaders exclaimed as he saw the object hidden inside until then. "Battleship or battle cruiser. Sure as hell."

"It'll be one of those things someday," another leader commented. "Right now, it's just a shell."

Startled late-shift workers were dropping tools and raising their hands as the soldiers swept among them. "No resistance here. No guards. Main construction dock is secured."

"Make sure there are no charges planted to sabotage that hull," Drakon ordered. "Go over the whole thing with some of those workers in tow."

Alarms finally blared as someone, somewhere realized that trouble had arrived. But with Drakon's engineers confusing the information coming into the control compartment, no one yet seemed to have grasped that an attack was under way. Bewildered automated systems trying to figure out exactly which emergency was the problem mixed the tones of various alerts, the onboard fire alarm switched to the object-collision alarm, which became the riot alarm, which changed to the decompression alarm, which turned back into the fire warning.

Where the hell are the snakes? Drakon wondered, scanning his display for any sign of them. "Do we have all control circuits locked down?"

"No, sir," the reply came from the combat engineer commander. "There are some redundant, totally independent circuits that we haven't been able to reach yet."

"Colonel Gaiene, make sure your soldiers get access to all circuits for the engineers as soon as possible. Bypass other objectives if necessary until we get everything under control."

One platoon found a snake barracks filled with ISS personnel hastily trying to don battle armor. After a single instant in which both sides stared at each other, Gaiene's soldiers launched grenades into the bunched snakes, followed by a rush in which the soldiers fired at anything that still moved, some of them continuing to flay the bodies with shots until their commanders slammed fists against their helmets.

Drakon snarled with frustration as he saw red markers on his display showing vital circuits and compartments not yet seized. But the civilians on this facility were all awake, some piling into the passageways in panic and slowing down Drakon's attack. He couldn't put off the next step any longer. "Broadcast the message."

Over the pulsing of the different alarms still clamoring

for attention, voices boomed over the internal announcing system hijacked by the comm specialists with Drakon's troops. "This facility is now under the control of soldiers of the Midway Star System under the command of General Drakon. Do not resist. Any citizens and soldiers who surrender will not be harmed. Return to your quarters and remain there. Do not offer resistance."

Another snake barracks, this one alerted but with only a few occupants, who fought viciously before being wiped out.

"Colonel, we've got a platoon holed up near engineering control. They're . . . Damn! Got a soldier down. These guys are fighting."

"Take them out," Gaiene ordered. "They had their chance."

Soldiers converged on the holdouts from three sides, overwhelming the defenders with a barrage of fire before charging in and finishing off any who were still alive.

Drakon watched it all, remembering so many fights just like it. Then the enemy had been Alliance soldiers. *We were taught to fight without mercy. They fought without mercy, too. Now we're fighting ourselves the same way.*

Is that why Black Jack told his people to start taking prisoners again and stop bombarding citizens? Because he realized that if merciless behavior becomes habit, you can end up turning those tactics on yourself? The Syndicate government has been willing to do things like that for a long time, and here we are, without the Syndicate ordering it or the snakes forcing it on us, repeating that pattern.

We've got to break out of it. "This is General Drakon. Everyone will provide opportunities to surrender to any defender at any point. Only if they keep fighting are they to be killed."

"General?" Gaiene questioned. "Your orders going in—"

"Have changed. We're not snakes."

". . . Yes, sir."

Drakon's eyes went to part of his display. He frowned, wondering what had drawn his attention, then saw an anomaly warning pop up near the main construction dock. "Heads up at the dock. There's someone coming your way!"

Moments later, a hatch blew open, and snakes and loyalist soldiers poured through it toward the massive hull under construction. Fire from Gaiene's soldiers pummeled them while Drakon started moving himself, calling to some of Gaiene's nearby units. "To the main dock! Now!"

Why should it matter? What could a few dozen snakes and soldiers do to something as massive and uncompleted as that hull? But they were fighting like hell to get to it, so there had to be some important reason. "Hold them!" he ordered the soldiers inside the dock. "Keep them away from that hull!"

"Too many!" one of Gaiene's soldiers cried, the signal cutting off abruptly on the last word as fire ripped into her.

Reinforcements entered the dock from three locations, one group led by Drakon. They could see the force of snakes and loyalist soldiers moving toward the hull, their advance hindered by the stubborn defense from Gaiene's original occupying force. Drakon's force had come in from the side, giving them clean shots at the attackers. Leveling his weapon, Drakon sighted on a snake dashing forward, his shot hitting home moments before two others, the combined blows taking out the snake.

The other two reinforcing elements opened fire as well, putting the snakes and loyalist soldiers in a cross fire coming from three directions on top of the shots still pummeling them from the defenders of the hull.

A loyalist soldier jumped up to run, only to fall as the nearest snake pumped a shot into him. A second later, the snake died, too, as the loyalist soldiers turned on the ISS agents among them.

"Hold fire!" Drakon ordered as the last of the snakes on the dock died and the loyalist soldiers dropped their weapons, then stood with empty hands raised in surrender. For an instant of time, the fate of the loyalists balanced on the knife-edge of veteran soldiers fighting their own instincts and experience to kill without mercy.

But no more shots were fired. As Drakon took a deep breath and refocused on the situation elsewhere, he heard one of the loyalists broadcasting an appeal in a shaking voice. "You guys know us! We've fought together! Don't scrap us!"

And the reply from one of Gaiene's soldiers. "Frost out, brother. We don't work for some CEO. We're General Drakon's troops. His orders are to accept surrender."

"Drakon? Praise our ancestors! Hey, the snakes said they needed to reach two places inside that hull. We don't know why. Here are the readouts."

"Let's check those locations," a captain ordered some of her soldiers. "You two engineers, come with us in case something needs disarming."

"General?" Colonel Gaiene's voice came.

"Yeah." Drakon finally relocated Gaiene on the map on his helmet display, seeing Gaiene leading a force down the passageway toward the primary control compartment. "They tried to get to the hull. Don't know why yet. How are things on your end?"

"We're about to knock on a door."

Drakon called up direct video from Gaiene's armor, seeing a soldier leveling a Ram tube at the reinforced hatch protecting the control compartment. The Ram fired, blowing the hatch completely off its mountings, and before the hatch had hit the deck Gaiene led a force through the hatchway into the main control compartment. Inside, screaming workers were trying to flee a half-dozen snakes in armor who were firing into them. "Try someone who can fight back!" Gaiene shouted as his first shot shattered the faceplate of one of the snakes.

The other snakes died in a flurry of fire, leaving a curious stillness around the soldiers. Through Gaiene's armor, Drakon could hear the shuddering gasps and pained cries of the surviving civilian workers, who were watching the soldiers with dread. "Start first aid and get some medics in here fast," Gaiene ordered his troops, then spoke to Drakon. "System operators. It looks like the snakes were going to kill them all, then try to blow the system controls. Totally pointless since we've already remotely seized command of those circuits. Just senseless, bloody slaughter." Gaiene took a step to stand over one of the snakes lying lifeless on the deck, pointed his weapon at the head of the dead body, and fired another shot. "Bastards."

Who would you be if you weren't you? Iceni's question came back to Drakon then. Who would those snakes have been? In a different place and time, would they have still been willing to do such things? Was it because they had been taught that such actions were right? Or had the ISS sought out those who were always to be found among humanity in every place and time, the ones who for a cause or for no reason at all would kill the helpless without blinking? The answer didn't matter just then. He and Gaiene had to deal with who the snakes were. "Good job, Colonel."

The main control deck had been one of the last places to be reached where resistance could be expected. Elsewhere, the flood of soldiers continued to spread rapidly through the rest of the facility, but aside from an occasional isolated loyalist soldier who stood with empty hands raised in surrender, no more defenders were left. "How's it look to you, Colonel Gaiene?"

"I've got teams checking a few last spots right now, General. But it looks like we've got this one put away."

A few minutes later, Gaiene called again. "All secure," he reported. "Odd that one force tried so hard to get to a hull that couldn't have gotten under way without several months of work."

"We should hear from the soldiers who went in to check on that real soon." Drakon studied the lists of data being downloaded from Gaiene's armor. "We took a few casualties."

"It could have been far worse, General. It was for the defenders." The elation and excitement was draining from Colonel Gaiene's voice, replaced by weariness and gloom. "I have a report from those who are inside the hull. They've found the packages the snakes wanted so badly."

Video popped up on one side of Drakon's helmet display. "Two nukes," an engineer reported. "Sealed behind false bulkheads. We severed the command links before they could be remotely detonated, so the only way the snakes could set them off was by getting to them."

"They sure didn't want anyone making off with this hull," the captain who had led the searchers commented. "If they'd blown those, it would have also trashed this whole dock facility."

"Get the nukes disarmed, disassembled, and removed," Drakon ordered. Had news of what Iceni had accomplished at Kane already reached Taroa, resulting in an extra measure of security against someone's stealing an uncompleted warship? Or did this just reflect snake paranoia of possible rebellion on the dock? He remembered the cooperation some of the prisoners had rendered and how they had turned on the snakes with them. "Colonel Gaiene, I want the loyalist soldiers who surrendered evaluated for candidates to come over to us. What I'm seeing shows that they're all Syndicate troops as opposed to Taroan locals."

"That matches my information," Gaiene said. "Apparently, the snakes didn't trust locals up here."

"They don't seem to have trusted the loyalist regulars all that much, either. With good cause."

Gaiene's smile mixed melancholy and satisfaction. "It couldn't have happened to a nicer nest of reptiles. We'll put the option of joining your forces to these soldiers and see what happens. I assume we want full screening of each and every one of those volunteers before we accept them?"

"You assume correctly. There have been way too many deep-cover snake agents showing up at Midway."

"And the civilians?"

"We'll screen them gradually. For now, I'll keep the facility at lockdown for another hour, then relax it by stages. That should keep any civilians from doing anything dumb and any snake agents among them from doing anything until we're ready to deal with it."

Feeling exhausted but grateful that coming down off the

adrenaline rush from an operation was eased by the need to concentrate on cleanup details, Drakon called the freighter. "Put me through to Senior Line Worker Mentasa." There were risks involved in using Mentasa, but those were more than balanced by the advantages in having someone known and trusted by the workers here. Mentasa also had firsthand knowledge of which specialists were most needed to finish out the work on the battleship at Midway.

"Here, General Drakon," Mentasa said, doing his best to stand in a military posture even though the cramped quarters on the freighter made that difficult, and even though his citizen-worker appearance made his attempts to look military seem a little silly.

"The facility has been taken. It's still on lockdown, but I want you to get on the comm system. I'm sending you an authorization so the blocks we put on it will let you through. Start talking to people you know. Tell them who we are, reassure them that they are safe, tell them what we want, find out what they've been building in the main construction dock, and see if anyone is interested in being hired to work at Midway. I also want to know everything you can find out about the hull in the main construction dock. Battleship or battle cruiser, how far along, how long it will take to finish, and whether Taroa has everything needed to complete it."

"Yes, General." Mentasa hesitated. "General, is it permissible to contact anyone on the planet?"

"Personal business or business?" Drakon asked, already knowing the answer by the look in Mentasa's eyes.

"Both. If that's—"

"It's fine. *After* you talk to the citizens up here and get me that information on the hull that's under construction, feel free to talk to citizens down on the planet. Let your people know that you're all right. By the time you talk to them, I'll have let the Free Taroans know why we're here."

Drakon took a few moments to check out his appearance, trying to look impressive but not too intimidating. The Free Taroans had open comm links, of course, broadcasting their propaganda and seeking recruits. Drakon's comm software easily hijacked one of the those circuits. "This is General Drakon of the Midway Independent Star System. My soldiers now control the primary orbiting dockyard in this star system. We have come here to assist the Free Taroans. The leaders of the Free Taroans are to contact me as soon as possible using this circuit."

That ought to produce a quick reaction.

How the Free Taroans would react to this unasked-for help had been the biggest variable in the planning. If the Free Taroans balked, if they were more afraid of Drakon's aid than they were eager to win, then things might get a bit complicated when he insisted on holding on to the docks.

He would have to wait and see. There were some things that couldn't be solved with soldiers.

CHAPTER SIXTEEN

THE response from the Free Taroans took about half an hour, about what he had expected from a group that seemed to think voting on everything was the way to do business.

He recognized the woman who answered, but in that haven't-I-seen-her-before way rather than precise identification.

She saluted him. "Sub-CEO Kamara. I once served in a force under your command, General Drakon."

Kamara? Now he remembered. Not the finest sub-CEO that he had ever worked with, but far from the worst. She had been good enough to impress herself on his memory. "You've joined the Free Taroans?"

"Yes. A number of the Syndicate troops did. We're tired of being slaves." She said that pointedly, eyeing Drakon as if it were a challenge.

"I'm not interested in becoming anyone's new master," he assured Kamara. "I brought forces to help the Free Taroans win here."

"That comes as a great surprise to us. Naturally, we're worried about other surprises. What is expected in exchange for your aid?"

Drakon smiled grimly. "What we get from the deal is simple. We win when you win. Midway doesn't want the snakes to achieve victory here. I shouldn't have to explain why. What we've heard of the third faction here makes it sound like they would be as bad as the snakes as far as we're concerned. Taroa is our neighboring star system. We'd like it controlled by someone we can work with."

"That's it?" Kamara's skepticism was clear.

"There are no preconditions though we'll be interested in negotiating agreements once the Free Taroans are in power."

"What about the docks?" Kamara pressed.

Drakon shrugged in a show of disinterest. He didn't want to get into his and Iceni's intentions for the docks until after the Free Taroans had committed themselves. "We're also here to recruit workers. Shipyard workers, specialists, that kind of thing. No draft. No slave labor. Hiring. If someone wants to come back with us on those terms, I don't want the Free Taroans telling them they can't."

Kamara didn't answer for a while. "Of all the CEOs I worked with," she finally said, "you were the only one who actually put himself on the line for his workers. Even though my common sense is telling me that you're only doing this because it's part of some scheme to control us, I don't think we can afford to turn down this opportunity. Nor can we prevent citizens who want to accept your offer of employment from taking that offer as long as it is actually a free decision on their part. But I don't have any final say. I'll discuss it with the interim congress, and we'll let you know our decision. How many troops do you have here?"

"Right now I have about half of one brigade."

"Only half of a brigade? That's not much, but it might be enough—" Her eyes shifted to one side. "We just spotted a force arriving at the jump point from Midway."

"Right," Drakon agreed, pleased that the others had finally shown up. "A heavy cruiser, three light cruisers, four Hunter-Killers, and five modified freighters carrying another two and a half brigades of troops."

Kamara watched him, tension back in her posture. "That's a substantial force. Enough to give anyone the edge here. I assume that if the Free Taroans don't agree to accept your aid, you'll offer it elsewhere?"

Drakon shook his head. "No. I told you. The Free Taroans are the only group here that we're interested in helping."

"And if we win with your help? How many of those soldiers stay?"

"On your planet? None of them." This dock, on the other hand . . . "We need them back at Midway when they're done here."

Another pause, then Kamara made a helpless gesture. "We probably have no choice but to believe you. Are we allowed to speak with anyone up there? Any of the citizens?"

"Sure. Why not? The snakes managed to kill a few of the workers here before we got them all, but everyone else is safe. I've had the place locked down while we ensured everything was secure, but I've started lifting that. I'll lift the comm restrictions, too."

"I will talk to the congress," Kamara said, but this time her tones carried more conviction.

LONG ago, a large staff might have been required to plan and coordinate the movements of almost three brigades of soldiers from the orbital facility to the planet's surface. But that kind of housekeeping work was what automated systems excelled at since the variables were few. Plug in current force data listing troops and equipment, shuttles and freighters, and the locations of all those, then let the software produce a detailed solution, issue the necessary instructions, and monitor progress. Malin and Morgan could easily keep an eye on everything to see if glitches developed and still have plenty of time to assist Drakon with other planning that was made much more complex by unpredictable human behavior.

The headquarters of the Free Taroans had once been

that of the Syndicate Worlds planetary forces, so it was well fitted out, though much of the equipment was older than that at the facilities on Midway since Taroa didn't have the strategic importance or the priorities for upgrades that provided.

Drakon looked at a map floating above the table in the main command center. The virtual globe slowly rotating beside it allowed someone to choose an area to zoom in on and change the area shown on the map, but it was set to show most of the occupied southern continent. Taroa's northern continent was big, but so high in latitude that it consisted of frozen desert plains and glacier-choked mountains. Aside from a few research and rescue stations with only a small number of occupants, no one lived there.

The populace so far had stayed on the much more pleasant southern continent, which straddled the planet's equator. At some point in the not-too-distant past as measured by the life of worlds, something had ripped the planet's surface there, causing masses of lava to boil up and form that new continent. Life had recovered from what must have been a catastrophic event by the time humans arrived to find a continent filled with knife-edged volcanic mountains and hills that separated lushly forested valleys.

"Screwed-up place to fight a war," Morgan commented. "You take one little valley, and there's a natural wall protecting the next."

Sub-CEO Kamara nodded. "That's one of the things that has kept us stalemated. It's very easy to defend the ground on this planet. The airlift available to us and the other groups got knocked out early, so we couldn't leapfrog over the ridges. A lot of the slopes between valleys are too steep even for armor to get up them, so it's foot soldiers slugging it out meter by meter, up one ridge and down the next. It doesn't take many ridges before you run out of foot soldiers."

Morgan gave Kamara a disdainful glance. "How many soldiers did you lose learning that?"

Kamara returned the look. "Us? Very few on offensive

operations. It's the loyalists that have gotten chopped up trying to reestablish control over the areas that belong to us, and the Workers Universal, which sent some human waves up the ridges before we killed so many they ran low on wave material."

"You've played it smart," Malin said.

"I don't know if it's smart. I convinced the interim congress to hold off on attacks since we seemed more likely to win by waiting out the loyalists and the workers. But I've been under increasing pressure to stage some offensive operations because everyone has been worried about a Syndicate Worlds relief force showing up to reinforce the loyalists and pound us flat." Kamara shook her head, sighing. "I knew I was just buying time. We couldn't win, and we'd keep getting weaker relative to the loyalists."

"You did the right thing," Drakon said. "Maybe you couldn't have won, but you damn well could have lost a lot faster if you'd bled your forces dry in futile attacks. The Syndicate Worlds government is busy in a lot of places and doesn't have nearly as much strength to deal with rebellions as it would like. Taroa would be pretty low on their priority list unless they happened to have someone out this way for another reason." A reason such as recapturing the Midway Star System, but there wasn't any need to bring that up. "Something else could have happened to even the odds for you. And it did."

"That was my thinking," Sub-CEO Kamara said, looking pleased at Drakon's words. "It's been a progressively more lonely position to hold, though. So many people want instant results, without thinking about the chances of success or the costs." She turned to the map, pointing out red splotches in some of the valleys where towns and small cities could be found, usually where those valleys let out on the coastline to allow easier access by water. "The main loyalist strongholds are in these areas."

"Why hasn't anyone tried assaults from the water?" Drakon asked. "Real narrow frontages, open fields of fire, jagged reefs just offshore, with thin channels dredged through them that make perfect kill zones, mines . . ." Sub-CEO Kamara shrugged, her bitter expression contrasting with the casual gesture. "It was tried a few times. I tried it, hoping the loyalists would be focused against ground attacks and overconfident about the effectiveness of defenses along the water. I was wrong. That's where we took most of our losses."

"Does CEO Rahmin still command the Syndicate loyalists?" Malin asked.

"She did until about two weeks ago. That's when a suicide squad from the Workers Universal infiltrated the loyalists' interim capital and blasted their way into her command center." Kamara didn't seem particularly upset at the loss of her former superior. "Now there's a snake running the show over there. CEO Ukula."

Morgan waved at the map. "If we take out the snakes, do the regular troops keep fighting?"

"That depends on whether they think they'll die if they try to surrender."

"Will they?" Drakon asked.

"Some units have committed serious atrocities. They'll have trouble trying to surrender," Kamara said as calmly as if she were talking about road conditions. "Others have been a lot better behaved."

Morgan smiled. "We can split the loyalist soldiers, then. All it takes is contact with the units that will be allowed to surrender."

"I can give you the identities of those units," Kamara said. "Managing hidden contact with them may be—"

"No problem," Morgan said, her smile still in place but now wolflike. "I can handle it."

Kamara stared at her for a moment, then looked back at the map.

Malin was running his finger across scattered purple blotches on the map, all of them concentrated in urban areas. "This marks areas controlled by the Workers Universal?"

"Roughly." Kamara's expression shifted to disgust. "If

we can roll up the snakes and turn everything on the Workers Universal, I think they'll fold pretty quick because they've hollowed themselves out. Sure, the workers have gotten lousy deals. But the ones who went with the Workers Universal are a lot worse off now. I told you about the human waves the WUs sent against us. Some real nutcases have taken over there. Their opposition in the workers' leadership was accused of treason, arrested and shot, or simply disappeared. These days, the ones left in charge are killing as many of their own workers in purges as we are in fighting them."

"Cannibalization of the revolution once the most radical begin competing for purity," Malin commented. "It's happened countless times in the past. Right now, many of those in this star system seeking stability are drawn to the loyalists as protection against the Free Taroans and the Workers Universal. But if the loyalists are defeated, then the choice for such people will be between—"

"Freedom and homicidal nutcases," Kamara finished. "I figure we'll look pretty good at that point to anyone wanting to choose sides." She glanced at Drakon. "The loyalists offered to conduct joint operations with us against the Workers, but I knew better than to bite that poison apple."

Drakon smiled crookedly, inwardly pleased that Kamara had not tried to keep that offer secret from her new allies. He studied the map, zooming in to identify some good locations for surgical strikes. "Colonel Malin, please get Colonels Gaiene, Kai, and Senski. We have a snake hunt to plan."

"We can't afford to lose a lot of infrastructure," Kamara said. "Neither can the loyalists, which is the only thing that has kept them from dropping rocks on us from orbit."

Morgan blew out a derisive breath. "You want us to defeat the loyalists without breaking anything?"

Kamara met her eyes soberly, nodding. "That's right. The loyalists are sitting on some of the most critical facilities on the surface. If all we inherit is ruins, then our victory would be as hollow as they come."

"The snakes have been following scorched-earth tactics every time we've fought them," Malin said. "Once they know defeat is inevitable, they try to take us with them."

"Then we try to make sure the snakes don't know they're losing until it's too late to do anything about it," Drakon replied. "Colonel Morgan, get the identities of the units you want to undermine from Sub-CEO Kamara and get started on that. I want to know what units those are, too, so we can work our plans around them and hit the other units first."

"How often do you want updates on what I'm doing?" Morgan asked.

"Let me know what I need to know when I need to know it. Otherwise, you're free to run with it."

She grinned. "No problem."

Kamara cleared her throat. "You've left two companies occupying the orbital dockyards. We'd be happy to send some of our militia up there to maintain control and free up your troops."

Drakon smiled at her. *I bet you'd be happy to gain control of those dockyards. Do you really think I'd just hand them over to you?* "With our warships protecting the dockyards, it's better that they deal with our own people there if any threats develop."

After a pause, Kamara nodded. "Certainly. I understand."

At least, she understood that the Free Taroans were in no position to demand the dockyards.

COLONEL Rogero walked alone back to his quarters after a coordination meeting with President Iceni's representatives. Meetings with people in locations remote from each other were easy to hold, everyone gathering in a virtual meeting place, but just as easy to tap into and monitor despite every possible security precaution. For routine matters, that was accepted as a fact of life. The ISS, and possibly someone else, would be listening. For anything important, or anything that shouldn't be overheard, it had become habit for people to choose actual meeting places at the last moment. Much more secure, but it could also lead to long walks as twilight darkened the sky and streets grew dim before the gloom deepened enough to trigger streetlights to life.

There were bars he could have gone to, restaurants he could have dined at, but Rogero preferred burying himself in his work. Every time he visited a bar or a café, he would find himself looking for her, knowing she couldn't possibly be there but still studying the crowd. *Someday, I'll buy you a drink,* Bradamont had said at their last meeting. *Someday, I'll buy you dinner,* he had replied. Neither had believed it could ever happen, but still Rogero found himself searching crowds.

She had been in the Midway Star System. She had sent him a message. But it was still impossible.

Tonight, then, he walked straight from the meeting to his quarters. But even though his course was a straight one, he didn't actually walk in a straight line or at a steady speed. Reflexes from the battlefield had become natural to him, so that as Rogero walked, he would, without thinking, speed up or slow down between steps, veer a bit to one side or the other, move slightly to keep objects between him and open lines of sight that could become lines of fire. It made it hard for anyone to target him on the battlefield and annoyed the hell out of anyone who walked with him at other times, but it took a conscious effort to not do it, so when he walked alone, he gave in to instinct.

As a result of one such sudden jerk forward, the shot fired at his head instead grazed the back of Rogero's skull.

He fell forward, rolling behind the nearest streetlamp base, weapon in hand as he searched the night for the assassin. The streetlights came on, triggered not by the oncoming night but by sensors that had detected the shot, and sirens hooted nearby. The police would be here soon, he would give a report, and they would search for the killer.

Rogero knew they wouldn't find anyone. This felt too much like the work of a professional. He raised his free hand to touch the bleeding scrape across the back of his head. Someone had tried to kill him, but who that was mattered less than who had ordered the hit. Or had he escaped death? Could the shot have been aimed to miss, a warning? If so, from who? And would that warning have been intended for him or General Drakon?

But whoever had fired had known he would be meeting with President Iceni's representatives and had known where that would be so they could predict what route Rogero would have to take back to his quarters.

"LAUNCH the bombardment," Drakon ordered. He stood in the Free Taroan command center, eyes on the big map display, which had rotated and risen so that he could watch everything play out. Ideally, he would be out there, with the attack, but there was too much going on this time, too many widely dispersed things happening, and he needed to be somewhere he could watch it all with the fewest possible distractions near at hand.

The tracks of kinetic projectiles fired by the warships in orbit appeared on the display, curving downward like a precise sort of rainfall. All of the projectiles were timed to hit at the same moment, and instead of falling across the three targeted valleys, they were aimed in curtains that dropped toward the defenses on the rims of the mountains surrounding the valleys and along the narrow coastlines where the valleys met the sea.

Massed along the other sides of those valley rims were Drakon's brigades, supported by some of the Free Taroan forces. Three brigades, three valleys, each valley held by an understrength battalion. Overwhelming force deployed against the most hard-core portions of the loyalist ranks. Victory wasn't in doubt, but if they couldn't time it just so, and the snakes blew everything to hell, then the victory would be a hollow one, as well as costing the lives of more of his soldiers.

Drakon's eyes rested on one of the falling projectiles.

Just a chunk of metal, aimed precisely, gaining energy with every meter it fell. There were a lot of meters between orbit and the surface, and the projectiles were already moving fast when they were launched. The seconds to impact vanished in a flurry of numbers spinning by too fast to read; then the rounds hit.

It was as if volcanoes had erupted in long lines along the ridges, rock and dust flying upward, the ground trembling, a sustained roar of noise rather than single crashes from impacts. The defenses along the ridges vanished, replaced by rubble.

He had been close to bombardments like that. Drakon could have closed his eyes and seen the rocks hitting, sometimes those fired by Syndicate warships to batter Alliance defenses before he sent his own soldiers in to attack and seize the ground, sometimes rocks launched by Alliance warships against him. Men and women as well as structures disappeared under those bombardments, not simply killed but their bodies blown into fragments, leaving battlefields empty and strangely devoid of the dead. *That's what hell really is. Not those places with fire and demons but just a place where death has been, and nothing remains because humans have wiped out all trace that humans or any other life had ever been there.*

I know how Conor Gaiene feels. I'm tired of turning places into hell.

But I don't know any other way to get this done that wouldn't kill a lot more people.

THE sentry gaping at the violence erupting along the ridges died without even knowing Roh Morgan was nearby. A moment later, the antiair vehicle the sentry had been guarding rocked as a limpet mine tore out its insides and killed its operator. Under the distraction of the bombardment hitting, commandos in stealth suits who had carefully infiltrated over the last few days struck at the same time, carrying out pinpoint attacks to destroy mobile defenses which had parked among the populace to discourage bombardments aimed at them.

A platoon of soldiers came pounding down the street, staring around for enemies. Morgan took careful aim and dropped their leader, who had made himself obvious by gesturing commands. Grinning, she gunned down two more soldiers, then shifted position as shots began hitting the area around her.

A panicked civilian racing across the street blocked her next shot. Annoyed, Morgan fired twice, both shots tearing through the civilian before slamming into the soldier behind him.

Green lights glowed on Morgan's helmet display, showing the other commandos in the valley had completed their hits.

But all of it had been a distraction, designed to keep the snakes confused and overwhelmed as reports of activity and threats poured in from all sides. She had learned that about people at an early age—how easy it was to divert and disorient them by throwing too many ideas and images and emotions their way. Men were particularly prone to losing the ability to think when women tossed the right enticements in front of them, but almost any human could be knocked off-balance by enough of the right kinds of mental overloads.

Not her, though. Morgan could always see her goals with crystal clarity no matter the confusion around her. It had all snapped into focus after she had been pulled from that asteroid. She had been reborn then because she had a destiny. Drakon's acceptance of her as an officer had been part of that destiny. He didn't know that yet. But she had known it for a long time.

She leaned back calmly against the nearest wall, completely unfazed by the small-arms fire being sprayed out from the survivors of the loyalist squad, tapping out a coded command. Puppet master limpets that Morgan and her team had previously attached to critical junctions in the loyalist command network went to work, sending out bogus commands and false updates. In the flurry of incoming reports, the snakes would see many that said everything was going well, and their minds would seize upon the things that they wanted to see in that mass of information overkill.

"THERE are the signals," Sub-CEO Kamara said, as major explosions occurred in all three valleys. "The commandos have softened things up inside the valleys."

Drakon nodded. "All brigades, go."

Shuttles hopped into the air, almost clipping the tops of the ridges as they crested the obstacles and burst through the still-falling dust to plummet toward the floors of the valleys. Many of those shuttles were Drakon's, but others belonged to the Free Taroans, battered remnants of the aerospace forces that had once protected the skies and low orbits of this world. Those Taroan pilots who had survived this long were either very lucky or very good, and both qualities served them now as they led the Midway shuttles into the attack. Only a few scattered shots erupted from any defenders who still lived and hadn't been disoriented or disabled or destroyed by the bombardments or the commandos.

COLONEL Malin paused, eyeing the vapor barrier guarding the loyalist headquarters complex in this valley. The water misting out from the barrier would allow detection of someone wearing even the best stealth suit, protecting the headquarters from infiltration.

But that barrier also clearly identified the headquarters and isolated it from surrounding structures. Even though it was well hidden from overhead view, Malin could precisely locate it from his position.

It had also made it relatively easy to spot the buried communication lines radiating out from the structure. Puppet master limpets were already at work on those, providing reassuring updates and blocking alerts and activation codes. Malin somberly eyed the readouts from the limpets, ensuring that the protocols and ciphers acquired after the ISS headquarters on Midway was overrun were working to undermine the snakes on Taroa.

Take nothing for granted. Have backup plans for your backup plans. For reasons unknown, higher powers had left Syndicate space to the whims of gods of chaos. Finding harmony again would require riding the waves of chaos, finding the means to ease the tempest by degrees, using the right forces to calm the storm.

Sometimes, that meant unleashing other storms.

He called the heavy cruiser, providing the coordinates for the drop, then faded away from the headquarters as fast as possible while not betraying his presence, while sending out an alert to the other commandos in this valley to beware of the impacts.

Seconds later, two bombardment projectiles fell through the atmosphere, moving too fast to be visible but leaving lethal streaks of light in their wake. The ground shuddered as the loyalist headquarters became a crater.

But on Malin's display, the limpets reported information still flowing to and from the now-vanished headquarters. *Clever. Even internal references have false position information. I need to find the real headquarters and get it shut down before it sends the wrong commands.*

Malin and his commandos went back to work.

"COLONEL Malin is showing red-status readout on mission accomplishment," Colonel Senski reported.

Kamara rapped on her controls as if that would change the information on her display. "Your bombardment destroyed the target at the coordinates he provided," she complained to Drakon.

"If Malin says the job's not done, it's not done," Drakon replied, eyes narrowed as he took in the situation in all three valleys. "Colonel Senski, continue your approach and carry out your assault."

"But, General," Senski protested, "if the assault goes in, and the snake headquarters is still functioning, enough accurate information may reach them to trigger a decision to go doomsday on us."

"The longer we continue the operation, the more chance we have of that happening anyway, Colonel. Get in there and take your objectives. If Malin needs something to cover his takedown of the snakes, your assault will draw their attention."

Kamara stared at the display, her expression grim. "There could be a snake doomsday device in this city," she said to Drakon. "The snakes want to recapture the rebellious portions of this planet if they can, not nuke it. But if CEO Ukula has time to realize what's going down—"

"We get a real big kick in the butt," Drakon replied, keeping his own voice casual. "I figured that might be the case. Pulling back now, hesitating now, will only worsen the risks."

She gave him a wry smile. "Since both of our butts are on the line, too, I hope you're right."

Me, too. "Malin will take out the snake headquarters."

THE main bodies of the brigades were arriving at their objectives, shuttles landing hard to spray out armored soldiers in overwhelming numbers. The defenders, hurt, disorganized, and getting contradictory orders thanks to the limpets on the snake command lines, resisted in some places and surrendered in others.

"Command links severed in this valley," Colonel Kai reported, looking perfectly composed even in the midst of battle.

"How can you be sure you got all the command links?" Kamara demanded.

"Because we have severed *every* comm link in this valley except our own. That part of your infrastructure will be much easier to repair than if this entire area is cratered," Kai replied.

Before Kamara could reply, another transmission drew their attention.

"Bloody hell!" Colonel Gaiene roared.

Drakon hastily switched focus to Gaiene's units, seeing a flurry of red markers intermingled with those of the soldiers with Gaiene. "Con, do you need me to send you the reserve?"

"Hell, no! They dropped us right onto the snake barracks for this valley instead of one street over! Lousy damned intelligence as usual!" Gaiene was firing as he spoke, pivoting to hit enemies popping up on all sides.

The snakes had managed to trigger local jammers. Between those and the disordered mass of soldiers and snakes mixed together, Drakon had trouble making out the situation as markers jumped, blinked out, and blinked back in again. "I'm sending in the reserve to you, Con." He only had two platoons, but that might be enough. Unfortunately, those platoons would take a while to get there even if the shuttles moved their fastest.

"Don't bother!" Gaiene retorted. "I've got plenty of ammo and plenty of soldiers. All we're running short of is targets!"

Kamara stared as the red markers dissolved from the display like soap bubbles hitting a hot plate. "I thought he was just a drunken letch."

"He's that," Drakon agreed, "but he's also a hell of a good soldier in a fight."

"Cut off everything!" Gaiene ordered his troops. "Sever any comm connection you find! We'll worry about where they go later."

Drakon looked at the situation in Gaiene's valley and in the valley where Kai and Morgan were operating. The loyalists and snakes were being rolled up very rapidly. However, as comm connections were broken, the ability of the limpets to confuse and deceive snake command and control was also being knocked out. *Malin. You've got very little time left before the snake commander figures out how bad things really are.*

FROM a covered position across the street, Bran Malin studied the nondescript building that his stealth suit's sensors told him was packed with defenses. He had seen armored figures moving within, flitting past windows almost too quickly to spot, and none had left despite the roar of battle as the main body of Colonel Senski's brigade had landed all around the valley. Partly that was due to the limpets leaving the snakes uncertain as to what was happening, but with combat near enough to hear, it was odd that not even one scout had been sent out to check on things personally. That could only mean whoever was inside had given staying hidden the highest priority.

Extensive landlines with full security shielding had led to the structure from the crater where the original headquarters building had been. Malin had followed them, and now he evaluated the building. There were apartments in the upper stories, providing both deceptive camouflage from overhead observation as well as citizens going in and out by day and night to further mask the nature of the structure to anyone spying from above. That meant there were probably still citizens in those apartments even though none could be seen.

Call in another orbital strike and ensure the snakes could not order any doomsday strike with their dying gestures? Malin looked at the apartments, knowing he had mere seconds to decide.

You do what must be done. Sometimes, some must be sacrificed. The decision and the wrong are mine.

He called the cruiser, then faded back only a short distance in the brief time before three more projectiles tore through the atmosphere, through the building, and into what must have been reinforced bunkers beneath. Malin lay flat as pieces of all that had once been in that location fell to earth in the wake of the bombardment, trying to keep his mind centered not on those who had died but on the larger purpose he served.

A blinking alert told Malin that the limpets were no longer able to find any snake command nodes active. Walling away any sense of triumph behind the same barriers where regret lay, he sent the mission-accomplished report.

DRAKON felt tension bleed out of him as Malin's mission-status marker switched to green. "All right. Let's wrap this up," he sent to his commanders.

"All done here," Colonel Gaiene reported on a private line that only Drakon could hear rather than using the command net. "We ran out of snakes to kill. The citizens are all being extremely well behaved. But we had about a company's worth of the loyalists surrender. They belonged to various units, but all of those units are on the Free Taroans kill-not-capture list."

Drakon glanced at Sub-CEO Kamara, who was busy talking to some of her own commanders about moving into the valleys that Drakon's soldiers had captured. "I suppose," Drakon said, "that all those who surrendered say some other guys committed any atrocities?"

"You suppose correctly. I could kill them all now," Gaiene added offhandedly, "or turn them over to the Free Taroans, which would just mean they died a little later, *or* I have some empty shuttles waiting in case wounded need to be evacuated to the orbital docks. We do need every *good* soldier."

"That would give us time to, uh, triage everyone," Drakon agreed. "Get those 'wounded' up to the orbital docks, but make sure they don't have weapons, and have a strong escort keeping an eye on them. Find out if they are really clean under full interrogation sensors, and we'll deal with any who aren't."

"As you wish, General. I'm so glad we had this conversation."

"I enjoyed it, too, Colonel Gaiene."

Colonel Kai reported in next, sounding slightly peevish. "We have a holdup." Through the remote video feeds,

Drakon could see a large building, the exterior already battered, from which weapons fire erupted every time any of Kai's soldiers showed themselves outside.

"Diehards forted up in a building full of citizens," Kai added, as if annoyed at the citizens for getting themselves into that situation. He probably was annoyed at them. Kai disliked anything that complicated the smooth completion of operations. "At least platoon strength, with heavy weapons. I can destroy the building easily enough, but you told us to avoid killing citizens." This time, Kai sounded accusatory because Drakon's instructions were preventing the simplest solution to the problem.

Sub-CEO Kamara had a stern expression. "He should get those loyalist diehards."

Drakon raised an eyebrow at her. "Even if he kills all the citizens in that building? It's pretty big. You're probably talking hundreds."

"We're willing to pay that price."

"That's noble of you," Drakon remarked with heavy sarcasm. "You're willing to let them die. I know you've been fighting a civil war here, but you'd better start thinking of those citizens as *your* citizens. Do you want your citizens to die, Sub-CEO?"

Kamara scowled. "They've got a building full of hostages. What else do you suggest?"

"That Colonel Kai promise them that if they leave the building, none of Kai's soldiers will fire upon them."

"You can't be serious! Do you know what the unit those soldiers belong to has done? We can't let them go."

Drakon's smile held no humor. "Did I say that? I agree that we can't reward anyone for taking hostages, especially people who've committed the sort of atrocities you've shown us records of. It won't be my fault if those loyalists don't read the fine print on any promises made to them."

"**I** cannot yet confirm that CEO Ukula is dead," Malin called in. "But all indications are that he, his personal guard, and his command staff died when we destroyed the alternate headquarters location. It will take time to sort out and identify DNA fragments amid the wreckage, though."

"Understood," Drakon said. "Nice job locating that secondary command location. The holdup had us worried. Did you run into any problems taking out the alternate headquarters?"

Malin's expression revealed nothing as he shook his head. "Nothing you need concern yourself about, General. I took care of it. Colonel Senski has informed me that her brigade is mopping up a few small pockets of resistance, but otherwise, this valley is yours, General."

"Thanks, I've always wanted one."

AFTER a series of back-and-forth negotiations with Colonel Kai, the loyalists came out of the building.

"They've got citizens around them as shields," Kai remarked disdainfully. "Even though I promised them my soldiers would not fire."

"You'd think they didn't trust us," Morgan replied. "Ready when you are, General."

"Wait until you have clean shots, then take them. Your call when to fire," Drakon ordered.

The loyalists were halfway to the shuttle that was supposed to lift them to safety when Morgan's hidden commandos fired, knocking down half of the enemy platoon in the first volley. The others hesitated, unsure whether to flee, fire back, or start slaughtering the citizens they were using as shields. By the time the survivors made up their minds, all but two were dead. One tried to surrender, but died before the dropped weapon hit the ground, and the other got off only one wild shot before also falling.

"All right. Do the act," Drakon ordered.

Morgan and the other commandos killed the stealth circuits on their suits, walking out toward the citizens standing frozen with fear amid the bodies of their former captors. Colonel Kai and his soldiers came from another angle, Kai raising his helmet shield to frown at Morgan. "I had promised them my soldiers would not shoot if they let the citizen hostages go free," Kai said loud enough for the citizens to hear.

"I didn't promise them anything," Morgan replied just as clearly. "And I don't work for you. These commandos are under my command, not yours."

"The Free Taroans did not want any citizens harmed," Kai pointed out.

"Then they should be happy," Morgan replied. "All we killed were the snakes and anyone helping them."

Kai shrugged, the motion oddly amplified by his combat armor, then turned to the citizens. "You are free to return to your homes. If there are wounded citizens inside the building, my medics will see to them."

"The citizens can't possibly believe that was real," Kamara protested back at the Free Taroan headquarters. "Your Colonel Kai sounded wooden, and Colonel Morgan sounded like she was joking."

"Colonel Kai almost always sounds like that. I don't keep either him or Morgan around for their acting ability," Drakon replied. "To those citizens, as scared and shook-up as they are, it probably sounded real enough. We just bought you some good publicity with the citizens in that valley. Make sure you don't waste it."

Sub-CEO Kamara nodded at Drakon, her expression thoughtful, then gradually acquired a gleeful look as she took in all the results of the operation. "That was the last pocket of resistance in the three valleys. This guts the loyalists. We've got their most important valleys, all of the support infrastructure in them, and we've wiped out their leadership. Their remaining forces can't hold out now. We've already heard from the commanders in two of the areas still held by the loyalists, asking for terms of surrender."

"Good." He couldn't feel too elated at the outcome. The casualty lists were coming in. Not too many dead and wounded for such an operation. But still some.

Kamara was happily talking to the other members of the Interim Congress of Free Taroa. Drakon gazed at the display, where the patches of loyalist-controlled territory had shrunk dramatically. Outside, the sun glowed dimly through the clouds of volcanic dust drifting across the sky.

CHAPTER SEVENTEEN

IT only took a week for the remaining loyalist opposition to crumble. At the end of that time, with the threat of Drakon's ground forces and warships looming over them, and with the Workers Universal making a series of ill-considered threats and a suicide bombing that angered rather than intimidated the WU's opponents, the last valleys controlled by the loyalists bowed to the control of the Free Taroans.

Sub-CEO Kamara promptly turned around the surrendered loyalist soldiers, combined them with her own forces, and charged into the areas still held by the Workers Universal. Drakon kept his own forces out of it as the Free Taroan soldiers, including those who had been recently fighting the Free Taroans, rampaged into the WU-controlled areas.

"We should be playing a part in this," Morgan grumbled.

"I don't want any part in it," Drakon replied sourly. "For people who were upset about atrocities, they seem way too eager to wipe out anything and anybody with any taint of Workers Universal."

"We could separate them," Malin suggested. "Keep the deaths down by stopping the fighting."

"They'd just finish the job when we left," Drakon said.

"Let them do it. Let them do it, then wake up in the morning and realize what they've done. Maybe in the long run, that'll save some lives."

"Do we have any word from the congress yet?" Malin asked.

"No. The *interim* congress is waiting until the WU is finished. I'll talk to them tomorrow, tell them what we want, then we can get the hell out here." Taroa was beautiful, but his thoughts of it were tainted by the toll of the civil war.

"General," Malin said, "we avoided this kind of thing at Midway. Because of how you and President Iceni handled things."

"Or because we had a lot more weapons and nobody would mess with General Drakon," Morgan said sarcastically. "Let's just tell these FreeTas what we want and tell them to deliver. If they're not grateful enough for our help, we can dump a load of hurt on their heads."

"They'll know they can't just blow us off," Drakon said. "They need us, our goodwill, because we're always going to be the star next door, and that's the other thing that they'll realize when they wake up in the morning."

"I love it when you're domineering," Morgan said, then laughed when he gave her a disapproving look. "I get what's going on. We own these guys even though the FreeTas get to keep pretending they're all independent and strong. And we own those orbiting dockyards, which I bet is the third thing the FreeTas are going to be waking up to. Nice job, General."

Malin didn't offer any rejoinder this time, instead watching Morgan with the intentness of a man trying to defuse an explosive.

"IT'S impossible to express our gratitude," another member of the interim congress intoned. "Now that Taroa is once more reunited, and free, we will never forget the aid that Midway offered to help bring that about."

Remembering came cheap, of course, and no one had yet suggested the idea of actual, tangible repayment. Drakon nodded, offering the members of the congress a small smile. "President Iceni and I were happy to assist. We want trade to get going again. Your ships will be welcome at Midway, and we won't use our warships to hinder any ships trying to get to you through our star system."

A few members of the congress got that, realizing that the statement implied that such traffic could be hindered at any time that Midway felt like it. Traffic could still arrive using Taroa's other jump points, but such travel would be much more difficult than for anyone using the speed and ease of Midway's hypernet gate.

One of the congress members gave Drakon a skeptical look. "What will be happening to the charges for use of the hypernet gate by merchant traffic? Now that your rates are no longer regulated by the Syndicate government?"

He wouldn't have known the answer to that except that Iceni had made a point of telling him before they left. "The rates are going to be reduced. It's not that we don't need money, but we won't be sending any of that on to Prime anymore. We can charge merchants using the gate less and still retain more to help pay for establishing Midway as a strong, independent star system."

"Why not charge even less and retain less?" someone challenged him.

Drakon couldn't help a narrow-eyed look at the person who had spoken. "You think you're getting a bad deal? I haven't heard anyone say anything yet about the soldiers we lost helping you gain control of your planet and star system."

The majority managed to look guilty though also defensive.

"Our military forces don't come free, and they're not cheap," Drakon continued. "I need enough revenue to cover pay, maintenance, operations, and a lot of other things. Prime isn't going to be defending Midway anymore. It won't be defending Taroa, either. You help us pay for defense, and we'll help defend you. Balk at that, and we may not have enough forces to spare when the Syndicate government shows up here again."

He had fallen back into CEO speaking habits without even thinking, talking as someone whose words were not to be debated or questioned. And the Free Taroans, with a lifetime of conditioning to fear and obey, sat straighter as their smiles faded.

Colonel Malin stepped forward slightly, drawing everyone's attention, sounding reasonable as well as firm. "As General Drakon said, we can no longer depend on Prime to pay for our defense. Instead, Prime has become a threat. We also have to deal with the enigmas. Yes, we are officially admitting that the enigmas exist and pose a threat to humanity. If they are to reach Taroa, they have to come from Pele, and through Midway. We must pay for the mobile forces to defend all of the star systems in this region out of our own pockets. Those mobile forces will be available to help defend you as well if we can reach the necessary agreements."

"Mobile forces aren't cheap," Sub-CEO Kamara agreed. "And we have none," she added for the benefit of the rest of the congress. "We've had a graphic demonstration of what the mobile forces under Midway's control can do to help us. I think it would not be wise to balk at paying less than we have in the past for use of Midway's hypernet gate when we are also gaining potential defenders as a result."

"Speaking of defense," another representative said, "we'll be happy to accept control of the dockyards from you as soon as we can lift soldiers up there."

"The dockyards?" Drakon asked.

A pause followed, then the representative spoke more cautiously. "Yes. The primary orbiting dockyards. They belong to us."

"We took them from the Syndicate government," Drakon replied. "They were never under control of the Free Taroans."

Kamara was watching him, her eyes hard. "You're going to keep them."

"We have every right to keep them," Drakon pointed out.

A woman representative burst out loudly. "You won't be able to sustain that facility without support from this planet!"

"You're not threatening me, are you?" Drakon asked. "What happened to 'thank you for the victory that gave us this planet mostly intact'? What happened to your gratitude? We're not taking anything that you ever possessed. If you want to talk about joint-use agreements, I'm sure we can come up with something, but control of those docks will remain in our hands."

"Threats would be meaningless," Kamara said, as much to the other representatives as in reply to Drakon. She leaned forward, hands clasped on the table, her eyes fixed on his. "We know that there's a partially completed battleship in the main construction dock. I assume you intend keeping that as well."

Drakon nodded. "There's a lot of work yet to be done before it can even leave the dock, but once the battleship is finished, it will be an important part of the defenses for our star system. And yours, should you choose to work with us."

"Choose?" someone asked scornfully. "We have no choices here."

"Yes, we do," Kamara corrected. "We had no choices before because all we could do was hang on against the Syndicate forces and the Workers United. Now we can decide how to deal with control of this planet, and the control of the star system that comes with that. The orbiting docks are critical, but we can't take them by force, not when Midway's ground forces and mobile forces protect that facility."

"We give in to blackmail?" the first man cried.

"We deal with reality."

No one replied to that for a while. Drakon waited, impressed by how well Kamara was herding the other representatives into handling the situation. She might end up in control of this star system on her own.

"There are strong grounds for negotiating the status of

the orbiting docks," another woman finally said, trying to look bold as her gaze flicked nervously toward Drakon. "Any forces from Midway that remain here to protect those docks will also, of necessity, protect us. Unfortunately, we are an interim government. We need to establish the exact form of our government, win the approval of the citizens for that, then hold elections for all offices. But it will be hard to gain the people's acceptance for the loss of the partially completed battleship."

"If I may suggest," Malin said, sounding somehow even more reasonable than before, "there is no certain time for such a government to be established, while the dangers that face us all exist now, and the need to keep commerce active and revitalized in this region is also a current requirement. You might consider granting a group of trusted citizens such as yourselves the power to reach temporary agreements on matters such as trade and mutual defense, those agreements to be subject to eventual ratification by whichever government is finally established. That would ensure that the government you establish has the final word but also enable us all to pursue actions necessary to the good of the citizens in the meantime."

The congress members looked interested and impressed by Malin's words. "But, the battleship . . ." one pressed.

"If the battleship were on the table," Malin said, "then agreeing to its loss might create problems for your government. But as General Drakon pointed out, our forces took that battleship from the Syndicate government. It was ours before we ever spoke with the Free Taroans, so you're not giving up anything."

Kamara smiled coldly. "We will discuss this, but perhaps we can agree that, officially, the battleship was never a Free Taroan asset. Our government doesn't need that kind of problem on top of everything else we have to deal with. Unofficially, though, the representatives of Free Taroa will expect some concessions for that."

"Unofficially," Malin replied, "we can discuss that."

"May we send representatives back with you?" another

representative asked. "To discuss these issues directly with President Iceni?"

"That's fine with me," Drakon said, wondering if they thought that Iceni would be any more willing than he to give away even a partially completed battleship hull. "We have some representatives with us from President Iceni who can discuss the trade agreements, and a proposed agreement on defense for you to look at. Colonel Malin will be your point of contact on that." The last thing that he wanted to do was get personally bogged down negotiating trade agreements and parsing which comma went where.

"General," another member of the interim congress began, smiling in the ingratiating manner that labeled him a trained executive. "Our own soldiers are limited in number, and we do face some security issues. You're already keeping some ground forces on the orbiting docks. Perhaps if some more of your ground forces remained on the surface on a purely temporary basis—"

Frowns were already breaking out on many other faces as Drakon interrupted the speaker. "No. All my forces except those providing security on the orbital docks are going back to Midway. That was the agreement." He made it sound like a great virtue, to be abiding by what he had said he would do, when in fact Drakon simply didn't want his soldiers tied down in garrison duty in former WU-dominated areas. He knew without asking that such places were where the Free Taroans would want to employ soldiers from another star system. *We've got what we want, and we've done as much dirty work as we're going to do in this star system.*

He managed to keep from going CEO on them again until the discussion ended, then Drakon left with a feeling of great relief.

He paused on the way out, ensuring that his security equipment was blocking any attempt at surveillance. "Good job jumping in there, Bran."

Malin shrugged. "In matters like mutual defense and trade, our self-interest coincides with that of the Free

Taroans. I didn't want them short-circuiting the possibility of agreements with their clumsy attempts to get something for nothing."

"Yeah. A few times in there I was really missing being a Syndicate CEO. I hope they get their acts together before this free star system goes completely down the tubes." Drakon checked his security readouts again, but they were still secure. Even though the Free Taroans had piously announced that they would never allow the sort of routine surveillance that had characterized Syndicate rule, he suspected that they would bend those beliefs just as soon as they thought it necessary. "How is the recruiting of information sources and active agents going?"

"We'll have a number in place here before we leave," Malin promised. "That's another advantage for us in increasing trade. The more merchant ships traveling from Taroa to Midway, the more opportunity our agents here will have to pass us information covertly, and the more ships going from Midway to Taroa, the more chances we have to send covert instructions to our agents here."

"Funny how that works out. Judging from what we dealt with in there, we're going to need the active agents getting to work right off the bat. We need them to push, cajole, bribe, convince, blackmail, or whatever works to get a government working here."

"Yes, sir."

"And not just any government," Drakon said. "It has to be strong enough to maintain control of this planet and star system, stable enough to hold together over time, and friendly enough to work with us. Strong enough, stable enough, and friendly enough. We need all three, and I'm sure President Iceni won't balk at whatever we need to spend to get that." That was something else the hypernet gate fees would be spent on, but there hadn't been any sense in bringing that up during the meeting with the congress. "Did you see how Sub-CEO Kamara was dominating the others?"

Malin nodded soberly. "Yes, sir. We want her working with us."

"Morgan would recommend getting her out of the way if she didn't play ball."

"Morgan would be mistaken," Malin insisted. "Someone like Kamara could make all the difference in the formation of a strong, stable government here. I didn't see any other players in there with her level of authority, and to the citizens here, she is the hero who defeated the loyalists. Get rid of Kamara, and there's no one to step into the void. The Free Taroans want a government with elections from top to bottom, General. They might just elect Kamara on their own if she's around to be a candidate."

"If they do that, and if Kamara proves to be what we need, then fine. If the Taroans work out an elected government, we might learn a few things from them. If it doesn't work, then we'll still learn a few things and have a cautionary example for anyone pushing for that kind of thing in our star system." Drakon studied Malin. "Speaking of which, you seem to have given that a lot of thought, Colonel Malin. And you seem to know a lot more about different forms of government than the Syndicate liked people knowing."

Malin nodded with a serious expression. "Everyone requires a hobby, General."

An evasive answer, one that revealed nothing. But clearly Malin wasn't going to say more unless pressed hard, and Drakon couldn't believe that Malin would betray him. "You picked a strange hobby. And a dangerous one. Just get enough agents in our pay on this planet, and get those agents working to make happen what we want to happen."

"Yes, sir. I'll be leaving here within the hour. There's some work in that respect that needs to be personally carried out in another city." Malin saluted and rushed off. Drakon had no doubt that by the time they left this star system, there would be a widespread and effective system of covert agents working to accomplish his and Iceni's goals.

It should have pleased him. Everything was working out. But Drakon felt dissatisfied. The Free Taroans had been extremely aggravating, outwardly thankful and yet carefully avoiding actually offering anything in exchange for the aid they had received. They had even balked at the simple truth that the orbital docks, and the battleship being constructed there, were now the property of those who had taken them from the Syndicate government. Yet the Free Taroans had also been so enthusiastic and idealistic. They were fools, doomed to disappointment when their dreams collided with reality, but . . . it would be nice to have something to be enthusiastic about. It would be nice to have something to believe in besides maintaining power, keeping his skin in one piece, and foiling his enemies. How long had it been since he had felt either enthusiasm or idealism?

Though he had felt something with Iceni. She seemed to be looking for that, too, some bigger reason to be in charge, some purpose beyond survival.

Unfortunately, Iceni wasn't here. She was light-years distant. Drakon looked around. Sentries stood here and there, watching for threats. He wasn't alone, but he didn't exactly have company either. Kai was half a continent away. Gaiene was probably already drunk and trying to see how many women he could get through in one night. Colonel Senski wasn't sufficiently well-known to relax with. Malin was off setting up the spy network. And Drakon didn't think he had the energy or patience to deal with Morgan's idea of conversation tonight.

The Interim Congress of Free Taroa had shown its appreciation for him by giving him the living quarters of the former star-system CEO for the night. That had cost them nothing, of course. Drakon hadn't been able to find out what had happened to that CEO. Everyone knew that the CEO had left for refuge with the ISS when the civil war broke out, but after that, the trail got hazy. The CEO might have caught a ride on one of the ships the snakes had managed to send out of the star system, but other reports claimed that the CEO had been executed for failure or treason or whatever grounds the snakes wanted to use and the body disposed of. Either way, there didn't seem much chance of the CEO's showing up again, and the living areas and offices had been gone over with a fine-toothed comb for surveillance devices and booby traps.

Drakon keyed in the access code and entered, looking around with amusement. The former CEO on Taroa had some luxurious tastes, especially considering that Taroa hadn't been that wealthy a star system even before the civil war hit it hard. The former CEO must have engaged in some truly epic skimming of tax revenue to afford such a setup. The bedroom featured not just expensive art and sculptures, not just a full bar well stocked even with liquors from Alliance planets that had been available only through the black market for the last century, and not just a bed big enough for an entire squad of soldiers to have used without squeezing together, but also an actual fireplace in one corner, framed by an expansive marble mantel.

None of it had done that CEO much good when the revolution started. As a matter of fact, the corruption this place implied had probably helped trigger the three-way fight that had sent the CEO fleeing.

Drakon strolled over to the fireplace, peered at the controller almost invisibly set into the marble, then activated it. A decent blaze erupted from the logs, filling the room with flickering light. Laughing self-mockingly at the indulgence, Drakon walked to the bar and examined the contents. Rum from Hispan! Amazing. Filling a tall glass, Drakon sprawled into a plush chair and gazed at the fire.

He had forgotten the problem with fires. When the flames danced, you could see things in them. After having risen to the rank of CEO, after having fought far too many battles, the things Drakon saw in the fire were not born of pleasant memories. Crowding to the forefront was that city. Where had it been? Some Alliance planet. Burning. Square kilometers in flames, no one to put them out, all automated firefighting systems destroyed, soldiers in armor moving among the holocaust, adding to the destruction as they struggled for control of the city ablaze around them. He had never seen so many things burning. Towering buildings, long stretches of low-slung housing, trees . . .

He remembered being told as he stood with his surviving soldiers amid the smoking ruins that the Syndicate ground forces had triumphed and controlled what had once been a city. A week later, with Alliance reinforcements storming into the star system, Drakon and the others still alive had been evacuated as the badly outnumbered remnants of the Syndicate mobile forces withdrew.

In official reports, it had been described as a Syndicate victory.

The first drink didn't douse the fires in his memories. He went back to the bar for a second. That was better. But recollections of old battles and dead friends still kept crowding in to destroy the tranquillity he sought, and that undefined sense of discontent with events at Taroa still troubled him, so Drakon got a third. He rarely did this, rarely drank so much, but that night he understood Gaiene better than usual. Even thinking about that new battleship, which might be a year away from being completed and operational, didn't help. If he couldn't find temporary tranquillity tonight, temporary oblivion would have to do.

He was well into the third large drink when the door alarm sounded. Nobody could have gotten to that door without passing a lot of sentry posts, so Drakon called out "open" and watched the locks release and the portal swing wide.

Morgan walked in like a panther fresh from a kill. The light from the fire glimmered on her black skin suit as the door swung shut again. Instead of being absorbed by the dull fabric, the firelight seemed to pick out every curve visible under the tight garment. "Hey, boss." She looked around with a comically puzzled expression. "I expected to see lots of ravaged women lying around here."

Drakon made a face. "That's not my style, Morgan."

"General, I know you like women."

"I do. But I don't force women. Never have. Never will. That's for weaklings and cowards." He finished the third drink in a single swallow while the little monkey in the back of his male mind made excited noises as it watched Morgan move a few steps closer with lethal grace.

"You could hire a woman. Or two or three," Morgan suggested with a sly smile. "Malin could get them for you. That man is a born pimp if I ever saw one."

"I don't need to hire women," Drakon said with some heat.

"Of course you don't. You can have any woman you want. They'd come to you willingly. Because you're a winner, General." Morgan had stopped a few feet from him, smiling down at Drakon where he sat. "And if you listen to those who want you to win, you can do anything."

Drakon tried to silence the jabbering alcohol-fueled monkey that was bouncing around so wildly in his head that he couldn't focus on the warnings his common sense seemed to be trying to get across. "Sure. Look. I'm tired and stressed. Why don't you—"

"I know you're stressed. How long has it been, General? I know men. I know how you get. A man needs certain things, and the bigger the man, the more he needs." Her smile had widened and taken on a quality that the monkey really, really liked. "You need a strong woman. A woman as strong as you are."

"Morgan—" Drakon began, then the thought of whatever he was going to say vanished from his mind as Morgan reached up and started unsealing her skin suit.

She ran the seal open from shoulder to thigh with one long, languorous motion, then slowly peeled off the suit. The firelight shimmered on her body, Morgan's eyes glinting with a muted red glow in the reflected light of the flames. "Let's celebrate your victory," she said.

He tried to say no, but the drinks had given the monkey enough power to silence any other voices in his head. And the monkey wanted her more than anything. Morgan pounced across the remaining distance between them, tearing at his clothes, and he could see nothing, know nothing, want nothing but the feel of her.

WHEN he awoke the next morning she was gone, leading to a very brief flash of hope that the whole thing had been an exceptionally vivid, detailed, and extended dream. But then he spotted the torn sheets, felt some bruises and scratches that hadn't been there the night before, and realized that he never could have imagined some of the things Morgan had done with him.

It wasn't the hangover that made him punch the wall hard enough to splinter the fine wood paneling.

DRAKON did not want to reenter the former CEO's bedroom suite once he had cleaned up and dressed. The office next to that set of rooms, though, had an impressive set of security equipment and would do fine for any work he had to accomplish. And there was definitely something that he had to do. "Colonel Morgan, I need to speak with you privately."

She arrived a few minutes later, outwardly acting normally. Normally for Morgan, that was. But he probably wasn't imagining the ghost of a smile that kept appearing whenever she looked at him. "Yes, General?"

He stayed as unbending as he could manage. "I wanted to ensure that you understood that the events of last night would not be repeated."

"Last night?" Morgan did smile openly this time. "Wasn't it worth repeating?"

He hoped his reaction hadn't shown. *I've never had a night like that, and I want it again, and again, but I won't.* "You know how I feel about sleeping with subordinates. I'm disappointed that you didn't respect that."

She looked puzzled. "Did I force you?"

"No." Arguing that she took advantage of his being drunk would sound silly as well as weak. "I made a mistake. It won't happen again."

"That's your decision, General."

"Do you mind telling me what you hoped to accomplish?"

Morgan grinned once more. "I think it was pretty obvious what I was trying to accomplish last night. And I succeeded. More than once."

Memories of that night warred with his desire to remain angry. "And that was it? That was all you were after?"

"Oh . . . yeah." Morgan's smile changed, and her voice grew serious. "General Drakon, everything I do is in your best interests."

"Then respect my wishes. I won't speak of this again."

"I like a man who doesn't boast about his conquests." Morgan pretended to flinch at Drakon's expression. "I understand, General. One-night stand. It's over."

"That's all."

Several minutes after Morgan left, Malin arrived. Was it just his imagination, or did Malin seem more formal than usual? Drakon had no illusions that no one else was aware that Morgan had spent a good, long time in his private quarters. Few besides Malin would fault him for that, and for some reason, that aggravated him even more. "What?" he asked Malin.

Malin paused at Drakon's tone of voice. "I have an update on the 'wounded' that Colonel Gaiene sent up to the orbital docks, General."

"Oh." The world went on, despite his own failures and discomfort. "Have they completed interrogating and screening them?"

"Yes, General. Full-scale interrogation, and none displayed signs of having been trained to mislead that." Malin checked his reader. "Of the eighty-seven who surrendered to Colonel Gaiene's brigade, six are confirmed as having actively participated in atrocities against citizens. Nineteen more witnessed such atrocities but did not participate themselves. The remainder belonged to subunits whose commanding officers evaded orders to carry out atrocities against Syndicate citizens. They neither witnessed nor participated in such actions."

Drakon sat back, trying to focus on those numbers. "Did any of those subunit commanding officers survive and surrender to us?"

"Two, General. One executive and one subexecutive are among the eighty-seven."

"Offer them comparable positions in our forces. I want the nineteen soldiers who witnessed atrocities rescreened. Make sure they didn't participate in doing things like that to our own citizens because they wouldn't, not because they just weren't personally asked. I want to know what soldiers in my command *will* do instead of wondering *what* they'll do. Offer positions in our forces to the soldiers who didn't commit or witness atrocities, but spread them around through the brigades, and if they accept, I want their service records altered to indicate they belonged to one of the units the Free Taroans said didn't commit atrocities." He didn't bother adding that such alterations should be undetectable. Malin was very good at such things and would make sure that no one could tell that the service records had been changed.

Malin nodded, making notes. "And the six?"

Turning them back over to the Taroans would be an admission that he had pulled loyalist soldiers up to the orbital docks, as well as risking the six soldiers' telling the Taroans that others from their units were still in Drakon's custody.

Besides, he had a responsibility to deal with this.

"Firing squads. Get it done, and get rid of the bodies. They died on the planet. Understand?"

"Yes, General." Malin turned to go.

"Colonel Malin." Drakon waited while he halted. "Is there anything else you want to say?" The invitation would give Malin a chance to talk, and for some reason Drakon wanted to know what Malin would say.

Malin took a moment to reply, then faced Drakon squarely. "I request clarification as to Colonel Morgan's future status, General."

"Unchanged."

Was that relief that flickered across Malin's features?

Another pause, then Malin spoke with extreme care. "General, I realize that I have no right to ask this—"

"It won't happen again," Drakon said. He definitely saw relief this time. And he had to tell someone. "I got drunk. I wasn't thinking. It's not going to happen again."

Malin looked down, nodding. "General, she has an agenda. I don't know what it is, but Morgan is after more than . . . sharing your bed for one night."

"And what is it that you're after, Colonel Malin?"

Malin paused. "What I do, General, is always in your best interests."

Drakon stared at the door after he had left, wondering why Malin and Morgan had used almost identical language to describe their intentions toward him.

That afternoon, he took a shuttle up to the orbital docks, wanting to be quit of the soil of Taroa. He was tired of dealing with people who couldn't be told to do what needed to be done but had to be convinced. A single, strong leader could get things done.

But they didn't have that at Midway, either. He had to get Iceni's approval for things like this. What if she had objected? How could anything with two heads function properly? And what if she heard about Morgan? He shouldn't care if Iceni heard, shouldn't care how she reacted to it if she heard, but all of those questions bothered him, further souring his mood.

Even a tour of the battleship hull didn't help. Going through it only emphasized how much remained to be done, how empty and incomplete the hull was compared to the one that Iceni had brought back from Kane.

It took a while to get all of the soldiers of the three brigades and their equipment as well back up to the docks and the modified freighters. The Interim Congress of Free Taroa dithered and debated, but thanks to copious bribes doled out by Colonel Malin and the efforts of agents working for him, the congress eventually approved the two temporary agreements on self-defense and trade, to last until a government was seated and voted them up or down.

"Major Lyr." Drakon waved Colonel Gaiene's second-in-command to a seat. "How'd you like to be a colonel?"

Lyr regarded Drakon with the wariness of a veteran. "What's the catch, sir?"

"Independent command."

It only took a moment for Lyr to figure that out. "Here, sir?"

"Right." Drakon leaned forward, resting his forearms on his desk. "You're a good soldier, a good administrator, and I know how much you've done to keep your brigade in top condition." He didn't add how important that had been in light of Colonel Gaiene's more-than-occasional lapses in periods without combat. Lyr knew that Drakon knew, and Drakon never bad-mouthed officers in front of their subordinates. "You'll keep two companies from Gaiene's brigade plus one company made up of regulars from Taroa who've been judged most reliable. This job will require someone who can operate on their own and also work with the Free Taroans. That part will be tough. You have to avoid being too overbearing with them because we want them thinking of us as partners, but you can't let the Free Taroans think they can tell us what to do. I think you can handle that."

Lyr nodded. "Yes, sir."

"There'll be a civilian left here, too. One of President Iceni's representatives whose job is to handle all of the trade and diplomatic stuff that doesn't involve military or security matters. Freighters should be making fairly frequent runs between here and Midway, so there shouldn't be any problem keeping me informed. Handle the little problems and try to spot big problems in time for me to act."

"So," Lyr said, "nothing too difficult or demanding."

Drakon smiled, knowing that Lyr meant the opposite. "Exactly."

"I'll do my best, General."

"I know, Colonel. That's why you got the job and the promotion." As hard as Lyr's job would be, Drakon thought, it probably wouldn't be as difficult as finding a replacement for Lyr as Gaiene's second-in-command. *But, what the hell, I need to grow more senior officers. Nobody ever claimed my job was easy, either.*

A week after Drakon had taken the shuttle up, his brigades were fully embarked, the agreements were in hand, and the freighters and warships broke orbit en route to the jump point for Midway. Having been moody for most of that week, Drakon wondered who would be happier to get back to Midway, himself or Kommodor Marphissa and the crew of the heavy cruiser, who would be able to bid farewell to him there.

CHAPTER EIGHTEEN

DRAKON'S mood didn't match his information.

"You seem to have succeeded in everything we agreed you should go to Taroa to do," Iceni said.

"Not everything," Drakon replied. "There wasn't even the beginnings of a stable government when we left."

"You could scarcely wait around until there was one. From what my representatives reported, Taroa is already leaning toward a formal alliance with us. That will be a start, and an incentive for other star systems near us to consider the same." Iceni rubbed her eyes with one hand. "In less positive news, I assume that you've heard from Colonel Rogero."

"And I assume that you've had no success in tracking down whoever tried to kill him."

She lowered her hand to lock eyes with him. "I gave orders that Colonel Rogero not be harmed. If anyone connected with me attempted it, they did so against my orders, and I will ensure that they regret it."

Drakon watched her for a moment before replying. "Are you implying that somebody connected with me tried to kill Colonel Rogero?"

"I have no information on it, General, so, no, I'm not implying that." She wondered why Drakon had jumped on that possibility so quickly. Was he worried about someone close to him? Was her own source in danger of being compromised?

He shook his head. "I find it hard to believe that some citizen took a shot at him. But more hidden snakes . . ."

"Could be involved," Iceni agreed. "Everyone is looking for such a nest."

Drakon nodded this time, rousing from his moodiness. "I wanted to make a point to mention how well Kommodor Marphissa did. We had zero problems with coordination and support. I've never worked with a better mobile forces commander."

"That's very good to hear. I was going to give her command of the battleship when it becomes operational."

"She should handle that easily," Drakon said. "But I hope she retains command of more than that. She handled formations and multiple units well."

"I'll remember that." Why was Drakon making such a point to praise Marphissa? They had both been on that heavy cruiser for a while. Drakon's staff thought that Marphissa was their agent already. Had he actually turned Marphissa against Iceni or made enough progress toward that to want her somewhere with greater authority in the mobile forces? "You brought back a lot of good shipyard workers. They'll enable us to get the battleship here operational much faster than anticipated."

"How soon?"

"Two months."

"That's still one hell of a big threat window," Drakon muttered, then, as if sensing that she might take that as criticism, glanced at her. "I appreciate that there's little else either of us can do to get it ready faster. But we'll want to get a lot of those workers back to Taroa as soon as we can to work on that second hull."

Iceni sighed. "A year to finish that one. Let's hope we're granted that much time."

"A year on the outside. Maybe we can push that, get more out of the workers now by offering real rewards." Drakon eyed her defiantly. "Maybe bonuses for workers instead of executives."

She raised both eyebrows at him. "I didn't know you were such a radical. We need the executives and subexecutives on our side, too. Perhaps bonuses for all based on actual results?"

That brought a brief, sardonic smile from Drakon. "Basing bonuses on results? And you're calling me a radical?"

"If you don't object, we can see how such a system might work, knowing that our people have been taught by the Syndicate system to game any method of evaluation. There might be ways to keep them focused on producing the results we want. Is there anything else?" Iceni asked. His odd edginess was making her jittery, too. Something had happened. But what? Togo hadn't reported discovering anything, but his sources weren't that close to Drakon. "It's good to have you back, General Drakon."

He nodded heavily, then got up to go.

She would have to check with her best source. And not by message. Something about this required a face-to-face meeting despite all the risks that involved.

BACK inside her own offices, the door sealed and alarms activated, Iceni sat down. Why was Drakon acting guilty? The most likely explanation, and the most frightening one, was that he had decided to move against her but felt unhappy about that for some reason.

She sat down, swiveling in her chair to face part of the virtual window wall located behind her desk. It currently displayed the city at night, as seen from some location high up, as if her offices rested in some high-rise with a perfect view instead of being safely located belowground. The lights of the city swept down the slope to the waterfront, where restless waves foamed with phosphorescence against natural rock and human-built walls. Her hand rested on one building glowing against the darkness, flattened so that the patterns on her palm and fingers could be scanned, and a patch of the virtual window vanished, to be replaced by a square of nothingness. After working through a half-dozen more access methods and verifications, a small armored door popped open.

Iceni pulled out the document within, an actual printout of a written work. Thumbing it open to a random page, she began finding the letters she needed to spell out a message. Forming messages using a book code was a tedious process, but still the only absolutely unbreakable code known to humanity. Her contact would only respond to a request for a personal meeting using that code.

Finally, she drew a mobile designed to be untraceable out of the same safe, punching in a number, then waiting until an anonymous voice-mail box announced its readiness. "One One Five," Iceni recited the page number, then, "six, ten, seventeen . . ." She went through every number matching the order of each word on the page, then hung up and tossed the mobile back into the safe.

Iceni paused as she was about to return the document to the safe. Countless things had been written by humanity in thousands of years, the vast majority kept preserved in virtual form, buried among a universe of preserved human thought, but bound printouts had never lost their grip on readers. That helped keep the use of a book code unbreakable no matter how fast systems could scan material in an attempt to break the code, since no two printouts had to use the same margins and page counts. All you needed were two that did match such things but didn't match any other printout of the same work.

Now she stared at the document, which she had chosen because of its great age, wondering what its creator would say if he knew his work was still being read by someone this long after it had been written on ancient Earth itself, in Sol Star System, home of humanity, the place the citizens still revered as the home of their ancestors. "*Incredible Victory*," she said softly, one finger tracing the words of the title. The name "Midway" on the book had caught her attention when she was seeking a document to use for this purpose, a reference to some other embattled place long ago with the same name as this star system. She didn't think of herself as a superstitious woman, but perhaps the title would prove to be a good omen.

ANY CEO with brains had at least one bolt-hole, a means to get out of their offices or living quarters without being spotted, an escape route known to no one but the CEO. Even Togo didn't know about the one that Iceni had used this time, because even Togo could not be totally trusted.

No one could be totally trusted. You learned that, or you didn't survive as a CEO.

Muffled in a coat against the evening breeze, her face half-buried in the raised collar, she walked through streets sparsely populated at that hour. Iceni felt naked without her bodyguards even though her clothing carried an impressive array of defenses. Any citizen who made the mistake of trying to rob or assault her would quickly learn just how big an error it was.

Surveillance cameras, both openly placed and concealed, gazed in her direction as she passed, but they did not see her. Embedded codes created by the ISS to ensure that they remained invisible to the police and other routine observation by creating blind spots in digital sensors were very useful for anyone wanting to move without being seen by the automated eyes of the police and other security forces.

Finally, she reached her objective, an inside corner in a mass-transit station, somewhere out of the crowd enough to avoid random contact or being overheard but close enough to others not to stand out as avoiding company, background noise providing a constant rumbling to help mask conversation. She leaned against one wall, watching passing people for the one she was to meet. Few gave her or the nondescript coat she wore a second glance. High-ranking CEOs and presidents didn't dress that way, and no CEO or president would be out in public without bodyguards or staffers.

A man wearing another unremarkable civilian coat sauntered into view, altering his course slightly to bring him close to her, where he leaned on the wall beside Iceni. Raising one cupped hand, he showed a small unit glittering with green lights.

Gwen nodded and raised her own hand, showing her own surveillance-detection and blocking readout, also displaying steady green. That was their insurance that every security system monitoring this spot had been temporarily diverted, spoofed, or blinded. The crowds walking by could see them, but no one monitoring their location remotely could hear or see them at all. As far as the surveillance systems were concerned, they weren't there. State-of-the-art equipment like theirs didn't come cheap, and finding out all the necessary codes to mislead the equipment wasn't easy, but those were some of the benefits of being a president. "Any problems?" she murmured.

"No," her source replied. He didn't seem nervous at all, appearing bored to the casual observer. "What is the difficulty? You know how risky this is."

"I need answers now, and I need to know that they are accurate answers," Iceni said. "What is Drakon doing?"

Her source paused, but more as if thinking than hesitating. "Nothing out of the ordinary. There's a lot of work to be done overseeing the return of our brigades to the surface and catching up on things here now that he's back."

"Is he moving against me?"

Another pause, this time apparently in surprise. "No."

"If you betray me now, either before I die or soon after I die, Drakon will learn who has been giving me information about him."

"I have no doubt of that." Her source shook his head. "He is not acting against you. That's not to say there is no threat. But it's not from him."

"Why is he acting odd?" Iceni demanded.

This was a longer pause. "He slept with Colonel Morgan."

"Oh."

She wondered what her tone had conveyed as her source gave her a sharp look. "General Drakon got drunk. She took advantage of that. He slept with her one time and only one time. That is what he feels guilty about."

"You're joking." She would have to be blind not to see how desirable Colonel Morgan would be to a man, and Iceni had lived long enough not to expect perfection from any man, especially when it came to his behavior with women. But she could still be disappointed when a man lived down to her expectations. "One time?"

"Yes. He will not repeat it."

She had picked up something in his own voice. "What disturbs you about that?"

"You know that I don't trust her. I am afraid she had some other goal when she seduced General Drakon and will try to use that night to her advantage."

"If he's going to take some crazy whore to his bed, he should expect problems," Iceni said, hearing her own voice get sharp and angry. It sounded like she was taking the incident personally, which was ridiculous.

"She's not crazy, at least not the way that you're thinking. Morgan acts in ways that cause others to underestimate her. For many of those others, underestimating her was the last mistake they ever made. She is very good at planning for both the long and the short term. She has some plan now. Do not take her too lightly."

Iceni made an irate sound. "Then perhaps we would be better off without her to worry about. No matter how dangerous she is, she can be eliminated. No one is invincible."

"I strongly advise against such a plan and such an action. I will not cooperate in it."

She felt frustrated now, as well as angry. "You hate her as much as anyone. You've tried to kill her already, and you're advising me not to?"

Colonel Bran Malin grimaced. "I did not try to kill her."

"Why not?"

Another pause. "Three reasons," Malin said. "First, she's

very tough and very smart. Any attempt would have a rough time succeeding, and the repercussions from a failure would be extremely serious. Second, General Drakon values her advice and abilities. If he found out that anyone had planned a hit on Morgan, he would be very unhappy. If he discovered I had a role in it, my access to him would be forever eliminated. He would not forgive anyone, not even me, for an attack on someone he considers a faithful subordinate. I very nearly lost my access because of the . . . misunderstanding during the attack on the orbital facility here. Drakon would never have believed me or forgiven me if, during that incident, I had not killed someone who definitely did intend on killing Morgan. If he suspected you in an assassination attempt, it might motivate him to strike at you in the belief that a hit on Morgan was just a prelude to a direct attack on him."

The arguments made too much sense to be ignored, though she doubted his explanation for the "misunderstanding" in which he had fired at Morgan. There was something else there, but she couldn't tell what it was. "What is the third reason?" Iceni demanded.

Malin's expression revealed nothing as he shook his head. "That is a private matter."

"I want to know it."

"I regret to disappoint you."

She set her jaw, wondering how far to push it, whether to threaten exposure. She still didn't know why Malin was feeding her information, but he had never told her anything that had proven to be less than accurate, and that kind of source that close to Drakon was invaluable. Malin surely knew as well as she did that she wouldn't want to lose that source unless his usefulness had ended, and therefore a threat to expose him would be a bluff. "You have no idea what Morgan's plan is?"

"All I know is what I know about her. She's ambitious. She has no moral qualms. She rarely fails in what she attempts."

Iceni breathed a soft laugh. "Why wasn't she a CEO?"

That led to another thought, a worrisome one. "Do you think that she means to supplant me?"

"It's possible. It may be that Drakon is her planned tool in that."

"Which one of us is in more danger from her then? You or me? Or Drakon himself?"

"I believe that Drakon is safe from her but cannot be certain. Between you and me, I don't know," Malin said. "If I am killed, look beneath the surface of whatever happens. I haven't been able to learn who tried to kill Rogero. Maybe she was involved in that, too. Rogero and Gaiene are very close to Drakon, Kai only a little less so. If my guesses are right, in the long run, Morgan is going to want to isolate Drakon from any influences but her, anyone who might lead him in directions other than whatever she wants." Malin looked directly at Iceni. "That includes you. I'm not sure of General Drakon's feelings, but, at the least, he respects you."

"But he doesn't trust me," Iceni said.

"No. He trusts me, and Morgan, and Rogero, Gaiene, and Kai."

"He trusts you, and you tell me his secrets," Iceni pressed.

Malin paused again. "I am loyal to General Drakon."

Are you? What is your long-term plan, Colonel Malin? Not that you would tell me. How much of what you've just said is truth as you know it, and how much is spin aimed at convincing me to do what you want? "Loyal to General Drakon? You have yet to prove that to me."

"It is probably impossible for me to prove my loyalty to him to your satisfaction."

"It would be easy," Iceni said. "Kill her."

"Morgan? No."

"Are you at least watching her?" Iceni demanded.

Malin's lips twitched in a twisted smile. "I do little but watch her. And I never turn my back on her."

"Then if you won't do what seems to be needed in regards to Morgan, at least keep a close eye on General

Drakon as well and see if you can prevent him from doing anything *else* stupid."

"I am watching him. I admit that I let my guard down at Taroa. But she won't get to him again like that, and if she tries, I have no doubt that General Drakon will reject her this time."

"You may have no doubts, but I have mine," Iceni said. *Men. If only they could be counted upon to use their brains to make their decisions for them.*

Granted that their male fallibilities made it much easier for women to use them as tools.

Women like Morgan.

Women like her. *You won't have Drakon, Colonel Morgan. I may not decide to want him, but you won't have him.* "And I will watch you, Colonel Malin," Iceni said.

Another very brief smile. "I never doubt that I am being watched."

"Keep me informed," Iceni finished, turning to walk off, knowing that behind her Malin would also blend into the crowd of citizens, there and yet invisible to the surveillance systems monitoring everything said and done in the city.

Almost everything, that is.

Iceni listened as she walked. There were important things that could be learned when you moved among the citizens, indistinguishable from one of them. They said things that you would never hear otherwise, things murmured too low to be distinguished from background noise by the omnipresent surveillance systems.

A lot of talk about Taroa, and most of that happy. *The snakes were gone from there. We had helped our neighbors and asked for nothing in return. That Drakon was a great general. There's a new trade agreement. Ships will be coming through more often again. Good news. Good news.*

Did you hear about President Iceni? What Buthol is saying? I don't believe it. But she was our CEO before she was our president. Everyone knows about CEOs. Isn't she different? Then why no election for president yet?

Iceni kept her head down until she reached the outer

entrance to the bolt-hole, passing through a dozen locks and safeguards of various kinds before feeling safe enough to remove her coat with a heavy sigh. Who was this Buthol? Why were the citizens so full of praise for Drakon but asking questions about her? Was that Drakon's work, sowing propaganda on his own behalf among the citizens?

It was late. She was tired and needed to think, to have time to absorb what Malin had said, to let her subconscious mull over how Malin had looked and acted.

President Iceni went to bed.

THE next morning, feeling oddly as if she were hungover without having been drunk the night before, thus getting punishment without benefit of having done anything to deserve it, Iceni drank a breakfast malt to wash down some pain pills.

She sat at her desk, wondering where to begin. The battleship. The latest report from Kommodor Marphissa had come in forty-eight hours ago. There was a constant status feed as well, of course, but . . .

Iceni caught herself on the verge of sending a hotly worded message to Marphissa. The Kommodor had done nothing to earn a tongue-lashing.

But that man she had heard about last night, on the other hand. Buthol?

A quick query on her news terminal popped up a list of articles as well as opinion pieces written by Buthol himself.

Buthol wanted elections now. Buthol suspected the President of diverting funds and demanded a full accounting of tax revenues. Buthol argued that only a full, perfect democracy of one person, one vote, in which every important matter was decided by the people rather than representatives, would be in the best interests of everyone.

The news reports all agreed that Buthol had few followers yet but was attracting more and more attention with his speeches and essays.

Iceni read it all with growing anger. *Who the hell does*

he think he is? Accusing me of corruption? Of wanting to be a dictator just because I won't hand the mob control of this star system the instant someone like him demands it?

"Togo! In here now!"

He arrived with a speed that suggested her tone of voice had been unusually demanding. "Yes, Madam President."

"Why the hell haven't you told me about this Kater Buthol?"

Togo blinked, then checked his reader. "Ah. Yes. He has few followers. He is being watched."

"He is getting a great deal of attention. He is personally attacking *me*."

"Madam President, you instructed us to let the low-level elections proceed without interference—"

"*Unless* something said or done constituted a threat!" She glared at Togo. "Hasn't this Kater Buthol broken *any* laws?"

Togo shook his head. "He has been very careful to tread just on the legal side of everything. You could order him arrested, but the charges would have to be based on fabricated evidence. I could have that evidence ready by this evening."

"That won't help! The last thing I need is to give this clown more attention by making him into some kind of martyr." She sat back and made a disgusted gesture. "This Buthol is exactly the sort of problem I don't need on my plate at the moment! Find a solution! That's all."

"Yes, Madam President." Togo left with more swiftness than usual.

She spent the rest of the day burying herself in work and trying to catch up on the low-level elections, which were supposed to alleviate pressure among the citizens for change. It wasn't at all clear that the elections were accomplishing that goal.

Most disturbing were the occasional suggestions that General Drakon would make a good president. That for the good of the star system, and with the looming threat of a Syndicate attack, a new leader might be needed who could deal with such dangers. Had Drakon arranged those whispers? That was worrisome. But not as worrisome as the possibility that the citizens were coming to feel that way on their own. Obviously, there was a need to raise her profile with the people. They needed to know who had won the battles here and at Kane, who had acquired the battleship, who had forgotten far more about mobile forces tactics than General Drakon had ever learned.

By the time Iceni went to sleep, she had worked up the outline for such a public-relations campaign.

THE next morning, she made the error of ordering a larger breakfast, only to almost choke on a bite of food as she scanned news reports tagged for her based on recent search activity.

Police report that last night political agitator and candidate for neighborhood representative Kater Buthol was the victim of a robbery in which he apparently fought with his assailant and was shot in the resulting struggle. Buthol died before police arrived on the scene.

Iceni stared at the news item, wondering why it felt not just surprising, but shocking. *I can't fault the timing. Now I won't have to lose any more sleep over that oaf, and Togo can—*

Togo.

What did I tell Togo yesterday? What did I say?

Something about finding a solution for Buthol?

Which Togo could have thought meant I wanted him to get rid of Buthol.

For once in my life, I didn't want to do that. For once, I wanted to handle it right.

And I might have ordered his death anyway.

She sat looking at her display. Calling in Togo again would serve no purpose. He knew the drill. This wasn't a routinely accepted thing like sending someone to a public firing squad for failing in their duty. Given the right excuse, anyone sufficiently low-ranking could be disposed of that way without any fuss. But not everyone who needed to be eliminated had committed an offense, and sometimes people who needed to be neutralized had powerful patrons. There were long-established ways of handling that to avoid any personal penalty for the action. If she asked Togo whether he had killed Buthol, or arranged for someone else to do it, he would deny it because that was what he would always do to give her deniability in the matter. She had not said, "Kill him." Togo would not admit that he had killed him. How many times had they played that game to ensure that any trips to interrogation rooms operated by the ISS would prove fruitless for questioners?

Did you order him to be killed?
I did not tell anyone to kill him.
The subject registers truthful.

Why did it bother her that Buthol was possibly dead at her hand? That damned Marphissa and her speeches about protecting the people.

But it was also about protecting herself, and her people. *I had meant to do something about that, to get assassination as a means of personnel management off the list of acceptable actions.*

Maybe Drakon did it. Buthol said some bad things about him, too.

She hesitated, then called Drakon.

"Is something wrong?" he asked as soon as he saw her.

That was bad. She was so rattled that she was letting it show. "I was wondering, General, if there were any personnel let go in your office recently?" That code phrase was an old one, a subtle means of asking about assassinations.

Drakon took a while to answer. "No. Not recently," he finally said.

Either he hadn't ordered it, or he wouldn't admit to it. She needed to talk to someone who would understand what had happened. But how could she admit to Drakon that she had possibly ordered a hit? Yes, CEOs ordering assassinations happened all the time, but it was still technically illegal even if a CEO ordered it. An admission of possible involvement would be evidence against her, handed to someone who could use that evidence to help gain total power in this star system for himself.

Had Malin told the truth about Drakon's intentions? Dared she believe that?

If only that big, stupid ape hadn't slept with Morgan. I could feel us getting closer, developing some sense of being able to trust each other a little—

A new thought arose, hitting her so abruptly that Iceni hoped her feelings didn't once more reveal themselves to Drakon. *Was that Morgan's idea? Did she sense that I was feeling more comfortable with Drakon and used having sex with him as a means to shove a wedge between us? She must have known that word of that event would get to me somehow.*

Is this part of Morgan's game? For me to mistrust Drakon, to stop working things out with him because he couldn't keep his pants on with her? But how could she be sure that I would hear something that I wouldn't dismiss as rumor . . .

Malin told me.

Was Malin a dupe in this, someone who could be fooled into being her messenger? Or is Malin actually working with her? Was that incident on the orbiting platform merely theater, a preplanned event that would make it appear that seriously bad blood existed between Malin and Morgan so that no one would suspect them of working together?

But how did Togo miss signs of that kind of collaboration? He never told me—

You can't trust anyone.

Anyone.

Iceni looked at Drakon, who was watching her and waiting for a response. Part of her, the instinctive part, told her to hold that man as far from her as possible and work at limiting his power and eventually neutralizing him completely. Drakon was the only one in the star system with the power to threaten her directly.

But what if that was the wrong answer? What if her only

real chance was to invest a measure of the little trust she could spare in a man who was either a lunkhead dumb enough to sleep with an insane bitch or cynical enough not to care that he was breaking one of the few rules he himself had set and was risking his own position for a short period of pleasure.

Or he was being manipulated, despite his power, by those beneath him.

"Many CEOs make the mistake of worrying only about those above them," a mentor had once confided to Iceni, *"when they should be worrying about what those below them are up to. It doesn't take a lot of strength to make someone stumble. All it takes is knowing when to drop a tiny obstacle in front of their foot. And who knows how to do that better than the people you might barely notice as they do your dirty work?"*

"General Drakon." *I am going to regret this. I know I am. Just do it. It's the last thing anyone will expect.* "I would like to meet with you personally. As soon as possible. Neutral ground, no aides or assistants."

He studied her, then nodded. "All right. The usual place? I can be there in half an hour."

"I'll see you there."

AFTER the conference room door sealed, Drakon sat down, watching her and waiting.

"I'm going to do something stupid," Iceni said.

"Really? That sort of thing seems to be going around," Drakon said in a half-mocking, half-bitter way. "I hope it's not as stupid as what I did."

"I'm going to tell you that I may have just killed a man with a carelessly worded statement." Iceni explained what had happened, then waited for his reaction.

"Why did you tell me that?" Drakon asked. "You know what I could do with that information."

"I am . . . trusting . . . that you will not."

He smiled for the first time that she could recall since

his return from Taroa. "You're right. That's stupid. Fortunately for you, I'm even stupider. I don't want anyone rummaging through the skeletons in my closet, so I'm not going to send anyone to go looking in yours. That's the kind of precedent that can bite back hard. As for what happened, or might have happened, to Buthol . . ." Drakon shrugged. "Don't lose any sleep over it. If you made a mistake, then you know what not to say next time."

Could he possibly understand? "Under what possible interpretation is a mistake that kills someone acceptable?"

Drakon looked away from her. "President Iceni—"

"Call me Gwen, dammit."

He seemed briefly taken aback. "All right. Gwen, do you have any idea how many battles I've been in and how many little mistakes I've made? And how many soldiers died because of those mistakes?"

"That is different. You were trying to do your job, you were learning—"

"It doesn't feel that way. Not if you're worth a damn." This time Drakon appeared surprised at having gruffly admitted feeling like that.

"Then you do understand. Forget what we've been taught. Forget all the lessons we learned on our way to the top of the Syndicate hierarchy. Is this what we want? The ability for someone in power to kill on a whim, or by mistake?"

She had expected some argument, expected defensive anger, but Drakon instead sat silent for a long while before replying.

"Neither of us is perfect," he finally said. "Both of us are human enough to make more mistakes than we should."

"Then should there be limits on our ability to make those kinds of mistakes?"

Drakon stared at her this time. "Is this tied in with what you were saying about changing the courts?"

"Partly."

"What is it, exactly, that you are asking me?"

Iceni took a deep breath. "Will you agree to order no

more executions *or* assassinations? Not unless we *both* decide that is necessary in each individual case?"

Another pause. "Did you discover who tried to kill Rogero?"

"No. But I'm wondering if someone else, someone who thinks that sort of tactic is run-of-the-mill business, someone who might work for you or for me, might have made that decision on their own."

"Because that's how things are done." Drakon made it a statement, not a question.

"And who knows who their next target might be?" Iceni added. "I want to know, if someone goes after me, that *you* did not order it. We've got the start of something here. We've kept this star system stable, we have the potential for alliances with two other star systems, and we can keep growing if we aren't destroyed. External threats are one thing. We have little control over that. But internal threats can destroy us, too. You and I have to place real trust in each other, and mutually agreeing to cease extralegal killings can be an important part of establishing such trust."

"Why should you believe me if I say I won't order killings?" Drakon demanded.

"Because I think you're worth a damn, General Drakon." *Why the hell did I say that?*

But after a moment he smiled. "I'll make you a deal, then. I will agree not to order any more executions or assassinations without your specific approval, and I'll reemphasize to my people that they are not to conduct such operations on their own. In exchange . . ."

"Yes?"

"Call me Artur instead of General Drakon. When we're alone, at least."

"I don't know. That's a big concession," Iceni said. "Who else calls you Artur?"

"No one. Not for a long time."

"Then I will agree." *But if you sleep with that female again, you're going to be "General Drakon" full-time.*

Before she could say anything else, her comm unit pulsed

urgently. She could hear Drakon's doing the same. "What is it?" Iceni snapped. "This had better be an emergency."

"It is," Togo said. "Update your system display."

Drakon, having listened to his own message, was already entering the command.

The image of the Midway Star System that hung above the table flickered for a moment.

"Hell," Drakon said.

At the hypernet gate, new ships had arrived. Iceni read the identifications glowing next to them. "A Syndicate flotilla."

"And they've got a battleship," Drakon said.

"So do we," Iceni replied.

"Their battleship probably works."

Iceni couldn't think of an answer to that. "Six heavy cruisers, too. How many light cruisers? Four. And ten HuKs." Even without the Syndicate battleship, that would present a tough problem for Iceni's warships since she lacked an operational battleship of her own. "They want this star system back badly."

"We're receiving a message from the flotilla," Drakon said, tapping another control.

A window opened before them, showing a familiar person in Syndicate CEO garb. "This is CEO Boyens," he announced. "To former CEOs Iceni and Drakon. I have been sent here to return this star system to Syndicate Worlds' control.

"You're both guilty of treason. If you want to make a deal, you'd better make me a very good offer and make it soon." Boyens offered them a standard CEO smile with a visible trace of smugness, then the brief message ended.

After a long moment of silence, Drakon glanced at Iceni. "Any suggestions?"

She shook her head. "Appealing to the better nature of CEO Boyens is unlikely to accomplish anything. He's far from the worst Syndicate official I ever dealt with, but he's very ambitious. What do we have to offer him?"

"As a bribe?" Drakon asked. "The most valuable things

in this star system are you and me. If you want, we can flip a coin to see which of us offers up the other."

"He doesn't need to settle for one of us," Iceni said. "Not with a force of that size. What we need—" She broke off as a new alarm sounded, this with a different note, a special note engraved in her memory. "No."

Drakon was eyeing the display, his expression even grimmer than before. "Yes. The enigmas are back."

The Syndicate force had arrived hours ago at the hypernet gate. The enigma force, coming in at the jump point from Pele, had also been in-system for a few hours, the light from its arrival only just reaching this planet. Boyens would be seeing them at about the same time, and realizing that his plans for reconquering the star system would have to change.

Iceni watched the symbols marking alien warships multiplying rapidly. "It's a strong assault force," she said, surprised that her voice sounded so steady. "They're not here to just hit-and-run."

"That's enough enigma warships to wipe out the human presence in this star system," Drakon agreed. "At least we can see them now that we've eliminated the alien worms in our sensor systems, but where the hell is Black Jack? What did he do? Stir them up and move on, leaving us to catch it when the enigmas retaliated for having their space invaded?"

A sensation of cold emptiness filled Iceni as she gazed at the display. "Or perhaps the enigmas proved to be more than even Black Jack could deal with. If the enigmas wiped out Black Jack's fleet, what chance do we have?"

Drakon surprised her by smiling, then she realized the expression was more the snarl of a wolf at bay than anything to do with humor. "Let's call Boyens and tell him he'd better ally himself with us if he wants to be a hero."

"And if he doesn't want to be a hero? If he'd rather run and live?"

"We die at the hands of the enigmas. If they've got hands."

Drakon paused, then shrugged. "Of course, with the odds we're facing, we'll all die regardless of whatever Boyens does. But he might help us buy a little more time."

"For what?" Iceni asked. "Do you expect help? From where?"

"I don't know," Drakon admitted. "Maybe your knight in shining armor will show up."

"I don't have any knights, General Drakon. A wise woman doesn't depend on someone's showing up to rescue her."

"What does she depend on?" Drakon asked, his eyes back on the display as if he were already thinking through their limited options.

Iceni also looked at the depictions of the attacking enigmas, the strong Syndicate flotilla, and their own badly outmatched defensive forces. "She depends on her judgment of whom she can trust, General Drakon."

Drakon gave out a short, sardonic laugh. "Then why are you here with me?"

"Why haven't you already pulled a weapon on me?"

He grinned with real humor this time, though a dark defiance of fate stayed in his eyes. "Because I never made a very good CEO. Go ahead and call Boyens while I get the ground forces fully activated."

Perhaps I do have one knight, Iceni thought. *A knight of darkness and shadow. But maybe it's just his armor that is tarnished. Maybe inside that armor is someone who is still capable of doing something that doesn't bring personal gain, who, as he told me, really does want something worth dying for. Or is he blemished inside as well and just recognizes that our very slim chances will become none at all if we turn on each other now?*

She said nothing more to Drakon before she called the Syndicate flotilla with an offer she hoped it would not refuse.

Read on for an exciting excerpt
from Jack Campbell's upcoming novel

THE LOST FLEET:
BEYOND THE FRONTIER: STEADFAST

Coming in May 2014 from Ace Books!

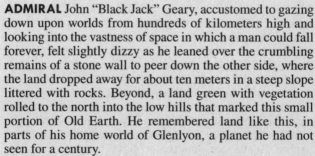

ADMIRAL John "Black Jack" Geary, accustomed to gazing down upon worlds from hundreds of kilometers high and looking into the vastness of space in which a man could fall forever, felt slightly dizzy as he leaned over the crumbling remains of a stone wall to peer down the other side, where the land dropped away for about ten meters in a steep slope littered with rocks. Beyond, a land green with vegetation rolled to the north into the low hills that marked this small portion of Old Earth. He remembered land like this, in parts of his home world of Glenlyon, a planet he had not seen for a century.

Geary squinted against a wind that brought scents of growing things and animals and the enterprises of people. Not like that inside a spacecraft, which despite the best air scrubbers known to science always held a faint taint of crowded humanity, caffeinated beverages, and heated circuitry.

"Not much left, is there?" Captain Tanya Desjani commented, looking at what had once been the wall's foundation.

"It's thousands of years old," Historic Properties Steward Main replied. He seemed as much a part of the landscape as the wall itself, perhaps because members of his family had served as Stewards of the wall for generations. "The wonder is that there's anything left at all, especially after the ice century of the last millennium. It got very cold up here when the Gulf Stream lost a lot of push. The rest of the world got warm and we got cold, but then this island has always been a bit contrary when it comes to the rest of the planet. Since then, everywhere else on Earth has been cooling down, and we've been warming up."

Geary smiled crookedly. "I have to admit it feels strange to be on a planet which has known humanity for so long that people can speak of the last millennium."

"That's all quite recent, compared to this wall, Admiral," Main replied.

"Hadrian's Wall," Desjani mused. "I guess if you want to be remembered for thousands of years, it helps to build a big wall and name it after yourself. I remember the Admiral and I talking about that empire of Rome, and I thought it must have been pretty small. Just part of one planet and all. But, standing here, I realize it must have felt awfully big to people who had to walk it."

Main nodded, running one hand above the fitted stones remaining in the wall. "When this was intact, it was about six meters high. Forts every Roman mile, and numerous turrets between them. It was an impressive fortification."

"Our Marines could have jumped over it in their combat armor," Tanya said, "but if all you had was human muscle, it would be tough, especially if someone was shooting at you while you tried to climb it. How did it fall?"

"It didn't. Rome fell. As the empire contracted, the legions were called home, and the wall abandoned."

Geary looked down the length of the wall, white stone against green vegetation, thinking of the massive demobilizations that had taken place inside the Alliance since the war with the Syndicate Worlds had ended. *The legions were called home, and the wall abandoned.* It sounded so simple, but it meant that defenses once regarded as vital were suddenly surplus, men and women who had once carried out duties considered critical were no longer needed, and things once thought essential were now judged too expensive. "The borders and their horizons shrank," he murmured, thinking not just of the ancient empire that had built this wall but of the current state of the many star systems in the Alliance.

Tanya gave him that look which meant she knew exactly what he was thinking. "They say this wall was garrisoned for centuries. Think of all the soldiers who stood sentry on it. Some of them might have been among our ancestors."

"Many people think Arthur might have been a king during those times," Steward Main said. "That maybe his knights held the wall for a while after the Romans left."

"Arthur?" Geary asked.

"A legendary king who ruled and died long ago. Supposedly," Main confided, "Arthur didn't die, but remains sleeping, awaiting a time when his people need him. Of course, he's never shown up."

"Maybe your need hasn't been great enough," Desjani said. "Sometimes sleeping heroes from the past do appear just when they're needed."

Geary barely managed not to glare at her. But his sudden shift in mood was apparent enough to cause silence to fall for a few moments.

Main cleared his throat. "If I may ask a question of you, what do you think our other guests think of all this?"

"The Dancers?" Geary asked. An alien landing shuttle hovered nearby, mere centimeters above the ground. "They're amazing engineers. They examined the remains pretty carefully. They're probably impressed."

"It's hard to tell, Admiral, since they're in their space armor."

"You probably couldn't tell even if you could see their faces," Desjani told him. "They don't display emotions the way we do."

"Oh, right," Main replied with remarkable understatement. "Because they, uh . . ."

"Look to us like what would happen if a giant spider mated with a wolf," Tanya finished for him. "We've speculated that we look as hideous to them as they do to us."

"Don't judge them on their looks," Geary added.

"I wouldn't, sir! Everyone's heard how they brought that fellow back. Better than many a human I've encountered, I'll tell you."

Main glanced at the sun, then checked the time. "We should move on when you're ready, Admiral, Captain."

"Give us a few minutes, will you?" Desjani asked. "I need to talk to the Admiral about something."

"Of course. I'll be right over there."

Tanya turned her back on the curious crowds hovering a few hundred meters away, citizens of Old Earth who were fascinated not only by the newly discovered alien Dancers but also by the humans from distant stars colonized by those who had left this world long ago. She turned her wrist to show Geary that she had activated her personal security field so their words could not be heard by others, or their lip movements or expressions seen clearly. "We need to talk about something," she repeated to him.

Geary suppressed a sigh. When Tanya Desjani said that, it meant the something she wanted to talk about was something he wouldn't want to discuss. But he stood close to the wall, right next to her, though he didn't lean on the ancient structure. That just felt wrong, like using a book from the far past as a foot rest. "Something about walls?"

"Something about here." She turned her gaze from the landscape and caught his eyes. "Tomorrow we leave Old Earth, return to *Dauntless*, and head for home. You need to know what people will be thinking."

"I can guess," Geary said.

"No, you can't. You spent a hundred years frozen in survival sleep. You've been among us for a while, but you still don't understand us as well as you should. But I know the people of the Alliance right now, because I'm one of them." Tanya's eyes had darkened, taken on a hardness and a fierceness he remembered from their first meeting. "I was born during a war that had started long before I arrived, and I grew up expecting that war to continue long after I was gone. I was named for an aunt who died in the war, saw my brother die in it, and fully expected any child of mine might die in it. We could not win, we would not lose, and the deaths would go on and on. Everyone in the Alliance, everyone but you, grew up the same. And while we were growing up, we were taught that Captain Black Jack Geary had saved the Alliance when he died blunting one of the first surprise attacks by the Syndicate Worlds that started that war."

"Tanya," he said resignedly, "I know—"

"Let me finish. We were also taught that Black Jack epitomized everything good about the Alliance. He was everything a citizen of the Alliance should be, and everything a defender of the Alliance should aspire to. Quiet! I know you don't like hearing that, but to billions of people in the Alliance that's who Black Jack was. And we all heard the rest of the legend, too, that Black Jack was among our ancestors under the light of the living stars but he would return from the dead some day when he was most needed, and he would save the Alliance. And you did that."

"I wasn't really dead," Geary pointed out gruffly.

"Irrelevant. We found you only weeks before power on that damaged escape pod would have been exhausted. We thawed you out, then you saved the fleet, you beat the Syndics, and you finally brought an end to the endless war." She ran one hand slowly across the rough stone of the wall, her touch gentle despite the force of her words. "Now, despite a victory that is causing the Syndicate Worlds to fall to pieces, the Alliance is also threatening to come apart at the seams because of the costs and strains of a century of war. In that time, you've come to Old Earth."

"Tanya." She knew he would be unhappy with this conversation, with being reminded yet again of the belief that he was some sort of mythical hero. For a moment, he wondered if an ancestor of his had stood here, very long ago, peering into that same wind for approaching enemies, burdened with the responsibility of protecting everyone else. "We came to Old Earth to escort the Dancers. If the aliens hadn't insisted, we wouldn't have come here."

"You and I know that, and some members of the Alliance grand council know that," Desjani said. "But I guarantee you that everyone else in the Alliance believes that you chose to come here, to Old Earth, the home of us all, the place our oldest ancestors once lived, to consult with those ancestors. To learn what you should do to save an Alliance which more and more citizens of the Alliance fear may be beyond saving."

He stared at her, hoping that Tanya's security measures really were keeping the nearby observers from seeing his expression. "They can't believe that."

"They do." Her eyes on him were unyielding. "You need to know that."

"Great." He faced the remnants of the wall, staring north to where the wall's enemies had long ago been. "Why me?"

"Ask our ancestors. Though if you asked me," she added, standing right next to him as she also gazed outward, "I'd say it was because you can do the job."

"I'm just a man. Just one man."

"I didn't say you would do it alone," Tanya pointed out.

"And our ancestors haven't been talking to me."

"You know," she added in the very reasonable voice of someone repeating common knowledge, "that our ancestors rarely come out and tell us anything. They offer hints, suggestions, inspirations, and hunches for those who are willing to pay attention. And if they care about us at all, they will offer those things to you, if you are listening."

"The ancestors here on Old Earth," Geary said as patiently as he could, "didn't get raised in an Alliance at war and indoctrinated about how awesome I am. Why should they be impressed by Black Jack?"

"Because they are our ancestors, too! And they know what Black Jack is! Remember that other wall they took us to? The, uh, Grand Wall?"

"The Great Wall?"

"Yeah, that one." She gestured to the north. "Now, this wall, the one that Hadrian built, was a real fortification. It kept out enemies. But that Great Wall over in Asia never could do that. The people there told us it was so damned big, so long, that it was impossible for the guys who built it to support a large enough army to actually garrison it. They sank a huge amount of money, time, and human labor into building that Great Wall, and whenever an enemy wanted to get through it, all they had to do was find a spot where there weren't any soldiers and put up a ladder so one of their own could climb up and over and then open the nearest gate."

"Yeah." Geary nodded. "It doesn't make a lot of sense, does it?"

"Not as a fortification, no." She waved again, this time vaguely to the east. "Those pyramids. Remember those? Think of the time and money and labor that went into those. And then those big faces on the mountain a ways north of where we first stopped in Kansas. The four ancestors whose images were carved into a mountain. How much sense did that make?"

He turned a questioning look on her. "This has something to do with me?"

"Yes, sir, Admiral." Desjani smiled, but the eyes that held his were intent. "That Great Wall said something about the people who built it. It told the world, we can do this. It told the world, we're on this side of the Great Wall, and all the rest of you are on the other. Those pyramids must have really impressed people a long time ago, too. And the four ancestors on the mountain? It didn't just honor them, it also honored their people and their homes and what they believed in. All of those things were symbols. Symbols that helped define the people who built them."

He nodded slowly. "All right. And?"

"What's the symbol of the Alliance?"

"There isn't one. Not like that. There are too many different societies, governments, beliefs—"

"Wrong." She pointed at him.

Geary felt that vast sinking sensation that sometimes threatened to overwhelm him. "Tanya, that's—"

"True. I told you. You still don't understand us." Her face saddened. "We stopped believing in our politicians a long time ago, and that meant we lost belief in our governments, and what is the Alliance but a collection of those governments? It can't be stronger than they are. We tried putting faith in honor, but you reminded us how that caused us to warp the meaning of honor. We tried putting faith in our fleet and our ground forces, but they failed, you know they did. We were fighting like hell and dying and killing and not getting anywhere. Until you came along. The man who we had been told all of our lives was everything the Alliance was supposed to be."

Tanya tapped the wall next to them. "Black Jack isn't just this wall, the guy who physically protected the Alliance from external enemies. He's also that Great Wall and those pyramids and those four ancestors. He's the image of the Alliance, the thing citizens think of that *means* the Alliance. That's why he is the only one who can save it."

He had to look away once more, to gaze across that sere landscape again, seeing overlaid upon it images of the battles he had already fought, of the men and women already dead. "Senator Sakai said something like that to me, but he was a lot more pessimistic." During the war with the Syndicate Worlds, the Alliance government had created the myths around Black Jack to inspire and unify its people at a time when the example of that sort of hero was desperately needed. Now the man that myth had been built around somehow had to save the Alliance that had created it. "Ancestors help me."

"Well, duh, isn't that what we've just been talking about?"

Geary felt a crooked smile form and looked at her again. "I never would have guessed what people born during the war were thinking. What would I do without you?"

"You'd be lost," Desjani said. "Totally, hopelessly lost. And don't you ever forget it."

From *New York Times* Bestselling Author

JACK CAMPBELL

THE LOST FLEET: BEYOND THE FRONTIER: GUARDIAN

Admiral John "Black Jack" Geary's First Fleet of the Alliance has survived the journey deep into unexplored interstellar space, a voyage that led to the discovery of new alien species, including a new enemy and a possible ally. Now Geary's mission is to ensure the safety of the Midway Star System, which has revolted against the Syndicate Worlds empire—an empire that is on the brink of collapse. Geary also needs to return safely to Alliance space with a valuable warship and representatives of an alien species, while adhering to the peace treaty with the Syndicate Worlds at all costs—even as the political unrest around him may spell the destruction of the Alliance.

"Jack Campbell's dazzling series is military science fiction at its best."

—Catherine Asaro, Nebula Award–winning author

jack-campbell.com
penguin.com

M1229T1212

From the *New York Times* Bestselling Author
JACK CAMPBELL

THE LOST FLEET: BEYOND THE FRONTIER: INVINCIBLE

Admiral John "Black Jack" Geary suspects that the Alliance he serves is deliberately putting his fleet in harm's way. An encounter with the alien enigmas confirms Geary's fears. Attacked without warning, he orders the fleet to jump star systems—only to enter the crosshairs of another hostile alien armada.

Now, with a group of his officers determined to eliminate this new threat at any cost, Geary must figure out how to breach the enemy's defenses so the fleet can reach the jump point without massive casualties—even though the enigmas could be waiting on the other side . . .

Praise for The Lost Fleet series

"A rousing adventure with a page-turning plot, lots of space action, and the kind of hero Hornblower fans will love."
—Willia of
ce

"Military science ficti of
—Catherine
ns

facebo

T1211